Shadow of the WHEEL

PAT KELLY

Published in Australia by Sid Harta Publishers Pty Ltd,

ABN: 46 119 415 842

23 Stirling Crescent, Glen Waverley, Victoria 3150 Australia

Telephone: +61 3 9560 9920, Facsimile: +61 3 9545 1742

E-mail: author@sidharta.com.au

First published in Australia 2019

This edition published 2019

Copyright © Pat Kelly 2019

Cover design, typesetting: WorkingType (www.workingtype.com.au)

Kelly, Pat

Shadow of the Wheel

ISBN: 978-1-925230-64-2

pp438

ABOUT THE AUTHOR

The author was born in Scotland a year before World War II started, but swears she didn't cause it ...

In January 1968 she arrived in Australia as a 'Ten Pound Tourist' with her, then, husband and four children.

After the breakup of her marriage after twenty-five years the author was contacted by a man named Mike Kelly, whom she had known in her teens and had had no contact with for nearly thirty years. Mike's marriage having broken up around the same time as the author's. On learning she was 'on the loose', he obtained her phone number by courtesy of his mother — International telephone enquiries — and the author's mother, so rang to see if she was okay.

One thing led to another, they were married in 1988 and returned to the Isle of Man to start a new life. On Mike's retirement, five years later, they followed the summers and spent half their lives in Australia and the other half in the Isle of Man.

In their months on the island each year, they ran a daffodil and plant nursery and were well known throughout the island for their roadside stall, where they sold their daffodils and plants.

As age caught up with them, they realised it was time to settle somewhere permanently. Being the warmer country, Australia won, and they moved there in 2014, to live in a retirement village in Lakes Entrance — one of the prettiest spots in Australia.

This, they both feel, will suit them until they climb in their boxes (but not for a long time yet) and move on to higher places.

BY THE SAME AUTHOR

Hedge of Thorns

The author, who hails from Scotland, spent many hours listening to her mother-in-law recount, in vivid detail, memories of her childhood days in the tiny village of Patrick ·during the First World War. In those days the village was dwarfed by the huge internment camp at Knockaloe, created for the accommodation of thousands of enemy aliens. That little girl grew up to marry and become the well-known personality Mrs Lou Kelly — mother of Brian, Mike and Juan. Brian is now the Canon of St. German's Cathedral, Peel; Mike raced in the Manx Grand Prix for eight years, drove the 'roads open' car and was finally the Deputy Clerk of the Course; Juan is a manager with the Milk Marketing Board and still lives in Crosby, only a few doors from the house his mother and grandmother bought in 1931. The author was so fascinated by these stories of life in Patrick at the time that she determined to preserve them for future generations, and in memory of a dear friend. 'Hedge of Thorns' is a true account of the impact_ that the Great War and the monster of Knockaloe Camp had on the lives of a Manx family which still followed the traditional crofting way. of life. It is a most moving and memorable story of the stresses and strains which shattered the peaceful existence of a family whose loved ones were caught up· in the emergencies of war. ·

*I would like to dedicate this story to my best friend,
my beloved husband Mike Kelly for all his years of love,
faith and encouragement.*

ACKNOWLEDGMENTS

My heartfelt thanks go to my husband, Mike, for many years of encouragement and faith in my writing ability. To my children, Dawn, Andrew, Alison and Kenneth for their support and encouragement.

Thanks also to my friends in The Lakes Entrance Senior Citizens' Club, who have been very interested and encouraging as my story took shape.

I would like to acknowledge the following for the help they have given in supplying me with information and helping me to bring this book to a what I hope is an enjoyable read.

The Manx Museum in the Isle of Man, who patiently supplied me with most of the information I needed about the 'Great Wheel'. I topped this off with information from their useful website.

The South Australian Maritime Museum in Port Adelaide, for steering me in the right direction as to shipping during the era I was writing about. Also, as to the conditions on board for steerage passengers and the hazards of the voyage. Thanks to the shipping information on their website, I learned about the mutiny on the *Navarino* and the fact that many of the passengers crewed the ship as it arrived in Port Adelaide.

The Australian history website, which gave me all the information I needed for my research into Kapunda and the history of copper mining in its early days.

Last, but not least, my editor Julie King, who has been a whizz. Julie has put in a lot of time and work to lift my story from a rather ordinary piece of writing, to a publishable script. I now regard her as a very valuable friend and look forward to working with her again in the future.

Chapter 1

⟡

Fingers trembling with excitement, Sarah tied the linen outdoor bonnet over the white cotton under-bonnet her mother always insisted she must wear.

Stealing a furtive glance toward the bedroom doorway, the girl plucked the little fly-specked mirror from the mantle shelf. The brown eyes that gazed back at her from the little metal square were alive with the excitement sparked by this very special day. Her face, it seemed to her, took on almost the same shape of the mirror; *too square*, she thought, saved only by the slight indentations of the dimples on her cheeks. Poking an odd stray wisp of dark hair inside the bonnet, Sarah made a face at herself and replaced the mirror. With a final furtive glance toward the bedroom, she moved stealthily toward the outside door and lifted the latch very gently, so as not to disturb any of the others.

The door creaked, and Sarah froze, hardly daring to breath, her heart pounding painfully in her throat. Holding the door half open, she stood motionless, listening warily.

'Is that you, Sarah?' her mother's sleepy, whining voice came at her from the bedroom.

Sarah caught her breath and gritted her teeth. Her fist clenched in frustration. 'Yes, Mam. I'm just leaving. Go back to sleep.' The girl looked pleadingly toward the bedroom doorway, worrying her lower lip with fine white teeth. 'Today of all days, dear God,' she prayed, 'let there be peace. Let this special day be happy.'

'Come in here then and let me see you before you go,' the grumpy voice commanded.

Foreseeing the scene that was to come, Sarah heaved a sigh so deep it racked her whole body as she moved toward her mother's voice. Dragging in one last huge breath, she sidled in through the bedroom doorway, adopting an air of cheerfulness she certainly did not feel.

Judith Fayle sat up on her lumpy bed, dragging a worn shawl around her thin shoulders to protect her from the early morning chill. Her lips, as was so usual these past two years, dragged down at the corners in an expression of constant disapproval.

'Where do you think you're bound, my fine young madam, in your best wool skirt and bodice?'

'To the ceremony, Mam. You know the wheel's to be set in motion this day.'

'Aye. And I know you're to work all day, too. You cannot work in good clothes!' Judith's voice was rapidly ascending to the high-pitched whine Sarah had grown to dread.

Sarah, looking down at her best clothes, could only shake her head and wish them better. She knew they were well worn even before they became hers — gratefully received cast-offs from sympathetic Aunt Jane.

'*Please* let me wear them, Mam,' she pleaded. 'I must look well today, for Governor Hope and his Lady Isabella will be at the ceremony. Also the Archdeacon, the Lord Bishop and his Lady, as well as Mr Dumbell, Chairman of the Directors. Oh — and the mines manager, Captain Rowe will be there too. Everyone will be wearing their very best clothes today.'

Sarah failed to mention that Patrick O' Malley also would be there and that just for once she would like him to see her dressed in something other than her rough work clothes.

'Yes! Yes, I know who they all are,' Judith said testily. She glared doubtfully at her daughter as she thoughtfully gnawed at her lower lip. She supposed the girl could be right for once. On such a very special occasion it was likely the people would all dress up a bit. It would not do for her daughter to be seen, dressed almost in rags, by such important dignitaries. Maybe if she looked well, Sarah might be one of those chosen to serve them their meal. That would likely mean some extra money.

With an exaggerated sigh, Judith grudgingly gave ground. 'I suppose you may then. Anyway, there would not be enough time for you to change now. But mind you don't spill food on your skirt and spoil it. And see you bring home all the money you get paid for today!'

Sarah's face fell, her wide, generous mouth drooping slightly at the corners. She had desperately hoped she might be able to keep a penny or two of her day's wage to buy some fancy combs. Now seventeen, she longed to have her hair fastened prettily, like the rich men's daughters she had seen riding in their grand carriages. Instead of just tied at the back with a frayed, faded ribbon.

'Can I not, please, keep a few pennies for myself? I am to be paid one shilling and sixpence for my work today and being a holiday, it is extra money.'

Judith snorted and shook her head. 'You know full well, my girl, that since your father was sent to jail in Liverpool, we need every penny you can earn just to survive.'

'Yes, Mam.'

Judith scowled, then gave an abrupt nod of her head toward the door. 'Go then.'

Sarah, hearing the tribe of younger Fayles stirring in the half loft, fled from her mother's room and hurried to leave the cottage. The last thing she needed was for the childer to throw on clothes and pester her to take them with her. At the doorway she paused long enough to glance round. Seeing seven-year-old Richard halfway down the ladder and dripping urine as usual, she whirled and fled from the house. Though Sarah felt sorry for her little brother, she could not help but feel a niggling irritation at his everlasting inability to control his bladder. On that special morning she was relieved not to be there to hear her mother's tirade when she saw the poor child's state. Nor to be given the job of cleaning him up.

The morning was glorious, with only an occasional cotton puff cloud to decorate the blue sky. Tightening her shawl against the chill of the early morning breeze, Sarah stepped excitedly down the hill, away from the croft and through the tiny village of Agneash. So excited that she almost danced.

With the hamlet behind her, walking for a few minutes, Sarah saw no signs of any human habitation. The green and purple hills slept, silent save for the music of a thousand birds. The distant bleating of a sheep; the warm glow of early autumn sun flooding the land, hills and sequestered glen with a fierce, clear light. The very earth itself looked young, virginal and unspoiled.

Then the girl rounded the last bend, stopping to absorb the breathtaking view between steeply sloping hills to where the glen finally ended, and the river tumbled gleefully to freedom in the Irish Sea.

The sea itself, alive with a million sparkles of the sun on the wave-tops, was a huge empty expanse, dotted only with a few fishing boats heralded by the endless noisy, wheeling squadrons of greedy herring gulls.

Huge grey cliffs reared their walls beyond the bounds of

the glen. They stood proudly, worn and pitted where huge seas had crashed against them throughout the centuries. Nestling between their outflung arms was a curving beach of white sand, and the tiny harbour.

Clinging precariously to the steeply sloping hillsides, a smattering of small, white painted cottages formed the village of Laxey.

Sarah hesitated for a few moments to again drink in the beauty of the scene. Surely there could be no place on earth more beautiful than her beloved Isle of Man. She could never envisage living in any other part of the world. This was home — this tiny island was her whole world.

As she stepped out briskly again, looking closer to hand she could see the huge, red and white waterwheel, which was to be the centre of the day's celebration. Beyond it, forming the only discordant part of the view was the growing pile of *deads* — the heap of rubble put aside after the metal ores had been extracted.

Making her way to the green near the wheel, Sarah found there were already very many people gathered in the area. Overheard snippets of conversation told her there were people present from every area of the island, many of them having travelled throughout the night to secure a good vantage point for the ceremony.

Benches had been placed all around the green and many of the mine workers, like herself, were bustling around, piling the large platters with beef, potatoes and other vegetables. Never in her life had Sarah seen so much food, or indeed, so many people.

Mistress Quayle, who was overseeing the smooth running of the banquet, first admonished Sarah for being tardy, then directed her into a commodious wooden building that had been erected at one end of the green especially for the occasion.

'The invited guests will be dining in there,' Mistress Quayle told the girl. 'Now, first I want you to help set up the tables, so you will be familiar with the layout of the room. Then after the ceremony I wish you to return there to serve at table.'

Sarah flushed with pleasure and drew a quick, excited breath. '*Me?*' she questioned. 'Serve the gentry?'

'Unless you have no wish to.' Mistress Quayle smothered a knowing smile. 'You have obviously taken great care to look at your best today. That deserves a reward.'

'Thank you, Ma'am,' Sarah said breathlessly, bobbing an unnecessary curtsy. Then, afraid Mistress Quayle might change her mind if she hesitated, Sarah dashed off with unladylike haste to the wooden building.

The interior quite took her breath away, so beautifully was it decorated. Coloured festoons and evergreen plants encircled the windows and roof, with a crown being placed at the top of the room. Adorning the opposite end of the building were the *Three Legs of Man* formed with dahlias of different colours; this being supported on either side by banners bearing the words *Shipping* and *Agriculture*.

Regaining her breath, Sarah set to helping prepare the tables with an unimaginable amount of silverware. This done, vast quantities of food were brought in on salvers, until the benches sagged and fairly groaned with the weight of it.

When all was prepared, the people left to join their fellow mine workers on the washing-floors to await the start of the ceremony.

Taking a final longing glance back into the building, Sarah thought there must be enough food to fill every starving belly in the world.

By the time she reached the washing-floors the morning had grown old and the sun was high in the sky.

All the mine workers seemed to be there, milling around the washing-floors, and their families. Sarah could think of no one who was not there — except for Patrick. But he would be there somewhere, she was sure. He had promised her he would come. Today would be their first chance to spend more than a few furtive, stolen moments together.

How Sarah wished her mother was not so aggressively against the Irish, who had been arriving in droves since the mines became prosperous. Perhaps then, she could have dared to tell her about Patrick and beg her to allow them a courtship. Now that was out of the question. As much as she hated deception, until her mother was in a better humour, things must remain as they were.

Trying not to look too obvious, she anxiously scanned the constantly moving sea of faces. *There must be fully five hundred workpeople*, Sarah thought. *No!* Probably nearer six hundred, all dressed in their holiday attire. Sarah felt knots of panic fluttering in her stomach as the time grew nearer for the ceremony to begin.

The Lord Bishop, his lady and family arrived, closely followed by the Archdeacon and many other gentlemen from the northern parishes.

Members of the two bands present gave an occasional toot, needlessly testing the tuning of their instruments to allay their nervousness.

All the while, Sarah looked around, excited by the pomp of it all, though at the same time not enjoying it to the full for fear that she would not find Patrick in the crowd. At last she glimpsed the thatch of dark red curls above the other heads and her heart leapt with joy.

'Patrick!' she called out in relief, feeling a hot blush rush up from her neck when many other heads turned to look at her.

Patrick looked around, then finding her in the crowd smiled, waved, then pushed his way through the excited throng to join her.

'I thought I was never going to find you,' he gasped. 'I've been looking all over, but the crowd is so thick.'

'So many people!' Sarah muttered, gazing about her in awe. 'I've never seen such crowds.'

Quite apart from the workpeople assembled on the washing-floors, the hillside all around the wheel was awash with bodies in clothes of every colour imaginable. Their movements were like the constant eddying of the restless seas.

'I heard tell there's something like four thousand people come to watch today,' Patrick said knowingly.

A short time later, just before twelve o'clock and amidst a deafening burst of cheering, His Excellency the Governor of the Island, Charles Hope arrived, accompanied by his wife, Lady Isabella. They drove up in a gleaming black carriage, with highly polished brasses and lanterns that glinted like fire in the sun. Two proud black horses pulled it, prancing spiritedly as it drew to a halt.

Immediately the two bands struck up.

Headed by George Dumbell and Captain Richard Rowe, and flanked by the bands, the workpeople marched from the washing-floors, up the slope toward the wheel.

Patrick tried to take hold of Sarah's hand as they marched, but she jerked it free, frowning up at him.

'People will see!' she hissed.

'I don't care if they do,' Patrick responded petulantly.

'Well *I* do. There would be the most frightful row if my mother should hear any rumour about us. She would make my life unbearable.'

'I have no fear of your mother. Nor am I ashamed of my feelings for you.' Patrick replied snappily.

'That's easy for you to say. You don't have to live with her, and you would fear her if you met her. She has not been quite well in her mind since my Daa was taken to jail.'

'She shouldn't take it out on you though,' Patrick muttered gruffly, then he fell silent. He well knew of Judith Fayle's reputation — she was the talk of the village.

Walking toward the giant wheel, Sarah gazed up in awe. The white-washed stone casement gleamed in the sun, the brilliant red wheel standing proudly above it. On the seaward end of the structure the 'Three Legs' symbol stood out in gigantic proportions. Its motto, *Quocunque Jeceris Stabit*, Sarah knew, meant *Whichever way you throw me, I will stand.*

Sarah felt her heart swelling with the pride of being a part of it all. The pride of being Manx and particularly of being a Laxey lass. For years she had watched the wheel, the brain child of Lezayre man, Robert Casement, grow from a pile of rubble into this magnificent land mark. She had heard many claims that it was the largest waterwheel in Europe. Looking up at its awesome bulk, she had little doubt it was. Perhaps, she wondered, was it the biggest in the world?

The procession drew to a halt at the base of the wheel. The band ceased its music. When Mr Dumbell and Captain Rowe stepped forward to greet Governor and Lady Hope, a deathly hush fell on the workers and the thousands who were gathered tightly on the surrounding slopes.

The silence was so complete Sarah could hear the whisper of the sea on the nearby beach, the husky roar of waves breaking on the headland rocks. Overhead a lone lark hovered, floating almost motionlessly in the clear sky, trilling his inimitable song, of the joy of just being alive on such a beautiful day.

The official party disappeared from view behind the wheel casement, but in a moment, Sarah saw them walking out along the first platform, led by Mister and Mistress Dumbell.

Patrick stood behind Sarah, pressed so close against her in the crush of people, that she could feel the strength of his hard miner's body against her back. Hidden by her shawl, he put his arms round her, clasping his wide, blunt-fingered miner's hands just below her breasts. Sarah leaned back against him, glowing with the pleasure of being closer to him than ever before.

A few short speeches were made by members of the official party, then Sarah saw His Excellency the Governor pull a small lever to let the first of the water flow onto the wheel. A thrill of excitement rose in her breast as the gigantic red-finned circle of the wheel took on life and started to turn.

Sarah gasped. Tears stood, unshed, in the corners of her eyes. For four years she had awaited this moment. Four years of watching spellbound as it had grown, rising like a phoenix from the ashes. Now the grand beauty had come alive. The huge wheel turned slowly, with majestic dignity, shaking sparkling droplets of water on the gentry and their ladies on the platform below.

Mistress Dumbell, Sarah noticed, was holding a bottle of champagne which was daintily decorated with lace. With the first movement of the wheel, the gentlewoman raised her arm and gracefully swung the bottle against the casement.

Starting slightly as the bottle smashed, Sarah felt Patrick's arms tighten about her, adding to the excitement of the moment.

'It's truly beautiful!' Head back, Sarah, like everyone else in the huge crowd, stared enraptured at the glistening giant.

'Yes, but I see an even more breathtaking sight,' Patrick agree huskily.

Looking around Sarah found him gazing down at her. Flustered and blushing hotly she returned her eyes to the official party.

'In honour of our Governor's Lady,' Mr Dumbell was saying, 'I name this magnificent waterwheel the *'Lady Isabella'.'*

At that same moment a flag was unfurled at the top of the construction, making known to the assembled thousands the title the wheel had been given.

Feeling her heart soar, Sarah lifted her arms, waving wildly and cheering until she was hoarse. All around her the strong lungs of the workpeople filled the air with a joyful din. Above it all the thundering boom of a cannon helped to proclaim to a breathless island the satisfactory accomplishment of a momentous undertaking. From that day forward the rich Laxey mines would be pumped safely dry by the *Lady Isabella* and could prosper in safety.

Sarah and Patrick watched in fascination as the official party wound their way up the spiral metal staircase to the upper platform, which stretched out over the wheel. After gazing on the brilliant scene below for a few minutes, they all descended, leaving the immediate area, the miners and other workers pressing enthusiastically toward the wheel. Swept along with the tide of excitement, Sarah and Patrick went with them, the girl only vaguely aware she should be returning to the wooden building to see to the needs of the honoured guests.

The magnetism of the newly named *Lady Isabella* was too strong, however, and Sarah found herself drawn eagerly up the spiral steps to the highest platform.

Looking down from the lower end, she had a sudden shock at the height. Viewed from below, the wheel had not seemed so high, but from her standpoint with the wheel, she seemed a fearful distance from the ground. The wheel, whose diameter she knew was over seventy-two feet, added to the depth of the casement and from that the ground below sloped away quite sharply on the side she was looking over. Although the turning of the wheel made not the slightest tremor, Sarah had the most awful sensation that the whole structure was swaying.

Feeling dizzy for a moment, she clutched a trembling hand to her mouth and attempted to step back, away from the rail. The crush of people around her held her firm. Panicking, she half turned, her eyes wildly seeking a way to escape.

Patrick, seeing her terror, folded her tenderly in his arms, holding her firmly, calming her with his strength.

Sarah clung; her face pressed hard against his strong chest until the faintness had passed. Then she smiled up into his gold-flecked hazel eyes; her heart warming and steadying by the gentleness and love she saw there.

'I'm fine now,' she whispered tremulously, taking care not to look down again.

Made reckless by the excitement of the day, Patrick bent and pressed his lips to Sarah's in their first real kiss. The girl felt her insides melt and her knees turn to water, while all around them people whistled and made good-natured lewd comments.

Breathless, and trembling with a passion that shocked her, Sarah put her hands against Patrick's chest, abruptly pushing herself free of his arms.

'Don't,' she whispered. 'Not here!'

'Where then?' He asked, his eyes pleaded hungrily, his grip staying firm on her arms.

'I don't know.' Suddenly aware of the many watching eyes she added, 'Nowhere, now I must go — I have work to do.' Sarah pulled herself free of his arms and pushed through the crowd toward the spiral stairway. Stopping after a few steps, she threw Patrick a confused glance over her shoulder, then shook her head worriedly and hurried away.

Chapter 2

Sarah edged through the mob on the platform, still filled with awe and shaken by the power of her emotions. It was hard to believe a lump of concrete and steel could affect her so strongly, though she did suspect her close encounter with Patrick may have had something to do with it. Pressed hard against the stonework of the wheel support, she squeezed past the excited throngs who were making their way up the spiral stairway.

Far below, she could see the official party making their way slowly toward the building where they were to dine, where she should already be waiting to attend to their needs. She must arrive before them! She had to, or else another girl might be taken in to replace her. There would be hell to pay at home if she did not bring the shilling and sixpence her mother was expecting, and she would surely receive a birching if she arrived home without it.

Fear lent wings to her heels. In a single bound, Sarah leapt down the last three steps, then picking up her skirts she sped across the grass toward the wooden room. From the corner of her eye she saw the Governor and his party stop to speak to a huddle of miners.

Snatching her chance, she darted past the officials, hastening toward her goal.

In the doorway Patrick caught up with her and gripped her arm, swinging her around to face him.

'Where will I meet you after?' He asked eagerly.

Over his shoulder Sarah could see Mister Dumbell and The Governor approaching. 'I don't know. Here, I suppose.'

'When?' Patrick kept a gentle grip on her arm.

Sarah shrugged and shook her head. 'I don't know. You'll just have to keep watching, for I don't know what time I shall be finished my work. I suppose it will depend on when the guests finish eating and what I am expected to do afterwards.' With that, she pulled her arm free and darted inside.

Mistress Quayle was thunderous when Sarah arrived in the hall, her thick brows drawn together in a scowl. 'Where have you been?'

'S–sorry,' Sarah stammered, 'but there are so many people and I had trouble forcing my way through the crowds.'

'The rest of us managed! Think yourself lucky I had not the time to seek a replacement for you.'

'Sorry. Thank you,' the girl mumbled, her head bowed, eyes fixed firmly on the ground.

'Well, now you have finally condescended to grace us with your presence, do you think you might be good enough to do some work? Most of the guests have arrived, except for the official party.'

Sarah quickly picked up a jug of ale and hurried to the tables. Many of the guests were already of a merry disposition, having already downed a goodly quantity of ale and French wines. All fell silent when Governor Hope arrived with the official party.

On arrival, Mister Dumbell took his seat at the head of the

table with, on his right, His Excellency the Governor and Lady Isabella and on his left, the Lord Bishop and Mistress Powis.

Sarah watched spellbound, while at the same time trying to serve to everyone's satisfaction. Never had she been so close to such famous people, and so many all at once. At seventeen, she was still young enough to be in awe at such greatness. Moving amongst the landed gentry of the island, efficiently filling their cups, Sarah found herself continually amazed at the pleasantness of some and the unbelievable bad manners of others. Bending to serve one foppishly dressed young man — already the worse with ale — she felt him brushing the side of her breast with the back of his hand. Repelled and angered, Sarah stepped back, stumbling and almost falling over his other hand that was fumbling with the tails of her skirt.

Snatching at her arm and gripping it painfully tightly, the youth tried to force his hand up inside her dress but was hampered to her relief by her many linsey-woolsey petticoats her mother insisted she wear.

'Let go of me!' Sarah hissed through her teeth, reluctant to make a scene.

'If you promise to meet me later. After the meal. Then I shall let you go.'

'I cannot! I *will* not!' Sarah's heart slammed against her ribs and she felt tears pricking at the corners of her eyes. Her stomach heaved threateningly.

'Of course you can. And you will. Else I shall ravish you here!' he hissed, his leering eyes devouring her bodice.

Sarah tugged frantically at her arm, feeling his fingers dig deeply into her tender young flesh. 'Please let me go. You're hurting my arm ...' she pleaded. Her eyes stung with hot tears of embarrassment and fear. All the time she could feel his other hand working its way beneath her petticoats.

'I desire to enjoy your favours. If I free you, you must meet me later. I shall pay you well.'

Spurred by fear and indignation, Sarah at last dragged her arm free, only to find her thigh tightly gripped by the lout's other hand.

'I am no doxy who can be bedded for money!' Sarah cried indignantly. 'Now take your hand off me this instant or I'll scream for help.'

At that moment she became aware that conversation around the table had ceased and the guests who were close enough to hear were studying her with a variety of expressions, ranging from shock, to anger and to undisguised amusement.

Suddenly an elderly gentleman seated on the far side of the youth bent to lift a riding crop from the floor at his feet, rose from the table and struck the boy hard across the face.

With an agonised squeal, the youth jerked backward, tipping his chair over, releasing his grip on Sarah at the same time. While he sprawled on the floor, hand to his cheek, Sarah backed, terrified, against the wall.

'I say, Henry,' one of the men blustered, 'that was a bit savage don't you think?'

Without a glance at his son, the man called Henry glared at his critic. 'No son of mine will treat any woman with such discourtesy,' he snarled. Taking a few steps toward the boy, he demanded, 'Now stand up like a man, Jeremy and apologise to this young lady.' He prodded the cowering youth with the toe of his boot.

Dragging himself to his feet and still clutching his flaming cheek, Jeremy sulkily mumbled, 'My apologies, Mistress.' But his eyes did not meet Sarah's, nor did he seem in any way sincere.

'I regret my son's ill manners.' Henry approached Sarah and

taking her hand, pressed a coin into her palm. 'Please accept this to help make up for the distress he has caused you.'

'Oh no, Sir, I cannot take this. My thanks to you just the same.' Sarah held the money toward him.

Henry shook his head, smiling gently. 'Please make an old man happy. Keep it, if only to ease my conscience. It is beyond me to understand how I could have sired such an ungentlemanly cur.' So saying, he bowed most courteously and resumed his seat.

'Thank you kindly, Sir.' Sarah curtsied as best she knew how, then hurried away, relieved to escape the embarrassing scrutiny of the gentlefolk. Stealing a glance toward the top table, she felt reasonably confident that Mister Dumbell and Captain Rowe had not noticed the commotion.

Mistress Quayle awaited her at the end of the room, frowning darkly. 'Would you be good enough to explain what occurred with young Master Kermeen?'

'Who?' Sarah frowned.

Mistress Quayle nodded toward Jeremy, who now sat with his head hanging almost into his cup of ale.

'Oh — him!' Sarah felt the blush burning to the roots of her hair. 'He tried to force his attentions upon me. Handling me like some cheap doxy. Until his father struck him and made him apologise.'

'His father, was it, who dealt the blow?'

'Aye.'

'You did not raise your hand to him?'

'No, though I would have soon if his father had not stopped him.' Sarah felt her lips tremble and clamped her teeth firmly on the top one.

Mistress Quayle glared over at the sorry-looking youth and shook her head. 'I'm pleased you did not raise your hand to him, child, but you would do well to stay well clear of that young villain. I have heard tales that there is much evil in him. He has caused his poor parents and many young ladies in the district a great deal of heartbreak. He's pure trouble. So be warned!'

Sarah shuddered. 'I certainly have no wish for his attentions. Who is he anyway?'

'The son of Mister Henry and Mistress Matilda Kermeen. A fine couple of gentle people from out Onchan way. Unfortunately, the son Jeremy, has fallen into evil ways. He seems to be a bad seed.'

'His father gave me this, to salve his conscience, he said.' Sarah held out the coin, finding to her amazement that it was a florin.

Mistress Quayle smiled grimly. 'Well that was a more pleasant way of coming by it than that young villain had in mind for you!'

Sarah shuddered, looking in awe at the coin. *A whole two shillings!* It was almost, but not quite, worth the horror and embarrassment she had suffered to gain it. That would make three shillings and sixpence she would have earned for this day's work. Half as much as she was paid for a full week's work on the washing-floors of the mines.

Patrick stood looking uncertainly around him for several moments after Sarah had dodged inside the building to start work. He almost hoped she would be too late and would be sent away. Then he would be able to spend the entire afternoon with her. But that was selfishness, he realised, because she had often told him how desperately her family needed money. He also had a good idea of what her mother would do to her if she went home without any.

Governor Hope and the official party were almost upon Patrick, standing in the doorway, before he awakened from his reverie. He had to jump hurriedly out of their way. Captain Rowe frowned as he passed but said nothing. Sighing, Patrick wandered off down the green toward where the benches groaned with enough food to nicely sustain the multitudes. He found there was a plentiful supply of good ale that stood to make his lonely afternoon more bearable. Also, much thought had clearly gone into the planning of the feast, with the Methodists and Totalists being well catered for with a generous quantity of ginger beer and milk.

Collecting a cup of ale, Patrick moved amongst the mine workers and their families. On such a beautiful day they were all dressed in their brightest holiday clothes; everyone in the gayest of moods. It was a surprisingly nice day, he reflected, for the twenty-seventh of September. Even the gentle breeze had not the slightest hint of autumn in it. The Good Lord had certainly sent weather fitting for such a special occasion. If only He had not seen fit to have Sarah working on this day!

Shaking his head sadly, Patrick replenished his cup and taking it and a goodly sized plate of beef and potatoes, sat on the grass in a position from where he could keep careful watch on the door of the wooden building.

High above the hillside a sparrow-hawk hovered, alert and watchful. Shading his eyes with his hand, Patrick watched it hang motionless in the still air, then plummet suddenly earthwards. In a moment it soared aloft again, a mouse or shrew tightly grasped in its talons.

Flocks of herring gulls swooped, screeching and squabbling to gulp down any pieces of food that were dropped or thrown away. Some snatched food from the hands of the revellers or straight from the tables. Around the table, people constantly waved their arms and shouted to keep the greedy birds at a safe distance.

With the door of the building tightly closed against him, the warmth of the sun and a few excess cups of ale making him drowsy, Patrick lay back on the grass to rest for a while.

Fluffy white cumulus drifted lazily across an otherwise unspoiled blue sky and Patrick closed his eyes against the glare. In moments he had drifted off into a dream-filled slumber.

Inside his sleeping mind, Sarah skipped and ran with him, laughing and carefree, over the heather and bracken-covered hills. Rabbits and peewit fledglings fled, startled, from their path. Suddenly the mother — Sarah's violent, ever-complaining mother — was no more. The dream world had faded her from existence.

Whenever he had asked Sarah to spend time with him, she always refused. Because her mother would be angry were she to be late home, the girl would not even linger to have a beverage with him in the tearoom in Laxey village.

In his dream the mother did not exist, and he was free to pursue and woo and, if she would accept a humble Irish miner, win his loved one.

The vision flitted across the hillside as lightly as a summer moth, Patrick in desperate, but happy pursuit. Catching Sarah, he pulled her into his arms. Tugging the strings of her bonnets, he pulled them off, liberating her shiny dark curls to fly freely in the breeze. With his arms tightly around her slim body, he lifted her easily, bending to kiss her deeply.

Sarah wound slender arms around his neck, tangling her fingers amongst his hair to hold him to her, and returned the kiss with an intensity to match his own. This time she did not struggle and pull away as she had done when on the wheel platform. This time she responded longingly.

Gazing down into Sarah's dark, sparkling eyes, Patrick suddenly realised how much he loved her.

Awakening abruptly, he was aware immediately of his embarrassing state of excitement. For just a moment he was disorientated, unsure of where he was. Suddenly alert, he sat up, pulling his knees under his chin and lazily scrubbing a hand over his scalp while he gazed around the field.

He felt he must have slept for quite some time, for it was late into the afternoon and games were well underway on the green. Thoughtfully he gazed up the glen and past the giant wheel and the mine workings which stretched its length. Several other wheels — far smaller ones — and engine houses were in view. Then beyond them, forming a magnificent backdrop to the industrial scene, stood Snaefell the Monarch of the Manx mountains. No more than a high hill, but to the Islanders it was the Mountain.

The wheel — the *Lady Isabella*, had an almost uncanny appearance, for there was an absence of any aqueduct to the top, or even in line with the centre of the wheel. A long row of arches approached it from higher in the glen, but they merely supported the long connecting rod that moved backwards and forward, applying the power of the wheel to drive the pump at the mine shaft, some two hundred yards distant.

Patrick was well enough aware though, that the water that drove the *Lady Isabella* flowed through an underground iron tube from a reservoir higher up the glen. On reaching the wheel casement, it rose up the centre of a tower, along under the platform and onto the wheel. All very ingenious, Patrick thought, and truly a credit to Mister Robert Casement.

Suddenly he also became aware that the door of the wooden building had opened, and the gentry were pouring out, many of them obviously in their cups and none too steady on their feet. This was the moment Patrick had waited for all afternoon and he moved closer, watching anxiously.

A threesome emerged, parents and son he guessed, the woman obviously distressed and the older man bristling with undisguised fury. Angrily he nudged the youth in the back with a riding crop, which propelled him stumblingly forward. The young one, nursing a livid raised weal on his face, shot a venom-filled scowl over his shoulder then slouched on ahead.

Eyeing them with interest, Patrick shuddered. Never, he hoped, would anyone ever look on him with such raw hatred.

The sun was well advanced in its trek down toward the hill-tops before Sarah finally emerged. The games on the green were petering out and the crowds beginning to drift homewards, many from the further distant areas having already left.

Patrick, with little patience, watched the pony carts, traps, Hi-Kelly carts and occasional fancy coach make their way, at differing paces, up the steeply sloping roads out of the glen. Others left on horseback, or the less affluent on sturdy Manx ponies. Most wandered away on foot.

The door of the building opened again and suddenly Sarah was there, looking warm and a little flustered. Stray curls poked entreatingly from her bonnet and Patrick thought she looked more beautiful and desirable than ever.

He stood up and waved frantically, starting to run toward her.

Seeing him, Sarah ran too and was breathless when she reached him.

'I thought I was never going to get away,' she said breathlessly. 'It took us so long to clear up in there, I wasn't sure if you would wait,' she said shyly.

'I had to,' he replied quietly. 'There is still the evening to come. The display of fireworks when it is dark. You'll stay and watch them with me, won't you? Please say yes.'

Sarah shook her head doubtfully. 'I don't know. My Mam

would want me home. She finds the childer too much for her to cope with these days.'

Patrick looked crestfallen. 'Just this once. Surely, she can manage them herself for a few more hours. Since I left the washing-floors and went down the mines to work, we have had no time to be together. I need to be with you. Please let me have these next few hours.'

Sarah, gazing up into his hazel eyes, saw the glints of gold and the longing in them. With a shiver of ecstasy, she remembered the kiss he had stolen and the feeling it had aroused in her.

'It would be nice to spend some time together. Mam will not know what time I finished working today. I expect she will be not too annoyed when I take the money to her. And I would like to see the fireworks!' She added.

'You'll stay, then?'

'Aye.'

Patrick gave a great whoop of delight, sweeping her up in his arms and swinging her in the air as though she was no heavier than a feather cushion.

'I have an extra two shillings, too,' Sarah said. 'And since I suffered great humiliation to earn it, I think I might keep it all for myself. Mam need not know I have it.'

'How did you come by it?' Patrick wore a questioning look, which soon turned to a scowl as Sarah related the tale of Jeremy Kermeen.

'You did not encourage him or let him do anything — well — unseemly?' he asked gruffly, his body stiff with jealous fury.

Sarah reeled away from him. 'Indeed, I did no such thing!' she retorted hotly, feeling it expedient to hide from him that the lout had in fact, fumbled his hand under her petticoats and well up her thigh. 'You should know me better than to ask. The mere look of him repelled me violently.'

Patrick nodded miserably. 'I know. I'm sorry. I didn't really doubt you. It's just ... well ... I love you so much it pains me to know another man has even touched you.'

Catching her breath, Sarah gazed up at him, eyes aglow. 'Did you mean that?' she asked breathlessly.

'What? Mean what?'

'That you love me? You just said it!'

Patrick was thoughtful for a moment, then laughing he asked, 'Did I really say that?'

Sarah felt her heart sinking. Nodding, she whispered, 'Aye ... Did you not mean it?'

His face hot with colour, Patrick pulled her close. 'Patrick O'Mally never says what he does not mean. If I told you I love you, my fair lassie, then that's the way it is!'

In the next few moments of joy they kissed deeply, unaware of the shocked faces around them. Then hand in hand they strolled to sit by a small copse of trees, high on the darkening hillside.

'We must find a way of spending more time together,' Patrick said quietly, slipping an arm around Sarah's shoulder.

The girl nodded thoughtfully, leaning against him to lay her cheek against his chest. He felt so firm and strong. With him she felt safe, protected from the evils of the world, and from her mother's fearful tempers. If anyone could make things work out right for her, it would be him.

'How could we arrange it? Mam would never allow me to see you not even in the company of a chaperone. When I am not at work, she needs me at home to help with the croft and the childher.'

Patrick nodded miserably. He knew the story well and had heard it often enough to know it word for word. Sarah repeated it every time he asked her to see him. From what he had heard of Mistress Fayle, he found it hard to believe she had ever been the good, loving mother that Sarah claimed. Was it possible for anyone to change so much? It had been a hard life for her he must grant. To lose four children and her husband in so short a time must be hard to bear, but surely it was unfair to vent her spite against life on Sarah.

He tightened his arms around his love. 'We *must* find a way,' he told her gently.

Sarah looked up at him, her eyes moist and trusting. 'Yes. We must.' Tilting her head back, she closed her eyes as his lips touched hers. Heart fluttering, she responded breathlessly to his intensifying kiss, wishing suddenly that it could be more.

Sensing her heightening desire, and uncomfortable with his own arousal, Patrick took reluctant control of his emotions. 'We'd better go back,' he sighed. 'It will soon be time for the fireworks.'

Sarah accepted his hand, outstretched to help her to her feet, and clinging together they made their way down the hill.

Chapter 3

The excited undercurrent of the crowd in the glen was infectious and Sarah soon found her senses tingling with anticipation.

Fireworks were a treat she had heard of but had never before seen. They would be the perfect ending to a truly wonderful day — the icing on the cake, as her mother used to say, in her happier days. Nowadays there was no cake, let alone icing.

The density of the crowd made it impossible for Patrick and Sarah to get anywhere near the viaduct on which the firework display was being held, and for a few anxious moments they sought a suitable vantage point.

'We should be able to see from there.' Patrick pointed up the hill. Laughingly they set off climbing, chasing each other upward, away from the crawling mass of people. They hurried because they knew the show would soon begin and they did not want to risk missing any part of it. Finding a good position with a clear uninterrupted view, they turned to watch and wait.

Nearby trees whispered mysterious messages and the night deepened, intensifying the light from the multitude of lamps below them.

The shoreline, quickly vanishing in the gloom, became no more than a faint incandescence, remote and unreal, just occasional choppy splashes in the dense, black ocean of the night.

Suddenly Patrick gathered Sarah in his arms, holding her so tightly she could feel the pounding of his heart hard against her. He kissed her, gently at first, then with a deeper, lingering sweetness and mounting ardour.

Sarah thrilled to the newly discovered joy in the warmth of his lips. She felt her whole being and self-control melt until nothing was left but a light-headed awareness of danger and delight. No longer a separate person, she became almost a part of him. Overwhelmed and shaken by the turbulence of her own emotions and from a long way off, she summoned her scattered senses and pulled herself away from him slightly. Dragging in a tremulous breath, she forced herself to a degree of calmness.

Sarah studied Patrick for a moment in the twilight. The sun, now set, left only a dusky ruby glow on the night sky above the mountain. The fiery redness this added to the auburn of his hair gave Patrick a wild, exciting look and she saw again with a joyous stab of wonder, how handsome he was.

'You feel as I do, I suspect,' he said quietly.

Sarah said nothing to this, merely moved a little away from him; needing time to calm the racing of her heart and allow the tumult inside her to die.

The darkness deepened and as the eagerly awaited moment approached — the time the fireworks were to be set off — the sounds of chatter and laughter from the glen below them modulated subtly downward.

A torch flared on the viaduct, causing a ripple of excitement to run through the gathering. This was followed by an anticipatory hush, so complete that the whispering of the distant sea could be heard like a siren song.

Suddenly, accompanied by oohs from the crowd, a spark flared, as brilliant as a fine summer's day, followed by a stream of multi-coloured lights popping high in the sky and cascading downward.

Looking down, Sarah saw an endless tide of young faces, like a field of autumn grain in the sun, turned upward to catch every moment of the excitement.

On the cliff sides, cormorants and gulls took off into the night on wildly flapping wings, screeching angrily, scolding the humans who dared disturb them so.

The display went on, with every imaginable kind of flashing light emanating from the viaduct. Huge fountains of multi-coloured illuminations; showers of brilliant silver light that looked like burning waterfalls. Wildly spinning wheels of fire and rockets flew high into the night sky, exploding noisily in a thunderstorm of colourful, fiery rain.

Sarah watched it all through the eyes of a child. Eyes wide with a mixture of fear and excitement. There was a special thrill in her heart because Patrick was with her.

A chill breeze sprang up and shivering, Sarah pulled her shawl tightly around her. Catching the movement from the corner of his eye, Patrick shifted so that he stood behind her, wrapping his arms around her, feeling her press back against him until their bodies were almost one. He felt the curve of her breast against his arm and had an urgent, rending desire to touch it with his hand. He quivered, his stomach contracting with the effort of retaining self-control and the fear of Sarah's reaction if he lost it. Then his body betrayed him, and he felt a tell-tale ache stirring in his loins. Embarrassed, he arched slightly to move the offending part away, but suspected he had been too slow.

Sarah, sensing rather than feeling Patrick's discomfort, thrilled with the realisation that she could arouse such a powerful reaction in him. Fired with a dangerous mixture of desire and mischief, she pressed back, moving her buttocks almost imperceptibly against him.

With an agonised groan, Patrick lost the battle with his hand. Taking control of him, it moved of its own accord, to cup her soft young breast.

Sarah stiffened, her spine tingling, knowing she should push his hand away. Knowing she should push him away. Slap his face perhaps. Her limbs had turned to jelly, and she was defenceless against his touch. Taking over her mind, her body responded shamelessly, and she found herself trembling against him, willing his fingers speed while, hidden by her shawl, they unfastened the tiny buttons of her bodice. At last his hand slipped inside, cold against the warmth of her skin, making her shiver with anticipation. Gently he teased the nipple and she moaned quietly, lost in a new ecstasy.

Then suddenly the fireworks were finished. Nothing remained but the smell of cordite and a few lingering wisps of smoke drifting across the face of a newish moon. The crowd was silent for a moment, with an uncanny hush, waiting for the next explosion of brilliance. Then realising after several minutes that it was all over, a rumble of voices broke out. A good-natured murmur of complaint ran through the crowd, trailing off to a low mumble as the people drifted away, alone and in groups to their homes.

Patrick and Sarah stayed for quite some time, alone in the dark, breathlessly revelling in their new-found intimacy.

Without a word, he turned her to face him. Bending, he kissed her breasts, teasing each one in turn with his tongue. Her shuddering pleasure aroused him even further and, now completely without control, he pulled wildly at her skirts.

The feel of his hand moving on her thigh brought to Sarah

first a thrill of pleasure that seemed to rise to her throat and stop her breath. Then a sudden, jolting memory of Jeremy Kermeen brought her to her senses like a dash of iced water in her face. With a violent shock of reaction, the mad longing died, and she twisted frantically from Patrick's grasp.

Jumping away, she faced him like a cornered animal, eyes blazing. 'Stop!' she cried. 'In God's name, Patrick, *stop*! Don't do these things!'

Puzzled, Patrick took a step toward her and she hit him then with all the power she could muster. Reeling back, tasting blood from where the inside of his lip was cut, he clutched at his face.

'Don't ever touch me like that again! Not *ever*!'

'But I thought——' Patrick broke off, confused and shaking his head. 'You let me. You seemed to encourage me. I thought you wanted it. I thought you were enjoying it, even.'

Sarah fought to control the tremor on her lips, a well of unshed tears in her eyes. 'I was. I did. But I shouldn't have. And you went too far. You should not have touched me in the first place and excited me so. I had thought you were better than other men, but you are not. It would seem you are interested in me only for what pleasure you can get from me. If that's what you want there are plenty of girls willing to sell it to you. I won't do it and I don't want to see you again. *Ever*!' Eyes ablaze, she stopped for breath.

Patrick heard her words as though from a great distance. Then the meaning sank home, and he started as though from a deep sleep. He reached out for her, but Sarah turned quickly and ran, stumbling toward the Agneash Road.

He stood, stunned for a moment, breathing deeply in the chill air, then sped in pursuit. Catching up, he gripped her arm and whipped her around so that he could look into her eyes. Pained eyes that looked blankly back at him, clouded with panic and shock.

'I'm sorry,' he said miserably, peering at her through the darkness. 'I didn't mean it to happen. I just couldn't stop myself and when you didn't stop me either ...' He shrugged and his voice tailed off miserably.

A tear escaped, trickling an unsteady path down Sarah's cheek. 'I couldn't help it. I knew I should stop you but couldn't!' Looking at her feet, she shuffled and whispered, 'I wanted you to, really... but not to go too far. You went too far! I'd better get home now. Mam will be angry I was not home long ago.'

'I'll walk with you to the door. Make sure you make it home safely.'

'No! Not to the door!' Sarah shook her head wildly. 'Mam must not know I was with a man!'

As they walked, she fastened her bodice with clumsy, trembling fingers. Below them at the bend in the road stood the mighty *Lady Isabella*, gleaming proudly in the moonlight, casting an eerie shadow across the glen. Just short of the gate, Sarah stopped beside a cluster of wind-battered elder trees. Looking around stealthily, she drew Patrick into their shadow.

'Don't come any further,' she whispered, 'for fear Mam hears and comes to find who's with me.'

Patrick caught her arm as she tried to step away from him. 'Will I see you again, Sarah?' he asked anxiously.

'Aye. Sometime.'

'When?'

Sarah twitched her shoulders uncertainly. 'I don't know. It depends when I can get the chance.'

Patrick studied her in silence for a moment. 'Are you still angry with me? I know I did wrong, but only because I love you. It felt right. Won't you forgive me? I promise I will never try to force myself on you again.'

Sarah gazed up at him, tenderness moving her heart. 'There's nothing to forgive. I was as much to blame, but we must never let it happen again.'

Hanging his head, Patrick nodded his agreement. Then because he looked so crestfallen, Sarah pulled his head down and tenderly touched her lips to his.

'When will I see you again, then?'

Taking a deep, shaky breath, Sarah sighed. 'It's so difficult now that we don't work together.'

'You'll have to find a way of escaping from your mother sometimes. We can't go on like this — just meeting for a few minutes now and again. Always with crowds of people around us. Never being alone together. Never able to show what we feel for each other.'

Sarah stabbed the toe of her boot into the carpet of autumn leaves. 'I know. I hate this deceit. It seems wrong to lie to my mother. Maybe she'll recover soon from the horrors that made her this way. I'll try to think of a way to spend some time with you, but I must not do anything that will cause her any more suffering.'

Patrick nodded. 'I know. And I respect your fine feelings, but I have feelings too. I need you, Sarah.'

'And I need you. Desperately.' She reached up to kiss him, taking his hand and pressing it for a fleeting moment against her breast. 'That was to show I really have forgiven you,' she whispered. Then before he could make more of it, she slipped away into the night, hurrying away from him with her heart in her throat — choking her.

From the end of the lane Patrick watched morosely, his heart in turmoil until she entered the croft, seeing her turn to wave from the open doorway.

For quite some time he stood in the dry, chill autumn air, aching with the longing to have Sarah pressed close to him again. Remembering, with a strange anguish, the warmth and softness and willingness of her body against his hands and lips.

Hearing voices raised in anger, he guessed Judith must be taking her daughter to task for her late homecoming. At last, the voices died and in the silence of the night Patrick turned to make his way back down the hill and around the coast to the cottage where he boarded, in Baldrine.

His feet were leaden. The climb up the steep hillside from Laxey wearisome. His heart pounded with the effort and with the deepening realisation of how impossible the situation appeared. The pain inside him seared like the aftershock of some deep wound. There was a haunting loneliness in the silence of the night. Alone. Yet not alone, for all around he could hear scufflings and scratchings. Creatures of the dark going about their business. Mice, shrews, frogs, the odd skittering of a lizard or a whirr of bats' wings close to his face. An occasional owl swooped, its wings a mere whisper in the night, to snatch a squealing rodent in its talons. Now and again tiny, baleful eyes, watching from the undergrowth, caught the glint of the moon.

Patrick settled himself on a rock to try to work out a solution to his problems. His life seemed to be full of woe, which he sometimes found difficult to come to terms with.

The hopelessness that Judith Fayle's hatred of the Irish was casting on his relationship with Sarah was just the latest in a long line of frustrations for him.

From the start there had been heartbreak, for almost as far back as he could remember. There had been the parents he could hardly remember, who had died back home in Ireland, during the cholera outbreak in 1833.

He had not been the only one to suffer, of course. There hardly seemed to be a family in Britain that hadn't. Most of his brothers and sisters had been taken too, though he could not clearly recall quite how many.

When he thought about it, even after all these years, the memory still turned his stomach. Though not much more than a baby at the time, the scene had etched itself all too clearly into his mind. Their dreadful moaning when their insides had been devoured and torn apart with the dreadful cramps the illness brought.

He could not really remember them, just the awful, lonely emptiness there had been when they had all gone. All except Colleen, that was. It was as though a limb had been ripped off, leaving a gaping, open wound in his life.

Engraved on his mind though, was the terror he had felt when they had all been taken away to a paupers' grave; he knew not where. Just that they were gone, and he and Colleen were alone in the world with no one to care about, or for them.

Someone, a neighbour Colleen had told him, looked after them for a few days. Quite a nice person, but with a large family of her own to care for. So very soon the policeman had come and taken them to the home for foundlings. There they had languished for quite some time. Then suddenly there was joy in their young lives again when hitherto unknown grandparents appeared from the country. The kindly couple had arrived one day, looked the miserable children over, claimed them as their long-lost grandchildren, then taken them back to their farm.

They had been like manna from heaven to the orphans, though Patrick had never quite been able to convince himself that they really were his grandparents. It did not matter a whit. To Patrick and Colleen, they had been the kindest people in the world — two elderly angels. And the children could have been no happier anywhere. Life was idyllic for years and the children thrived. The brother and sister had gone to school and,

Patrick was sure, were given a much better chance in life than they would ever have had with their own parents and the vast number of siblings who had died.

Besides their schooling, which had cost their elderly benefactors dearly, they had learned the skills of farming. For some years their futures looked rosy indeed.

Then disaster had struck yet again. Colleen had ridden out on her horse one crisp winter's morn as was her wont each day. Hours later he had seen the horse, unaptly named Lucky, galloping across the fields, to arrive at the farm in a trembling lather of sweat.

For hours that seemed to stretch into an eternity they had scoured the countryside; Patrick, the farm hands and his grandparents. When he had found Colleen lying beneath a tree, her head was twisted at a grotesque angle, and an angry weal lay across her face where a tree bough had hit her with great force. Her body had already begun to stiffen with death and the morning frost.

Nothing could comfort the old folk. Try as he would, Patrick could not rouse them from their despair and they swiftly faded away. Within weeks both were in graves alongside Colleen, the farm left to Patrick.

Alone with his sorrow, with everyone whom he had ever cared for dead, the young man often found himself wondering in moments of depression, if there was something about him. If perhaps *he* brought ill luck to those he loved. Was he a Jonah he wondered? Then in more cheerful moments he would tell himself that was just superstitious nonsense.

Heartbroken and empty, he had been unable to settle. Feeling the need to get right away and make a completely new life for himself, he had sold the farm and wandered aimlessly for a few years. When work came his way, he took it. At other times he lived on the proceeds from the sale of the farm. Finally, with little money left, he had come to the Isle of Man; the washing sheds of Laxey mine; and into the life of Sarah Fayle.

Thinking of Sarah, Patrick shook himself out of his mournful reverie. Rising now, he looked around, remembering he had been on his way home.

Below him now he could make out the sea, dappled in platinum moonlight, chopped to a shower of rippling brilliance by the undulating surface and the swirling wind.

For a few moments his cares faded in the beauty of the evening, but then they all closed in to weigh him down again. *Whatever her problems,* he decided, *Judith Fayle had no right to treat her daughter so badly. Nor did she have the right to be a blight on her daughter's future.*

Pausing on the hillside, absently watching the moonlight playing on the water, the occasional shadow of a sea-bird flitting across his vision, he thought of Sarah. He loved her. He really loved her. Deeply. Without reservation. He knew that now. Somehow, he must rescue her from the fearful life she was living.

The answer came to him with a suddenness that shook him to his boots. He would marry her! That would be the solution. Yes. That was it. He loved her. He wanted to spend the rest of his life with her. So, he would marry her. What could be more sensible? Her mother could surely have no objection to that.

With a lighter heart, Patrick fairly strode the last few miles to Baldrine. Tomorrow he would ask Mistress Corlett — his landlady — if he might bring home a wife to share his room with him. She was a sour old puss, but fond of money, so he felt certain that were he to offer higher rent she would have no objection.

Once he had arranged with Mistress Corlett, he would ask

Sarah. Then her mother. As soon as was possible the marriage would be arranged. Yes, that's what he would do.

Patrick had never considered himself as a marrying man, but then he had never known a girl like Sarah before. A girl with so much gentleness, patience, love and, Patrick shuddered as he thought of her ferocious defence of her mother, of such great loyalty.

Somehow, he must win her and make her his wife! Life would be nothing without her — hardly worth living. His heart filled with an awesome emptiness at the mere thought of it. He must not lose Sarah as he had lost everyone else. If need be, he would even try to help Judith Fayle with her croft and her house-full of children.

Well pleased with his decision, Patrick hurried home. Wishing to have Mistress Corlett in as good a mood as possible in the morning, he let himself into the little cottage in Baldrine very quietly indeed so as not to disturb the ill-tempered lady.

Sleep eluded him that night, for the following day, he hoped, was to be the most important of his life.

Chapter 4

Sarah stepped inside the doorway, then turned to gaze momentarily toward where she had left Patrick.

'Where have you been until this time of night?' The harsh question bit into the night.

Startled by the sound of her mother's voice, Sarah whirled around, to see her huddled over the loom in the corner.

'Oh, Mam. I didn't see you there. You frightened me!' Sarah clutched a hand to her chest and gulped down a breath as her heart slammed against her ribs.

'An' so you should be frightened, my girl. Stayin' out until this time. You must have finished work long since. It has been dark for many hours. What do you think your reputation will be now? Coming home so late! Have you no sense of decency, girl? Where have you been?'

'We–I was down by the viaduct. There were fireworks after dark. I've never seen them before, so I went after work to watch.

The slip of the tongue had not been lost on Judith. 'We? You said we! Who were you with? Why did you not come straight home?'

Sarah desperately sought an answer. 'I went with–um–some of the ladies from the washing-floors.' Colour burned in her face. Lying did not come easily to her, having been brought up to abide by honesty.

'And what of the red-haired man? Who was he? Did he go with you to watch the fireworks? Havin' fun when you should have been here helping me with the croft an' the childher.'

'Red-haired man?' Sarah frowned, trembling as she tried without much success to feign ignorance. Worms squirmed in her stomach.

Fury flared in Judith's eyes. 'Don't try to act the innocent with me madam! I saw you myself. I took time from the croft to watch the ceremony, for it was the biggest event the district has ever known. I may have been a long way off, but there is nothing wrong with my eyes. I saw you kissin' a man! A large man with red hair. It was most *certainly* you I saw in his arms, makin' a spectacle of yourself!'

'I'm sure you were mistaken, Mam,' Sarah lied desperately. All the worms turned somersaults.

'Indeed, I was *not*. I saw you clearly. Acting like a trollop! Makin' love in broad daylight. In front of hundreds of people. The only mistake I have made is to believe I could trust you. Have you thought how smeared your name and the family's reputation will be now?'

'Oh, *that* man!' Sarah attempted to pretend a remembered triviality. 'It was just for a moment. In the excitement and danger of being so far above the ground, for a moment I felt a little light-headed. The man, one of the miners I think, lent me support and when I was steady again, he stole a kiss. He meant no harm. I hurried quickly away from him.'

'On the wheel, you say. You lie!' Judith's fury was rising now. 'It was not on the wheel I saw you, but on the green! In the afternoon. And it was no brief encounter — it was lingerin' an' filled wi' passion! I had been wi' the childher to get some food an' saw you from across the green. I sought to take you away from the man, but lost sight in the crowd an' could not find you.'

'Oh, Mam!' Sarah cried miserably. 'It's not what you think. Please don't be upset.'

'Upset is it? I see my eldest daughter makin' love in front of some of the best people — and some of the worst gossips on the island and you tell me not to be upset!' Judith's voice rose by degrees until it was a high-pitched screech.

'Please, Mam … be calm.' She reached to touch her mother's hand, but it was snatched away from beneath her fingers, as though burned.

'Don't touch me girl! I don't want you near me! Where did you go with that man while I was searching for you? I want to know where you went …' Her voice was low now, every word punched out with venom.

'We–we just walked up the hill a bit and talked until it was time for the fireworks.'

'Who with?'

Sarah frowned, puzzled. 'Well, with him. The man you saw me with.'

'And who else?'

Sarah shrugged nervously. 'No one else.'

'You went into the hills with a man? A miner?' Judith's eyes blazed, and her tone was ominous. 'An' no one else with you? Alone in the hills for hours. With a strange man! God preserve us girl. What were you thinkin' of? What have you done to us? Have we not had enough pain to bear recently without you bringin' shame on us?'

'I've done nothing wrong, Mam. Honestly. We were only talking and there were lots of other people around — only they weren't actually with us.'

'You *swear* that's the truth?' Judith was calming now.

'Aye, Mam. I swear we did no wrong. Sarah thought, blushing slightly, of the intimacy they had shared on the hill above the viaduct. It had not seemed so wrong really, and she did not feel she was being too dishonest with her mother. She had come to her senses before they had done anything *too* wrong.

'I needed you here to help with the animals and the childher.' Judith whined accusingly.

'I'm sorry, Mam, I'll work harder tomorrow.' To placate her mother she added, 'I have the money here for you.'

Judith's face lit up. 'They paid you today?'

Sarah nodded, smiling as she tried to hide her relief. The worst was over, she thought.

'And you brought it all home?'

'Aye. You asked me to, and I know how much you need it.'

'We do that. Good girl.' Her hand, trembling slightly went out toward Sarah, palm upward.

Sarah dug her hand deep into the pocket of her skirt. Carefully feeling the three coins that lay snuggly in its depth, she picked the two smaller ones. For a moment she hesitated, conscience dictating that she should give all three to her mother. Then she thought of the difficulty and unpleasantness of having to explain how she came by the extra florin. Pulling the shilling and the sixpenny piece from her pocket, she timidly placed them into the outstretched hand.

Judith smiled hungrily as her fingers closed around the coins. 'You're a good girl,' she said and just for a moment Sarah had a glimpse of the mother she had known before all the recent tragedies had turned her into an angry harridan.

Pushing her hand back into her pocket, and with a small glow of satisfaction, Sarah fingered the warm florin still nestling there, the movement causing her shawl to slip from her shoulders and fall to the floor.

Suddenly the smile drained from Judith's face, and it became a black mask of fury. Her hand whipped out, slashing across her daughter's face with all the strength she could muster. The girl's head jolted back sharply.

'You *slut!*' she hissed, her eyes flashing.

Sarah gingerly felt her cheek and tears sprang to her eyes. 'I've done no wrong, Mam. I thought you believed me.'

'Aye. I did. An' more fool me! For a moment I *did* believe you. Until I saw what your shawl was hiding. Comin' home in such a state of undress indeed. Flaunting your sins. An' in a house with young minds to be warped.' Judith's fists were clenched, her arms waving wildly as she spoke.

Following her mother's glare, Sarah saw with dismay the buttons of her bodice. Fastened with fumbling fingers as she walked home, some of them were in the wrong holes, the garment awry.

'It's not as it looks, Mam. Honestly it isn't.' Sarah's mind sought desperately for a plausible explanation.

Judith laughed, a hollow sound that made her seem barely sane and that frightened her daughter even more than her wrath. 'Honestly, you say? It seems that you no longer know the meaning of the word. You left home this morning in a state fit to serve royalty and you come home now looking like something off the streets!'

'I can explain, if you will listen please,' Sarah pleaded desperately.

'There is only one reason I can see that a girl would stagger in, half disrobed, after hours alone in the dark with a man. *Fornication.* That is the word for it. You will be branded. I always knew you would come to no good one day.' Mingled with Judith's righteous anger, Sarah sensed a feeling in her akin to jubilation because she had been proved correct.

'No, Mam, it's not what you think. *Please* listen,' she begged.

Sarah could sense the younger children in the half-loft upstairs shifting, awake now and listening quietly. From the corner of her eye she could see Alexandra's head poking over the edge, her eyes wide with a combination of fear and excitement. The terrifying thought flitted across her mind of the pleasure that witnessing this scene would almost certainly give her younger sister.

Judith eyed her suspiciously. 'I'm listening. I'll hear your explanation.'

Sarah heaved a sigh and thought quickly. 'There was a young man at the luncheon given by the company. Jeremy Kermeen, Mistress Quayle said he was called. He tried–well he was in his cups. Probably not used to all the ale he had drunk, Mistress Quayle said. He–well he tried to take advantage of me.'

'After the meal, was this? Was that the man I saw you kissin'? The one who forced himself on you?'

'No, Mam. It was during the meal. When I was serving him with ale, he tried to touch me wrongly an' to put his hand up my skirt.'

Judith's nostrils flared. 'I trust he did not succeed?'

'No. I told him to stop an' tried to pull away from him. He would not let me go. His father was also present and saw what was happening. He came and hit him across the face with his riding crop.'

Judith eyed her daughter doubtfully. 'I'm not sure if I believe you. Such a to do. Whatever will people think? Even if your story is true people will think you encouraged him.'

'The gentlefolk who were near knew it was no fault of mine. In fact his father—' On the brink of blurting out the tale about the florin, Sarah stopped abruptly.

'What about his father?'

'He, well, he made a great point of apologising before the gentry for his son's behaviour. He made his son apologise too.'

Judith fixed her daughter with a long, penetrating look that turned her bones to jelly. 'Well, it sounds a strange enough story to be true, I suppose,' she said grudgingly.

'Ask Mistress Quayle. She'll tell you it's true,' Sarah said hopefully.

Judith tossed her head angrily. 'Indeed, I will ask Mistress Quayle no such thing. Get to bed now. And you!' With this last, she glared up toward the half-loft and Sarah glimpsed Alexandra's grinning face just before it disappeared from view.

Crawling miserably into her cupboard bed, Sarah felt relieved that, being the oldest now, she did not have to share the loft with the four younger children.

Listening to her mother's deep, even breathing from the next room, she reflected tearfully on the last disastrous four years that had wreaked such devastation and heartbreak on her family.

Despite the appalling conditions under which they had had existed, their life in Douglas had been fairly happy. Even with nine children under the age of fourteen, her mother had always been well in command of every situation and always cheerful. The type of person to whom everyone, from very young to very old, came to tell their troubles.

Theirs had been a tiny, dilapidated cottage with no water piped in. Every day water had to be collected from the well in wooden buckets. Nor did the house have any drainage, as many of the homes in the newer areas had. It was always smelly, for the open drain where everyone emptied their slop buckets and chamber pots, ran down the middle of the street. There was a continuous stream of effluent from further up the street oozing past their door, but the stench meant little to her, for it had always been there. It was just a part of life and she had been born to it.

In Douglas in those days though, her mother had been kind and gentle and loving. The kind of mother any child would wish to have.

Then the fever had come to town, as it did every year. Some said it came from the stinking drain, which seemed very possible. Others said it was brought by the seamen, but no one seemed to really know.

That year, 1850, it had crept its insidious way into the Fayle's home.

First Sarah's eldest brother, George, had caught the awful disease. Within days, five of the younger children had also fallen to it.

Sarah, aiding her mother's desperate efforts to save her children from the fever, had to watch in horror as her siblings vomited everything that passed their lips — including water. She had listened and tried to give comfort as they screamed and writhed in agony.

Sarah had desperately sponged burning faces; held wet cloths to their mouths for them to suck; wiped their lips in a vain effort to stop them cracking and had felt helpless to ease their pain in any other way. Tearfully she had washed sheets that were foul with the mixture of faeces and blood that had been excreted from their poor little bodies.

Finally, with no tears left to cry she had watched, stunned as within three days four children followed one another to the grave. With each death, her mother's eyes had died a little more and sunk deeper into her head and she moved as though in a dream. Or was it, Sarah wondered, a nightmare.

By the time they had all been laid to rest and the last posy of wildflowers placed lovingly on the mound, the Fayle household had become a silent, sombre place indeed.

Sarah had watched her mother shrink and shrivel inside;

her hair turned grey, then white. The gentleness that Sarah remembered so well was gone. Distant, held beyond a wide chasm, she was almost unreachable now, with the only flicker in her eye that of hopelessness.

Judith, from the day her fourth child died, begged her husband to take her away from Douglas. *Away!* Any place. She cared not where. Just a place where her five surviving children would have a better chance of staying alive.

Sarah too had pleaded to be taken away from the stinking, disease-ridden streets of the island's largest town.

George, after whom the now-lost eldest son had been named, had also felt the same need to be gone.

After some searching, he soon found them what was to be a wonderful new life. A life in the open country. After several days absence, he had burst through the door shouting joyfully about the croft he had found in Laxey.

'Wait until you see it,' he told them enthusiastically. 'It's small, but it's clean. Right at the end of a narrow track with not a neighbour in sight. High on a hill above the village an' no dirty stinkin' waste runnin' past the door. The view from up there must be the best in the world. It's got a good-sized piece of land too, so we'll be able to do a bit of croftin' and make some extra money from that.'

Judith had looked perplexed. 'But what about a job? You'll need to work. We'll need money.'

George swept her up in his arms. 'Taken care of, love. Got a job in the mines. Money's not great, but we'll be able to grow a lot of our own food.'

'How did you know about it?' Judith was starting to feel some enthusiasm now.

'I got offered a job in the mine and the gaffer there told me this man was goin' to some place called, America I think he said. An' him, the owner, was lookin' for someone to rent it to. I went to see the man an' he gied it to me. A low rent too!'

'An' is this a good job? In the mines I mean. Will you be able to do it? You've only ever been a fisherman.' Judith began to worry.

'Well. Could be it's time for me to learn new tricks,' George said happily. 'They say they'll pay me twenty shillings a week. It's not as much I got from the fishin', but what we make from the croft will make it up. We can grow some vegetables. Get some chickens an' maybe a goat for milk. An' we'll be out of Douglas and its sicknesses. Life will be good!'

Sarah clearly remembered the day they had put their meagre few belongings on Harry the knife sharpener's cart. The excitement of the younger children, milling around giggling and squealing, getting under everyone's feet. And her father laughingly shouting at them and telling them to behave themselves and give a hand loading the cart.

Tears ran down her cheeks to soak her pillow and her hair as she remembered that wonderful day. The day had shone bright and warm as Daa had lifted the children into his cart. The sky seemed bluer than it ever had before. With some of the family beside and some following eagerly behind, the pony had plodded northwards from Douglas. Singing as they went, they left the smelly, disease-riddled streets of the town, travelling out around the bay and up over the beautiful, clean and fresh hills.

Laxey had been a breathtaking sight. They had topped a hill and suddenly had seen below them, gleaming in the sun, a collection of clean-looking white cottages scattered around the steep hillsides to the narrow winding glen.

In the distance, lording it over the island, towered the mighty mountain — Snaefell. Green and purple, she seemed an implacable wall, lifting black shadows into her cap of white clouds and the glorious, distant reaches of the sky.

In the bay, the mist-shrouded water was as smooth as silk; the cry of a distant oyster catcher strangely muted.

The children, who had never been to Laxey, stopped to survey the scene below them in breathless awe. Waking them from their reverie, Harry threw all his weight and strength onto the brake handle. Clicking his tongue, he flicked the reins and started the pony down the steep, crumbling road.

Through the village and past the foundation of the wheel the tired and untidy straggle of people went. On and up past Agneash to where the tiny cottage stood in happy isolation half a mile on from its nearest neighbour.

It was going to be the start of the most wonderful and healthy new life. A place where they hoped sickness and death would not be able to find them.

Sarah turned restlessly to her other side, pushing wet hair away from her face.

Such a wonderful day that had been. Everyone singing and rejoicing. Nothing but happiness to follow, they thought. Perhaps in such a peaceful place Judith would be able to heal the raw and weeping wounds in her heart.

Before long the children, Sarah included, had started school in the neat little schoolhouse the mining company had built, mainly at the urging of George Dumbell.

Though Sarah was old enough to work in the washing sheds at the mine, George insisted, to her great joy, that she should continue her schooling.

Cows, sheep, hens and a goat were purchased from the family's meagre savings. Everyone worked, throwing themselves with great enthusiasm into the task of making the croft a paying venture. Each one thrilled to the sense of independence and self-sufficiency their labours helped to bring. Grain crops were planted on most of the land, with the stretch nearest the cottage being given over to the cultivation of vegetables.

Judith, who was quite knowledgeable in the craft of weaving, made a few useful shillings each week to add to George's income and whatever the croft produced.

The children's cheeks soon glowed with rosy health, even the two sickly ones who had survived the fever. A spark of life returned to Judith's haunted eyes.

Sarah turned on her back and stared at the roof of her cupboard bed, just becoming visible with the approaching dawn. Remembering when things had started to go wrong, she shuddered and felt another tear escape.

All had been well until the Irishman came. '*That One!*' her mother called him, with venom on her tongue.

Sean Casey.

George had met him in the inn and brought him home with him one day. Judith had disliked him from the start. She had seemed to know instinctively that he would bring trouble to her family and had tried desperately to stop George falling in with Sean's wild schemes.

Sarah smiled ruefully into the gloom. At first, she had liked the Irishman, finding him fascinating with all his blarney and flattery. Often when he came to visit, he brought comfits and boiled sweets for the younger children and lengths of bright ribbon for Sarah and Alexandra's dark hair. Until finally — young though she was then — he had made her uneasy with his hungry eyes and she had seen in him what her mother had seen from the first.

George though, felt he had a heavy burden to bear. Ever eager to increase his income and improve his family's way of life he could only see good in Sean. Try as they might, neither Judith nor Sarah could make him see his friend's evil side.

Remembering, Sarah drew in a deep breath, letting it out after a moment through trembling lips. The day was etched forever in her memory, when George had rushed into the cottage shaking with the excitement of his latest plans.

'*We're going to be rich!*' he had yelled. 'Rich beyond belief!'

'How so?' Judith had looked up quickly from her spinning, watching him apprehensively.

'Sean has a wherry an' wants me to skipper it for him.'

'Skipper the Irishman's boat? But what about the mine?' Fear showed in Judith's eyes.

'Aye.' I'm givin' up minin'. The job on the boat has far better money an' it's safer than mines,' George had replied cheerfully.

'What would you be doing with a wherry then?' Already Sarah could see a seed of suspicion growing in her mother's mind.

'Takin' cargoes across for him. Sometimes to Scotland. Sometimes to England.' George's gaze had become shifty and now rested on the fire.

'What kind of cargoes?' Judith's eyes had narrowed, and she jumped to her feet. George had merely shrugged, so she continued, 'You're goin' smugglin' aren't you?'

At first, he had tried to deny it but could not lie to Judith for long. Then an argument started that lasted way into the wee small hours of the morning, growing ever louder, until Judith had realised how upset the children were becoming and called an end to it.

So, George had had his way and gone smuggling. The first two trips were uneventful and lucrative, but George's luck ran out on the third. He was caught in the Mersey, tried in Liverpool and sentenced to fourteen years imprisonment with hard labour.

When the Constable came to tell Judith, she had taken it with a deathly, frightening calm; merely nodding her head slowly and responding with 'I see' to everything he told her. She had known it was coming. Of course she had. Ever since the day George had brought that evil Sean Casey into her home.

Sean had escaped capture and disappeared like a wraith of mist, never to be seen again on the island.

Overnight Sarah saw her mother change from a gentle, loving person to a demon, hidden behind cold, wild eyes and a wall of anger and hatred.

At last the sun wandered up out of the Irish Sea to squeeze through the tiny window and bring an end to Sarah's long night of misery.

Today, she thought. *Today maybe Mam will be better.* With a sigh, she pushed back the curtain of the cupboard bed and went to waken the younger children.

Perhaps, she hoped, if she prepared the children for school herself and let her mother sleep on, last night's troubles might be forgotten.

Richard, the last child down, had just reached the bottom of the ladder as Sarah was stepping into her skirt. The florin fell from her pocket, clinking and rolling as it hit the slate floor. Heart thudding leadenly, Sarah moved quickly to put her foot over it, all the while praying that no one had seen.

'What was that?' Alexandra asked, her eyes narrowing.

'Nothing. Get on with your breakfast,' Sarah replied sharply.

'It was not nothing! I saw it an' I heard it.' It was money an' you put your foot on it,' the younger girl said, unnecessarily loudly.

'Hush or you'll waken Mam,' Sarah tried to silence her.

'Why don't you want her wakened? You don't want her to know you've got that money, do you?' Alexandra asked spitefully.

'I just don't want you to waken her. She deserves and needs some extra rest.'

'Well there's no chance of that today, with all this arguing going on is there? Now you can let me see what you're hiding under your foot, Madam.'

Startled by the sound of her mother's voice, Sarah swung round, her heart leaping to her throat.

'There's nothing, Mam.' She lied desperately. 'Why don't you go back to bed an' I'll bring your breakfast in to you.' Her stomach was heaving in panic.

'If there's nothing there you won't mind moving your foot then will you?'

Sarah hesitated a moment longer, then defeated and sick with apprehension, she lifted her foot.

Judith swooped on the florin and rounded on her daughter, eyes blazing. 'A two shilling piece! An' you were going to keep it for yourself?'

Sarah hung her head, no longer able to lie.

Suddenly smitten by another thought, Judith pushed the coin almost into Sarah's face. 'Where did you come by such a fortune?'

With a tremulous sigh Sarah told her the full story of her encounter with the Kermeen family.

Judith studied her through narrowed eyes for what seemed like half a lifetime. 'You lie!' she spat out finally.

'No, Mam. It's the truth. I swear it!'

'No man would give you a florin for such a reason. There is only one thing he would pay for so richly. Now I know beyond doubt why you crept home in such a state of disarray last night!' Judith's face darkened and Sarah became more frightened with every moment that passed.

'You *whore*!' Judith hissed. My daughter — a whore. I never thought I would live to see this day!

'No, Mam, I'm not! I didn't! I have *never* done such a thing.

Not with anyone. Especially not for money. Please believe me ...' Sarah bit her lip to stop the threatening tears.

'*Believe you?*' Judith screeched. 'Why should I believe a word you say? All you do is lie to me. All my other heartbreaks and now *this!*'

Without warning she leapt forward striking Sarah's face, first with the palm of her hand, then with the back of it on the return swing. Her wedding ring cut a vicious line slantwise across the girl's cheek, from the corner of her mouth to her ear.

Sarah backed away, trembling toward the door, wheeling around to flee when her mother picked up the broom and swung it at her. It caught her a mighty blow across her back just as she tumbled out onto the pathway.

Turning for a last silent, agonised plea to her mother, she saw the broom raised again and took to her heels. For some strange reason the scene that imprinted itself most vividly on her mind was of Richard standing, screaming, eyes wide with terror amidst a steaming puddle that spread rapidly across the flagstones. Beyond him Alexandra grinned triumphantly.

Chapter 5

✦——◇——✦

Patrick drew a deep breath and cornered Charlotte Corlett in the kitchen the morning after the *Lady Isabella*'s christening.

'Ah, Mistress,' he began, 'I have the greatest favour to beg of you.'

Charlotte Corlett glared suspiciously from under lowered lids. 'A favour, you say?'

'Aye,' Patrick's copper thatched head nodded vigorously.

'What sort of a favour can I be doing for the likes of you?' she asked cautiously.

'The very greatest, Mistress, and while you're at it you can make more money for yourself too.'

'Oh aye?' Mrs Corlett's look was both suspicious and mocking. 'How so?'

'Well, I have a lass in mind I wish to wed. And I–we would deem it a kindness if you would allow me to bring her to live with me here, after the nuptials have been attended to.'

Charlotte eyed him with open aggression. 'Wed? A woman? You want to bring a woman here? To share my home with me?'

'With *us*.' Patrick corrected. 'She is a kind and gentle girl.

And hard working. You would like her. I know she would be more than willing to do her full share of the housework.'

'Help me? *Pah*! Interfere and hinder me, more like,' Mistress Corlett grumbled. Suddenly her face lit up with the memory of the other thing he had said. 'You made a mention of more money...'

'I did indeed. It goes without saying, of course, that I would not think of asking you this favour unless I was prepared to pay you extra for your trouble.'

'Extra, you say? How much extra?' Mistress Corlett made no pretence at nicety.

Patrick thought he could almost see pound signs flashing in the woman's greedy eyes and knew he almost had her won. Four shillings a week, Mistress Corlett.'

Charlotte Corlette nodded thoughtfully. 'When's it to be?'

'When's what to be?' Patrick asked, startled to have won so easily.

'The wedding, of course. You said you were getting wed. So, when is it to take place? The marriage?'

Patrick found himself flustered. Suddenly it occurred to him that perhaps it might have been prudent to have first asked for Sarah's hand. But would that really have been best? He had felt he really should have a home to offer her before proposing marriage.

'I–well, we–have not decided on a date yet. But I should imagine it would be as soon as we can possibly manage it.'

Charlotte Corlett's eyes narrowed. 'Not sure of a date, but as soon as possible, eh? Have you been misbehavin' with the girl? Is she, perhaps, with child?'

Patrick glared at the woman, his face red with anger. 'No. She is not. Does a girl have to be pregnant before she can be wed quickly?'

'No. But that's most often the reason for a rush!' Charlotte snarled. 'There's many a child conceived the wrong side of the blanket what's been claimed to have come before its due date. You're certain it's not that with your girl, are you?'

'Of course I'm certain. Beyond any doubt.' Patrick felt his fists ball. How he would love to tell this nosy old harridan what to do with her home!

'Then how come you're so uncertain about the date the marriage is to be?'

Patrick shuffled uncomfortably, suddenly feeling a trifle foolish. 'I haven't asked her yet,' he mumbled, 'But I shall as soon as you, good lady, tell me there will be a home here for me to bring her to.'

'Who's the girl? Would I know her?'

'Sarah Fayle. From just above Agneash.'

'I've heard the name.' Charlotte Corlett's brows met in an untidy tangle as she searched her memory. 'Aye. I recall now what I've heard of them. From Douglas are they not?'

Patrick groaned inwardly and nodded, knowing what was coming.

'Yes. I'm mindful of them now. A whole tribe of them there was. Lived next to my sister. Then the fever wiped out half of them, so they came to Laxey to live. That's them isn't it? Your girls' family?'

'Yes,' Patrick agreed. 'They wanted to get the children who survived away into the country. Felt it would be healthier for them,' Patrick agreed, feeling things were going his way. No one, he was sure, who knew Sarah could help but like her.

'The father's in jail now isn't he? A convicted criminal!' Mistress Corlett growled.

'Aye.' Patrick's heart sank like a lead bubble. 'But only for smuggling.'

'I see. So, you consider smuggling a respectable crime, do you?'

'Not respectable — no crime is respectable. But he was a good man. He cared for his family and was only trying to give them a better life.' Patrick's discomfort increased with every moment that passed.

'Better! *Pah!*' Mistress Corlett snorted again. 'Him in jail now in Liverpool, and his wife gone mad as a shrike because of it. Made things worse for them instead of better. Should have been content with earning an honest living like the rest of us have to. Does the girl work for her keep?'

Patrick sighed, struggling to control his anger. 'Aye. Sarah works in the washing-floors of Laxey mine. I must get away now, Mistress or I'll be late to work, so what's your answer to be?'

Charlotte's lips worried thoughtfully at her thin lower lip. Eyes narrowed, her face was a picture of avarice. 'You can bring her here to live, as long as you're lawfully wed, but for a girl from that family it will cost you five shillings a week. Take it or leave it. If she's earning, you'll still be better off than you are now. But if I should find out later that the girl is in the family way; you'll both be straight out on the street. I'll have no dirty, smelly, squalling brats in my house! Is that clear?'

Patrick glared at the woman, hating everything about her. 'More than clear, but I'll take it,' he answered coldly. 'Five shillings a week it is.'

Well it didn't have to be forever, he thought. It was obvious Mistress Corlett would make Sarah uncomfortable. All he wanted was somewhere to take his love, so that they could be together, until he could find a better place. There had been cottages left empty by people migrating to America in the bad times, but most of them were tholtans, ruins now, or had been taken by the flood of miners moving into the district from all over Britain.

Picking up the canvas bag containing his butties, flask of water and work clothes, Patrick hurriedly left the cottage.

With a spring in his step and whistling the tune of a mercy mining song, Patrick set off at a brisk march on the miles to Laxey. Today, somehow, he would find a way to have a word with Sarah. And to tell her — no ask her — if she would consent to honour him by becoming his wife.

Curlews whooped their strange call as he walked. Wood pigeons flew out from almost under his feet on madly whirring wings. Overhead, gulls wheeled and circled in their endless search for food. The sun shone warmly even at such an early hour and Patrick knew that today was going to be especially wonderful. Today Sarah would agree to be his wife.

Smiling, with a soft look of wonder in his hazel eyes, he reflected on the spell Sarah had cast on him. Never would he have considered himself the marrying kind. The girls in his past had been plentiful, always pretty and usually very willing to join him in sexual frolics. He had learned from some, taught others, enjoyed them all. Never had he had any inclination to make one his wife. Indeed, he had always been strongly determined never to give up his freedom for any woman. Life was too short for ties and responsibilities.

Then into his life had come Sarah Fayle with her gentleness, purity and love for all the world and everything in it. Her ferocious and touching loyalty to the mother who ruled her like a crazy tyrant was beyond his understanding. Puzzled though he was, he could not help but respect her for it.

At first, he had to admit, it had been her looks and, perhaps even more, her body that had attracted him when he had first spotted her. With her dark, quiet beauty she had stood out from amongst the other women and children on the washing-floors. She was taller than most women, too, with an entrancing softness blended with a natural poise and strength. But once he had got to know her, and she had rejected his subtle hints of the pleasures he offered, he knew he had met someone special. Even denied physical fulfilment, he had been unable to break himself away from Sarah and had felt not even the slightest inclination to seek the company of any other female. He'd followed her, sought her out to talk to. Chased her like a love-sick school boy, he realised.

Patrick suddenly laughed out loud at the thought and a rookery of startled crows took noisily to wing, flapping overhead, scolding heatedly. A hedgehog, which had been ambling across the path just ahead of him, looked up in timid dismay, then scuttled hastily on its way and disappear into the undergrowth. *Yes*, he admitted, *a schoolboy with a crush.*

When he had been transferred away from the washing areas and sent to work down the mine, life became a torment. Sarah would not see him outside of working hours for any more than just a few moments of conversation. More often than not their shifts did not coincide, and it had become almost impossible for him to see her at all.

Just to spend a few moments in her company, he had often sneaked, embarrassed, onto the washing-floors and had to endure the merciless taunts and many a ribald comment from the women there.

Then there were the times he had walked from Baldrine when his shift had made it possible, hanging around waiting for Sarah to finish work so that he could walk her home. Afraid her mother might see, or get to hear of their association, she had never allowed him to accompany her any further than Agneash village.

In fact, he realised suddenly, last night was the first time he had ever really been alone with her. What a delightful evening it had been too. Patrick shivered with the memory of it. The sensual warmth of her soft young body under his eager hands. That same body trembling with desire at his touch. Then he had spoiled it by losing control and allowing his passions to rule senses and his hands and trying to take the affair too far.

The only answer was to make her his wife as quickly as possible. *Yes! That was it!*

Cresting the last hill above Laxey, Patrick stopped, looking down into the glen, with the magnificent wheel casting its long shadows on the ground. The deads from the mine — the piles of waste left after the ores had been extracted — were like an open sore; the only scar on an otherwise perfect scene.

Below him a few fishing boats lay at anchor on the calm silver sea, riding the gentle waves like sleepy seals. Gulls rode the air currents, wheeling alertly, watching for any movement that might hold promise of a meal.

An ore ship lay wallowing like a stranded fish in the little harbour and Patrick found himself shaking his head at the hazardousness of the loading operation.

The ships had to sail in carefully at high tide, to be beached when the sea receded at ebb.

The bagged ore was taken, in horse-drawn trucks on a three-foot-gauge railway down the Glen Road to the beach. With the cargo aboard, the ship then had to wait for the next high tide to re-float her. A great deal of damage was often caused, especially during stormy weather, but in the absence of a proper harbour, it was the best that could be managed.

Several minutes tiptoed past while Patrick dreamily watched the early morning bustle in the glen. His eyes fixed thoughtfully on the distant hills and the heather clad Snaefell, while his mind reflected on a hoped-for happiness with Sarah and a limitless future together.

A watery sun rose to tinge the mist with pale, shimmering gold. A cormorant flew over — black and ugly, screeching angrily and swooping close to him with its vicious beak.

Patrick, disturbed from his reverie, realised he might have strayed too close to its nest, though he imagined the chicks would be grown up and gone their own way by then. He became aware, also, that he had lingered too long and would be late at the mine.

Silently cursing himself for a fool, he set off briskly down the hill, his long legs quickly eating up the distance.

It had been his intention to try to catch Sarah before she began work but now, because of his dreaminess, it was going to have to wait until later.

On arrival, Patrick headed straight for the mines yard, which lay downhill from the wheel, to purchase the dynamite, powder, fuses and candles he would require for his day's work. How much better it would be, he thought, if the company supplied these necessities.

His next call, before descending into the mine, was to the blacksmith to collect the tools he had left there for sharpening.

''Twas a good day for it yesterday, lad.'

'For what?' Patrick frowned, puzzled, at the smithy.

The man shook his head, smiling. 'Mind still in the nest with some doxy is it, lad? Better wake up before you start blasting or you'll have half the mountain down on your head. Nice day to start the wheel turning, I was meaning.'

'Oh, aye. Nice day for that,' Patrick agreed.

The blacksmith handed over an armful of tools. 'That's fourpence altogether. A penny for the pick and the dozen jumpers for threepence.'

Patrick picked up the assortment of ironmongery, packing them into the canvas bag with the rest of his tools and took his leave of the smithy.

Striding quickly across the footbridge that spanned the Laxey River, he entered the changing-room to don his rough, dust-ingrained underground clothing of trousers and jacket. Gathering his candles together, he tied the wicks, fastening them securely to the buttonhole of his jacket. They would provide the only light he would see during the long day spent in the otherwise pitch-blackness of the mine.

Then he walked quickly up through the mines yard, along the main adit and into the cross-cut adit that led to the shafts.

The moment he stepped from the gentle spring sunlight into the tunnel, he felt the chill dampness and smelt the mustiness of the mine — and danger. Shivering slightly, he headed toward the shaft that led to the section where he was currently working. He paused only momentarily at a recess in the cross-cut adit, where wet clay was held, to collect a ball of it.

A long queue of men was waiting to descend when he reached the shaft, so Patrick's late arrival passed unnoticed. While loitering in the line, he checked the candle on the front of his hard felt cap. There was only a tiny stub. Not enough to last any decent length of time, so he pulled it off, attaching a new one to the hat with the ball of wet clay. After checking it was firmly held, he pulled the cap tightly onto his head.

When his turn came in the queue, he took a strong grip on the top of the ladder, stepping carefully onto rungs, which were slick with moisture and slime. A few were starting to rot through in places.

Down, down and yet further down the treacherous ladder he descended, into the bowels of the earth until, nearly an hour, and two thousand feet later, he arrived on the lowest level. After a walk of several hundred yards along the level, he came to his allotted workings; the area he, as 'Bargain Man' for his pitch of four miners, had managed to win for them at a fairly good rate of pay.

Percy Quirk, Caesar Cottier and Robert Kelly, the other three men in Patrick's pitch, were already there and had started hammering in the jumpers — long cold chisels — to make holes for the dynamite.

Percy glanced up as Patrick moved to join them. 'We was beginning to think you wasn't coming, boyo,' he said amiably.

'Sorry. Got held up a bit talking to my landlady.'

'We had it in mind your dark-haired maid from the washing-floors might have over-tired you last night!' Caesar laughed quietly, his eyes twinkling.

Patrick merely shook his head, but the black look he shot Caesar told his three friends that Sarah must never be the target of lewd jests.

The day dragged by exceedingly slowly, with Patrick's mind rarely fully on the job at hand. It was safe enough to daydream, he thought, while the jumpers were being hammered in to make the six holes, three to four feet in depth, to take the sticks of dynamite.

It was only when the holes were ready to be rodded out and packed that the job gained his full attention, for this was the point at which deadly mistakes could be made. The volatile materials rarely gave the opportunity for a second mistake. Fingers, eyes and even lives were too easily lost.

Patrick placed a stick of dynamite into each hole. Choosing a tamping bar made of copper, for a steel one might make sparks and cause a premature explosion, he pushed the dynamite to the farthest ends of the wounds in the rock face. Following this, he pressed a detonator and length of fuse into each hole, packing it with straw wadding. Finally, each hole was clayed up.

Patrick knew the other three men would have moved back

up the tunnel as his work neared conclusion, but even so he looked around to check before lighting the fuses.

There was no one near and well along the level he could see three shadows, bobbing grotesquely in the flickering light of the candles as they moved away from him.

'*Down!*' Patrick yelled, then as the shadows all dropped, he removed his hat, touched the ends of the fuses to the lighted candle, then turned to flee along the narrow tunnel. No matter how often he performed the task, dynamiting still terrified him. His heart was in his mouth as he fled, fear lending wings to his heels.

The double sound of a successful firing came as he threw himself flat to the ground just short of where the other three men were huddled. First there was the muffled rumble and knocking of the explosion through rock as the detonators ignited the dynamite. Then the full-throated roar when the rock shattered and flew. The ground trembled as the explosion reverberated around the confined space, and dust flew on the blast of displaced air.

All bar one of the four candles blew out. Caesar passed his cap around for the others to re-light, then the four men went back to survey the lode, stumbling over fallen rocks along the way.

Well pleased with the quality of the ore they had uncovered, Patrick returned to his land of fantasy.

Even his friend's ribald good humour and gentle teasing during the lunch break did not fully penetrate his dream world. His meal of dry jam butties and water passed his lips, unnoticed. All his thoughts were with Sarah and the question he had to ask her that evening.

When it came time to knock off for the night, Patrick was the first one to the ladder, climbing it more quickly than he ever had before. Even so it took almost the full hour.

On the surface once more, he rushed to wait for his lady at the gate to the washing-floors.

Impatiently he lingered there, kicking happily at the dust, drawing circles in it with the toe of his boot. He longed for the ringing of the bell which would signal the end of the day's work.

Gazing aimlessly around, his eyes took in the Mine Captain's house, set atop Captain's Hill and overlooking the washing-floors. Set in spacious grounds, it was currently occupied by Captain Rowe and his family. On its lawns, Patrick could also see the tiny church the company had built for the miners.

From the carpenters' shop came the noises of men kept busy with saws and hammers at the saw-benches, manufacturing the posts, boardings, ladders and other wooden chattels necessary down at the levels.

Blackbirds and thrushes sang a tuneful melody, while sparrows chattered in the nearby trees. The first robin sat on a bush across the road, heralding the winter that was just around the corner.

At last the welcome sound of the bell came and the work people began filing out of the washing-floors and up the hill.

Anxiously Patrick waited, the question he had held to all day itching at his lips to be asked. Then finally he saw Sarah, arm linked with that of motherly Mary Cubbin from the last cottage at Agneash. She shuffled through the gateway; her face turned toward her friend. With joy in his heart, Patrick rushed forward to meet her.

Sarah raising her head at his approach, looked at him through pained eyes and his cheerful greeting died on his lips.

Chapter 6

S arah stumbled from the croft; her body racked with sobs. Clutching her face, she stopped to lean shakily against one of the gnarled elder trees at the end of the lane. Glancing back toward the house, she saw Alexandra in the half-open doorway. Just before her stomach cramped to toss out what little breakfast she had eaten, she had a vivid picture of Alexandra's leering joy at the beating she had brought upon her sister. And of poor Richard wetting himself in terror.

'Why, Mam? Why won't you believe me?' Sarah sobbed aloud. 'And why were you so determined to cause trouble for me, Alex? What have I ever done to make you hate me?' She knew that had it not been for her own pleas for Judith to allow Alexandra to stay at school, the younger girl would have been sent to the washing-floors at the mines long ago. 'You would have hated that, Alex. You know you would,' she whispered, still wondering at the betrayal.

Straightening, she donned the bonnet she'd had in her hand when she fled. After poking the stray curls out of sight, she smoothed her skirt and stumbled down toward Laxey.

Half a mile down the lane, Mary Cubbin was leaving her

cottage in Agneash and on seeing Sarah approaching, raised a plump arm in greeting and slowed per pace to wait for the younger girl.

'What a beautiful morning it is,' she said cheerfully as Sarah came near.

Sarah automatically raised a hand to cover her face. 'Mornin', Mary,' she replied tremulously.

Something in Sarah's attitude made Mary look more closely, then hurry up the track toward her.

'Whatever has happened?' she put her fingers under Sarah's chin, then stared, aghast at her friend's cut and bruised face.

Sarah thought quickly. 'I fell,' she mumbled.

'Fell?' Mary asked doubtfully.

'Aye,' Sarah whispered, nodding her head gingerly.

'Fell?' Mary repeated. 'You did not injure yourself like that with a fall. How could that be?'

'I tripped in the dark last night and hit my face against a tree.' Ashamed of lying, Sarah kept her face downcast.

'It didn't happen last night, did it?' There was statement rather than question in the homely Mary's gentle words. 'That wound on your cheek is fresh. 'Twas done this morning. Any fool can see that.'

Looking at her hands Sarah noticed, for the first time, the sticky ooze of fresh blood. Unable to find her voice, she nodded her head, sniffing miserably.

'Was it your Mam did this to you?' Mary asked quietly.

Sarah gulped, gnawing nervously at her top lip. 'Aye,' she whispered.

'That woman should be horse-whipped!' Mary stamped her foot angrily.

'She thought she had good reason.'

'Good reason? Nothing would be a good enough reason for

this. Come away into the cottage an' let me clean you up as best I can.'

Sarah followed Mary into the tiny, dark cottage, seating herself wearily before the table.

Mary lit a candle, the better to see what she was doing, then bustled around angrily. Filling a tin basin with water from a pot that hung over the peat fire, she gently washed the blood from Sarah's face with a clean piece of rag.

'There now. That's as good as I can get it, I think. Let's have a look at you.' Placing the pads of her fingers beneath Sarah's tortured chin, Mary gently tilted her head back and turned her face toward the tiny window.

'How do I look? Does it show too badly?'

Mary clamped her lips. 'Well, you're no picture. But many times better than you looked when you came in. Now, we'd better hurry or we'll be late to work. On the way you can tell me how all this happened.'

If it had been anyone else asking, Sarah would have been likely to tell them to keep a mind to their own affairs. With Mary she knew it was genuine concern and not malicious nosiness that made her ask. Without Mary's friendship and support for the last two years, Sarah knew her life would have been unbearable. No friend could be better.

Omitting only to tell Mary of the intimacy she and Patrick had shared on the darkened hillside; Sarah related the horrors of the previous twenty-four hours. Telling of her mother's accusations of how she had come by the florin, she burst into an uncontrollable flood of tears.

Sobbing miserably, she said, 'I know I was wrong to try to keep the money to myself, but just for once I wanted something pretty and new for Patrick to see me wearing.'

Mary bridled. 'If he's the man you think he is he'll like you no less without pretty frills. But how could your own mother treat you like this?' she asked. 'I cannot understand how any mother could do such a thing to her child. Not for any reason. Doesn't she know how lucky she is to have such a good, loving daughter?'

'Mam refuses to believe how I came by the money. She believes I was doing — well, you know. You believe me though, don't you?' Sarah asked desperately.

'Of course I do, love. I know you would never do any such thing. I would gladly have given an arm to have a child like you,' she said sadly. 'Unfortunately, the Good Lord never saw fit to bless us.'

Puzzled, Sarah studied her friend for a moment. 'I have watched you with children. I know you love them, so how is it you have none of your own?' she asked quietly.

Mary shook her head, her eyes moistening, showing a sudden inner agony, as they looked back through time.

'We could start them alright. I was good at getting pregnant.' Mary gave a hollow laugh. 'But that was all. I couldn't hold them in my belly. Over twelve times I was with child, but the babe flushed away within weeks. Then the Lord gives one a year to monsters like your mother!' Mary finished bitterly.

'I'm sorry,' Sarah whispered, horrified. She wanted to leap angrily to her mother's defence but could not find the right words at that moment.

'It's all water under the bridge now, love. It happened a long time ago.' Mary was calm again, her anger spent.

'My Mam wasn't always like this. She was good and kind like you. Even when there were nine of us to care for, she loved us desperately. Nothing was too much trouble for her in the care of us. That's why she took it so bad when four of her babes died. Then with my Daa being taken away, and not knowing whether he's dead or alive, it was just too much for her to bear. She doesn't want to be the way she is; you know. It's something she cannot help.'

'Aye love, I understand. I didn't really mean it when I said she was a monster. It's just that it upsets me when I see you so unhappy.'

'It's just an illness. I know it is. She'll get better soon. Someday we'll all be happy again.'

'Aye,' Mary agreed doubtfully. 'Now if anyone asks about your face, we'll tell them something startled you and you ran into a tree branch. The wound doesn't look as new or as bad now.'

Not many people asked, for most knew of Judith and her insane rages. It was not only her own children who suffered from her moments of madness, but anyone who unwittingly happened to arouse her fury. She was notorious in the district. Sarah always feared she would one day say the wrong thing to the wrong person. There were many about, who would not hesitate to give her a beating.

While most of the older women on the washing-floors felt sorry for Sarah, some of the younger lasses were of a more dramatic turn of mind. Sarah could hear them with no trouble. Though she tried to ignore them and keep her mind on her work, they talked loudly enough to ensure she would hear.

'I bet it was that big Irishman did it to her!' she heard one girl, much younger than herself, declare knowingly

'The red-haired one?' asked her companion, eyes agog.

'Aye. They was kissing up on top of the wheel yesterday. Brazen as you like, I heard.'

'And on the green afterwards,' another girl joined in the scandal-mongering with enthusiasm.

'I'd bet you a golden guinea she led him on too far, then tried to back out when it was too late!'

Sarah kept her head bowed over her work, so they would not see the tears that pricked her eyes. Anger started to bubble in her breast. How dare they speak of her like this. What did they know of her? Or of Patrick!

'Aye. An' him being Irish an' all. An' you know what a temper the Irish have. And a red-head too!' This last snippet was spoken with relish, suggesting that red-headed Irishmen were veritable demons.

'Most likely he had to beat her to allow him his way with her!'

The other two girls nodded their agreement.

'It's my feeling she led him on too far an' got herself ravished,' continued the first girl.

'Asked for it too, if you ask me. The way she was carryin' on with him yesterday. An' with everybody watching too. Probably even the Governor an' his Lady saw them makin' love on the green!'

Sarah could take no more. Whirling, arms akimbo, she confronted them. 'You know *nothing* about me! Or Patrick!' she shouted.

The girls sniggered. 'Oh, but we do. We know all about you. And your mad mother!'

Mary heard it all and decided it had gone too far. She could not let the comments and nastiness pass without punishment. Moving with remarkable speed for one of her bulk, she rounded on them, giving each one a hearty clout across the ear.

'You three witches need your mouths scrubbed with carbolic and I'm just the one to do it for you!' Mary snarled. 'If I ever hear any of you talking so filthy again, I'll soon let your Mams know of it.'

There was no more such talk within Sarah's hearing, but from the covert looks and the sniggers to be heard around the washing-floors, she knew the rumours were spreading, and undoubtedly growing with each telling. As these things inevitably did.

Why, why, why, she wondered, had she been foolhardy enough to permit Patrick to embrace her in public. It seemed the whole world had seen. No doubt the gossips would also have noted how willingly, even passionately, she had responded. Now she was shamed. Never again would she hold her head high.

Painfully and slowly the long day trailed past. The cutting chill of a brisk north wind combining with the discomfort of Sarah's bruised face started her head aching.

Pausing on occasions to press her fingers into her skull, Sarah glanced around the washing-floors. As ever the area was a hive of industry, with even the Laxey river walled and boarded over to provide more work space. Water, as in the rest of the mine workings, was everywhere. It was water that powered the wheels and supplied the processes to wash the ores.

People scurried everywhere, keeping going the complicated series of machinery that had been designed by Robert Casement to sort and wash the ore.

Horse-drawn wagons were arriving constantly, filled with the precious ores. These were then tipped into sloping stone bunkers from where they were raked onto the revolving tables where Sarah was usually employed.

After sorting, the metal ores were taken by barrow to the jaw-crushers. These powered by a much smaller waterwheel than the Lady Isabella, broke the ore into small, pebble-sized pieces.

With a shuddering sigh, Sarah took a last glance at the odd assortment of women and children around her, then returned to the work in hand.

At last the bell tolled to signal the end of the long cold

working day and with relief the workpeople downed their tools, straightened their backs and shuffled stiffly toward the steep path away from the washing-floors.

Mary caught up with Sarah, linking her arm through the girl's. 'Are you going straight home?'

Sarah nodded, sighing. 'Yes. I must. Else Mam will be angry. And no doubt think I've been up to even more mischief!' she added miserably.

'I'll walk with you to Agneash. Give you some company on the way.'

Sarah squeezed Mary's arm with hers, signalling her unspoken gratitude.

'What are you going to do about your Mam?'

'Do?' Sarah frowned, failing to understand the question.

'Aye.'

Sarah shrugged helplessly. 'What can I do? There is nothing I can think of. I–we all shall just have to make do as best we can.'

'Have you seen a doctor about her?'

'A doctor? No!' The girl shuddered at the thought of it.

'Well, you could do that,' Mary suggested kindly.

'No!' Sarah stopped dead in her tracks, rounding angrily on her friend. She jerked her arm free. 'Not that!'

Mary resolutely took hold of her again, making her continue the walk toward the top of the viaduct.

'Why not a doctor? You have said yourself you consider her sick. She has been for a long while now. Do you not think perhaps she needs the help of a doctor to make her well again? If it's the money, we have a bit put by. 'Tis for a rainy day we always said, but they don't get much rainier than this, do they?'

Sarah shook her head sadly, feeling tears burning the backs of her eyes. 'Thank you so much, Mary, but it's not the money. What if he couldn't make her well?' she whispered, admitting the possibility to herself for the first time. 'Supposing he said she would never be right in the head?'

'Then at least you would know the worst and could arrange your lives to suit. You would not have to go on living with this empty hope.' Mary's voice was little above a whisper, her eyes beseeching as she spoke.

Sarah's tears flowed freely then. 'But if she could not be cured, the doctor might say she must be locked away,' she said hoarsely.

'May that not be for the best? If things stay as they are what will this life do to that little brother of yours? His name escapes me for the moment. The one who pisses his pants.'

'No!' Sarah sobbed, shaking her head. 'My Mam must not be put away. You know where they take them don't you? People like her. Like she is now.'

'N–no. I don't think I do,' Mary replied doubtfully.

'They throw them into jail in Castle Rushen. At Castletown!'.

'In jail? For being sick? Wherever did you hear a story like that, child?'

''Tis true. One of our neighbours in Douglas went that way. The doctor said he was mad and too dangerous to be left loose. So, he sent him to Castle Rushen, for that's where lunatics are put. They lock them up beside common criminals!'

'Surely that can't be true.' Mary was ashen.

'Aye. The girl's right. There's no place else to put them,' cut in one of the other women who had been eavesdropping on the conversation.

Bristling, Sarah turned and shot daggers at the women. Moving closer to Mary, she lowered her voice to a whisper.

'I can't allow her to be sent Castle Rushen, you see,' Sarah explained. 'I can't let my Mam be locked away with criminals. I must protect her from that. So, you see, I cannot have a doctor to her.'

Mary nodded. 'Aye lass, I can see that,' she agreed kindly.

Another of the women walking behind had moved closer and managed to hear the whisper. ''Twould be for the best if she was thrown in jail. Then she couldn't hurt anyone else,' she said cruelly.

Turning quickly, Sarah found herself almost nose to nose with the woman.

'My Mam is a good woman. Good! She has hurt no one,' she growled as the woman took a quick backward step.

Choking back a sob, Sarah speeded her step, dragging Mary who stumbled breathlessly along on her short, plump legs.

'Wait up a bit, lass,' the older woman gasped, pulling back on the girl's arm. 'My legs is older and shorter 'n yours. Don't let cruel people like her upset you. Some folks have such miserable lives themselves they're not happy unless they're hurting somebody.'

At that moment they stepped out onto the road and Sarah raised her head to see Patrick standing a few feet away, his face alive, excited and smiling.

Then his eyes took in Sarah's state. The bruising, the vicious cut across her cheek and eyes red and puffed with tears. He saw the strain and misery in those dark eyes and his smile froze and faded.

'God in heaven, what has happened?' He rushed forward; eyes dulled with concern. Without thinking, he tried to take Sarah in his arms, but she stiffened, pushing him away.

'Don't touch me. People are watching,' she hissed.

'Who did this?' Patrick growled, his face burning with fury.

Unable to speak for the moment, Sarah raised her shoulders in a gesture of despair.

''Twas her Mam,' Mary volunteered quietly.

Patrick snorted angrily; his hands fisted. 'Why? For God's sake?'

Mary looked questioningly at Sarah and, seeing the girl's slight nod, offered a quick explanation.

'She was given a florin by one of the gentry yesterday as an apology for his son harassing her. When she gave it to her Mam, well, she would not believe the reason he gave her it. Her Mam was sure it must be payment for … 'services'.'

'How could she think that of you? You of all people?' Patrick's eyes blazed with anger.

Sarah shrugged, sniffing back another sob. 'I don't believe she really does think much anymore. The whole world is just a black place to her now. How can she be stopped? I'm at my wits end to know what to do.' Sarah sobbed through chattering teeth. Mary put a hand on her arm in sympathy.

'I said before what should be done,' spat out the woman who had spoken earlier. 'Have her thrown in the dungeons with all the other lunatics!'

Patrick rounded on the woman his eyes blazing.

Fearing what he might do, Mary stepped in front of him. 'Leave her!' she shouted. 'Scum like her aren't worth the trouble they'll cause you.'

After another blistering glare at the offender, Patrick returned his attention to Sarah, who stood looking ashen and shocked. 'I have an answer to your problem,' he said quietly.

Sarah looked up at him through eyes that were dull and without hope. 'What answer can there be?' she asked woodenly.

'Walk with me so we can talk alone.'

Sarah glanced around and, seeing many curious eyes already watching them, shook her head. A cloud crossed before the darkening world, turning it suddenly cold.

'I cannot dare to be seen alone with you. There is too much talk already,' she muttered dejectedly.

'You may hurry ahead of us and wait at my cottage,' Mary

suggested in a whisper. 'You can talk there and there'll be no one to see.'

To allow them privacy, Mary wandered off as soon as they reached the cottage. To fetch herbs, she said, from the kitchen garden.

'We'll have to talk quickly, else Mam will want to know why I'm late,' Sarah said as soon as they were alone.

'I was thinking last night. About us and the way we were together. The way we feel about each other,' Patrick started.

'We must never do anything like that again!' Sarah interrupted him, her dark eyes flashing. 'I don't know what came over me to allow you such liberties. I've never done such a thing before.'

Even as she spoke her body betrayed her and she experienced the same longings as she had the night before. Her whole being ached for the sensations his hands had created. The colour rose hotly from her neck, flushing up to the hair on her brow as she looked up at him, feeling again a deep desire to touch him. To hold his hand or reach up and run her fingers over his cheek. Just to fondle him and have him touch her and bend to press his lips to hers as hungrily as he had last night. Sadly, she met his eyes, praying he could not see her longing.

'I did not mean to take advantage,' Patrick said shamefacedly. It just happened. I promise it won't ever happen again. The guilt of what your mother has done to you — to your face, can be laid at my door. I have the answer to our troubles, I think. It only needs you to give the right answer to my question.'

'What question?' Sarah frowned. 'You have asked me nothing.'

'Then I must remedy that, my Lady,' Patrick told her, his high spirits returning. With a flourish he went down on one knee and taking Sarah's hand in his, kissed her fingers. Feeling a thrill of excitement at his touch, she shivered pleasantly.

'Please, My Lady,' he said quietly, 'would you do me the honour of consenting to be my wife?'

Sarah gasped, shocked and delighted at once.

Could he really mean it? Her eyes searched his, trying to read there whether he was serious or just messing about. His expression was all the answer she needed! How she had longed for this moment. Loving him. Wanting desperately to be his.

The word 'yes' sprang to her tongue, but she could not speak it.

'What's wrong? Why don't you answer?' Her hesitation brought Patrick anxiously to his feet. 'Please say you will.' He was pleading now, his heart twisting in agony.

In the next few long, intolerable moments, he became aware of sounds, as though magnified and distorted. Of rooks and jackdaws screeching in the nearby trees. Wind soughing like a love song in the branches of the trees outside the cottage. Mary clipping herbs, whistling quietly to herself, in the kitchen garden.

Then he saw Sarah, as though from a long way off, shaking her head. Tears welled in her dark eyes; suffering etched in every line of her face.

'Why?' Patrick mouthed, his voice failing him.

'Mam needs me. She would not manage without my help. Or my wage. The children would be too much for her to handle alone.'

'You can't sacrifice yourself to her needs forever,' Patrick pleaded. 'You have a life of your own you must live! And God knows she doesn't deserve much consideration.'

'Oh, but she does,' Sarah replied quickly. 'You never knew her as she was. But I remember so much. I am mindful of all the sacrifices she made for me through the years. It is only the dreadful mental tortures she has had to suffer, for the love of her family, that have made her as ill as she is.'

'Please don't refuse me, Sarah. Don't destroy your future. Or us. Or what we have together. Could have together!' Patrick pulled her to him, holding her so tightly she could scarcely breathe. She tipped her head back and he kissed her almost savagely, bruising her lips.

'I could not even if I would, for Mam would never allow me to marry an Irishman!' she sobbed.

Patrick pressed his face to hers and their tears mingled to drip onto her bodice.

Suddenly he pushed her away from him. 'Is that your final word then? You will not marry me?'

'I would if I could. How I wish I could. But I cannot!' Sarah replied, her lips quivering.

'Then there can be no point in me waiting around, loving you and longing for you can there? I'd best leave!' He growled bitterly. Spinning on his heel, he rushed from the cottage.

Sarah slumped into a chair; her body wracked with sobs.

Chapter 7

⟡

Patrick stumbled down the road, a hissing curtain of black rain driving into his face. Water streaming from his head and down his neck drenched him right through to his tattered long woollen underwear.

On a morning like this he would have been happy to have been unemployed and would have made no argument about staying snugly in Mistress Corlett's kitchen, watching the weather through the window. Except that she would not have permitted him, he thought ruefully.

It had seemed a long, cold winter since the day Sarah had rejected him. No, perhaps that was an ill choice of words. He had sensed her desire to accept, but he had come second in the race for her affections.

Patrick tried not to think of that day for the memory of it always made him feel angry. Angry and frustrated. He loved Sarah. Needed her and had been certain her feelings matched his. He shook his head, at a loss to understand how anyone could turn their back on love for the sake of what? A lunatic. *Yes, that was the word — lunatic!*

There had been times, during the bitter months of winter,

when he had seen Sarah leaving the washing-floors and his desire for her had been almost overpowering. He had wanted to rush to her and carry her off, against her will if need be.

Always Mary Cubbin was there. Fat Mary. Like a wide round guardian angel, ever holding Sarah's arm as though to protect her — but from what? From him? *Most likely*, he thought angrily. Mary was astute. She must have been easily able to see the longing in his eyes when he looked at Sarah and had appointed herself the girl's guardian.

There were moments when he had seriously considered reporting Judith Fayle to the authorities. They would soon see she was a dangerous lunatic and take her away. That would leave Sarah free! Then he would remember where they would take her. And he knew Sarah would hate him forever if he caused her beloved mother to be locked away in the cold stone dungeons of Castle Rushen.

Autumn, which had retained the warmth of summer until that awful day in Mary Cubbin's cottage, had broken soon after, and to Patrick the winter that followed had seemed endless.

Floundering through a river of muddy water that gushed down the road, staring through rain-bleared eyes, he made his way across the mines yard and over the footbridge to the changing room. His underground clothes were almost as wet, in their canvas bag, as the stepping out ones he was wearing, but he changed into them just the same, shivering in the cold of the unheated wooden building.

At least in the mine, he thought thankfully, once you went deep, the temperature could be relied upon to stay quite warm and without change throughout the year. Even in damp clothes he would not feel too chilly by the time he had reached his pitch.

Having fastened the candles securely to his jacket, Patrick picked up his tools and walked to the door of the changing room. There was little improvement in the weather, so after taking a deep breath, he bolted across the open ground to the main adit.

The narrow entrance, being only a path on which the ore wagons ran, was crowded with miners all hurrying to work. All as wet as he. Patrick pushed along with them, sloshing through pump water and tripping over rails.

At last, reaching the end of the cross adit, he moved away from the rough rock wall to the lip of the shaft. Then squeezing through a hole that was no more than two feet square, he gripped the top of the ladder. Swinging himself onto it, his foot found the shaky, weak spokes to start the long descent. So used was he to the treacherous slipperiness caused by an accumulation of clay and oozing damp, that he negotiated it easily and without much thought or concern.

It was on these long downward climbs that Patrick most often found himself thinking of Sarah. In an hour of flickering semi-darkness with one man climbing above and one below him, there was little else to do but think.

He had seen her only from a distance, but not to talk to, since that day late in September. Not that he didn't want to — he did. But talk was not enough. He knew that if he were to attempt conversation, he would soon be asking her to walk out with him, pleading with her. Then finally growing angry when she again refused his proposal, as he knew without a doubt that she would.

Patrick's hand clenched tightly on the slimy rung when he remembered. Sarah weeping and himself no better, though there had been a certain numbness that day. But his grief had been like a wound; the real pain slow to come, and even after all these months it was still spreading, raw now, tearing at him, rending open the very depths of his being. He'd had to lose her before he realised just how much a part of him she had become. This was much worse than merely losing a limb.

Just the sight of her now turned a knife in the wound in his heart. To try to just talk normally with her would be torture. The day might come when he could, but not for a long time yet.

Deeper and deeper into the bowels of the earth he clambered, with the flame from his candle giving only enough light for him to see just the shadowy form of the man climbing above him. It was an eerie sensation.

Boots shuffling on rungs, kicking against the rock faces as they were sometimes pushed too firmly onto the ladder rung. Muttered curses as a loose rung turned at the touch, or a hand was cut on one of the binding spokes that were worn to the thinness of a knife. An occasional guffaw, as a joke was told, would burst on the scene with startling loudness.

Now and again a sudden draught of air would rush down the shaft, dowsing many of the candles. But as the miners moved deeper into the mine this happened less and less frequently, until not at all. Until there was no air movement.

There was an uncanny stillness to the place, made stranger by the throaty rumbling and wheezing and slurping as the pumping machinery, driven by the huge waterwheel, drained the water from the depths of the mine. Patrick had heard rumours it could move anything up to two-hundred and fifty gallons per minute.

Reaching the lowest level, Patrick caught his breath while waiting in the close, stuffy atmosphere for his three friends to finish their descent. Together, they filed along the passage toward their 'pitch', Patrick silent and morose, the others laughing and joking, telling and retelling stories of their adventures, mostly with buxom wenches.

Strange, Patrick reflected absently, how men's tales of their sexual successes seemed to grow with each narration. He supposed he must have behaved in the same way before his obsession with Sarah. *Sarah.* He felt his eyes moisten and tried to move his mind to other matters.

Time and time again, paying scant attention as he stumbled, partly bent, through the narrow passages, he hit his head on sharp pieces of rock protruding down from the roof. If it hadn't been for the hard felt hat, he thought, his head would surely have been a mass of bleeding sores.

Patrick managed to put thoughts of Sarah aside, momentarily, when they reached their workings. This was a good pitch, he thought with satisfaction. It had taken some hard bargaining to win it for them, but it was well worth the effort.

Percy, Caesar and Robert had leapt around like scalded leprechauns whooping with delight when they had seen the ore uncovered by their first blasting.

A trickle of sweat meandered down Patrick's back. The warm, humid air was thick and heavily scented with the smells of spent gunpowder, burning candles and good honest sweat.

Looking to the 'drivings', where they had dynamited just before knocking off the previous night, Patrick saw that the complete face of rock they had uncovered was sparkling, alive with rich, raw metal.

Stepping forward, he touched the wall, drawing his fingers down it with almost the touch of a lover.

'This one's extraordinary,' he said with quiet reverence. 'Almost pure metal. Lead and blende. 'Tis my betting there will be a high yield of silver in it.'

'Aye.' The three men nodded and voiced their agreement. Their faces glowing with the same degree of awe and almost sensual pleasure as Patrick's.

'Nearly as exciting as bedding a doxy!' Percy exclaimed.

'Naw! Nowhere near,' Caesar disagreed. 'Though this lot would surely pay for a few grand nights,' he added with enthusiasm.

Patrick glowered. 'Is that all you two ever think of?'

'What else is there? Anyway, 'twas all that was in your mind too, until that dark-eyed maiden addled your brain,' Caesar retorted.

Patrick turned away, feeling his temper rising. 'Aye well that's in the past now,' he growled.

Robert, the thinker of the foursome, watched Patrick cautiously for a moment, trying to guess what was in his mind. He had observed him for months, building a higher, thicker wall around himself.

Sarah suddenly had become a forbidden topic when Patrick was within hearing. The other three friends had often speculated, of course, when he was not around, but were unable to find any real understanding. Robert had on occasions, noticed his friend watching Sarah from afar. Had seen a look of helpless, empty longing on his face. Then had seen him turn and walk away with no attempt to catch her attention.

Patrick swung his pick into the quality ore that shone at him from the walls, resolutely levering loose large chunks.

While he worked, a little distance apart from his companions, Robert covertly studied him, attempting to gauge his mood. Finally, he moved around to work beside the Irishman.

'What happened?' he asked quietly.

'To what?'

'To you and Sarah? I mean ... I am asking what in heaven's name occurred to come between you two?'

Patrick frowned irritably and turned away. 'None of your affair. I have no wish to talk of the matter!'

Robert rubbed his chin thoughtfully with thumb and

forefinger. 'It's not just idle curiosity,' he said at last. 'I'm your friend. I know the maid was more to you than a mere tumble in the grass.'

Patrick, finding himself unable to speak for the moment, merely shrugged. A tear stung his eye and he found himself shaken that the loss of her could still affect him so strongly after such a length of time.

'There was never even a tumble in the grass with Sarah.' Patrick admitted, laughing shakily. 'She was very special, you know.' His eyes misted.

'I can see you still care deeply for the lass,' Robert continued. 'Is there no way you can make up whatever argument it was you had?'

Patrick stood, for a moment, with his head bowed and pick still held on high. Then taking in a huge deep breath, he let it out in a shuddering sigh. Turning he stared, almost belligerently, at his friend. 'There was no quarrel!' He said shortly.

Robert glanced nervously at the raised pick and, smiling apologetically, Patrick lowered it to his side.

'Then why? I have seen the way she watches when she's sure you aren't looking. I cannot believe she does not care.'

'She cares alright. Or she did then. But not enough!' He added, his voice betraying a trace of bitterness.

'I don't understand.' Robert shook his head, frowning.

'I don't think I do either. Wouldn't you think that when two people are in love it should be the easiest thing in world just to get wed?'

'Tell me the problem. Maybe between us we can think of a way to solve it.'

Patrick shook his head. 'As long as Judith Fayle lives, there is no solution!'

'The mad woman from Agneash?'

'Her mother! Aye.'

'Tell me it all. It will help you if you talk of it. I promise you'll feel the better for it and it will go no further than my ears, I promise.'

With another sigh, Patrick set upon the ore again with his pick, unburdening his heart to Robert as he worked. All the long months of loneliness, frustration and bitterness poured out. His friend let it all run without interruption and Patrick found it a mercy to be able to talk at last, like a letting of blood; like the cleansing of his soul after a leeching.

Robert shrugged and sighed when the narration was finished. Shaking his head, he said, 'I'm sorry, but I can suggest nothing. There appears no way out. Especially as the mad woman hates Irishmen so. Unless Sarah would agree to wed without her Mam's consent after her twenty-first birthday.'

Patrick said nothing, knowing it would not happen. Robert glanced over his shoulder to where the other two men were working, then moved closer to Patrick. Having eyed the Irishman speculatively for some moments, he clutched his arm to stop the swinging pick.

'I have another suggestion,' he said quietly 'Not concerning Sarah, but it would require you to put her from your mind forever.'

Patrick had little interest. He did not feel he was quite ready to let go, completely, of his hopes for a future with Sarah. Politeness made him consent to hear his friend out.

'This is a good pitch, you must agree,' Robert began.

Patrick nodded.

'The ore is good quality — almost pure.'

'Aye.' That fact was indisputable.

'An' we'll be well paid for it — mainly, of course, because of your good bargaining.' Robert bobbed his head slightly in recognition of this.

Patrick remained silent, waiting patiently to hear what his friend was leading up to.

'Well,' Robert continued enthusiastically, 'I've been saving.' He stopped suddenly, glancing over his shoulder to ensure the other two men were not within earshot.

Patrick waited, watching his friend intently.

'I have a mind to migrate to Australia!' Robert finished in a rush.

'Australia?'

'Aye.'

'You? Leave the island?' Patrick shook his head in disbelief.

'Aye.' Robert nodded enthusiastically.

'So, how far away is this Australia then? Is it many days' travel? I heard it was halfway around the world and takes months at sea to get there!' Patrick shook his head again. '*You?* Travel halfway around the world? In a boat? I don't believe it!'

Shooting another furtive look over his shoulder, Robert quickly put a finger to his lips. 'Aye. Why *not* me?' He asked indignantly.

Patrick gave a snorting laugh. 'You're such a serious sort. I suppose I never thought of you as a wandering man. Have you the money for the fare?'

'Not yet. But the way this pitch is shaping I should make up the shortfall quite quickly. Come with me, Patrick.'

Startled, the Irishman dropped his pick, which flew across their workings.

Percy and Caesar stopped what they were doing to look curiously at the other two. 'Sorry. My hands are sweating, and it slipped.' Patrick smiled apologetically and retrieved his tool.

'Why me?' He hissed at Robert. 'I've never even thought of Australia. Why not Percy or Caesar?'

Robert grinned. 'We'd make a good team. You an' me. Both

fancy free. There's money to be made. A lot of money in mining there. Not this rubbish we have to slave for here. There's copper an' silver an' gold in Australia. Enough so you can just about pick it up off the streets. We could come back, if we've a mind to, millionaires in a year or two.'

'I don't know.' Patrick frowned. 'It sounds tempting, but it will take some thinking about. It's not the sort of decision you make overnight. Have you asked either of them?' Patrick nodded to the other two, who were starting to eye them suspiciously.

Robert shook his head decisively. 'They're married, though you'd never know it to hear them talk. It'd be no good having women along on such a venture. Tie a man down too much, it would. They've got childer too, so there's always their safety to consider. If you want to follow the goldfields over there a man's got to be free. Think about it, will you, and let me know when you decide.'

'Gold on the streets, eh?' Patrick teased.

'Well, maybe not quite that,' Robert laughed. 'But I've heard tell that it's often found lying, shining on the surface. Tears of the sun, 'tis known as in places. And the mines are shallower and safer than these. A good life, I believe. 'Specially for a single man!'

'Aye. It well bears thinking about,' Patrick said thoughtfully. 'But first I must be sure there is no possibility Sarah might change her mind. When must you have my answer?'

'Not until I have saved the full fare, plus a bit to keep body and soul together until I have my first strike of gold. I should like if it is possible, to leave before winter.'

'Before winter,' Patrick repeated, nodding thoughtfully.

'You would fare best away from here, if the lass won't wed you.' Robert said gently. 'For the wound will never heal when you see her every day.'

'Aye.' Patrick nodded and chewed thoughtfully on his lip.

Chapter 8

❖

George Fayle sat hunched on his bed, if such it could be called. It was damp, cold and infested with all sorts of vermin he could have more comfortably done without.

Scratching his head, he grimaced and glanced nervously toward the tiny window of his cell. He tried to guess what time it might be, by the lightness of the scrap of sky he could see. It was blue, but pale with a pinkish tinge, so it must be very early still, he decided.

Rising, he paced the pantry-sized square, excitedly making plans in his mind. The sun was shining so today must be the day. When this road was finished there might not be another one to mend. After today he might not have another day outside the jail. Or another chance!

Taking a chip of hard stone from under his thin straw mattress, George scratched a line, alongside hundreds of others, in the rock wall of his cell. This would be the last, he told himself. The last line. His last day in jail — his heart skipped an excited beat at the thought.

In his mind he added them all up. Nine hundred and fifteen. Sighing, he shook his head sadly. Nine hundred and fifteen days he had spent in this hell hole! Two and a half years!

George again counted the stones that made the slimy, oozing walls of his tiny cell. He had done this the first day he'd been locked in, and the rocks had become almost like friends to him. Despite their dampness, he almost felt a warmth, a companionship about them. When he had needed a friend to talk to, they were always there to listen, without interruption.

At first the cell had not seemed so bad, for he had grown used to close confines and rock walls closing in on him when he'd worked in the mines. Then the numbing shock of his capture and trial had worn off and the realisation had come that, unlike the mine he could not just put down his tools at the end of the day and go home — he was here for fourteen years!

An awful black, empty loneliness had settled on him then. He felt as though the whole world had receded into an impenetrable blackness and forgotten George Fayle ever existed.

During the days that followed he had felt he was losing his reason in the shuddering, relentless semi-darkness. That was when he had realised that to keep his sanity, he must have friends to talk to. The stones of the wall had been appointed, and he had counted them often, to help pass the time and alleviate the loneliness.

There had been a time when he came to a different answer every time he counted. It had only lasted a few days, but those days had brought unreasonable panic and had seemed to draw the walls in ever more closely around him. If the count was short, he felt he had lost a friend. An iron band tightened round his chest and his lungs had to labour painfully to keep breath coming. Frantically he counted and recounted, filled with an irrational terror. The missing friend must be found!

Then one morning, early, he had heard the bolt draw back on his cell door and without warning he had been taken out, with a gang of other men, to work on the road.

His spirits had soared, and despite the coldness of the day, he had revelled in the feel of the winter winds and sun on his face. Life returned to his leaden mind and soul and even working in rain or sleet or snow was a pleasure. Anything was wonderful, even hands and feet that were blue with frozen pain. *Anything!* Just as long as he was outside the walls of his cell.

On his first day on the road gang he started to plan an escape. His heart pounded with joy just at the thought of freedom.

George drew a deep breath and, leaning on his pick handle, looked furtively at the motley collection of people around him. Prisoners and guards alike, they all looked equally cold and miserable. With luck the cold would make the guards less alert.

This was the break he had prayed for every day of the almost-three years he had spent in Liverpool jail. It was only the thought of being regarded as a trusted prisoner and sent on an outside work-party that had kept his fiery temper in check on many an occasion. Often, he had come within a hair's breadth of cracking the jaw of a sneering, sarcastic guard. Or of fighting back when he was pushed around or beaten.

Now finally he was outside the prison walls. The guards, as he covertly watched them, appeared complacent and disinterested.

Good. All he needed, he thought, was to wait until the road they were rebuilding passed through an area with reasonable cover. Then he'd be off. He knew his time in jail had not softened him physically, for he had been careful to keep himself well exercised in his cell. Exercising had helped to pass the dreadful, dreary long days.

Looking into the distance, George saw the fresh falls of snow on the hills. It would be cold, but not unbearably so, he told himself, for his years at sea had hardened him and the winters in his cold, damp cell had kept him tough.

At last the road passed a tree-lined gully, winding steeply down between the humps of sullen hills. Thick trees and shrubbery grew right to the roadside. The long-awaited moment had arrived.

Eyes half closed, George swung his pick, watchful all the while of where the guards' attention lay. After what seemed like a lifetime, they huddled together, backs turned, hands cupped around the cigarettes they were trying to light.

The other prisoners all seemed engrossed in either their own misery or whatever task they were about.

George watched them for a moment as they battled the fickle, swirling wind. Without a sound, he laid his pick on the ground and slipped noiselessly into the bushes.

Instinct told him to run. To put distance between himself and the work-party as quickly as possible. But common sense made him creep stealthily. No sense in crashing through the undergrowth drawing attention to his escape. With luck, if he went quietly, it might take a while before he was missed.

A twig cracked behind him — not a natural sound — and George felt the hair on the nape of his neck stiffen. Heart thundering in his throat, he slithered speedily under a bush. Before he could properly hide himself, the pursuer was upon him.

George met his gaze, absently registering the tall, muscular body and cerulean eyes under a thatch of grubby, straw-coloured hair.

'What the *Hell* are you doing here?' he hissed.

'Same as you,' the boy whispered, grinning cheerfully.

'Go back!' George ordered. 'They'll notice quicker with two of us gone.'

The boy shook his head stubbornly, smiling still. 'If I go, you go.'

'Escape was my idea. Don't you spoil it for me,' he growled.

'I won't. But I'm coming along. I can likely help you.'

'A man can get along better on his own. I don't need some kid with mother's milk still wet on his jowls.'

'I'm *not* going back!' The boy stared arrogantly at George; his smile gone now. Absently he drew a hand across his mouth, as if to wipe away the milk.

The older man sighed angrily. 'This is no place to argue. Come on then, we must put in as much distance as we can before they notice we've gone.'

Before they had reached the bottom of the gully, they heard a hue and cry break out behind. There were moments of angry, confused shouting, then George's teeth clenched when he heard the staccato sound of shots being fired. Holding his breath, he waited for the tearing pain which would tell him his escape was over.

He could not go back to jail. Would not! To be shut up again, treated worse than an animal. Birched for escaping. Or trying to, rather. Given a longer sentence. Better he be shot! He would die first!

Suddenly he realised that the firing had stopped and slowly he let his breath out, whistling softly between his teeth. There had been no sound of any bullets among the trees close by.

'They have no idea where we are!' he hissed triumphantly to his companion. Becoming aware for the first time that he was gripping the boy's arm and digging his fingers in hard, he let go, smiling apologetically. It had been an automatic action to ensure the boy didn't take fright and run. To break cover could have meant death.

The young man rubbed his arm ruefully. 'Do you think it will be safe to move yet?'

George was still for a moment, listening to the sounds of the countryside. After a spell of fearful, indignant squawking, the birds had fallen silent. They now perched, watchful and sullen in the trees. Through the stillness, the sound of a horse's hooves started up. Suddenly, spurred from a standstill to leap into a full gallop.

'One of the guards has gone for help. We'd better move — and quickly, for they'll have the dogs on our heels in no time. By the way, you have not yet told me your name.'

'Josiah Panter. Jos, they call me.'

'George Fayle. Now let's get away from here. I'll be a fair mite happier when we reach the cover of them woods.'

The two men shook hands briefly, then moved stealthily down toward the tree-lined glen. Once they were over a hummock and out of any possible sight from the road, they stood up, breaking into a run. Leaping over tussocks and rocks they fled, stumbling and sliding on the ice-slicked slopes and across a stretch of open ground to the welcome protection of a spinney.

Once in its shelter they stopped, each leaning on a tree, painfully dragging huge gulps of freezing air into their lungs.

'So far so good,' Jos gasped, a note of triumph in his voice.

'Don't go getting complacent just yet,' George warned quietly. 'There's still a long way to go.'

'Where are you bound for?'

'The Isle of Man.'

Jos looked puzzled and shrugged dismissively.

'It's halfway between England and Ireland.' George volunteered. 'And you? Where are you going?'

The boy pulled a face, turning his lips down at the corners and shrugging again. 'Nowhere in particular. I have no home. No family. Just wanted to get away from jail and when I saw you slip away, well it seemed like a good idea. I hope it is alright if I come with you?'

George sighed and shrugged. 'Well, you're here now aren't

you? You've come this far. You might be useful, sure enough. It'll be easier if I have someone to help handle the boat.'

'Boat? You have a boat waiting?'

George shook his head and grinned. 'No, we'll have to find one, then borrow it!'

Jos ran a shaky hand through his hair. 'Borrow? You mean steal. God! We'll be hanged if they catch us!'

George shrugged and grinned. 'Your choice. You can go back if you like. Or go your own way.'

Jos shook his head decisively and the pair pressed on toward the sea, scrambling and sliding on the icy, rugged hillsides. Following the glen river, they skirted sheer gorges that were frosted thickly with gleaming sheets of periwinkle ice.

With fingers too numb to grip the rocks properly, they both took several tumbles, collecting many painful cuts and bruises. Each time they helped each other up, continuing their journey at the greatest speed they could muster.

Where the river twisted back on itself, like a shimmering snake, they climbed over the hills between coils, sliding and rolling for added speed down the far sides. Plumes of loose snow drifted in their flanks like smoke from a funeral pyre.

At one point, when the river swung away inland, they left it and struck out across open country. Laboriously they skirted the foot of a mountain whose peaks loomed, beaten by age, scraped by merciless weather and crowned now, in bitter frost. Whipping winds, that forever swirled, feathered layers of fine powdery snow from the mountain's slopes. It turned them into rising sheets, hurling them forward like ghostly giants.

'We could have picked a better day,' Jos said, shivering.

'There might not have been a better day! Or even another day with a chance of escape.'

In late morning they came to the river again, emerging from the wood near the foot of a waterfall. They needed to reach the other side but were not sure how. So deep was it, and so fast the current, that there was no chance of crossing from where they stood.

George lingered for a while gazing up, enraptured, at the fall. A grinding roar of grey and white water dropped sheer down the craggy face. Thundering and hissing, it split on the plunge pool, bursting under a natural rock bridge into the lower gorge, where it boiled, frothing before them.

'Best go down river,' George said thoughtfully. 'At least if we can't get across, it should bring us to the sea.' He had to shout to make himself heard over the deafening roar of falling water.

The younger man nodded, and they pushed into the sodden green undergrowth, shivering and wet through from the blown spray.

Suddenly George became aware of another sound. What he had taken as the fluting of the wind through the tree branches, suddenly took on a new, more sinister meaning. In a quiet spell when the wind died momentarily, he identified the new noise as the baying of hounds.

Catching at the back of his companion's shirt, he drew him abruptly to a halt.

'What is it?'

George put a finger to his lips. 'Listen!'

The two men waited, in similar attitude, heads cocked to one side, eyes searching back the way they had come. A whining wind gusted again, but the men remained motionless. Alert still. Listening.

During another lull the sound came again. Distinct now. George's teeth rattled as the spine-chilling baying invaded his ears. His stomach clenched in terror.

Jos looked around frantically. 'Where now? There's no escaping from them brutes!'

'There's just one chance,' George said quickly. Grasping his new friend's arm, he tried to propel him forward. 'The river.'

Jos, looking blank, stood his ground. 'River?' He asked vacantly.

'Aye. The hounds can't smell us to follow us through water.'

With the wind now howling ferociously, and the air so cold on their faces that their beards and eyebrows froze, the men darted forward. Over the bleak countryside they raced as though death itself was on their heels.

On the river bank they faltered momentarily. George, looking down into the turgid, swirling grey water, felt a flutter of fear eat into his confidence. Then he had an awful insight into what lay ahead if he were to be recaptured. 'Come on boy. Faint heart will win us nothing.' With a firm grip on Jos's arm, he plunged into the torrent.

For a moment he seemed almost suspended in air, then he was into the freezing water and under it. Gasping when the cold caught him, he inhaled a lungful of the freezing liquid. The awful weight of the water was upon him and he could not breathe. He felt the blackness of death as a suffocating mass around and above him.

Fighting a threatened unconsciousness, he pushed upward, straining and clawing. Panic caught him in its grip. Then there was joy as he broke the surface, coughing out the icy river and inhaling the chilled air in great lungsful. Struggling toward the bank, he felt slippery rocks under his feet and thankfully dragged himself upright. It took a moment before George realised he had lost his grip on Jos. Frantically he looked around, his heart lifting when he caught sight of the boy, struggling in the water.

'Over here, boy!' he called.

Jos flapped his arms ineffectively. 'I can't,' he called despairingly. 'I have no strength left. I'm exhausted.'

'*Try harder, boy!*' George screamed. 'Only a few feet further and you'll make it.' He threw himself forward thrusting through the icy water until, at last he was able to grasp the lad's jacket and pull him into the shallows.

Jos squatted in the water, leaning on one arm. While he coughed and spluttered half-melted ice drooled from between his chattering teeth.

'How are you, lad?'

Jos nodded breathlessly. 'Alright.' He whispered it so softly it could have been the sighing of the wind. 'I am——' he choked, whooped a bit then inhaled his first deep breath. 'Alright,' he finished wearily.

'We must press on,' George said almost apologetically. 'There's no time to lose. But at least we have crossed the river. The guards won't be in a hurry to do that!'

For over an hour they stumbled and sometimes crawled along the shooting shallows of the river as it sliced ever westward. They were careful always not to touch any part of the banks, which were wide now and brown with mud and silt.

Eventually they came to where a narrow stream joined the river. George took a long look, then nodded in satisfaction.

'This way. The hounds should have lost the scent by now, but we'll stay in the water a little way further down the stream. Don't touch any overhanging branches.'

Jos dragged in deep breath. 'I don't think I can walk much further.' His voice came out in puffs of steam on the chill, dense air.

George nodded. 'We'll rest soon.'

They floundered on for a time, often crawling on all fours in the icy waters of the river bank. Finally, all strength sapped, the two men dragged themselves up the steep embankment. Flopping to the ground, weak and panting, they lay exhausted at the crest of a rise.

Totally exhausted, they slept for some time. When George opened his eyes, he found his lashes, beard and brows were rimed with frost. His feet and hands pained him terribly, but he knew it had to be borne. After resting for a while, he propped himself onto one elbow, listening to and watching the woodland.

'We must go on, boy. They'll still be after us.'

Jos nodded from behind closed eyelids but made no effort to move.

George tried to stand, but his dead feet would not hold him. A wave of dizziness and pain caught him, and his knees buckled. There was a blackness in his brain and a strange buzzing, like a nest full of wasps, in his ears. He clung, shivering, to a tree waiting for the weakness to pass.

At last some strength returned and he nudged the younger man with the toe of his boot. '*Move,*' he said urgently, kicking Jos hard enough to hurt a little.

Sighing, Jos pushed himself upright and struggled wearily to his feet. 'I don't think I have the strength to go further.'

'Yes, you have,' George told him decisively. 'Keep your wits about you and your eyes and ears open.'

All afternoon the wind strengthened. A gale now. Gusting. Swirling. First propelling them forward at a run, almost out of control. Then pushing them backward. Often thrown off balance, they fell, tearing their faces and hands on bushes and brambles.

From time to time George caught Jos gazing behind, eyes and ears alert. Once he thought he heard the dogs, but it might have been wind, so he said nothing. Best to keep his fears to himself.

Late in the afternoon the day darkened prematurely. George, looking at the sky, shuddered. Thick purple and black clouds raced from the west, lowering menacingly, gathering themselves for a storm.

The two men pressed painfully onward, their hands and feet, mercifully unfeeling, lips frosted and clothes crackling with ice.

Suddenly Jos slumped forward, falling against a drift of snow. 'I can't go on,' he said pitifully.

George caught his arm, pulling him to his feet. 'We must keep moving — else we'll perish in this cold.'

He half-carried Jos through the drag of heavy snow, stumbling across a trackless downward slope. Dazedly they pressed on, drifting snow blowing, stinging their faces. Deaf from the wind and blind with the winter darkness, it was animal instinct alone that lifted one foot after another and kept them going forward.

Suddenly, the storm that had long been threatening, broke around them, lashing their faces with black sleet and wiping out all visibility.

The narrow rocky track they had been following became a gushing torrent, almost washing their feet away from them. Coming to a shelf in the hillside, George peered along it, seeing a shadowy blackness.

'*We've got to find shelter!*' he yelled above the din of the downpour. With a jerk of his head indicating the path they were to take, they inched along the narrow ledge and quickly the dark area took on definition. To George's relief it was a cave of some considerable size, stretching far enough back into the hillside to give them reasonable shelter from the wind and rain.

'Pity we have no way of lighting a fire,' Jos said miserably.

George did not reply at first but walked away from Jos into the cave's dark interior. With relief, he heard the whistling of the wind diminish. The acrid odour of minerals awakened his miner's senses and for a moment he was back in the beautiful

Laxey Glen, digging once more, for lead and silver. Shaking himself back to reality, he returned to where Jos was huddled just inside the cave's mouth.

'Come further back in, boy, to where the cave narrows. If we huddle close together there, we'll maybe stay warm enough to survive the night.'

Jos forced himself painfully to his feet, his mouth moving in the semblance of a grim, chilly smile. Then he followed George to the farthest small nook of the cave.

Huddled tightly together to lend each other heat, they fell into a restless sleep of exhaustion.

'Dear God,' George begged wordlessly as he felt consciousness deserting him, 'please let us live to wake up in the morning.'

Chapter 9

<hr>

Mary looked thoughtfully at her young companion. During the winter, she developed a deep fondness for Sarah. The girl had leaned on her when she needed support. Kind-hearted Mary had always been more than happy to lend an ear, and to help her find the strength to carry on.

In her blackest moments the lass had turned to her. Talked to her. Cried on her shoulder. When she had refused Patrick's proposal of marriage, Mary felt she had never seen anyone in quite so much pain.

Mary had watched in horror as Patrick had stormed out of the Agneash cottage in a rage. His last words had been angry and bitter. But it was an anger brought on by frustration and loss, not hate. By hurt and unrequited love. Mary had seen his pain and had felt for him. Not though, as she had ached for Sarah. For Patrick, though rejected, would forget in time. He was free to find another girl. Another love. Time would heal him, and he would go on to make, she hoped, a happy life for himself.

Not so for Sarah. The reason she could not wed Patrick would remain with her for as long as Judith Fayle walked the earth. For her there would not be the normal girlish romances. Nor Marriage. Nor even, probably, an exciting roll in the hay. She had made herself a prisoner of the mad woman of Agneash, because of daughterly love and a strong sense of duty.

Mary smiled, recalling the times, oh so many years ago, when she and James had sneaked off running hand in hand to a field, a haystack, a dry patch under the trees. Anywhere, within reason, that they could be alone. She had thrilled to his touch. The feel of his hands exploring her and hers him. His body against her, inside her. The sensation of warmth and fulfilment. Feelings she still had even after all these wonderful years of marriage when James was near. Especially in bed at night. Time and age had taken no toll on their lovemaking. It was beyond Mary to imagine life without it, or without the comfort and strength of her man.

Then the day had come when, she remembered, filled with horror she had realised she must be pregnant. Followed by the thrill when James had said they must be married. Not because of the coming child, because he loved her. The child only made it necessary to wed sooner.

Then she remembered the heartbreak, two days after the wedding, when the child, which they had already grown to love, was rejected by her body. The spiritual pain was worse than the physical agony she had endured. And the awful feeling of guilt because she had allowed James' baby to die.

James had never wavered in his love. Not even when all the other babies had followed the way of the first. He had remained entranced with her. She had long since lost count of the number of times she had miscarried. Now, when her flux did not come she no longer became excited, or even mildly hopeful, for she knew this one would go the same way as the rest.

Sighing, Mary looked sideways at Sarah. If that first child

had survived it would, she supposed, have been about Sarah's age by now.

How she wished——. *No. That was pointless.* As her mother used to say, 'If wishes were horses, beggars would ride'.

When they reached the top of the viaduct Sarah's eyes, as ever, roved amongst the miners' seeking — always seeking. Then when she saw Patrick standing a little way off, she would look away before his eyes could meet hers.

Mary noticed the girl stiffen, her head suddenly dropping, and saw her intense study of the rough, stony roadway. Then looking along the road, she saw Patrick, cap in hand, watching Sarah, raw longing in his eyes.

'You should speak to him sometimes,' she said quietly.

Sarah shrugged. 'What would be the point? He needs to get on with his life without me.'

'It's plain to see he's yearning for you. He's been seen with no other lass since you turned him down.'

Unspeaking Sarah shuffled along, head hanging, clinging tightly to Mary's arm. For once the older woman found it irritating. She felt like pushing the girl away from her, preferably into Patrick's arms. A woman her age should not be the only companion for a girl so young. The child should have friends of her own ilk. Peers. Not a woman near her mother's age. She should be living, not merely existing. Taking the world by the throat and shaking it.

I know what I'd like to do with that mother of hers, Mary then shook her head as if to banish the spiteful thought.

'Why don't you go over and talk to him now? You can surely still be friends?' Mary persisted.

Sarah shook her head, biting her lip to hold back the tears. 'He wants more than just friendship. I can't give him that.'

'You could, if only you would. Even if you can never wed him, you could be a companion to him. Talk to him. You need him. I have no doubt you love him.'

'Aye.' Sarah nodded sadly. 'For all the good it will ever do. Waiting for me would be a waste of his life.'

'If you would only take the time to talk with him. At least make an effort. I'm sure you could make it work.'

'Not with my Mam. She would never hear of it.'

'Then don't let your Mam know. You must make a life of your own. You deserve a husband and childher and most of all — happiness.'

'I'll think about those when my Mam is cured.'

Mary tutted irritably. 'Sometime — *never!*' she snapped.

'She's getting better ...' Sarah said without much conviction.

Mary studied the girl, frowning. 'Wishful thinking, perhaps?' she suggested gently.

'No. Really. She's quieter now. Much more in control of her feelings. Her outbursts of rage are less frequent. It's weeks now, since she hit me.'

'That sounds promising, I must admit. The beatings used to be daily for a while.'

Sarah nodded. 'That was when she had it in her mind I was whoring. I think I have won back her trust. She is much calmer now. Even gentle and loving sometimes. More like she used to be.'

'I do hope you're right,' Mary said with feeling. 'I would like to see you smile again.'

'Time and love will win through. You'll see. As long as she can see I care — we all care — she'll be completely well again quite soon.'

'They say love can move mountains,' Mary agreed. 'If you can bring your mother back to normal that will have been a hellish big mountain.'

'I wish that you'd known her before all this. You would have
loved her. Everyone did. They will again. Soon too.'

'Good. Then when she does recover, you'll be able to take up
with Patrick again.'

The animation drained from Sarah's face. 'No. Not Patrick,'
she whispered.

'Why ever not? He's a nice, well-mannered, presentable
young man. I cannot imagine that a woman in her right mind
would not take to him. And it's clear he thinks you make the
sun shine.'

'He's Irish,' Sarah said simply, 'and it was that Irishman, Sean
Casey, who got my Daa into this trouble.'

Mary stamped her foot crossly. 'Surely she cannot hold that
against all his countrymen?'

'I don't think I could even take Patrick home, let alone suggest we should be wed. The danger it might break her mind
again would be too great. That's why it is pointless for me to
take up a friendship with him again. I would be raising his
hopes falsely. He and I can *never* be!' Sarah clamped her teeth
onto her top lip to stop it trembling.

Mary fell silent. It was clear the girl was not to be swayed.
The bitter cold of the day making her shiver, she tugged at
Sarah's arm. 'Let's hurry. 'Tis too sharp a day to be standing
here arguing.'

The other workpeople fell away, one by one, each leaving at
his own turn-off, until Mary and Sarah were the only ones left
still plodding up the hill.

In the barren branches of a gnarled blackthorn tree a robin
chirped cheerfully, mindless of the melancholy of the two
women. Bluetits, struggling for food in the hard, frosted landscape, flitted from tree to tree, following the women in the
eager hope that they would throw some crumbs.

Sarah, who had been off somewhere in her own dream world of wishing, became suddenly aware of footsteps on the path behind. Turning, she saw Patrick, a few yards behind, his face a mask of apprehension and silent pleading.

Tightening her grip on Mary's arm, Sarah hastened her steps. 'Can I come in with you for a while?' she pleaded.

Almost at a run to keep up, Mary glanced over her shoulder. Seeing who it was they were fleeing from, she stopped abruptly.

'Talk to him!' she ordered.

Sarah tried to pull away, but Mary held fast until Patrick came up to them.

'Please, Sarah. Please let me talk to you. It's important. Just this once. My whole future — our whole future — will depend on your answer.'

Sarah felt herself trembling. There was nothing she wanted more. But it would be folly, she thought, to stir up old memories. It would just rub salt in old, unhealed wounds. *No good could be gained from it.* Shaking her head, she said, 'Nothing has changed since the last time we talked. Surely we have nothing to discuss?'

'We have,' Patrick told her, sounding more confident now. 'There is a great deal we must talk about.'

Mary moved toward the cottage door and Sarah looked at her pleadingly.

'Talk to the man,' Mary ordered. 'Surely you owe him that much.'

'Please, will you not just walk out with me?' Patrick asked when they were alone.

Sarah sighed, her resolution starting to weaken at the nearness of him. Her body shook with her longing to feel his arms around her and his lips on hers. In a moment she became startlingly aware of the true reason she had refused to speak to or have him near her all these months.

Tortured, she whispered, 'Where is the use? There will never be a future for us together. No amount of talking will change that!'

They had reached the copse of elder and gently Patrick took her elbow and drew her amongst the leafless trees, so they could not be seen from the croft.

'What is the point in us talking?' Sarah asked plaintively. 'There can never be more. I told you last time, in Mary's cottage. It will only keep the wound festering and cause us both more pain if we continue to see each other.'

'I heard from James that your mother seemed better.'

'Aye. Better than she was. Almost her old self again. But she will never be strong enough to accept an Irishman into our lives.'

'You can't know that for sure. At least say you'll see me. Spend time with me. Even if only for a few minutes now and again.' Patrick had kept his grip on Sarah's arm and he now drew her closer to him.

For a moment Sarah resisted, trying to pull herself free, but it was a half-hearted effort. In a moment she was in his arms, the whole length of her body pressed tight against his, emotion and desire shaking her whole being.

'I need you,' Patrick groaned into her hair. 'We need each other. Please, my Sarah, don't turn me away again. These months without you have been torture.'

'And for me,' Sarah admitted. 'I wanted you yet felt it unfair to hold you on a string when there can be no future for you with me.'

Patrick put his fingers to her lips. 'I wish you would let me decide what's fair for me.'

'You should have found yourself another girl. You still should. One who would be free to be your wife.' Her whole being recoiled at the thought of this, but she knew for his sake it had to be.

'I have thought of it. I must admit that, but I can't. I love you too much and my feelings for you just will not die. There never has been, and never will be in the future, another girl I feel I can love enough to spend my life with.'

'How can you know if you won't even try? You have hung around wishing for me and given yourself no chance to get to know any other girl.'

Patrick smiled grimly, remembering the girls he had tried since Sarah's rejection of him. Though keen to give him the pleasure of their bodies they had been failures. Every encounter just nothing. They had managed to arouse him enough to perform his task. But that is just what it had been — a chore. Having taken to the hay with him, they had expected it of him, and he had performed. No true satisfaction. A slight physical pleasure, nothing more. That too, spoiled because during the act he had tried, without success, to imagine himself with Sarah and had only ended up feeling soiled and somehow, that he had cheapened her image. After the third such misadventure he had given up trying.

'I love you and I want to be with you. If I cannot wed you — and I won't believe that will never be possible — then at least let me walk out with you. You must give me an answer. I *must* know. And I must know now, so that I may make my plans.' His voice, it seemed to Sarah, had an edge of desperation.

'Give me time to think about it please.'

Patrick shook his head, his copper hair flopping over his anxious hazel eyes. 'No more time, Sarah. There is no more time. It's now or never. I *have* to know today.'

'Why so suddenly?' A gnawing apprehension crept into Sarah's stomach. 'Why must I decide in a moment?'

'Because Robert Kelly has asked me to go to Australia with him. There are rich pickings to be had there. Gold lying loose on the ground, just waiting to be picked up. And if you will have no more of me, then I shall go. I'll never be able to rid my mind of you if I stay here.'

Patrick shifted his feet uncomfortably. Fear held an icy grip on his heart. What if her answer was 'no'? Could he bear it? Or would he lose control of his senses, follow his instincts, grab her and carry her off?

Sarah gasped, and looked up at him in wide-eyed horror, a tight band gripping her heart and squeezing. She had heard of Australia, of course. The new world. A country where men became rich quickly. Or were killed trying! Died violently at the hands of savage black men! A land so far away. *So out of reach.*

'Australia? It's so far!' she whispered hoarsely, her voice quivering. 'There would surely be no return from there?'

''Tis unlikely I'd return. I have to know your answer now, so I can plan and save for the fare if I have to go.'

Sarah was thoughtful. Undecided. Shaken to the core. Her mind refusing to work, she couldn't think sensibly. Her heart took control and all it told her was that she could not bear to lose him. Must not lose him.

'Australia?' She repeated, dazed.

'Aye. Australia. You must see it would be impossible for me to stay here if you forsake me.'

Sarah nodded, her dark eyes brimming with tears. Instinctively she pressed closer to Patrick and felt his arms tighten comfortingly around her.

He bent his head to lay his cheek against hers and Sarah felt her heart stirring at the touch of his skin. Without thought, she tilted her head and felt the joy of his lips against hers. Gently at first, then more hungrily as his passion increased. His tongue touched her lips, tasting then probing and she moved hers to meet it.

Their kisses increased in intensity until Sarah found herself carried away with the strength of her emotions and desires. Completely out of control of her mind, she was powerless to control her body; months of heartache and yearning for Patrick welled up and boiled over in a moment with his nearness and manliness.

Raising her hand, she drew her fingers gently down his face, tracing his strong jawline. Then she stroked his hair in a fusion of tenderness and desire. But desire was uppermost and impossible to overcome. To be so near to him again. The answer to a prayer.

Her bonnet had come adrift during the wildness of their embrace and his hand, moving in her dark curls, became more urgent.

He gazed down at her with a look, almost of agony, his eyes revealing an eagerness as great as hers. Letting her fingers caress his neck, she knew they conveyed her longing. Standing on tip-toe, she reached up to kiss him again, ardently and probingly.

Patrick's response was instantaneous, as though a dam had burst, sweeping away all self-control and doubt. He took her head between his hands, moving his mouth from her lips, to nibble her ear lobes, then to kiss her throat.

A jackdaw, attracted by the movement, alighted on a nearby branch, watching curiously. Head cocked on one side; his glittering black eyes fixed beadily on the strange behaviour of the humans below.

One of Patrick's hands slid behind Sarah's head, holding her while his lips and tongue found hers again. The other moved gently to her breast.

Sarah drew a quick breath, shuddering with the need for him. Feeling his shaking fingers fumbling with the buttons on her bodice, she moved to help him, her hands taking on a life of their own. With the buttons undone, it was she who pulled the camisole and vests aside to allow him the freedom of her breasts.

Patrick drew back slightly to look, his eyes glowing with pleasure as the moon broke from behind a cloud to shine on their milky whiteness.

Somewhere close at hand an owl hooted, and Sarah wondered at her vivid awareness of the quiet whoosh of its wings as it plummeted to earth to snatch some unsuspecting creature.

She felt Patrick's mouth and his tongue gently caressing her breasts, his hand now grappling with her skirt. Oblivious now to anything other than her desperate need for him, she reached down to help him. When his hands moved along the length of her bare thigh and worked their way gently amongst her dark pubic curls, she felt herself swept by a surge of the most indescribable pleasure. There was a vague awareness that someone was moaning. A low, throaty animal sound. Suddenly Sarah realised it came from her own lips.

'Sarah, I need you.' Patrick's whispered voice held a sob. His breath was hot in her ear and she could feel his maleness hard against her.

'And I you.'

He looked around desperately for somewhere to lie, but there was nowhere. All around was either snowed or crisp with hoar frost. Gently, but forcefully, he pushed her back against a tree, and she could not resist.

Opening his coat, Patrick wrapped it as well around her as he could, and she found her hands, no longer under her control, pulling at his shirt and vests. When finally, they had wormed their way inside his shirt, Sarah almost choked with excitement at the feel of his hot skin. Gasping for every breath, she enjoyed touching him, her hands moving restlessly on his chest and back.

Suddenly Patrick froze, peering over Sarah's shoulder. Clinging to him still, the girl turned to follow his gaze, but could see nothing.

'What's wrong?' she whispered.

'I thought I heard something.'

For a few moments there was nothing, though the pair stayed motionless. Tense and alert, listening intently.

A sound came to them through the clear winter air, of boots clinking on the loose stones of the path.

'Someone's coming,' Patrick said quietly. 'We must be quiet until they're gone.

Quite suddenly Sarah became aware of her state of undress. Looking down, she found her bodice lying wide open, with her breasts laid bare, pointing proudly. Lower, she saw her skirt and petticoats hitched almost to her waist. Really aware, for the first time, of what she had been about to do, she shook now with fear, not passion.

'No one must see me like this,' she hissed. Panicking, she tried to pull away from Patrick, roughly pushing her skirt down. Pulling frantically at her bodice, she tried with trembling fingers to fasten the tiny buttons.

As the footsteps came nearer, Patrick grasped her elbow, drawing her further into the cover of the bushes. With a finger to his lips he signalled her to crouch down.

Sarah flopped down, making herself as small as possible. Listening nervously for the person to pass, she heard the whispering of voices and muffled sniggers.

The sounds of feet stopped on the path, only feet from where Sarah and Patrick hid, and for a few moments there was a strange silence.

'In here. No one will see us.'

Sarah recognised Alexandra's voice, sibilant and urgent.

Two people sneaked past. If Sarah had reached out, she could have touched them, and the moon gave light enough for her to recognise that the second person of the couple was Ned Collister, one of the lads from the washing-floors.

There were sounds of whisperings and muted giggles, followed by a long, pregnant silence and strange rustling sounds.

'For a ha'penny you can have a look. A feel costs a penny. And if you want me to rub your thing it will be a penny more.' Alexandra's instructions, though spoken quietly, showed no embarrassment or lack of confidence.

'I've got threepence. Can I poke it in you for that?' the boy asked eagerly.

'Don't be stupid!' Alexandra's voice was shrill and scornful. 'But I'll rub you twice as long for threepence,' she finished hopefully.

Ned was silent for a moment before he grudgingly agreed. 'But you'd better make it good!' he warned.

There followed a spell of grunting and heavy breathing, during which Patrick plucked at Sarah's sleeve and they crept guiltily, like thieves in the night, from the thicket and down the road some distance.

Sarah found herself trembling with a great fusion of emotions. There was shock at what she had almost allowed Patrick to lead her to do. Horror that she had so badly wanted it and come so near to allowing; helping even; it to happen. Fright at being so nearly caught. Frustration because her body still desperately wanted Patrick and was denied him. Embarrassment for so many reasons, but most of all because Patrick had heard her sister selling her favours. Behaving like some common doxy! Frightened in case, after the sinful caress she'd just permitted, he might think she was no better than Alexandra.

Her stomach squirmed at the thought of Alexandra and what

she was doing. What she was obviously in some habit of doing. A burning rage overcame her, and she wanted to rush back to the thicket and drag the young tramp out by the hair. Kick the lout where it would hurt him most while she was at it!

'She's only twelve years old!' she told Patrick in horror. Revulsion brought a taste of vomit to her mouth.

Patrick held her gently. 'There's nought you can do about it, love.'

'There should be. She's my little sister and she's whoring! I should be able to stop her.'

'What can you do? Go in and drag her out perhaps?'

'Perhaps that's just what I should do.'

'And how would you propose to explain how you knew she was there?'

Sarah thought about it for a moment, finally raising her shoulders in a shrug of despair. 'She must not know I was there. Especially not with you.'

'Then do nothing. For if you try it will only cause more trouble for yourself. She has clearly been at it for some time. So, if you stop her now she will still do it again tomorrow with someone else. She is not the first, nor will she be the last maid to have lost her virginity by the age of twelve.'

'But to be selling herself for money!'

'Would she listen if you talked to her about it?'

Sarah was thoughtful for a moment, then shrugging forlornly, shook her head.

'Then you can do nothing better than to dismiss it from your mind.'

'What must you think of my family?' Sarah asked miserably.

'I care only about one member of your family. I love you Sarah. Promise me we can meet as often as possible.'

'I can promise you that, though it might not be very often.

But ask no more of me. Please don't ever expect marriage of me.' Sarah knew she should be sending him away and refusing to see him again, for both their sakes. But she no longer had the strength nor the will to fight their love for each other.

'I'll wait for you tomorrow,' Patrick said quietly, and Sarah nodded.

'I must go now else Mam will wonder what's become of me.'

Patrick turned to walk with her, but she put her hand on his chest to hold him back.

'Don't come back up with me. Alexandra might see.'

Patrick closed his arms around her, kissing her, his tongue busy and she felt the fire of longing rise again. With an effort she pushed him from her and turning, stumbled away from him up the lane.

Judith looked up from her spinning as Sarah entered the croft. 'You're late. No trouble at the mine was there?'

Sarah shook her head. 'No, Mam. I just stopped to talk a while with Mary.' Shaking her head, she wondered when and how it had become so easy for her to lie to her mother.

Alexandra slipped in through the doorway, breathless, flushed and with an aura of excitement.

'You're are late too; have you been running?' Judith asked.

'Aye. I saw Sarah ahead and I was trying to catch up,' the girl lied.

Sarah felt a sickness in her stomach. An anger, a fear and a shame on her sister's behalf.

Chapter 10

George opened his eyes to the sound of sea-birds and the low murmur of a brisk wind eddying around the cave mouth.

Realisation of where he was slowly coming to him. Fearing it was all just a dream, he opened his eyes reluctantly. But they were not cell walls he saw around him. He was out of prison! They were out of prison, he corrected, remembering Jos. *Free!* But for how long? Had they shaken off their pursuers?

He tried to stand but his limbs seemed to him to have frozen in the one position. Locked around his companion as the other man's were clutching him.

Slowly, gingerly, he attempted to move his arms and legs. Needles of pain shot through him like a million shards of broken glass, though his extremities seemed to have no feeling at all. Looking at his hands, he saw they were the colour of midnight.

Jos did not move. Panicking and fearing him dead, George put an ear to his chest. The heart beat seemed slow. But it was there, and it was steady. His chest moved with a gentle, almost imperceptible rhythm. With a sigh of relief, George unwound his cramped limbs and forced himself to his feet.

Staggering slightly on numbed, swollen feet, he stumbled and almost fell, hitting his ribs against a protruding rock. Breath momentarily lost to him, he waited, half bent over, until the pain subsided. Then he shuffled to the mouth of the cave.

Over to his right, roiling clouds hung, pearled lavender in the morning light. The sun was still a ghost, ascending low on the horizon, through a thick haze. George stood motionless for a while, thoughtfully watching the grey, ashen world change to a water colour in the muted dawn light.

A kite soared watchfully aloft, wheeling at George's appearance, to hover some distance away.

With very little view of the surrounding countryside, George edged warily forward. Ever watchful for any sign of movement around, he moved only inches at a time. Suddenly finding nothing below his forward foot, he glanced down, his heart lurching with horror; pounding in his chest. For what lay before him was the beetling edge of a precipice. It was a far drop to the stark and desolate winter landscape below.

Leaping back rapidly, George looked in horror along the ledge they had followed to the cave, his lips curling in a thin and weary smile. The shelf they had stumbled along in the darkness was little more than two feet wide.

'Well if the Good Lord allowed us to negotiate that safely in the dark, he must mean us to stay alive — and free!' he told himself.

George's mind, now come to full alertness, was working quickly. His dark eyes; Sarah's eyes; were clear, their gaze sharp and quick.

Their pursuers would not have given up the hunt, he realised, though they would almost certainly had rested for the night. They would have slept warm and comfortable. They would be fresher.

At that moment the sun broke through a rent in the clouds at the edge of the sky. In its light George could see the glint of a river in the valley below, widening as it flowed toward his left. Beyond it was a glimmer of sea, painted a lurid purple in the filtered light. The sea! There was a fluttering at his heart. It was still some distance away, the Irish Sea, but within sight now. And beyond it, just a few short miles further on, was home. His island. His beloved Isle of Man. The Isle would protect him. He would be safe — if he could but reach it.

Thinking of home sparked a lurch of longing in his heart and brought back the urgency of their situation. They must not linger here any longer or they would surely be caught. Returning to the cave, his step quicker and more assured now, he shook Jos.

'C'mon, boy. Stir yourself.'

Jos opened his eyes, dazed and disorientated at first. Then awareness came. Groaning, he stirred, stretching his cramped limbs. Flexing his fingers and ankles, he forced himself upright.

'Do not think me a fool, but we must flee from this place at once.'

'Are our pursuers near?' Jos was instantly alert, looking anxiously toward the mouth of the cave.

'Not yet. But I'm thinking they won't be too far behind. They'll be better rested, well fed and not as stiff as us. We had best be on our way while the morning is still young. We must quickly put as much distance as possible between them and us.'

Jos nodded his agreement and headed toward the mouth of the cave.

'Careful how you go, lad,' George warned. 'There's a hell of a step down from the cavemouth.' He lifted his arm in a sweeping outward gesture.

Being careful not to look down, the two men edged their way back along the ledge they had so heedlessly stumbled the length of the night before.

A herring gull swooped angrily and Jos, unnerved, swung his arm at it and stumbled. Dodging him, it lifted again with a bad-tempered squawk.

'Careful, boy,' George warned as he grabbed the lad's arm.

The late February morning was clammy with a muscle-aching, bone-chilling mist that penetrated every fibre of their bodies. Jos shivered, longing to slap his arms about his shoulders, but not daring lest he should unbalance himself.

What seemed like a whole lifetime later they had reached the end of the ledge and were back onto the steeply sloping hillside.

Eyes screwed tightly against the bright, pale sun; George studied the valley. A few trees were scattered around, but with long spaces between and few places to hide. It had to be crossed though and then they could follow the ever-widening river to the sea.

George could almost imagine he could smell the seaweed and taste the tang of the salt spray on his lips. Apart from his family, his one and only real love had been the sea and the ships who sailed her. It had only been the loss of his children and Judith's desperate fear of living in Douglas afterwards that had made him agree to move to Laxey.

From the clean, endless freedom of the vast bright sea, to the gloomy claustrophobic confines of a lead mine. George shuddered involuntarily at the thought. He had been a good miner. He was sure of that. But it was not the life for a seafaring man. Nor for anyone, come to think of it. Man was not meant to live in a hole in the ground. That should be left to moles, rabbits and the likes.

He turned his head to take in the breathtaking display, a

ripening spray of red and gold in the east as the sun crept from behind a layer of lacquered clouds, rising well above the horizon.

'We'd better get a move on.' George moved off down the sharp incline. Jos followed close behind, both men had great difficulty with their footing on the frozen clay and greasy boulders.

After safely reaching the floor of the valley, they made better speed. Racing across open ground, they hurled themselves over fences and into the cover of any shrub or copse of trees they could find. George repeatedly glanced behind, watchful for any sign of pursuit and listening constantly for the baying of hounds.

The mist would be helpful, he thought, though it would also allow the hunters to draw closer without being seen.

When they reached the river, they found the banks; mostly loose treacherous shingle and ice; dropping almost sheer to the rapidly flowing water.

'No need to cross the river,' George said confidently. 'If we follow it to the sea, we should be able to find a boat we can borrow.' He saw Jos smile at his choice of words.

Rounding a bend in the river, George stopped abruptly, his heart warm and soaring with joy at the sight that confronted him. Lifting a hand to shade his eyes, he pointed.

'Look-ee there, boy!'

Following his gaze Jos saw the sparkling sea no more than a mile away. Winking at him, as he looked, the grey waves, tipped with reflected light, shattered by the wind, to a million glittering crescents that bobbed and danced. Into it intruded the dark bulk of a small wooden jetty. Moored there were several small craft. 'Will they be large enough to carry us safely to your island?' He asked incredulously.

George's eyes were aglow with excitement. 'Big enough to take us and small enough for two to handle easily.'

Suddenly he stiffened, his head half turned. Jos was silent, listening with him. The sound came again, distant, but as distinct as the crack of thunder on a rain-washed night. The howling of a dog!

George studied the horizon. A red slash of whore's lipstick rimmed above the dark, threatening inland mountains. No chance of seeing their pursuers amongst that lot!

For long moments the two men stared into each other's faces, each hoping his did not reveal the consuming terror he saw in his companion's.

'The sea. A boat.' George said quickly, 'We must be well away before they get here.'

As one, the men ran. Racing with all the energy they could muster. Bounding over every obstacle, hearts pounding, lungs straining. Fleeing as a fox before the huntsmen. Jumping fallen trees and rocks, barbed twigs and branches slashing faces and arms. Small animals scampered, startled, from their path. Birds flew from the trees in angry, noisy clouds. A low wall loomed ahead and Jos, reaching it first, placed his hand on the top, vaulting it cleanly. In an instant of complete terror, his feet discovered nowhere to land and he found himself hurtling downward, a scream torn from his lips.

A small tree brushed past and he clutched at it, like a drowning man at a straw. His shoulders, wrenching painfully, took the strain; though he felt one dragged from its socket; halting his plunge. Trembling, he looked around, trying to see a route out, noticing the tree was pulling out from its clay bedding.

Reaching forward, he managed to grip a rock. Feeling around with his foot, he found a toe-hold in a small fissure, just as the tree finally pulled loose from the cliff. Crying out with fright, he hurriedly transferred his weight, snatching at the cliff-face with his free hand. The first attempt was futile, but he managed to attain a feeble grip at the second.

The weather chose that moment to vent its spleen on him and the storm that had been threatening all morning finally broke violently. His insides churned in horror as he choked in the crush of whipping hail and frozen snow lashing at his face, tearing at his hands. Desperately he flattened himself against the rock, scrabbling frantically for toe and finger holds.

Shale was breaking away, above and below him, bouncing stingingly against his head. He could hear it falling, clinking against rocks, splashing into water far below.

He clung there, his body heavy and tired, hardly feeling a part of him anymore. He dug his fingernails into the rock; felt them tear but kept his grip. Sick, terrified beyond reasoning. Crucifying himself. Only an animal instinct for survival keeping him fighting. His numb fingers were losing their grip and, battling desperately to keep a hold, he balled his hand in a tight fissure in the rock.

As the volley of rubble increased, raining relentlessly on his head, his foot slid from its precarious hold. His hand finally torn from its grip, he fell away, sliding and bouncing to the river's edge.

Leaning over the wall above, but far out of reach, George watched in horror as his friend tumbled from the rock wall. In slow motion, it seemed he skidded and spun, appearing like a rag doll in a gale.

Hanging into space, almost overbalancing, George could only just make out the motionless body in the shrubbery below. 'Oh, dear God!' He whispered, his voice cracked and dry.

Spurred into action, he bolted, panicking along the banking, finally finding a less steep way down. With little regard for safety, he scrambled most of the way, slipping and falling through briars and thorn bushes in his blind haste.

A squall threshed along the river when George reached it and finding he could not walk against the fury of the storm; he was forced to crawl on his hands and knees to where Jos lay.

The boy was a mess! His face was a pulp of cuts and grazes, his right hand gushing blood. Looking further along his body, George felt himself blanch, for the boy's right leg, between knee and ankle, jutted at right angles, the foot spiralled at the ankle, facing completely behind him. The boot, probably mercifully, was ripped off.

'God help him,' George murmured under his breath. Fighting the nausea and faintness that threatened to overpower him, he knelt.

Suddenly becoming aware that the lad was conscious and watching him, he smiled, hoping Jos would not read his true emotions.

'It's bad isn't it?' Jos asked quietly through gritted teeth.

'Bad enough,' George replied non-committedly. 'I think your leg's broken. Does it hurt much?'

Jos shook his head, wincing at the movement. 'My hand hurts — and my shoulder, but I can't feel the leg. I've made a mess of our Great Escape, haven't I? Trust me to botch things up.'

"Tweren't your fault, boy,' George said gruffly. He found himself bathed in burning perspiration, despite the coldness of the day. Quickly he removed his coat and shirt. Then replacing the coat immediately, he tore his shirt in strips. With some of these, he staunched the bleeding of the hand.

With that accomplished, he turned his attention to the leg. He dreaded what he was going to find, but even then, was not prepared for the sight that accosted his eyes when he ripped open the trouser leg.

The tissue of the leg was ballooned, already turning black, sharp splinters of bone had ripped through muscle and skin, to protrude far out from his shin. The ankle had fared no better. It was shattered and completely spiralled.

Turning away quickly, George stumbled into the bushes dry retching as his stomach tried to pump out what was not there. Finally, summoning his courage, he forced himself back to Jos.

'Sorry, boy. Got caught short. Had to go for a piss.' He fumbled with his fly buttons, making a pretence at fastening them.

Jos shook his head. 'I'm not fooled, George. I watched your face when you looked at the leg — I'll be going no further.'

'I've set broken limbs before. At sea and in the mines. I can splint yours, but it will hurt.'

Jos looked hopeful. 'I can bear the pain.' Trying to ease his position slightly, he groaned. 'My shoulder hurts worse than anything. I think it's broke too.'

George nodded miserably. *What else could be wrong?* It was quite on the cards Jos had internal injuries too.

'I'll have a go at the leg first,' he decided. Handing the boy a stick he added, 'Bite on this for the pain.'

He knelt and nervously gripping just above the ankle, asked, 'Are you ready?'

Jos nodded; terror clear in his eyes. He clenched his teeth tightly on the wood.

George wiped the perspiration from his face. Gritting his teeth, he started putting traction on the leg. His stomach heaved as he felt and heard the bone grating under his fingers.

Jos gave one blood-curdling scream then mercifully lost consciousness.

George worked quickly. Pulling the shin straight, and the ankle as well as was possible. Then ripping some reasonably straight branches from the bushes, he placed several of them the length of the limb, binding them in place with strips of his shirt. He rubbed his chin thoughtfully as he surveyed his handiwork. Not very pretty but at least the foot was facing the front again.

Moving then to the shoulder, he found it to be dislocated. Jos's strong muscles resisted his tired attempts to pull it back into place. As a last resort, George had to stand over Jos with a foot firmly planted in his ribs and throw his whole weight against the arm. Grunting with the effort, he felt it move and was relieved to feel it jump back into place.

The storm died as suddenly as it had come, leaving in its wake an uncanny calm.

Jos came around a few moments later. His eyes were dazed and absent at first, but reality quickly came, and with it the full agony of his wounds. He cried out at first, then muted it to a low groan.

A dog, sounding in the near distance, answered his cry, barking excitedly.

Biting his lips to prevent any further cries, his eyes fixed on George in silent plea.

'I'll find a way to move you,' George assured him. 'Somehow, we'll do it.'

'Find a stout branch and with your help I can walk,' Jos said gamely.

Leaning on a stick and with George taking most of the boy's weight the pair shuffled painfully and slowly over the rough ground toward the sea.

Behind them the sound of the dog grew louder, and they could hear men's voices too. With only about one hundred yards to go to the edge of the beach Jos stopped, painfully lowering himself to the ground. 'I can go no further,' he said quietly.

'You *must*.' George commanded. 'We're nearly there.'

Jos shook his head. 'The hunters are too close. They'd catch us in the open long before we could reach a boat. You might make it alone. Leave me and go quickly.' His face was grey with pain and fear.

'If I go — you come too,' George said stubbornly.

'Then we'll both be captured. Where's the sense in that? You can be of no more help to me now. Go!'

George hesitated for a moment, his mind working quickly. *The boy was right, of course.* There was no chance of them both escaping, and Jos needed medical attention. He would get that, of sorts, in jail. Even if he could be got to a boat, which was unlikely, the journey would be hard and there was every chance he might die on the way. His decision finally made; George stood up.

'Very well, boy. But when you get your freedom again, and if you need a home come and find me. Just ask in Laxey for George Fayle.'

Jos nodded, waving his hand dismissively.

George took one last lingering look at the boy then with deep regret, he fled. Making no further effort to conceal himself, he raced through the last few yards of cover before the beach. In the open he sped as fast as his legs could carry him, reaching the end of the jetty without any sound of an outcry from behind.

There were four boats, but George went to the one at the extreme end of the pier. Taking time only to check there was no one aboard, he jumped hurriedly into her. Crouching on the deck, he froze, listening intently.

Voices were vaguely discernible in the distance, but there was no sound of alarm. The dog was silent. He dared a look to whence he had come but could see nothing through the gloom.

'Dear God, make sure they discover the boy. He'll not survive long in this,' he begged in a whisper. Then swiftly and efficiently he cast off the mooring lines and pushed the boat free from the jetty.

After allowing the boat to drift on the outgoing tide for a few minutes, George hoisted the sail. In the wake of the storm there was almost a dead calm and the canvas flapped uselessly.

A search of the boat produced a little dried fish and an apple, so he settled himself in the bows to eat. The fish was salty, but his stomach was glad of it — would have been glad of almost anything — and the apple refreshed his mouth afterwards.

When the oblate sun crept through a rift in the clouds, glowing amber from its light, the morning was less chill. George lifted his head and the sun blinded him. Lowering it, he looked again at the water, blue green and sun-dazzled golden. George had a feeling, somehow, of euphoria. As if nothing in the world could harm him now. A calmness had taken him, and he was content to drift through the day without thinking. He started to doze.

When he awoke the sun was already well past its zenith. He sat quite still for a moment watching the bright wisps of sunlight rippling like molten lead on the surface of the water.

The day passed slowly, with the little boat merely meandering over the Irish Sea. George kept his eyes well skinned but saw no evidence of any pursuit. There was nought moving on his side of the horizon but a few scattered black clouds and a handful of noisy gulls and cormorants.

A brisk breeze stirred, growing swiftly to a strong wind, which brought him quickly to full attentiveness. As he spun the wheel to straighten her to the wind, the bow dipped precariously, then righted itself, the stem coming up in a shower. The cascade streamed over the gunwale, running aft and departing through the scuppers.

The wind gradually increased, and the little boat ran quickly across a swelling sea, an occasional strong gust snatching and billowing the sail.

Evening came, with still many miles to go, the weather changed fast, blowing a dangerous swinging wind. Glittering ranges of black anvil clouds piled higher and nearer.

Marbled storm clouds stood on an oyster-grey sea, making it impossible to see where water ended, and sky began.

Suddenly black winds smashed head on, lashing George with a stream of stinging, frozen pellets. The storm smote the ship with monotonous abandon, the gale shrieking in the rigging in inexorable fury.

Because of the unpredictability of the wind, it was now essential that the wheel be manned at all times, but the storm sail also had to be reefed. Leaving the wheel, George staggered to attend the sail. The seas rose and the ship, unmanned, began to flounder and yaw. Lying heavily in the crashing waves, she began to take on water. As the man worked frantically, sleet came in sheets and the day was filled with the hiss and drumming of the downpour.

Exhausted, George knelt for long moments with his arm around the wooden mast, feeling it tremble. Listening to the rhythmic creaking of the fittings, the soughing of the waves against the hull, the desolate call of the wind.

Slithering on his buttocks along the deck, George reached the wheel, wrestled with it briefly, soon regaining control of the boat. Day was almost gone before the storm blew itself out. Calm descended and the clouds, almost by magic, broke up and disappeared. The sky burned purple and black and dark red in the last of the sun. It was a minute crescent now against the horizon as it lowered itself behind the welcoming, shadowy bulk of what George knew could only be the Isle of Man. *Home.*

Beneath a cold carpet of stars and in the platinum luminescence of the moon, George peered into the night. Faint lights well to the south, he felt sure must be Douglas. That would put him, he reckoned, approaching the coast somewhere north of Onchan. Fine. That would serve his purposes well. It wouldn't be too far a walk from there to Laxey.

Landing on the Island's treacherous coast at night, he knew, was a hazard-fraught game, but no more so than waiting at sea until morning. And at least on land he might have some chance of finding shelter from the cold that was already biting into his bones.

As the island loomed large before him, trembling from combined fear and excitement, George strained his eyes toward the moonlit coast. The breakers lashing the cliffs sounded thunderous and terrifyingly close.

Suddenly the little boat heaved herself into the air, shuddering. George tasted acid in his throat at the sound of the bowels of the craft being torn out on rocks. Then she tipped on her side and he was catapulted into the icy brine.

Down he plunged into the black depths, watching the moonlight receding away from him. The gulp of air he had desperately snatched into his lungs was fast diminishing and he felt consciousness deserting him.

George came around again quickly, gasping and choking, the sea filling his mouth and throat. He fought his way toward the dim, rippling pool of emerald light. Up from the awful depths. The eerie, liquid silence. From the buoyancy of death. Out, coughing and retching, into the clean sweet air and the churning of the waves. Back into life itself.

Then miraculously there was land under his feet, and he was stumbling and crawling, helped by the action of the waves, up the beach.

Falling to the sand, his lungs working like bellows, he vomited the last of the sea water before he passed out.

Chapter 11

Sarah fairly strode up the lane from the washing-floors, her gaze intent on the roadway above. Scurrying to keep pace, Mary finally gave up. Leaning on the fence puffing, she called, 'You'd better go on alone, your legs are longer than mine — and younger.'

Looking round guiltily, Sarah stopped and apologised laughingly. 'Nor have they so much weight to carry,' she reminded her friend cheekily.

'No need to be impertinent, just because you've got your man to meet,' Mary grumbled, but there was a friendly twinkle in her eye.

Sarah lingered, kicking the ground restlessly.

'Don't wait for me lass,' Mary puffed. 'You hurry on and meet him. He'll be getting anxious.'

''Twill do him good,' Sarah said chirpily, but all the same she was impatient, and her heart was fluttering with the thought of being near him again. 'We'll walk up along with you. Best if he and I aren't seen walking alone together for fear the news gets back to my Mam. If Alexandra was to see us, she'd be likely to tell.'

Sarah's face clouded for a moment at the memory of her younger sister and the depths to which she seemed to have sunk. But she knew there was nothing she could do to alter that, and she would not let it spoil her happiness that day. All she could do was pray her mother never learned of it. It would be the death of her, Sarah was sure.

Patrick was waiting, eagerly watching the women trudging up the pathway. His eyes lit with joy when he spotted Sarah amongst the crowd, he straightened and strolled toward her.

'Hello, Mary,' he nodded in the direction of the older woman, but his eyes stayed, simmering, on Sarah.

'Right glad I am to see you two sorted out and showing a bit of sense at last,' Mary said briskly. 'You can walk with me as far as my cottage, for appearances sake, then after that it's up to you what you do!' She winked at Patrick, and Sarah felt the heat of a blush rising in her face.

The sun shone softly out of a deep cerulean sky, bringing some heat to the closing of the day — the first warmth for many a long month. Sarah put her head back, enjoying the warm glow on her face for the last few moments before the sun dropped below the hilltop.

As they walked up the hill, they heard from all around them the gentle dripping and the pitter-pattering rhythm of melting snow falling from the tree branches. Now and again there was a dull thud as a solid pat of snow slid from its winter perch, tumbling to shatter on the ground. Sarah took it all in wonderingly, hoping that winter was loosening its bitter grip at last. Was spring around the corner? She did hope so.

Sparrows chirped and fluttered around them, already looking slimmer, as though they had started to cast their winter coats. In the hedgerows the first green shoots of spring-blossoming wildflowers were poking through the soil. It would not be long, Sarah thought, before the hibernating animals came out to investigate the new season.

Chattering excitedly while they walked, Sarah glanced furtively around, then unable to stand being distanced from Patrick any longer, slipped her hand into his, pressing herself close against his side.

Watching from the corner of her eye, Mary smiled with satisfaction. Nothing, she was sure, would ever part that couple again.

Harry the knife sharpener, was just leading his pony past Mary's cottage as they approached. Looking frightened and bewildered, his face lit up when he saw Sarah.

'I'm truly glad I've found you, lass,' he gushed, trying to hurry the pony toward the trio. With the cart well laden, the animal pulled back, tossing its head irritably. Laying back its ears, it dug in its heels and refused to move.

'Me?' Sarah was puzzled. 'What do you want with me, Harry?'

Harry looked uncertainly at the other two. 'Maybe we'd better talk alone, miss,' he suggested.

Sarah looked blankly at her companions, then shrugging, allowed Harry to lead her aside.

'I've got someone in the cart what belongs to you,' the man confided. 'An' I don't rightly know what to do wi' him.' Reaching into the cart, he lifted his work apron and straw bag of tools and pulled aside the corner of an old rug.

Puzzled, Sarah leaned over and peered into the cart. '*Daa!*' she gasped, her knees sagging. Hanging to the cart for support she took another, better, look. There could be no mistake, the figure squeezed between the grinding wheel and the side of the cart was quite definitely her father.

Leaning into the cart, she touched her father's face. So severe was George's pallor, his skin had a blue tinge and felt frozen against her fingers. It was fissured with deep, angry looking scratches and cuts.

'Is he dead?' She clasped a hand to her mouth and gazed fearfully at Harry, her brown eyes made darker with unshed tears.

Harry shrugged. 'He wasn't when I found him, Miss. But he's been in there a long time and 'tis a cold day. I covered him up as well as I could to keep him warm, but he was in a bad way when I found him.'

Sarah glanced toward where Mary and Patrick watched curiously.

'We'd better bring him to the croft. Would you mind bringing him up there for me?'

'Can't take him there, Miss. I thought home was the best place to fetch him, even if I was risking your Mammy throwing a hatchet at me. But when I reached the gate the Constable was there. I heard him tell your Mammy he had to search the croft. They must be looking for him.'

Sarah remained leant over the cart, her head spinning, mind working furiously. Her father was still alive. Very faintly she could feel his breath against her hand.

'I can't keep him with me, Miss,' Harry was saying. 'If he ain't warmed soon he won't survive. An' if the Constable searches my cart, I'll end up in jail wi' him.' Harry was hopping from foot to foot in agitation, his gangly limbs almost twitching. A nervous tic kept jerking the corner of his thin lips.

Sarah nodded. What Harry said made sense. But what to do? She looked speculatively at Mary and Patrick. Could they be trusted? Would it be fair for her to ask for their help, she wondered? To take such a risk. Sighing, she realised she had no choice.

''Tis my father,' she said at last. 'He must have escaped from jail and he's near frozen to death. Harry cannot take him home because the Constable is there.'

Mary hurried to look, her face crumpling in horror when she saw him.

'Oh, that poor man,' she clucked, reaching into the cart and feeling the coldness of him. 'Quickly you must bring him inside.'

'It will put you in danger if he's found,' Sarah warned, but her heart lifted with relief and gratitude just the same.

Mary tutted and frowned. 'We would be very poor neighbours indeed if we could not help a friend in trouble. Bring the cart right to the door, Harry, so we can slip the poor man indoors without anyone seeing.'

Harry's long, kindly grey face lit up with relief. 'Very good of you, Missus. It's real glad I'll be to hand him over to someone what can help him. He's real sickly. Wouldn't have survived much longer in the cold, but I didn't know what to do with him when I saw the Constable there.' He dragged the reluctant pony close to Mary's door.

After his many months in jail, George was not much more than skin and bone. Picking him up easily, Patrick carried him into the cottage and lowered him gently onto a fire-side chair.

'How did you come by him?' Mary asked as she hurriedly arranged gorse kindling in the grate.

'Found him by the roadside, Missus,' Harry explained as the women prepared to see to George's comfort.

'First we must get these wet clothes off him,' Mary suggested, adding, 'Go on, Harry, we're listening.'

'Well he was staggering along, only barely conscious. When I came around the bend, he didn't seem to know who I was at first. Tried to hide, but of course he was too weak to move quick enough. Then when he recognised me as a friend, he begged me to fetch him home. I was coming to Laxey anyway, so it was no hardship.'

While he spoke, the two women and Patrick had managed to rid George of the icy wet clothing and had wrapped him warmly in blankets.

'We'll bring the truckle bed in front of the fire, as close as it's safe to,' Mary instructed.

When Patrick had it in place, they lifted George onto it, lying him as comfortably as possible. Mary banked the fire with peat.

Sarah gazed around the cosy room, seeing it really for the first time. Around the edges of the high mantle-shelf was a gay little trimming of checked cotton, a match to the curtains at the window. And standing proudly atop the shelf were a fine display of delicate china ornaments. Against one wall stood a dresser, with a fascinating assortment of mugs, hanging on hooks along its length.

Dried herbs and strips of dried fish hung from the wide beams and there was a stone crock of flour in the corner. A large, warmly glazed stone jar contained drinking water from the spring. Sarah thought she had never been anywhere quite so comfortable or homely.

'What will James say about this?' Sarah suddenly remembered Mary's husband.

'He'll say we've done the right thing. Don't you worry. James would never have turned him away either. Go on, Harry. We're still listenin'.'

'There's not a lot more to tell, I don't think.' Harry rubbed his furrowed brow, frowning, trying to remember. 'Before he fainted, he said he escaped from jail an' made his way to the sea, with all kinds of adventures on the way. Then he pinched a boat, rode out a storm comin' over, was shipwrecked and washed ashore north of Onchan Head somewhere. He said he must have been unconscious all night on the beach. Then when he woke this morning, he was trying to make it to here. I came along and the rest you know. He collapsed straight after he told me his story and hasn't woke up since. I hid him in case anyone was lookin' for him. Just as well I did, too!'

'Oh, poor Daa.' Struggling to hold back her tears, Sarah knelt on the floor beside the truckle bed, lying half across her father's body, her face against his. She hoped that, even in his unconscious state, he might sense her presence and the warmth and love she felt might flow from her body to his and give him the strength to fight.

Sarah lingered, knowing she would be needed at home with her Mam, but reluctant to leave her father. Through the window she could see the sky had darkened.

'His colour's coming back a bit, though he's still awful pale,' Mary said, studying him. 'You'd best go to your Mam. She'll be frightened and wondering what's happening — what with the Constable calling and you so late home. I'll bathe your father's face and take care of him for you.'

Sarah nodded, kissed her father's cheek and stood up. 'I don't know how to thank you, Mary. No one could ask for a better friend.' A tear threatened, and she choked it back with a sob.

Patrick went with her to the door. 'I'll walk with you.' He put his arm around her as they walked, and Sarah drew comfort from his nearness.

Patrick suddenly caught her arm, jerking her to a halt.

Startled, Sarah looked up at him. She opened her mouth to question him, but his finger was to his lip. Silently he drew her to a gap in the hedge and into the field beyond.

Straining her ears, she could make out the sounds of someone approaching down the lane. *Hoof-beats!* Themselves hidden from sight; they had a reasonable view of the lane in the early moonlight.

They stood; bodies pressed closely together while the sound

of the horse grew louder. Then it drew level to the gap in the hedge and Sarah could clearly see the Constable.

He stopped momentarily, turning to look back from whence he had come. Then frowning and shaking his head, he dug his heels in the horse's ribs and continued his journey.

Patrick and Sarah stood without a sound until the hoof-beats had faded in the distance. Then Sarah sighed tremulously, though still she said nothing, content to be in Patrick's arms and to rest her head on his shoulder. He nuzzled her neck and ear, allowing his hands to wander impatiently about her body, his excitement and desire mounting, He could feel the whole length of her against him, stirring him to hardness again.

Sarah felt herself lost, submerged and drowning in feelings of a depth beyond her control. Pressing closer to him, she raised her face to be kissed, lost in the pleasure his lips brought.

Patrick's senses were more alive and urgent than he had ever known them, awakening in him a strange mixture of tenderness and passion. One part of him wanted to fondle and caress her gently. Another part wanted to push her to the ground, or against the hedge and make love to her. Desire almost won the battle, but sense and love convinced him that this was neither the right moment nor place to take her. Giving her a long, passionate kiss, he let his arms drop away.

'I'd better get you home to your Mam while I still have the strength to control my actions,' he said gruffly.

Sarah was thankful for his strength of will, for she knew she could not have been the one to make the break. The fervour of his embrace had thrilled, but in no way satisfied her. She wondered then how she could have held him away from her all those months and was certain she could never be without him again.

Patrick left her at the gate, lingering only long enough to

give her a kiss that held such passion it turned her bones to jelly again.

Judith was weeping and in extreme distress when Sarah arrived home, her eyes red and puffed.

'What's wrong, Mam? What's happened?' Sarah ran to take her mother in her arms.

'The Constable was here,' Judith sobbed. 'Searched the croft, he did. Even in the cupboards. He turned everything out. Look at the mess he's left.'

Sarah glanced quickly around, fury boiling in her at the state of the cottage. Swallowing her anger, she said quietly, 'Don't be upset, Mam. We'll soon tidy it.'

'And you're late *again*,' Judith accused, suddenly seeming to realise. 'I needed you here on time today. You could have talked to the Constable. He frightened me so!'

'I'm sorry, Mam, I got held up in the village. Harry the knife sharpener stopped me. What did the Constable want?'

Judith frowned as a memory flashed back. 'Harry came to the gate while the Constable was at the door, but he turned and left without calling. I wonder why? Did he tell you why?'

'Aye. But you haven't told me yet why the Constable was here.'

Judith's eyes filled with tears again. 'He says your Daa ran away from the jail!'

'That's nothing to cry for, Mam.'

'Aye. It is. The Constable says he's most likely froze to death, for there would be no warm refuge for him. Nor for the young fellow who went with him. An' in this weather too.' Judith broke down sobbing again.

'Mam, my Daa's not dead,' Sarah said softly. 'But he is very ill.'

Judith's head shot up and she frowned at her daughter without understanding. 'How could you know this?'

'I've seen him!'

'When? Where?'

With joy Sarah saw a spark of life in her mother's eyes. 'Today. Just now. That's why I'm late getting home.'

'You said you were talking to Harry.' Judith was still not grasping the significance.

'Harry had him in his cart. That's why he didn't come in. Why he left so quickly when he saw the Constable here.'

Judith's breathing quickened, and she started frantically toward the door. 'Well we must bring him in right away. We must get him in out of the cold. He must be freezing. Ill did you say?'

'He's warm now, Mam, and being well looked after.'

'Where then? Where is he? I must go to him.'

'I'll take you. But we'll have to be careful we're not seen. People might guess.'

Mary had cleaned George up well, though his face was still a vivid mask of cuts and abrasions. The blueness had gone from his skin and his breathing improved, though he was still deeply unconscious and shivering frighteningly.

Judith stood in the middle of the floor looking down on him. She cried unashamedly, tears running unchecked down her face to drip onto her bodice, while her body was wracked with huge shuddering sobs.

Mary, who at first was apprehensive of the other woman, soon warmed to her. She could see now the person Sarah had tried to tell her about. The gentle loving wife and mother. Heartbroken to see her husband in such a state, yet joyful because he was alive and free. It was clear that she still loved him very deeply. Crossing to Judith, Mary put her arm around her shoulder. 'Come and sit by his bed, love, and I'll make you a hot cup of camomile to buck you up a bit.'

Judith moved to obey, rewarding Mary with a watery smile.

'Thank you so much for caring for him. We'll take him home as soon as we can find a way to carry him.' Judith trembled uncontrollably, her teeth chattering as she spoke.

'It might be safer to leave him here until they stop searching for him,' Mary suggested. 'If the Constable came back there would be no escape for him from your cottage and it's unlikely they will look for him here.'

'Do you not work? Who will care for him during the day? He cannot be left alone.'

'Aye. I work beside Sarah. But you could come to tend him during the day while the childher are at school. You would need to be careful not to be seen. It's lucky we're well out of the village and have no near neighbours, but you would still have to watch. People come into the fields picking berries an' they're a nosy lot!'

With a groan, George heaved over onto his side. Sarah and both women looked to him, startled and hopeful, but he lay at peace again, still deeply unconscious.

When they left Mary's cottage, Sarah felt as though she had been given her mother back from the dead. There was a spring in her step and hope. Her dead eyes had come to life again. As they strode along the last half mile to their croft Judith clung to her arm, chattering and planning joyfully for the future.

The Constable arrived at the croft well before the sun was up the following morning, having carefully searched the surrounding area before he hammered on the door.

Sarah sat up quickly. Startled, with eyes wide she looked fearfully at the bolted door.

Judith staggered through from the bedroom, trembling and dragging a shawl round her shoulders. 'Who is it?' she whispered, not yet properly awake.

Sarah shrugged. 'I don't know,' she murmured in reply. Aloud she called, 'Who's there?'

'The Constable, Missus! 'Now open the door! This minute!'

Sarah leapt from the bed, moving quickly to obey lest he should think they were up to some mischief. As the Constable stepped into the cottage the heads of the four younger Fayle children appeared over the edge of the half-loft.

'I've come to search!' the man said abruptly.

Sarah looked at him angrily, her dark eyes flashing fire and her narrow chin set firmly. 'You searched yesterday.'

'And I'm searching again today!'

'At this time in the morning? It's still dark. You've no right coming dragging decent folk from their beds like this!' Sarah snapped defiantly.

'Decent folk?' The man scoffed. 'A mad woman and her brood. Wife and spawn of a convicted criminal! Decent folk indeed! I have the right, doxy, to search where I like and when I like. 'Tis more likely I am to catch a criminal before he has time to wake. Now move aside. And you lot up there,' he added, looking at the line of faces at the loft's edge, 'Had best get yourselves down here right sharpish.'

The children all scrambled hastily down the ladder to stand, miserable and frightened in the cold morning air that whistled through the open door. Richard, tears streaming uncontrollably, stood amidst a steadily growing, steaming puddle.

Watching him, the Constable snorted derisively, and Sarah moved to put a protective arm around the terrified, embarrassed child.

His search completed and fruitless, the Constable stormed from the house in a raging temper.

'But I'll be back.' He snarled, wheeling his horse. 'And I'll keep coming until the bastard's either recaptured or found dead!'

After shooing the children out of earshot, Sarah and Judith

quickly confirmed their plans for the morning, then Sarah left early for the mines, keen to look in on her father before work.

Dawn was a saffron rent in the clouds that morning. Clouds scudded rapidly across the eastern sky, black and roiling, threatening some violent weather to come.

A thrush sat on the branch of a leafless hawthorn, his black beads of eyes warily following Sarah's progress. Trilling his inimitable song, he puffed his feathers against the chill of the strong morning breeze.

On arriving at Mary's cottage, Sarah looked around carefully then quietly let herself in, her eyes going immediately to the truckle bed before the fire. George still lay there, in much the same position as she had last seen him. Mary knelt by his side, the intentness on her face switching to a bland mask on Sarah's entry.

'How is he?'

'Very sick. He has the most awful fever. Maybe pneumonia. He really should have a doctor.'

Sarah moved to kneel at the bed, putting an anxious hand to his brow. Though clammy with perspiration, it burned against her hand.

'I think it would be safer not to,' James said quietly, emerging from the bedroom. 'A doctor would be obliged to inform the Constable he was here. Then poor George would be back in jail and the rest of us along with him, no doubt. The law wouldn't take kindly to what we're doing. All his suffering would have been in vain. And do you not feel that perhaps the poor man would rather be dead than back in that place?'

Sarah studied James momentarily. His slightly too-ample frame leaned on the doorpost, his grey eyes sympathetically watched the patient. A look of genuine concern reflected in his florid face and Sarah knew instinctively it was not of his own safety he thought, also certain he was right about her father preferring death to imprisonment.

George, in the following days, continued to worsen, though Sarah and Judith slipped in and out whenever they felt it was safe, to give the love they felt he needed and to help Mary nurse him. They watched in fear as his fever burned relentlessly and his laboured breathing became a whistling, painful wheeze.

They could never stay overnight because the Constable came and went at all hours to the Fayle cottage, never a trace could he find of his quarry.

'I think it would be better if you did not hold too much hope,' Mary warned gently one morning. 'He seems too weak to fight the pneumonia. I wish we could have the doctor to him.' While she spoke, she watched Judith carefully, fearful she might not have the strength to bear such news. Despite her earlier misgivings about Sarah's mother, she had to admit that in the week since George's return, she had grown to rather admire her.

'He'll not die!' Judith told her with determination. Looking to where George was battling agonisingly for every breath, she added, 'I will not allow him to!' Then she smiled.

Judith seeming to draw her old strength from the nearness of her beloved man, displaying a stoicism Sarah remembered of old and had thought lost forever.

Sarah had left with reluctance for the washing-floors that morning, Mary almost having to drag her away.

'But what if Daa should die while we're gone?' she asked plaintively. 'I fear for Mam if he does.'

'There's really naught we can do but pray, love,' Mary said kindly. 'Whether he should die while she's alone with him or in company will make little difference. And if it has to happen 'tis best she be with him at the end.'

Sarah sighed unhappily. 'I suppose that's true,' she agreed.

Hurrying anxiously up the road that evening, with Mary almost running behind, Sarah saw her mother lingering in the gloom just inside the partly open doorway.

Why was she here, Sarah wondered? Their plan had been for James to watch over George when he wakened from his night shift to allow Judith to be home for the children after school. Heart in mouth, she quickened her pace.

'Mam. What's happened? Why aren't you home with the childher?' she asked anxiously.

'I was, but I had to come back. I told Alexandra to look after them while I went a message down in the village. Come in quickly.' Judith plucked urgently at Sarah's sleeve.

Alarmed, Sarah bounded into the cottage.

George was partly upright, propped against his pillows and on seeing Sarah he struggled to sit upright.

'The fever broke after you left this morning,' Judith babbled joyfully. 'He's had broth and camomile.'

Sarah ran to the bed and dropping quickly to her knees, she put her arms tightly around her father. 'Welcome back,' she whispered on a sob, as a tear slid down her cheek.

Pain rippled through George's chest, making breathing still a labour, but he clung tightly to his beloved daughter.

Much of his strength had been sapped by his ordeal. He knew it would be many a long day before he returned to full health. But recover he would. This moment, wakening amongst his family, made all he had endured worthwhile.

'When I'm well enough,' he gasped painfully, 'We'll have to consider the future.'

The three women studied him, failing to understand his thoughts.

'We'll have to leave Laxey,' he explained, 'For I'm known here. It would be dangerous to stay.'

Chapter 12

✦—•—◇—•—✦

Patrick kicked savagely at the loose stones in the roadway. His round, freckled face, usually good humoured, was glowering.

'Will you tell her, Mary?' he pleaded.

Mary raised her shoulders in a brief, dismayed shrug, sighing helplessly. 'I don't know what to advise. Really I don't.'

'Well I've hardly seen her since her father turned up! It's been over two weeks now.' Turning again to Sarah, he said, 'I need to spend time with you, Sarah. I *must*.' He turned again to Sarah glaring demandingly yet pleadingly into her eyes.

'Patrick I've tried to explain. Why won't you listen to me? You must try to understand.'

'I've tried to be patient, but I'm starting to believe you don't really care about me!' Patrick snapped. 'If you really loved me enough you would want to be with me. You would find a way. If you truly loved me!' he finished bitterly.

Mary looked up sharply. 'Now just stop that right there! That kind of talk will get you nowhere. Blackmail, that's what that is. Emotional blackmail. Of course, the girl loves you. And wants to see you. But she loves her mother too an' she has to think of her — and her father. You should admire her for her love and loyalty to them. Just for once try thinking about Sarah's feelings. Don't you think she has enough pain just now without you turning the knife in her wound? You're not the only person in the world you know!'

Patrick almost shied away, so shocked was he by Mary's vehemence. Then he rallied. 'Well, shouldn't she think of me too?' Turning again to Sarah he said, 'From Monday I will be on the night shift for four weeks. There will be no chance then for me to see you after work. Four whole weeks!'

Sarah's face fell, and a tear stood in her eye. 'Perhaps by then things will have sorted out.'

'I have a better idea!'

Both young people turned to Mary, waiting expectantly.

'Well I was talking to the Constable this very day and he said that wreckage had been found, washed up north of Onchan, of a boat that was stolen from Across, around the time your Daa escaped. 'Tis their reckoning now that his boat sank, and he drowned. So, I should think it unlikely the police will be calling to search again.'

Sarah heaved a shuddering sigh of relief. 'Is this true, Mary?'

'You have my word.'

'I don't see how this helps us. Sarah and me.' Patrick said morosely.

'Well, just think about it. George will be well enough to leave here soon, as long as he stays well hid. He can't sleep on our truckle bed, hidin' from the world forever.'

Sarah's face lit up. 'We'll be able to take him home then?'

Mary held her hands up, palms toward Sarah. 'Whoa girl, not so fast. I reckon it wouldn't be a good idea for him to be home. If the childher knew he was here, they might accidenty let it slip at school.'

'What then? Where else is there for him to go?' Bewildered, Sarah shook her head.

'Well, James an me's been talking. Up in the spinney just above your cottage there's a little tholtan. It isn't much, but the roof is sound. I think the owners went off to that America place an' left some bits of furniture. We can give him the truckle bed an' between us we could make him right cosy there.'

'I still don't see——' Patrick started.

'Let me finish, boy!' Mary said sternly. 'Probably not many people know it's there an' you can't see it from the lane. An' no one goes up that lane as far as your place anyway. He could go out on the hills snaring rabbits and maybe some seagull eggs. Help your Mam to feed you all. Dig peat. Help to provide for his family.'

Sarah was quiet, thoughtful and looking a little uncertain. 'But what if someone saw him and told the Constable?'

'We've thought about that too. While he's been ill, he's grown a beard and don't look nothing like he did before. Would you recognise him if you hadn't been seeing him these weeks? Lots of strangers go rabbiting in the hills. If he met anyone it's not very likely they would know him. An' on the hills he could see a body coming from miles off an' stay out of his way.' Mary's grey eyes shone with enthusiasm.

Patrick drew a deep breath. 'I still don't see how it helps us!'

Mary looked at him pitifully and shook her head. 'Well, don't you see, they'll have much lost time to make up, George and Judith, I'm thinking. If you get my meaning?' She winked at Patrick who smiled sheepishly.

'And?' Sarah eyed Mary suspiciously, her dark eyes sparkling with excitement at whatever plot her friend was hatching.

'And they might like to spend some time together in the evenings. No one there to watch the bedroom door shut behind them!'

Sarah blushingly saw Mary's plan. A knot of excitement tightened in her stomach. 'I'll talk to Mam and see what she thinks. I think though, that she is likely to want my Daa living with us.'

Mary nodded. 'Make sure you tell her how dangerous it will be for him to live at home. No one, 'cept us, would have to know he was there.'

'If she was out back at the tholtan I could slip away a bit and spend time with Patrick before he starts down the mine at ten o'clock.'

'I could come early to Laxey, then we could spend even more time together,' Patrick finished the line of thought. Throwing his arms around Mary, he tried to swing her off her feet. Then discretion being the better part of valour, he settled for planting a resounding kiss on her plump forehead and telling her he loved her.

His face saddening for a moment, he said. 'I don't like deception though. Now your mother is so much better I don't see why we can't just be honest. There is nothing I would like more than to have your parents' permission to walk out with you.'

Mary, looking thoughtful, shook her head slowly. 'Better to leave it until things are settled again. First, we must find how the thought of an Irishman will affect her now George is home. Perhaps we could enlist his help with your Mam if he holds no bitterness. He might hate Sean Casey for landing him in jail, but with luck he won't blame all Irishmen for it. Let's try to find how the land lies before we produce you.'

'I'll go and talk to Mam now,' Sarah turned to hurry away, but Patrick caught her arm, spun her around and kissed her longingly.

'Good luck,' he said quietly.

Sarah almost skipped up the lane to the cottage. 'Please,

God,' she prayed quietly. 'Please let my Mam agree. Mary's right, it would not be safe for him to live at home amongst us.'

Judith shook her head when Sarah told her of Mary's suggestion. 'No. No, that wouldn't do for him,' she said decidedly. The children say it's haunted. They won't go near it, for they're too scared.'

'That's all the better then isn't it? There would be no danger at all of them going up there and seeing him. I don't believe in ghosts an' I'm sure Daa doesn't either. It could be made quite comfortable.'

Judith still had doubts, so it was arranged that they should all get together at Mary's house to discuss it.

To Sarah's relief George was all for the idea.

'Well love, you have to see Sarah and Mary are right. I would love to be home with you and be a family again, but you must remember I'm an escaped convict. It would only need one of the childher to tell a friend I was back an' I would be back in jail before you could count to ten.'

Judith gave a tremulous sigh. 'I can see that. But we can't spend the rest of our lives living a hundred yards apart.'

'I know love, but it wouldn't be the rest of our lives. Just a few months. Mary and James have been wonderful friends to look after me as they have, but I'm well now and you can't expect them to put up with me forever.'

'I know. I understand that but how can we ever be together?'

'Well, I've been doing a lot of thinking while I've been sick. While I'm in the tholtan you can come and spend time with me when the childher are at school. An' in the evenings, sometimes. When I've got my strength back, I'll walk over the hills to Peel. There's a big fishin' fleet there an' no one knows me there. I'd get a job at the fishin' real easy.'

Judith nodded sadly. 'Aye. The fishin' an' the sea! That's

where your heart really is. An' I made you leave it. If I hadn't none of this would be happening now.'

'No, you made me do nothing, lass. The decision was mine,' George said quietly. 'I wanted you an' the childher safe. Until we go to Peel, I will be able to help you with the croftin'. If I stay out back no one can see me from the road. Plant some crops. Milk the goat, maybe.'

'So, if we go to Peel, we'll be back living in the town I suppose.' Judith sounded resigned.

'No, I've thought about that too. I'll find us a little place just out of town, maybe at Patrick or Glen Maye. You will be safer from diseases there.'

'Let's pray,' said Judith suddenly, echoing Sarah's thoughts. 'That nothing will ever part us again. Our family has had more than its share of ill-fortune. We must hope there will be no more heartbreak. We must stay together forever now. Never another Irishman to tear us asunder.'

Sarah started, her eyes going guiltily to her mother. Could she have heard a rumour about Patrick? With relief she saw that Judith was looking, not at her but, commandingly, at George who smiled apologetically and nodded his agreement.

'No, love,' he said quietly. No more Irishmen and no more smugglin'. Though I must find a way to make a living. It must be the fishin'.'

As easily as that the decision was made.

George was smuggled up the lane, behind their croft and into the tholtan under cover of darkness two days later. It wasn't a palace, but it was dry, reasonably draught free and fairly cosy. It would do nicely until he could find a job and a home in Peel.

* * *

The schoolteacher, Jenny Mills, stood just inside the door nervously wringing her hands. The poor woman had heard many tales about the 'mad woman' who lived on the hill and was not sure she should have dared to come. However, she knew it her duty to tell the parents when their children did not turn up to school as they should.

'I'm not trying to cause trouble,' she said quietly, eyeing Judith carefully and poised to flee at any moment if need be, 'but Alexandra has not attended school for some time. I'm not sure if you are aware of this and felt I should let you know.'

'Not at school?' Judith frowned. 'I don't understand. She goes every day with the other three childher. She must be at school!'

Jenny shook her head. So far so good. The mad woman wasn't going at her with a meat cleaver. 'No. I'm sorry. The other children attend well but Alexandra does not.'

Judith sighed and nodded. 'Thank you for letting me know. Leave it with me. I'll speak to her an' find out what's going on.'

'I want a word with you,' Judith said. She spoke quietly, though under the surface she boiled.

Alexandra had just come home from wherever she had been and now stood akimbo, glaring defiantly at her mother. It was not hard to know trouble was brewing.

'I had your teacher here earlier.'

'Oh her!' Alexandra dismissed her with a toss of her head.

'Yes, her. She tells me you have not been going to school.'

'So?'

'So where have you been spending every day?' Judith struggled to contain her anger but managed to keep a calm façade.

'About!' The look on Alexandra's face was one, almost of hatred.

'About where?'

Alexandra shrugged. 'None of your business!'

Sarah gasped, not believing what she was seeing and hearing. The other children sat silent and wide eyed, too scared to move.

Alexandra turned toward the door, but her mother moved swiftly to block her.

'I want an answer. Where do you spend your days?'

'With my friends, in the village and around the hills.'

Well, that's probably the truth, Sarah thought. *How well it is Mam doesn't know just what you get up to with these friends. Her heart would be truly broken. And Daa's.*

Alexandra, who had grown overly used to having things too much her own way, said no more and flounced off to the loft in a sulk.

Judith sat for a while immersed in thought. Sarah could see her shoulders trembling and moved to put an arm around her.

'Try not to be upset, Mam. Life is just starting to come good for you again.'

Judith reached to squeeze her hand. 'You're a good girl, Sarah.' In a whisper she added, 'I have to talk to your Daa about this.' At this, she slipped out, leaving the children, still huddled together in shock.

George, when he heard her story, was both shocked and furious. 'And that was all she would tell you?'

'Aye. If you knew what I've had to put up with from her recently. Comes home late from school. At least that's where I thought she was. She sneaks out whenever my back is turned and refuses ever to tell me where she's been. There's no saying what mischief she might have been about while I've been nursing you. I really don't know what's come over her.'

'I suppose she's at an age she might be starting to take an interest in boys,' George suggested.

'Boys? Dear God, I hope not. She's only thirteen! What are we to do with her?'

'Well, she's had her chance. If she won't go to school, she will have to go out to work! It's as simple as that.'

'But you so wanted her to have an education,' Judith frowned worriedly.

'I did. She doesn't. An' if she won't go to school, she will bring us in some money. God knows, we need it!'

When Judith returned to the croft a short while later, there was a determination to her step. 'Alexandra, I want to talk to you. Come down here.'

An unintelligible, mumbled complaint drifted down from the half-loft.

'I said, come down. Now!' Judith insisted.

Alexandra climbed down the rickety ladder and faced her mother with an arrogant look.

'I've had a think about it, and you say you no longer want to go to school, is that right?'

Alexandra looked startled, then agreed with her mother.

'Fine. I won't make you go back then. Instead you will go to work at the mines and start bringin' some much-needed money into the family.'

Alexandra stared at her mother in undisguised horror.

'Indeed, I will *not*!' she shouted, her eyes blazing. 'I'm not going to spend my life on the washing-floors, with my hands in water in every kind of weather, sorting stones from metal. I'm not going to work at a job that gives me red, raw, ugly hands like Sarah's! And for only seven shillings a week!'

'You will do as you're told, my fine lady!' Judith snapped, showing the first sign of temper Sarah had seen since her father's reappearance. 'We must all pull our weight.'

'Well I shan't work in the mines ever!' Alexandra shouted defiantly.

'You will if you're told to!' Judith raised her hand but managed to stop short of swinging it.

Sarah watched in silent horror, knowing she could never defy her mother in such a fashion.

'Shan't! Not ever! I'd *die* before I would work in those damned mines!' Alexandra stood her ground, head poked forward defiantly. Pushed beyond the limit and without warning, Judith's hand flashed out, sweeping stingingly across Alexandra's mottled, angry face.

Sarah leapt to her feet, the chair crashing backwards away from her. For a moment she saw the mad look in her mother's eyes — one she had hoped was gone for ever.

Alexandra rubbed her cheek, glaring at her mother from below hooded lids. Her eyes were narrowed, filled with venom. 'You'll live to rue this!' she hissed, then turning, she fled out into the night.

Judith collapsed into a chair, her head in her hands. 'Do you think she's sneaking out to meet boys? Do you know anything about this Sarah?'

Sarah, feeling her chest constrict, shook her head vehemently. 'Oh no, I'm sure it's not that!' She crossed her fingers behind her back.

Turning to the other children, Judith said quietly, 'You must have known she wasn't going to school.'

Three heads nodded.

'Then why did you not tell me?'

'Because she said if I did, she would cut my bits off an' m–m–make me eat them!' Richard said tearfully.

Judith sighed miserably and asked the little girls, 'And what of you two? What did she threaten you with?'

Louisa gulped. 'She said she would boil us and eat us!' she hung her head and tears slipped down her cheeks to plop onto her dress.

'Oh, dear God!' Judith sat with her elbows on the table, her face buried in her hands.

'It's late now,' she said after a while. 'I'm tired and I need to get to bed. I'll leave a lamp burning and come to sort this business out the moment she condescends to return.'

When Alexandra did arrive home the hour was very late indeed. Sarah, pretending sleep, but peeping out from the cupboard bed, was horrified at the dishevelled state of her sister's clothing and hair.

Alexandra edged the door open carefully peering round it, her expression a mixture of apprehension and defiance. Finding the room empty, she stepped inside, shutting the door quietly behind her. Her bonnet was askew, skirt crumpled, and bodice half unbuttoned.

From the next room Sarah could hear her mother's gentle snoring and was relieved she had not awakened as Alexandra sneaked in. She could not bear to think what it might do to her mother to see her daughter in such a state. There could be no doubt what she had been up to.

Looking flushed, her face a mask of arrogant insolence, Alexandra had made no effort to tidy up her clothes and was clearly spoiling for a fight. For several moments she stood, her eyes fixed steadfastly on the bedroom door. She walked to it, passing close to Sarah's bed, to stand holding the door handle.

Sarah held her breath. Surely the younger girl was not going to be brazen enough to awaken her mother, not in her present wanton state.

Sarah closed her eyes, feeling sick, a little voice inside her head pleading with Alexandra to just go quietly to bed. When she looked again the girl was leaning toward the door with her ear pressed to it.

Seeming to suddenly sense Sarah's eyes on her she whispered,

'Silly cow's asleep. Thank God Daa is away else there'd be another brat on the way. The only sensible thing then would be a visit to Lucy Costain. Anyway, if she can sleep so easily it shows how worried she was about me!' Turning on her heel, she shot off up the ladder to her mattress in the loft, leaving Sarah trembling.

After that Sarah found it almost impossible to sleep. Alexandra's vehemence frightened her and no matter how hard she tried she could not shake off the deep longing for Patrick to be there to give her comfort.

When sleep finally took her, it was a disturbed nightmare her eyes closed on. Broken with wild cries and crazy images she tossed and turned, knowing Patrick was in terrible danger — sensed rather than seen. Or was it her father? The face was unclear and seemed to keep changing. The Constable entered her tortured sleep, to chase and kill, but even he was faceless.

A sudden unearthly screech wakened Sarah, and immediately she was bolt upright in bed, her jangled nerves shaking her uncontrollably. She could neither see nor hear any movement in the cottage, so rising from her bed she crossed to the tiny window, pulling back the fresh blue and white checked curtain. At first, she could see nothing but the ghostly shadows thrown randomly around by the full moon.

The awful sound came again and following its direction she was able to make out a screech owl on the bare hawthorn, its head atilt watching for prey. It rose, suddenly, diving into the shrubbery and the girl heard a small scream as a tiny beast died. Then the bird rose again, powerful wings beating slowly, and flew to rest again on the thorn tree to feed.

Drawing a deep thankful breath, Sarah let it out shakily, then made her way back to bed to wait, wakefully for morning.

Escaping from the croft early, before the rest of the family stirred, she felt a great weight lifted from her. There would be Hell to pay in the confrontation when Alexandra and her mother met, and she was thankful to be out of it.

Mary shook her head, tutting irritably when Sarah told her of the set to with Alexandra.

'That young 'un is going to bring nothing but heartache,' she said, shaking her head angrily. 'Both for herself and anyone else who's misguided enough to care about her.'

Sarah frowned suddenly, a memory coming of something else her sister had said. 'Who's Lucy Costain? Have you heard of her?'

Mary looked at her sharply. 'Where did a girl like you hear that name? Why do you want to know?'

Quickly Sarah told of Alexandra's comment, at which Mary snorted furiously.

'Lucy Costain is a woman of the type who should be put in a spiked barrel and rolled down Slieu Whallian with the rest of the witches!" she said shortly.

Sarah had heard the story of Slieu Whallian. In days gone by a woman suspected of being a witch was put in a barrel, with many spikes on the inside. The barrel was rolled down the long, steep hill called Slieu Whallian. If she was alive when she reached the bottom, they knew she was a witch and was then put to death. If she died on the way down, she had been wrongly accused and was given a Christian burial.

'Is she so evil?' Sarah asked, wide-eyed.

'Worse! Her type is the evillest to walk this earth!'

'In what way? What does this woman do that is so terrible?'

'Kills babies!'

Sarah tripped over a stone in her shock, almost falling full length in the roadway.

'How so? Murder? Surely she would be arrested?'

'Nothing so open and clean as murder,' Mary corrected,

her voice taught with fury. 'She kills them afore they have the chance to be born!'

'She takes unborn babies?' Sarah stopped dead in her tracks, staring shakily into the distance in shock. Her eyes dazedly took in the dawn, now a saffron rent in the clouds to the east. The sea glistening in its light like a field of wild poppies.

'Aye — abortion they call it.' Mary's expression now was one of sadness. 'I would have given my life to bear a babe, and that witch does away with them as if they were just some piece of rubbish.'

'Where does this Costain woman live? How would Alexandra know of such a person?'

Mary gave no answer, but she had no need to. Her expression said it all.

The world closed in around Sarah and for a moment she thought she would faint. Bile rose to sour her mouth.

'Alexandra?' she rasped past a tongue that cleft drily to the roof of her mouth. 'But she's only just turned thirteen years of age!'

'It happens lass. I'd heard talk of Alexandra being seen leaving the Costain woman's house. And I knew it was not at her mother's bidding she went. I had no intention of telling you. I wanted to spare you that. And your Mammy too.'

'Oh God — Mam! What will it do to her if she learns of it, Mary? She's only now becoming herself again.'

'Then we shall have to try to keep it from her.' Mary's voice was firm, authoritative.

'Aye,' Sarah agreed sadly and a lone gull mewing mournfully overhead seemed to echo her melancholy mood. 'Tell me, Mary,' curiosity made her ask, though her heart did not want an answer, 'How does she do it?'

'Who do what?' Mary frowned.

'This Lucy Costain. How? Does she cut the babe out? Alexandra has never stayed away from home for even one night.'

'No, 'tis done with a potion. A mixture of ergot with camomile to make the taste bearable. It makes the womb take spasms and brings on the bleeding.'

Sarah nodded dazedly. Alexandra not yet full grown. Whoring. *Killing babies*! 'She doesn't know what she's doing to herself, Mary.' Sarah shook her head in horror.

'Happen she doesn't. But she wouldn't listen if you tried to tell her because she thinks she's found a good way to get rich quickly.'

Dawn's rosy light picked out the shadowy forms of the mine buildings, reflecting like fire from the white casement of the giant wheel, throwing its long shadow over the glen. The two women lingered for a moment to enjoy the spectacle.

At that moment the miners, having finished their core, were starting to file wearily from the changing shed.

'I'll just wait and see if I can catch Patrick when he surfaces. Maybe he'll be able to meet me tonight.'

Mary nodded. 'I'll get on down then, love. Don't be late to work though will you. No point to getting yourself in bother with the overseer.'

Sarah saw Patrick as he sauntered from the adit, standing head and shoulders above his companions, his red hair like a halo in the early morning light. Catching her breath slightly at the effect he had upon her, she moved timidly toward him.

'Sarah!' His voice was pitched high with pleasure and surprise at seeing her there.

All at once she found herself in his arms, her face buried in his chest and her whole frame shaken with silent weeping, not caring who might be watching.

'What's happened?' Patrick's voice held a note of fear.

For a moment she did not answer, merely staring into his eyes with raw, open love, the hint of a tear on her cheek. Then with a quick shake of her head, as though to clear her thoughts of irritation, she pulled away from him slightly.

'There's no time to talk of it just now. Nor is this the place. Alexandra was awful to my Mam last night and there is going to be the most terrible trouble. I need badly to tell you of it. Please can you meet me at Mary's tonight?'

'Aye, love. Of course I shall. I'll be there by eight of the clock.'

'And I'll come as early as I can manage.'

Patrick watched worriedly as she walked away from him toward the washing-floors.

Chapter 13

Sarah, sitting on a low stool in the inglenook, watched her mother a trifle apprehensively as she attempted to gauge her mood. Though there seemed no apparent tension in the atmosphere, no mention was made of Alexandra, or how much of a row there had been that morning.

Alexandra had gone to school, it seemed, but when she came home, she was in a poor mood, sullen and resentful, but her mother seemed not to notice it and showed no sign of any ill-feeling.

Merely grunting a reply to their greeting, she went straight to the table, burying her nose in a book. From that point on she ignored everyone until after tea when she stood up, announcing she was going to see a friend about some work they were covering at school. Before anyone had a chance to raise a complaint, she had grabbed her shawl and flounced from the cottage.

Judith looked toward the door and sighed. 'I pray the fairies don't get her,' she murmured, and Sarah knew she meant it.

During the evening Sarah made a diligent attempt at intelligent conversation; made difficult with her mind in such a frenzy of anticipation; and with such fear in her heart that she would not be able to escape to meet Patrick.

Finally, grasping her courage, Sarah took a deep breath, held it for a moment then allowed it to escape slowly from her lungs.

'Would you mind very much if I went out for a short while?' She asked quietly, trying to sound as casual as possible.

Her mother lifted her head and looked at her enquiringly. 'I don't know that it's safe for a young woman to wander along in the dark. Have you somewhere special to go?'

'James is below ground tonight, so I thought I might walk down and keep Mary company for a little while. Would you prefer it if I didn't go?' Sarah held her breath apprehensively, her fingers firmly crossed behind her back.

'No, lass. You go. Mary has been a good friend to us, and I know she'd appreciate your company. I'm sure you'll be safe enough. I've heard of no brigands around these parts. And if any man had rape in mind he would hardly wander so far from the village on the off chance of meeting with a maid. I might just take a stroll out back — catch a bit of fresh air. If you meet up with that sister of yours tell her to come home quickly. And mind you don't get took!' Judith instructed.

Sarah nodded, smiling at her mother's fears that the fairies might take her. A great believer in the fairies, her mother was; like many of the Manx. Picking up her shawl with hands that trembled slightly, she left quickly. Once clear of the cottage, she flew down the path, past the copse of gnarled elder trees and down the road toward Agneash.

The wind made strange shadows whenever the moon managed to struggle, for a moment, from behind her mantle of cloud. It reminded Sarah of the fairies in the glen and the poor reputation they had concerning children and maidens.

With her mother's parting words still loud in her ears, Sarah sped as quickly as she dared, for between the brief flashes of moonlight the darkness was complete. But with Patrick waiting, she hoped the Little People might be given no chance to take her.

Arriving agitated at Mary's cottage, she paused momentarily to recover her breath. Stopping for a moment she smoothed her skirts and tucked stray curls inside her bonnet. With unsteady hands she gave a quick knock then lifted the door-latch and opened it slowly, her heart bursting with anticipation.

Patrick was there before her, pacing the floor impatiently. His face lit when she arrived, and he smiled lovingly. For a moment he stood unmoving, his eyes filled with longing, silently drinking in the beauty of the tall, slender girl before him.

Even in her poor, shabby clothing she looked magnificent to him. Moving forward, he took her in his arms and as she tilted her head, his hungry lips met hers.

Mary tactfully kept her head lowered to her stitching, while James sat at the table, tacking the wayward sole back on his working boot.

It was a prolonged breathless embrace before, mindful they were not alone, they broke apart. Patrick rubbed his cheek briefly against Sarah's. After a long, unsteady sigh, he put her away from him. Standing with his hands still on her waist, he looked down into her dark eyes, a mixture now of love, excitement and the underlying worry that lay behind them.

'Mary has told me the gist of what has been upsetting you,' Patrick said quietly.

'What are we going to do about that child then?' Sarah asked, relieved she had been saved the trouble of explaining it to him.

'I can't see that there is a lot we can do. We have known for some time what she is up to. Now we know for certain it goes further than just looking and touching. But I can think of nothing to suggest what we can do to stop her.'

'She's going to ruin her life completely if she continues.' Sarah's hands fluttered in a gesture of helplessness.

'Well, I'm sorry to say it, but I should think she has most probably succeeded in doing so already,' James said, frowning at the boot. 'Once a maid's reputation has so badly gone there can be no way of redeeming it.'

Mary shot him a quick warning glance, twitching her hand slightly in annoyance.

'Has she such a terrible reputation then?' Sarah asked quickly, her eyes intent upon James.

'That wasn't the way James meant it,' Mary cut in before he had a chance to reply.

'I want the truth. Please don't hide things from me. I must know. What do you know of it, Patrick?' She stepped back then from his hold, watching his expression, waiting.

Patrick shrugged, studying an imaginary speck on the floor, teasing it with the toe of his boot.

'He has probably heard what the rest of us have in the changing shed.' James rescued him, needing to say no more.

Suddenly seeing all, Sarah nodded miserably. 'Men as well as boys!' It was a statement, not a question. 'And her antics are discussed in lewd fashion amongst the men in the changing sheds?'

Patrick drew a tremulous sigh. 'That's about the strength of it, love.'

'There will be no saving her, I'm afraid,' James continued gently. 'She's well fallen and making good money while her Mam thinks she's in school.'

'Oh Hell!' Sarah slumped into a chair, cradling her head in her hands. 'What am I to do?'

'Nothing, if you take my advice.' Mary sat next to her, putting a plump arm round the girl's shoulder. 'Say nought to her or it will only cause trouble in the house. Your Mam could not help but feel it. She would have to tell your Daa and what purpose would it serve for them to know? They'll learn of it soon enough. Let them have some time of happiness before then. God knows, they've had more than enough misery.'

The evening was gone all too quickly, and time came near for Patrick to leave for the mine.

'I'll see you safely to your door,' he offered eagerly, but Sarah shook her head.

'Thank you, but I think after what I have learned today, I would rather be alone for a while. And perhaps you might care to think again about whether you want it known you are walking out with the sister of a whore!'

'I know what I want!' Patrick's voice was tight with passion. 'And I care not what anyone thinks of you. It is what I know of you that matters!' The gold flecks in his hazel eyes glittered as fiercely as his anger. 'What your sister is, or does, makes no difference to me! You are you! And I love you!'

After he had left, Sarah stayed on for a while with Mary and James, needing time to recover her wits before she faced her parents.

Mary, motherly and anxious as ever, made a cup of camomile to warm her. Before she left James too, offered to walk with her to her door, but she again refused.

Once outside their door she stood motionless for a moment, a little afraid of the moonlit semi-darkness, but glad of the anonymity it afforded her. Taking a deep breath, she held it for a long moment, as though hoping it would cleanse her soul of her sister's muck.

Not yet feeling she was ready to go home and live a lie, Sarah wandered down toward Laxey. Changing her mind at the corner she went off up the lane that led to the reservoir which held the water to power the mighty Lady Isabella.

Before her stood Snaefell, silhouetted and towering like a gaunt and forbidding black giant guarding her island in the moonlight.

Reaching the reservoir, Sarah sank wearily down on a rock near the water's edge. Drawing her shawl more tightly around her shoulders, she sat completely still to listen to the multitude of night sounds.

Unseen frogs croaked in many keys and pitches, puffing their throbbing chins to attract a mate to their embraces. Small creatures of the night, now out of hibernation, scuffled and scratched nearby, while the whirring wings of their predators often could be heard.

As Sarah gazed over the gleaming stretch of water, she began to feel better, smiling as a ray of moonlight played on a pair of polecats frolicking on the bank. The tangle of gorse and new spring growth full of secret places to hide.

Soon, she supposed, they would breed, then there would be a whole family of the sleek little creatures gambolling there. Why, she wondered, had God made it alright for animals to follow their instincts and breed willy-nilly, but indecent for people to do the same. It really was a frustratingly complicated world for humans.

Sarah fingered her threadbare grey wool skirt with distaste, thinking absently of the rich, brightly coloured dresses she had seen real ladies wear. What would she give to be a lady? To wear silks and satins and brocades. Ride in richly decorated carriages pulled by shiny, high trotting horses, with glittering brasses on their harness. Oh, to live in a fine mansion, the likes of which she had only and would only ever read about.

If only! She stopped her line of thought with a doleful sigh. It would never be. Someone had once told her 'if only' were the two saddest words in the English language. How true that was!

It would take a kind fairy with a powerful magic wand to give her just a small part of that sort of grandeur. Everyone knew that Manx fairies were mostly mischievous. Those who were not downright evil!

Smiling, she remembered the oft-told tale, about the wonderful goat of Laxey. Owned by an old woman, this goat was the purest of whites, with amber eyes and huge, curving horns. No other goat on the island gave such rich, creamy milk right throughout the year.

The old woman called her goat 'Lhiannan-Shee', which was 'Fairy Sweetheart' in Manx. The people in the glen told her it was unwise to call an animal after 'Themselves' (the fairies), but so much did she think of her goat that she disregarded them.

To the old lady's dismay, she found out the people were right, for when the moon was full Lhiannan-Shee used to leap the wall and disappear. In the morning she would be back, ready for milking but with a strange look in her eyes.

The house where the old lady lived was away up the valley, well past the Fayles' croft. Sometimes the old woman had to walk down to the village for a few provisions. One winter's day, darkness fell before she could get home. Suddenly, as she neared her cottage, she heard gay, lilting music. Rounding the bend in the road, she saw light flooding from her home. Creeping a little nearer, she saw the goat standing in the middle of the floor with a wreath of flowers around her neck, her amber eyes aglow. Little people crowded near her, dancing and singing. Others were spreading food on the table and building the fire with peat. Angry with the thieving beggars, she tried to rush into the cottage, but was swept backwards by some strange force. When she regained her senses, the cottage was empty, the lights dowsed and the fire almost out. On checking the shed where the goat should be, she found the door wide open and the animal gone.

The fresh cream and pat of butter she'd had in her larder was also gone and long after the old woman went to bed, she heard whisperings around the house.

In the morning the goat was back.

For a while the old woman thought about selling the goat, but despite the trouble with the fairies, she was fond of the animal. And besides, she knew she would not get such fine milk from any other.

On the next occasion the old woman went to the village she not only tied the goat with a strong rope, she pushed a heavy stone against the shed door.

Arriving home, she found the little people there, just as on the previous occasion, only this time they took with them when they left, a fresh baked bonnag as well as butter and cream.

The shed door stood wide open, the goat gone and only the rope remained.

This time, still not wishing to sell the goat, she took her to the parson, asking him to put 'good words' on her to keep the fairies away.

The man of the cloth told the old lady that if she left the goat with him for a week, he would have her cured. This the old woman did, but when she returned to the village the following week, she found it deserted, with no sign of life whatsoever. Though all the doors stood wide open, there was no sign of smoke from any chimney.

Then suddenly she heard music, the same type as she had heard in her cottage. Looking toward the sound, she saw all the villagers, led by the parson and the white goat, which had a garland of flowers around its neck. The church bells started to ring and immediately the white goat vanished.

All the people stopped dancing and returned to their shops and houses as though nothing had happened.

When the old lady asked the parson for her goat, he discovered her gone, with only the rope he'd left her tied to remaining. The old woman knew then that Lhiannan-Shee had been a fairy goat.

Had not the sexton been locked in the church when she led all the people away, and rung the bells to break the spell, there was no knowing where the goat might have taken them. As it was the wonderful goat of Laxey was never seen again.

Sarah wakened from her reverie, glancing round apprehensively. There were many tales of the Manx fairies stealing babies and children and maidens. Stories she sometimes felt could be true.

Suddenly the sounds Sarah heard around her in the dark took on a new meaning and she jumped nervously to her feet. Something moved at her feet, rustling the grass and she jumped back, startled. Aware now, of the shadows moving strangely in the breeze she was certain she could detect the shapes of little people, their faces made white and their green coats and red hats muted to differing shades of grey by the eerie light of the moon.

Jumping to her feet she spun around and heart in mouth, lifted her skirts and raced up the hillside away from the reservoir. Leaping over the stones she saw, tripping over those she did not, she slowed only when she reached the comparative safety of the road and Agneash. Even so she felt eyes watching from the shadows all the way up to the croft and was almost certain she could hear the melancholy music of the story.

Drawing level with the elder trees, there was a definite whispering and fear stopped Sarah in tracks. Her heart thundering in her ears, she stood listening intently, too frightened to move.

Somewhere nearby Sarah heard a sound of muffled giggling,

and a rustling. A gruff adult voice said, 'I've spread my coat, so get yourself on the ground and be ready for me, girl.'

Her stomach in the grip of a million butterflies, Sarah passed slowly on up the lane, picking her way as quietly as possible, hearing feminine squealing that sounded very much like Alexandra! And the strange grunting sounds of a man.

It was with great relief Sarah found the croft in darkness, her mother safely abed and ignorant of what was occurring just a few yards away.

Slipping quickly out of her clothes, Sarah was in bed and feigning sleep when Alexandra let herself in some considerable time later.

Sarah found herself wondering absently what her sister did with the money she earned. Did she save it? If she did, just where did she keep it hidden? In such a small croft and with so many nosy children, that would be no easy task.

Alexandra, to her sister's astonishment, carried on her double life with no appearance of shame.

Sarah, however, felt guilty because of her knowledge, and soiled by association. In the washing sheds she often caught people whispering, staring at her, then averting their eyes when they saw her looking. In the village, too, she felt she was being discussed. She was the sister of the doxy who lived in the croft 'up along' and therefore, it seemed, to be tarred with the same brush.

Mary tried to tell her she was imagining it all, but she knew from the lewd comments often directed at her that she was not.

When Patrick arrived at Mary's cottage one night with his fists grazed and a bruise on his face, Sarah knew the cause of it right away, though he refused at first to admit it.

'Was something said about me?' She asked quietly.

'Why should my fights concern you? Why would you think that?' he asked, feigning surprise

Sarah gave a bitter, snorting laugh. 'Because I'm neither stupid nor deaf. I know what is being said about me behind my back. I know that many class me with my sister. After all we are of the same blood aren't, we? We look much alike. Therefore, in the eyes of this village, we must behave in the same fashion!'

'Don't let it upset you, love.' Mary gripped her hand, squeezing it fondly, while Patrick moved to enfold her within the safety of his arms. Sarah immediately burst into tears against his chest, her whole body shuddering with the force of her hurt and anger.

'I'd like to take that little doxy and shake her 'til her bones drop out!' Patrick said angrily.

Mary tutted, scowling at him and shaking her head angrily.

'I'm sorry, Sarah. I shouldn't call her that. I forget, sometimes that she's your sister.' Patrick apologised.

'I'm glad someone can forget it,' Sarah said bleakly. 'For no one else in the village can. Call her what you like. It's what she is!'

Patrick insisted on walking Sarah to the safety of the croft that evening, for knowing the types Alexandra was mixing with, he feared whom Sarah might meet on the path.

Pausing by the gate, they listened for a while to make sure the copse of elders was unoccupied before they moved into their shadow.

'We shall have to be wed, Sarah,' Patrick whispered, bending slightly to lay his cheek against hers. ''Tis the only way to silence the venomous tongues.'

Sarah shook her head sadly. 'It is a poor reason to be wed.'

'Not the reason Sarah. You know that! I've wanted you for my wife for some long while now, as you well know.'

'There is still the problem of my Mam's hatred and fear of Irishmen.'

'Perhaps if you explain the situation, she will be happy to consent.'

A tear leapt into Sarah's eye. 'Aye. Perhaps.' she whispered. 'But I cannot do that without them knowing about Alexandra!'

Patrick gave an anguished groan. 'Damn Sean Casey! Damn him to Hell! And damn Alexandra too!' Gathering Sarah into his arms he kissed her with a passion that was born of anger and frustration.

Lips bruised, and hardly able to breathe, Sarah struggled to free herself from him. 'You're hurting me,' she gasped when she finally managed to free her mouth from his.

'Sorry love,' he mumbled, then gently he caressed her cheek and ear and neck with his lips. His hands moved slowly on her body, coaxing the tension and misery from her.

Sarah enjoyed his kisses and the warm feeling of security it gave her. But she felt no arousal. The mental image of her young sister taking, between her legs, any rough miner with the right price, quenched the flame of her desire.

'I'm sorry, Patrick. I have no wish for any type of lovemaking tonight. The thought of being touched makes me feel even more soiled.'

Patrick removed his hands as though they had been scalded. Stepping back, he studied her for a moment in the moonlight. 'Then I'll bid you goodnight' he said tightly. Turning abruptly, he stormed off, away from her down the hill.

Her body racked with sobs, Sarah watched him until he vanished amongst the shadows far along the lane, but he did not once look around.

'Dear God,' she muttered, 'Don't let him meet up with Alexandra on the way, for in his present mood there is no saying what he might say or do.'

Chapter 14

Primroses presented their bright, sunny faces along the roadsides as spring progressed. Long before they were finished came the azure blanket of bluebells, the merry little celandines and the delicate beauty of wood sorrel. The tenacious, everlasting Manx gorse was always present, despite the amount that was burned to warm the homes of the islanders through winter.

Sarah and Patrick met when they could, but it was nowhere near as often as he would have liked. Opportunities were few, especially when he was on a spell of night shifts in the mine.

'I wish we could be alone together more often,' Patrick whispered in a fit of pique one day as they strolled up the lane. 'The most I see of you is when we walk up from the mine and Mary is always with us. I understand you don't want us to be seen alone in case a rumour gets back to your mother. But she must know about us one day. I had thought that with your Daa back things might be better for us.'

Sarah sighed, hearing him speak of the feelings she too felt. 'Aye I wish it too. With all my heart I do. But you know why it must be this way.'

Patrick shook his head. 'You know I would marry you tomorrow if you would only say yes. Now your Daa is home, surely your Mam could manage fine without you.'

'I'll talk to Daa and find out if he is bitter to all Irishmen. If I feel it safe, I'll tell him about you and ask him to help. Maybe he'll be able to bring Mam to her senses.'

'You'll do that soon?'

'Aye. I have to be careful when I go to the tholtan. I can only go when the childher are not around, lest they wonder about me going there.'

Patrick nodded his understanding.

'Mary and James are good to let us be together here sometimes and afford us as much privacy as is possible. It would not be right to impose on them too often though.' She gave a wry smile. 'It's probably safer if we're not alone together you must admit!'

'It might be safer, but it's not the way I want it.' Patrick steered her from the lane into the thicket, his arms instantly around her, crushing her, his lips against hers and his tongue searching hungrily.

Sarah felt herself melting, the fiery warmth of her passion all-consuming and she responded without thought.

Surfacing momentarily for air Patrick gazed down at Sarah. His gold-flecked hazel eyes saw his own eagerness reflected in her large, dark brown ones.

'I love you, Sarah Fayle, with every fibre of my being,' he said huskily. He ran gently loving fingers down the smooth curve of her cheek, her throat, and on downward until he held her breast cupped in a hand that trembled with desire. Fumbling quickly, he opened her bodice to slip his hand inside.

Sarah gasped and clutched him to her, reaching up with one hand entwined in his hair to bring his lips back to hers. Her other hand, with a will of its own, found its way to where it could gently caress his hardness she felt pressed against her.

With a low, throaty groan, Patrick abandoned himself to the pleasure of her touch. Their hearts, only inches apart, thundered so loudly Sarah was certain the sound must be heard throughout the village.

It was only the sound of children's voices in the lane a short time later that brought them back to earth. Jumping suddenly apart, they stood looking toward the sound. Patrick put a finger to his lips and drew her further away from the lane.

In a few moments Richard, Louisa and Elizabeth came running around the corner, giggling and chasing each other.

Having the children so near broke the spell for Sarah. When Patrick reached for her again, she pushed his hand away.

'No, Patrick. This is not right.' Blushing, she turned away from him and fastened her bodice. 'I think it's best if I walk the rest of the way on my own.'

Patrick watched her walk away from him, his mind a turmoil of frustration, anger and love.

Lying awake that night Sarah, still in a state of avid excitement, found it impossible to sleep. Whenever she started to drift away, Patrick would leap back into her thoughts and she wondered how it would feel to be completely possessed by his body. To be alone with him, without fear of interruption, and to make love to its final tingling conclusion. And oh, how her body longed for it to happen.

Somehow, she must find a way to cure her mother of her revulsion for the Irish.

It was these thoughts chasing each other through her mind that had her wide awake when the storm started.

Its onset was sudden. An unheralded, ear shattering, earth trembling crash of thunder that brought Sarah instantly upright in bed her eyes wide open, staring terrified into the darkness of the night. Her first thought was that the mine must have blown up and she was thankful that neither Patrick nor James were on core that night.

Suddenly the black square of the window was lit with a blinding flash that ripped the night sky asunder with another explosion. Before the earth had stopped trembling, the heavens opened to unleash a torrent on the sleeping island.

For three weeks the rain did not stop. Mary and Sarah, by the time they had walked down the hill each morning, arrived at the washing-floors a sodden mess.

There was no escape once they were there, for they worked outdoors and had no cover. Many of the women and children employed there fell ill with fevers and deaths were not infrequent.

Mary, usually strong as an ox, succumbed eventually and was taken with a chest infection, which the village doctor, John Bryant, gravely diagnosed as double pneumonia. Judith, pleased with the opportunity, if not the circumstances, to repay a debt, took it upon herself to minister to Mary during her illness.

Sarah, pushing thoughts of Patrick aside in her concern, hurried from the washing-floors each evening, almost running up the hill to help with the nursing. Relieving her mother whenever possible, she prepared steaming bowls of Friar's Balsam to help clear her friend's congested lungs. Changed sweat-dampened sheets and coaxed Mary to sup small quantities of thin broth. And when she could think of nothing more, just knelt on the floor beside the bed with her hands clasped in simple, silent prayer. To the relief of all, Mary proved to be no less resilient and every bit as much of a fighter as ever and she was soon past the crisis. It was quite some time though before she was properly on her feet and strong enough to manage without some considerable assistance.

To Patrick's pleas that she should spend some time with him, Sarah turned a deaf ear. Her reply always, 'There will be all our lives ahead once Mary is well again. But until then I cannot think about us. Mary has been such a good friend to us, I must put her first for this short while.'

Disgruntled, Patrick snarled, 'It seems to me you can always find someone who must be put before us! Or are they all just excuses you make to keep me dangling on a string? Let me know when you do decide to consider me — *if ever!*' With that he wheeled, almost running from her in his anger.

With no risk of being seen from the lane at the front and while the children were at school, George painstakingly dug the land behind the cottage. He planted crops as the wild wet winds of April progressed toward a balmier May. The wet weeks that so devastated the mine workers had come at just the right time for him.

His frustration grew as, more and more, he wanted to go out into the world and earn money, instead of hiding away. A worthless fugitive was how he grew to regard himself. A dreadful millstone round the necks of his family. He found it hard to be so near his family, but to stay hidden from them. Hard to leave four of his children thinking he was dead. His only contact with his wife seemed stolen and furtive. Day by day his pride in himself as a man and a provider became ever more bruised.

Visits from Sarah brought a ray of sunshine into his life, but only briefly. When she left again, she took the light out with her.

Watching him anxiously, Sarah and Judith saw him becoming increasingly unsettled, withdrawing into himself.

'I cannot go on living this way!' George announced suddenly one evening. 'This is no life for a man, hidden away. Terrified always that I might be seen. Knowing the lies that will have to be told if I am and the trouble it would bring to you all.' Judith and Sarah looked at him warily, their eyes darkening with fear.

'You must stay hidden. You know full well that if you're seen and recognised, you'll be arrested and sent back to jail. I couldn't bear that!' Judith shuddered, remembering how ill she had become the last time he was taken away.

'Nor could I, love. Nor could I,' George agreed feelingly. 'But no more can I go on hiding behind the skirts of women or ducking out of sight in the fields whenever I see anyone in the distance. Or living close to my children, watching them from the cover of the spinney, but not being able to take them in my arms. Do you have any idea how hard that is for me?'

Judith nodded, a trembling hand clutched to her mouth and Sarah could feel the agony in her heart.

'Please, Daa,' she pleaded, 'Can't you be patient a little while longer?'

'How much longer, Sarah? Can you tell me?'

Unable to find words, Sarah drew a tremulous breath, shaking her head miserably.

'It will be forever, if we stay here. Can't you see that? I would spend the rest of my life watching the people I love wearing themselves out to keep me fed and clothed. In many ways that would be worse than being locked up.'

'Well we would rather have you here. We don't mind working do we, Sarah?' Judith looked pleadingly at her daughter.

'We'll think of something, Daa. Don't do anything rash.'

'Nothing rash, love. But we must move away from here. Go where I'm not known. Take a different name. To the mines at Foxdale, perhaps. Or to Peel to the fishin'. The fishin' would be better — 'tis what I know. The reason I went smuggling was to give you all a better, easier life. And I wanted you, Sarah, to stay at school to get a good education. You're a clever girl. You have the sort of brain that might have made you into a school mistress or a nurse. Instead I have to watch you wasting your life on the washing-floors of a mine.'

'I don't mind, Daa. Truly I don't.'

'But I *do*!' George said angrily, banging his fist on the table. 'It makes me no kind of a man to live this way. Our only answer is to leave Laxey! I'll go soon to look for work and find lodgings elsewhere.'

Thinking of Patrick, Sarah's heart sank leadenly to the pit of her stomach.

'Not Back to Douglas?' Judith asked fearfully. 'I could not bear to live there again.'

'No. Not Douglas,' her husband assured her gently. 'I know how you feel about the town. Besides, I am too well known there. We must go where I am not known.'

Having learned from James that Patrick was on the afternoon shift that week and finishing at ten o'clock, Sarah was waiting for him when he left the changing shed the following night.

Seeing her, he gave an abrupt nod of his head and said, 'Evening Sarah.' Turning on his heel, he made to walk away from her.

'Can I talk to you please, Patrick?'

Patrick hesitated for a moment, looking searchingly into her eyes. 'Seems to me you're all talk and not much else,' he snapped, then he strode away with Sarah almost running half a step behind.

'*Please*, Patrick,' she beseeched.

'Say what you have to while we walk. I'm in a hurry.' Patrick increased his pace.

Sarah stopped, standing hands on hips while she watched his angry back receding. 'I shall run after no man,' she called icily. 'And if you walk away from me now, you'll never see me again, Patrick O'Malley.'

Patrick took several more steps, and for a few awful moments Sarah thought he would walk on. Vaguely she was aware of other miners smiling and nudging each other knowingly.

'If he don't want you, I'll be happy to give you a good wild roll lass,' one young larrikin called, leering at her. 'I reckon it might be a bit of fun to try the other sister for a change. See if you're as good as the young 'un!'

In a flash Patrick had rounded on him, his huge hands gripping the youth's shirt fronts, face burning and sweating with fury.

'Don't, Patrick!' Sarah leapt forward to grasp his raised fist. 'Don't be in trouble on my account. He's only saying what everyone else is thinking. It's just the name my sister has earned for me.'

The young miner, still in Patrick's grasp, was pale and trembling. For a moment the Irishman looked at him, anger and contempt etched in every line of his face. Angrily he threw the lad roughly from him, sending him sprawling full length in the mud.

'Now you'll apologise to the lady if you want to keep your face in one piece,' he ordered, his face thunderous.

'Sorry, Miss. Real sorry, I am.' The lad painfully pulled himself to his feet, dipped his head quickly in respect then scuttled off after his mates, who elbowed him and laughed derisively.

'What was it you wanted, Sarah?' Patrick asked, his voice soft now and his hazel eyes gentle.

'Oh, Patrick,' Sarah sighed, 'I just don't know where to begin.'

He took her hands in his, waiting in silence for her to find the words.

'My father is dreadfully unhappy and unsettled. It weighs heavily with him to live as a fugitive, seeing Mam and me working to keep him. Last night he was talking of moving away, he thinks to Foxdale or Peel, where he's not known.'

'Surely he wasn't serious?' Patrick felt his heart lurch and stared into Sarah's eyes, willing her to deny it.

'Most decidedly he was. He feels less than a man with things as they stand at the moment.'

'Do you really think he will go then?'

'Aye.' Sarah nodded her head, chewing miserably on her bottom lip. 'Without a doubt.'

'When?'

'As soon as he can arrange something. I think he might wait until Harry comes to sharpen the knives, then beg a ride with him in the cart.'

'And you, Sarah? What will you do? Will you go with him?' Patrick's voice, no more than a whisper, was charged with emotion.

Sarah nodded and the tear that had been threatening escaped, running its course down her cheek to drip from her chin. 'I must. If the family moves on, I must go with them. There will be no lodgings for me here.'

'Then what about us? You and me. Where will that leave us?'

Choking back a sob, Sarah shrugged weakly.

Miners passing from the changing rooms, hazarding guesses about her tearfulness, made lewd comments. Sarah, so distressed was her state, failed to notice, but Patrick, who had been trying in vain to ignore them, grew increasingly irritated.

'This is a poor place to talk,' he said finally. Taking her arm, he guided her across the grass and past Cronk e Chule farmhouse toward the Lady Isabella. Leading her under one of the huge arches of the wheel casing he pulled her into his arms, kissing her softly but urgently.

'You won't really leave, will you? I couldn't bear it if you did.' His words stuck in his throat, cracking his voice.

'If my family go, I shall have to,' Sarah agonised.

'Surely there must be some other way. Your mother's no longer alone. She doesn't need your strength now.'

'But if anything else goes wrong ...'

Patrick groaned. 'Sarah you cannot run your life on ifs. None of us can tell what the future might bring. We can only hope for the best. We can only live one day at a time. Your mother's future is with your father. And yours is with me!'

Sarah was thoughtful. Her heart told her Patrick was right. She so much wanted to believe it could be so. But her head kept sounding a caution. She was not yet twenty-one, so would have to do whatever her parents wanted of her until then.

'You must talk to your mother, Sarah. Make her see you have a life of your own. That she must set you free you to live it. She must let you make your own choices and your own mistakes.'

'I know you're right, Patrick. But I still remember her as she was when she was ill. The mad woman, everyone called her. And I worry about how she might be if——'

Patrick put his fingers to her lips to silence her, then removing them, kissed her long and lingeringly. Holding her at arms' length, he looked at her quizzically.

'There you go again, Sarah Fayle,' Patrick said sternly. 'Concerning yourself with ifs. Don't torture yourself this way. Just this once think first of yourself. Let your Daa worry about his wife. We could be wed before your family leave Laxey, then my concern would be with my wife.'

Sarah nodded, her eyes brightening with the flame of hope that was kindling in her heart.

'So, you will talk to your Mam? Make her see your side of the matter? I'm sure once she meets me, I can convince her that not all Irishmen are bad.'

Sarah frowned, her teeth worrying her lip and Patrick felt an aching tug at his heart.

'You will, won't you?' There was a note of desperation in his voice now. 'Talk to her, I mean.'

Sarah nodded, noting with a smile, his sigh of relief.

'I'll talk first to Daa. He'll know best what to do. His first concern will be for my happiness and he's a fair man. Now I'd better be off home, for I told them I was visiting Mary.'

Under the arches, in the shadow of the magnificent water-wheel Patrick took his girl in his arms, kissing her with all the depth of feeling in his soul.

Chapter 15

◈━━◇━━◈

Studying her father's expression, Sarah tried to guess his reaction to the news she had just given him.

'An Irishman you say?' His brow furrowed.

Sarah nibbled her lip, fighting to control the inconstant pounding of her heart. She gave an apprehensive nod.

'How long has this been going on?' George looked sternly at his daughter.

'Nothing has been going on, Daa. Well not the way you mean it.' Sarah felt like a naughty schoolgirl at attention before the headmaster.

'That's not the way I meant it at all. Unless your conscience is troubling you?'

A burning flush rose from her neck to the top of her scalp as Sarah shook her head vehemently.

'Right, now back to the case of the Irishman. He's a miner and he wants to walk out with you?'

This brought another emphatic nod from Sarah. At least her father had not ranted, though he had looked a trifle displeased. Perhaps things might work out as she wanted them to after all.

'How long have you been — er — fond of each other?'

'I've known him over three years now. Ever since I started working on the washing-floors. He worked there too, until just over a year ago.' Sarah said in a rush. Finishing with a note of sadness she added, 'But since he went to the core, we have been able to spend very little time together.'

George smiled knowingly, 'The supposed visits to Mary before she took ill?'

Startled, Sarah looked up at him, feeling her face colour. She nodded miserably, unable to meet her father's eyes, not seeing the affectionate and mischievous twinkle in them.

'Why, love? Why couldn't you just have brought him home and let us meet him? You're quite old enough now to have a beau. Why the secrecy?' Then an awful thought crossed his mind. 'It wasn't because of me was it? Were you afraid he would see me and inform the Constable?'

Sarah was moved by the concern in his rugged face. 'No, Daa, 'twas nothing to do with you. Patrick knew all about you, for he was with us when Harry brought you home. In fact, he was the one to carry you from the cart and take the wet clothes off you.'

'Why then could we not be told of him sooner? I should have liked to thank him for his help. He is clearly to be trusted or I'd have been back in jail almost as soon as I was free.'

Sarah's chest heaved in a huge sigh. 'Because of Mam. You don't know what she was like while you were gone, Daa. She was so ill and lost control of her senses completely. People who knew of her called her the 'mad woman', or the 'crazy woman of Agneash'. She had such tempers. And such a hatred for the Irish. 'Twas because she blamed Sean Casey for you bein' sent to jail.'

'But I've been home three months or more now. Couldn't you have told us sooner? We should have known. We should have met him!' George said feelingly.

'I feared how it might affect Mam to know I was in — to

know I cared for an Irishman. She was so strong in her hatred. I couldn't forget how wild she'd been, and I feared that knowing about Patrick might make her ill again.'

George studied his daughter for a long time, not knowing quite what to say. It broke his heart to know he had brought her and indeed the rest of his family so much unhappiness. With a catch in his voice he told her to bring her man home as soon as possible.

'If he's to be my son I want time to know him before he becomes it,' he said with a forced cheerfulness.

'But Mam?' Sarah asked warily.

'Leave your mother to me,' George said grimly. 'If you love this Patrick, I'm sure she'll soon grow to love him as well.

Sarah met Patrick when they finished work on the Saturday. Holding tightly to his hand as they walked up the hill, she felt the thrill of a child being taken on its first picnic. How exciting she found it to be able to walk openly with her large, gentle, red-headed beau. To see the open envy in the eyes of some of the other girls and to know that she could now proudly claim him as hers.

'What did your Mam say, then?' Mary was asking, her eyes aglow with pleasure.

'Daa didn't say. Just that she'd agreed it would be alright for me to bring Patrick home today. She hasn't even mentioned it to me herself.' Sarah's face clouded momentarily. 'I do pray all will be well.'

'Now don't be worrying,' Mary instructed cheerfully. 'Once your Mam meets him, she can't help but like him.'

'I promise to be on my best behaviour,' Patrick said solemnly, but there was a twinkle in his eye. If truth be told though, he had to admit to feeling more than a little nervous of meeting this mother who hated all Irishmen.

'I'll wish you the best of luck then!' Mary called after them when they left her at her gate.

The birds and summer flowers were out in all their wild profusion and Sarah gazed around, her happy brown eyes taking in their splendour.

A gay tangle of dandelions, campions and comfrey adorned the roadside embankments, lending to the girl's joyous mood. Wrens, sparrows and chaffinches moved warily from their path, chattering cheerfully, while in the distance they could hear the call of corncrakes and curlews. A raven flew overhead, crying his strange, croaking call that always sounded, to Sarah, like a frog.

Patrick paused when they reached the stand of elders. Drawing Sarah into their cover, he closed his arms around her. Again, she felt the breathless tight, excited feeling she always had when he was near.

A blackbird, looking down from her perch a few feet above them, sang a touching love sonnet.

'Just a few moments of loving, my sweet, to give me the strength to face your mother,' Patrick whispered.

Sarah giggled. 'She's no monster, you know.' Then a memory of the past cast a shadow over her face. 'My mother is quite sane now.'

'I know, love. I didn't mean it that way. Just that it's a little nerve-wracking to face, for the first time, the mother of the maiden you wish to wed!'

Joy lifting her spirits, Sarah melted into the heat of his embrace, forgetting all else for a few moments in the urgency and pleasure of their combined desire.

For long moments the only sounds to be heard amongst the elders were the droning of honey bees and the distant mournful mewing of sea-gulls. It was Patrick who first found the strength to break the spell, pushing her gently from him.

'We'd best go in, love. Let's get this over with.'

Sarah nodded mutely, unable to trust her voice for the moment. Feeling breathless, she stood very still, her eyes sending tender love messages into his while her heartbeat returned to normal.

Stepping back from her, Patrick looked uncomfortably down at his shabby, worn work clothes. 'Do I look well enough?'

Sarah nodded and opened the door.

Judith stood up from her loom and moved toward them. Sarah could see she was nervous but trying hard. She smiled when she was introduced, but it was a forced, tight-lipped gesture, almost as if she was trying to achieve it past a mouthful of lemons.

'It was nice of you to come,' Judith said tensely.

'Thank you for inviting me.'

'Irish aren't you?'

Sarah closed her eyes, her mind in torment. 'Please, God, no. Don't let her spoil it,' she prayed.

Patrick bowed his head in silent acquiescence.

When Judith merely nodded and held out her hand, Patrick brought it to his lips to kiss her fingers and she smiled quite gently.

Sarah lifted her eyes toward heaven, her mouth forming the words 'thank you.'

Alexandra chose that moment to pop her head over the edge of the half-loft. Seeing Patrick, her eyes burned with interest and she hurried to the ladder. Lifting her skirts rather higher, Sarah thought, than necessary, she sped to floor level, almost displaying her buttocks.

'I'm Alexandra,' she introduced herself, looking coquettishly into his eyes.

Patrick tensed, startled by her similarity to Sarah. This was the first time he had seen her, up close in daylight. If he had ever tried to picture Alexandra, he would not have visualised Sarah's face on a smaller younger body, as indeed that was how she looked. The likeness was incredible, though Alexandra's brown eyes lacked the velvety warmth of Sarah's.

The younger girl's eyes were hard. Cold. Shrewd. A light of evil glittered in them.

Inclining his head politely, Patrick said, 'I'm pleased to meet you. I've heard quite a bit about you, Alexandra.'

Sarah shot him an alarmed look, but he had no intention of saying more.

Alexandra walked around him, eyeing him appraisingly. Studying him from head to toe, as a farmer would a prize bull, her eyes, embarrassingly, missing no detail.

Patrick felt his flesh crawling with embarrassment.

'Very nice, Sarah,' Alexandra said finally, her eyes resting suggestively on Patrick's lower mid-section. 'Very nice indeed.' She nodded her approval.

Sarah, shooting a frightened glance at her mother, saw to her relief that her attention was elsewhere. Glaring furiously at her sister, she moved protectively closer to Patrick who, red-faced, had turned away from Alexandra's searching gaze.

Patrick was subjected, for the remainder of his visit, to a wanton exhibition of Alexandra's blatant body messages.

Serving his meal, she contrived to lean so close across him that her breast was almost pressed against his face. Her hand accidently brushed his so often that in the end he was forced to hide his under the table. Sarah witnessed the performance in silence, a knot of anger tying her stomach in a hard ball.

She wanted so desperately to rush to Patrick's rescue, but knew her mother was noticing nothing of what was going on. To make a scene would more than likely bring her wrath on

Patrick instead of Alexandra. More and more she felt nothing but disgust for her sister.

What she did not see, luckily, was that during the meal Alexandra was teasing Patrick beneath the table. Hidden by the table cloth, she made frequent, fleeting assaults, most of which he was unable to counter without it being noticed. Disgusted with himself, he felt his body responding and to his embarrassment knew this had not escaped Alexandra's notice.

Judith was slow to warm to Patrick, though when the time came for him to leave, she wasn't openly hostile as he had feared, melting to coldly polite, bidding him, without enthusiasm, not to leave it too long before visiting again.

While Patrick was saying his goodbyes, Alexandra slipped out, calling over her shoulder that she was just running down to visit a friend in the village.

'Well don't take long. And do be careful!' Judith called after her.

Patrick and Sarah shot each other a look — he shaking his head dazedly, she feeling sick.

'If she had only waited a few minutes I'm sure Patrick wouldn't have minded accompanying her safely to the village,' Judith suggested, frowning.

Patrick, sighing with relief at his narrow escape, could do no more than mutely nod his agreement.

Sarah walked with him to the gate, wishing to have just a few moments alone with him. It had been a hot summer's day, but with the fall of evening, a chill wind blew in from the sea to sweep away the heat of the day. Shivering slightly with a mixture of cold and anticipation, Sarah contentedly melted into Patrick's arms as soon as the door closed behind her mother.

'Well, let's hope that next time I visit, that sister of yours will not be home,' Patrick said feelingly.

'She did rather flaunt herself at you,' Sarah acknowledged angrily.

'Flaunt? I could think of stronger words!' Patrick's stomach churned, and his face burned at the memory of what he had been subjected to during the meal. Then anger flared at himself as the memory stirred of the treacherous part of his body that his mind could not control. He felt dirty and as though he had been unfaithful to Sarah.

Tightening his arms around Sarah, he crushed his lips to hers, opening her mouth with his tongue. Feeling her tongue responding. Their two tongues meeting, exploring each other, tasting each other.

Their two bodies pressed closely, Sarah could feel his arousal, as she knew her tremor betrayed hers. Longing desperately to experience everything, she moved her body against him, swaying gently and thrilling to his response.

A rustling in the undergrowth stilled their movement, freezing them like statues in a pose of exaggerated concentration.

Though they heard not another sound, the spell was broken. Pulling away gently, Sarah whispered, 'Not tonight, Patrick. My Mam will be out looking for me if I'm out too long. Please understand.'

'I do,' he said softly. 'We must not rush it first time. It must be special.' Looking at her, he saw the glint of a tear on her cheek and bent to kiss it away. 'When the time is right, it will happen, love. Now go. I'll watch until you're safely indoors.'

Patrick stood motionless for some time after the door of the croft had closed to take Sarah from his view. Breathing deeply in the cool, summer scented air, he gazed up at the diamonds that littered the black velvet sky.

He could wait. No matter how his body might try to control his mind, he would wait. Sarah's first experience of complete lovemaking must be unhurried and clean and beautiful. A sensation she would remember only with pleasure.

At last! At last! At last things were going right. Judith Fayle had accepted him, though unwillingly, and had even thought him suitable to walk with her younger daughter to the village. Soon he could ask for Sarah's hand and know with almost certainty that both her parents would approve.

Turning, he started down the lane, whistling quietly, wrapped in his own joy and contentment. A shadow detached itself from the others beneath the trees, to stand silently in the lane a little way ahead of him.

Patrick started, then faltered in his stride, straining in the moonlight to recognise the shadow.

'Alexandra? Is that you?' Patrick's nerves jangled a warning.

'Aye. Where're you bound for?'

'Home.'

'You're not in any hurry, are you?'

'Aye. I have Baldrine to go to. 'Tis a far stretch.'

'I'll make it worth your while to linger a spell!'

'No!' Patrick took a step back, repelled by this awful child and her offer.

'You know you want me,' Alexandra insisted, edging closer to him.

'I most certainly do not!'

'Well your thing does! I felt it swell up when I touched it under the table.' She was near him now, leering up at him with those cold, dark eyes.

'You had me at a disadvantage! I certainly had no desire for such intimacy!' Patrick cried hotly, remembering the discomfort and embarrassment she had put him through. Backing off, he found himself up against a tree.

'He had!' Alexandra looked pointedly below Patrick's waist.

'I'm good at it, you know. You would enjoy it. Much more than you would my cold sister. I saw her tease you to a frenzy then run off and leave you!'

Feeling sick, Patrick realised the girl had been near them in the trees, spying.

'I wouldn't make you stop.' Alexandra moved closer, lifting her skirts. In the moonlight he saw her slender white legs, leading to a triangle of dark curls.

Patrick found himself trembling amidst a whole plethora of sensations. Revulsion! Anger! Sadness for the family who loved this mindless, immoral child, who must inevitably be hurt by her. Strongest of all was self-hatred, for he also felt lust. He found he could not tear his eyes away and excitement grew in him to a fever.

Pressing herself hard to him, Alexandra took his hand, guiding it between her legs, her other hand fumbling with his fly buttons.

Patrick's mind told him furiously to push her away and he thought he tried to, but his muscles wouldn't obey his bidding. If only she did not look so much like Sarah! He closed his eyes, hoping his will power would strengthen if he blocked out the image.

Alexandra's hand found its mark and Patrick stiffened, feeling his resolve weaken even further. His own hand moved, against his wishes, caressing the girl.

'Let's go further into the trees, then we can lie down without being seen,' she moaned huskily. You can do it for free and I promise it'll be a lot better than anything you'll ever get from Sarah!

Patrick came to his senses suddenly, Sarah's name acting like a bucket of icy water.

'Get away from me!' he cried. Grasping the girl by the shoulders, he thrust her roughly away from him. 'Stay away from me, you dirty little doxy,' he snarled.

'You wanted it a minute ago,' Alexandra reminded him, her dark eyes veiled.

'Not from you!' Patrick's eyes smouldered with fury. 'You put me out of my mind for a moment. I feel shamed and soiled for even thinking of it.' With rapid movements, he tucked himself away, tidying his clothes.

'If you don't do it, I shall scream and tell them you tried to force me. Mam will hear me from the house. That will soon put an end to things between you and my fine sister.'

Patrick snorted scornfully. 'Do it then, Madam. Scream if you wish. I won't be blackmailed.'

Alexandra eyed him suspiciously. 'Even if it means Sarah being forbidden to see you?'

'I don't think it will come to that.' Patrick laughed harshly. 'You see Sarah and I know all there is to know about your little business in the village. We know of you selling your favours to the miners. And about the babes Lucy Costain took from you. If you accuse me of anything, I shall tell your mother everything. It won't take her long to find out I am telling the truth. Then do you think they would believe a word of your evil tales?'

Alexandra stood her ground for a moment, staring defiantly at him, then her shoulders sagged. 'I *hate* you!' she hissed, then smoothing her skirt carefully, she turned toward the croft.

'Don't you ever again try to compromise me as you did today,' Patrick called as she walked away from him. 'Next time your mother will quickly learn what your hands are doing under the table!'

When she had gone, Patrick found himself trembling, filled with self-loathing for what he had almost allowed to happen. And with a child just turned thirteen. If only she had borne less of a resemblance to Sarah!

'Dear God,' he thought. 'Punish me any way you feel fitting, but just don't let my innocent Sarah ever suffer the pain of learning what almost happened here this night.'

198

Chapter 16

Sarah and Patrick drifted through the golden summer in a euphoric haze, their happiness almost complete and their future secure.

Now a frequent visitor to the Fayle's croft, Patrick had quickly been accepted as one of the family. Even Judith treated him with a wary friendliness. Alexandra alone, made no effort to make him feel welcome. It was a great relief to him though that she disappeared with a sullen look, either to the loft or more often, the village, whenever he appeared.

Patrick had agonised for weeks after that awful night about his lack of control over Alexandra's advances. With every day that passed, his conscience burned a deeper hole in his mind, until he found himself becoming irritated over tiny things — even with Sarah.

Finally, almost overcome with self-revulsion, and a desperate need to talk, he confessed to Mary and James.

'I'm not sure which has made me feel the most guilt-ridden. The fact that I almost betrayed Sarah's trust, particularly with the girl being her own sister. Or because, in years at any rate, Alexandra is no more than a child.'

Mary shook her head sadly. 'Well I can't say I condone what

you did, but at least you put a stop to it before any real harm was done. That girl is going to bring a mountain of heartbreak one day. You stay well away from her, lad, if you don't want to be the one it falls on.'

Patrick laughed hollowly. 'Don't you fear. That one will never get close enough to me in the future to try that sort of trick again. Thank you for listening to me. I was badly in need of an understanding ear. Now I told you of it; confessed my sins; I feel as if a window has opened in my prison and let in a ray of sunlight.'

When, a few minutes later, he arrived at the Fayle's croft, Alexandra glowered hatefully then took her leave immediately.

'It's strange the way the girl behaves,' Judith commented thoughtfully, as she watched Alexandra hurry off toward Laxey. Then she laughed. 'I suppose she'll be about that age. 'Tis my guess she has a crush on you and don't like to see you looking all lovey at her sister.'

Patrick shifted uncomfortably in his seat; Judith had been a bit too close to the mark for his liking.

'No doubt she'll get over it in her own good time,' Judith decided, nodding to herself.

When he had time on his hands, Patrick spent time with George and they soon became close friends. George could not have approved more of his daughter's choice for a husband. It would be with his approval that they could be wed.

With Patrick's arrival on the scene, and another man to plan and talk things over with, George decided to see out the summer in Laxey. It would be time enough, he said, to move on before winter came, for he would not be able to have a fire in the tholtan.

Tired of being tied near the croft he became more daring as summer passed, making his way through the spinney behind the tholtan, he made expeditions into the hills with Patrick and Sarah to dig peat and cut gorse for the winter fires.

Judith ever cautious and fearful for his safety, persuaded him to wear a wide-brimmed hat whenever he ventured abroad. This, to Sarah's amusement, he pulled almost over his eyes on the odd occasion they saw anyone in the distance. As far as she was concerned the bushy beard was disguise enough.

It was a joyful summer for the young lovers. Often, they took the two little girls, Elizabeth and Louisa, on walks with them.

Sarah loved their jaunts into the hills, often leaving her bonnet off, to her mother's profound disapproval, and allowing her curls to blow free in the wind.

Running in the young bracken with Elizabeth and Louisa she pointed out to them the different types of beauty God had put on their island for them to enjoy.

A field of yellow corn, swaying gently in the warm breeze, reaching its ripening ears toward the sun. Sparrow hawks hovering watchfully and the skylark with its sharp clear call. Raucous crows and rooks and jackdaws, swooping across the heath looking for creatures that had died, to fill their stomachs and clean up the countryside, removing the remains that would otherwise rot and foul the fresh, sweet smelling air.

Enraptured, Sarah, Patrick and the two little girls watched the trout in the streams, playing lazily until their alert eyes observed a movement. Then with a lightning fast flick of their tails they would disappear. Their eyes lit with fascination at the sight of the patient, nervous herons that stood motionless in the water, waiting for a careless trout or stickleback to drift by. Until the humans came too close when, with a wild flapping of their huge wings they would rise fearfully from the stream with water dripping from their legs, sparkling in the sunlight.

George, often watching from a nearby thicket, surveyed his children, sometimes with his eyes brimful of tears. He was touched by their innocent excitement and remembered the awful days in jail when he was locked away from such pleasures.

One day, high on the slopes above Laxey flanked by Louisa and Elizabeth, Sarah turned to gaze in wonder at the glen below. The huge wheel, with all her splendour predominating, her shadow reached long fingers across the mine workings. Scattered around her, like the subjects of a powerful queen, the collection of lesser wheels that powered the mine's machinery. Buildings, chimneys, adit entrances with the rails for the ore carts running from the main one. All looking, from where she stood, like children's toys.

It was all very still, with no movement or smoke, for being Sunday, the mine was closed.

Down the glen from the Lady Isabella was the untidy heap of deads, the viaduct and beyond that the washing-floors. Her gaze moved on, following the valley to where the river emptied into the sea. Screwing her eyes up slightly against the glare, she looked lingeringly on the vast expanse of ocean, today calm and pale, so that it was hard to tell where sea ended, and sky began.

A lapwing, or peewit as the children were wont to call it, fussed around, frightened, yet reluctant to leave, so Sarah knew they must be close to its nest. Suddenly, squealing with delight, Elizabeth saw a tiny, mottled chick run toward its mother.

As if by magic the baby bird disappeared, and it took a careful search to find it, lying on its belly, pressed close to the ground, looking unbelievably like a piece of sheep dung.

'Come and look,' Sarah called quietly to the two little girls. 'But don't touch. We mustn't frighten it too much.'

While they watched the chick lay motionless, the only thing giving it away the rhythmic movement of its breathing. Its mother fluttered and called nervously a few feet away, trying to distract their attention.

When they were just a short distance away from the chick,

a lone seagull soared high overhead. Instantly the mother lapwing flew to intercept it, continually diving to attack the much larger bird, until she had driven it well away from the area of the nest. With the danger over, she quickly flew back to her family, still keeping a wary eye on the humans.

It was so peaceful that Sarah felt sure there could be no place closer to heaven without actually being there.

The peat pile grew and dried nicely, so Patrick and George, facing the problem of bringing it down from the hill, built a sledge. It was rough, but strong. Sturdy enough, they felt sure, to bear the rigours of the rough heath.

'Well at least it's mostly downhill,' Sarah encouraged when they had the first load aboard and it turned out to be heavier than they expected. The biggest problem, they found, was going down the steep slopes without it running away from them. They solved the problem by tying a rope to the rear and using Patrick as an anchor.

Sarah followed in their wake, giving little assistance, but making plenty of impertinent comments and splitting her sides with mirth.

Toward the end of August George became unsettled again. With most of his crops gathered and winter not so far away, his thoughts turned once more to earning and providing for his family. There were no longer seagull eggs to be gathered and soon there would be no rabbits either. He was becoming a burden, he felt and the thought of months of enforced idleness ahead was more than he could bear.

One afternoon, with the children at school George sat in the cottage with Judith and Sarah. He was quieter than usual, Sarah thought, subdued and thoughtful.

'When's Harry due round?' he asked suddenly. His question, coming out of the blue, startled them all.

'Fairly soon, I should think. He hasn't been for quite some time.' Judith studied him apprehensively.

'Good.' George nodded, satisfied.

'Why do you ask?'

George was silent for a moment. 'I've been thinking a bit recently. It seems to me that with winter not too far off it might be a good thing if I started looking for a job away from here. And a house.'

'I thought you were settled here now. There's been no talk of moving for a while.'

Sarah, seeing a tremor at her mother's lips, moved to hold her hand.

George shook his head sadly. 'I know, lass. 'Twas not so bad in summer. But I can't be shut in here all the long winter months. It would be like being in prison still. I need to be free to roam the countryside without fear of discovery. I want to have some friends. To be able to go the tavern for a pint of jough from time to time. Most of all to support my own family. You must understand.'

Judith nodded. Understanding, but at the same time fearing the future. Afraid for George. Afraid for her own peace of mind.

'What about you, Sarah?'

Before the girl could answer George said, firmly but gently, 'Sarah will stay here and wed Patrick. He's a good man and she has her own life to lead now, love, and every right to it.'

Judith nodded mutely. Of course, he was right, but could she bring herself to leave Sarah? She well knew how much strength Sarah lent her. It would pain her terribly to consider moving on and leaving a child behind.

Harry the knife sharpener came just over a week later and cheerfully agreed to take George to Peel.

'You might be lucky in finding a house there,' he said encouragingly. ''Tis in the mining areas the housing problems are. And I think you'd surely be happier on a boat than down a hole in the ground wouldn't you, George?'

'Aye,' George agreed wholeheartedly. His eyes sparkled with hope. 'My one real love, next to my family of course,' he paused to look around, 'is the open sea, the boats who sail her and the feel of a well-scrubbed deck rolling under my feet.'

'It will be a long journey, you understand? We won't make it to Peel in a day, for I have to see to my business all along the way.'

'Aye', George nodded. 'But I don't want to take the coach for fear I'm recognised.'

Packing a few clothes and provisions in a canvas bag, he took his leave of his Judith a few hours later.

'I'll get things sorted out as quickly as possible and return to you soon,' he promised, seeing Judith's lip quivering.

The pony looked round balefully, putting his ears back when he saw the extra passenger climb aboard.

'You'd best lie in the back an' keep covered up until we get clear of Laxey,' Harry advised.

George nodded and lay on the hard floor, while Harry threw down a horse blanket and a collection of tools, making sure no part of him was showing.

Satisfied, Harry climbed aboard and grabbed the reins. 'Gid-up, Junket,' he called, slapping the reins on the pony's rump. Junket did a little war dance to convey his annoyance, then gave a huge, shuddering sigh and moved off toward Laxey.

Judith stood in front of the cottage, tears streaming, waving although she knew George couldn't see her, until the cart was out of sight.

Arriving home from work some hours late, Sarah found

Richard and the two little girls sitting miserably on the doorstep.

'What's wrong?' she asked apprehensively.

Richard shrugged. 'Dunno. There's something wrong with Mam.'

Sarah rushed in, to find her mother huddled by the loom, her face a mask of misery, the empty look back in her red-rimmed eyes.

The clock turned back for her and in fear Sarah took her in her arms, tenderly picking stray wisps of tear-wetted hair from her cheeks with slender, shaking fingers.

'What's happened, Mam?' she asked fearfully.

Judith cast a glance toward the doorway where the children sat, then nodded to the back door. Together they walked to the vegetable garden and sat on the rickety bench there.

'Your Daa's gone,' Judith sobbed, her whole frame trembling.

'Gone? Gone where? When?'

'Harry the knife sharpener came today an' your Daa went off with him some hours ago. He's gone to Peel to try to find a fishin' boat and a house for us on the west.'

Sarah was puzzled. Surely that was good? That was what he had said he was going to do wasn't it?

'Don't cry, Mam. It's nothing to cry for. He'll be back, safe and sound in a few days.'

Judith nodded. 'Aye love I know. Sense tells me so, but I can't help remembering the last time he went. Dragged off by the troopers he was an' sent to Liverpool. Then he came back years later near dead from the cold.'

'That won't happen this time!' Sarah put as much certainty as she could into her voice.

Judith gave a tremulous sigh. 'No, love, I'm sure it won't. Now you go out an' meet your young man. Summer's nearly gone.

On such a nice evening you should be walking in the hills, not sitting here with me.'

'Will you be alright?' Not certain whether her mother's mind was strong enough yet to bear this set-back, Sara's eyes were dulled with concern.

Judith managed a watery smile. 'Aye. I'll be fine enough. You give me the strength to cope. You go now. I've a fancy to be alone for a while.'

Sarah hesitated for a moment then rising, went inside to make a butty.

Meeting Patrick in the lane she told him sadly. 'My Daa's gone. Harry the knife sharpener came and Daa's gone off with him.'

Patrick drew a quick breath. 'How's your Mam taking it?'

'She's very upset, but I think she will be alright. I think she needs time to herself, for she told me to meet you and go for a walk.'

Patrick nodded in relief.

'I've made a bit of a picnic,' Sarah continued.

'Well let's take a bite to eat then go and fetch some peat down. There's still a lot there, cut and dried,' Patrick suggested. 'You would be able to help me a bit with the sledge, wouldn't you?'

'Aye,' Sarah nodded thoughtfully. 'But if Mam and Daa leave Laxey, they won't need all this peat will they?'

Patrick was quiet for a moment then, turning her to face him, said earnestly, 'I was thinking of finding out if we might take over the lease on their croft when they leave. We'll be wed by then and we must live somewhere. The croft's a better place to live than most people have.'

Sarah gasped, and her eyes sparkled. 'Do you think we'll be able? Wouldn't it be wonderful? Our own croft!' She was almost hopping with excitement.

'I'll see what can be done,' Patrick promised. 'But don't get your hopes too high. And if your parents don't leave, of course, there will be no chance at all for us.'

Patrick slung the sledge rope over his shoulder and with his free arm around Sarah, led her over the bracken, now browning with the advent of autumn. There was a pleasant heat in the evening sun. As Sarah strolled, her long dark curls blew across his face sometimes, caught by the odd rogue gust, exciting him with its touch.

At times the joy in her heart took her skipping ahead of him, like a young child, her long slender legs carrying her easily over the heath.

Patrick watched appreciatively, thrilling to every movement of her supple young body, until she came running back, to throw her arms round his neck and plant her soft, warm lips urgently on his.

Arriving breathless at their peat plot they looked laughingly at the mountain that was still to be moved.

Eyes alight with the pleasure the hills always brought to her, Sarah looked down on her valley and beyond. Through a rift in the hills she could see the northern area of the island, where it was flat, featureless and, after the long hot summer, brown and dry-looking. It had its own type of beauty, she supposed, but she liked the wild ruggedness of the hills. They were shaded brown now with ageing bracken and purple with the millions of dainty heather bells.

An occasional hardy mountain sheep dotted the slopes, contentedly nibbling at whatever greenery it could find.

Turning to look at Patrick, she found him studying her, with a strange, distant look in his eyes. Motionless, his body tall and muscular, he appeared like a statue. A stone God, Sarah thought, placed there by some ancient peoples, the only moving part of him his coppery hair, teased by the wind.

'Why do you look at me so?' Sarah asked, her insides stirring uneasily.

'It was just going through my mind that you must be the most beautiful creature God put on earth,' he said, a quiet reverence in his voice.

Turning away from him, blushing femininely, Sarah watched a group of rooks circling in their everlasting search for food.

A hare leapt suddenly from a scrub of gorse, racing a zig-zag path away from them, never pausing for a moment to see if they were following.

'Look, Patrick!' Sarah squealed in delight, pointing, watching him go. 'He's the largest I've ever seen. Like a big dog! I didn't know they could grow to such a size!'

'I wish I'd had a gun with me,' Patrick growled. 'He'd have grown no bigger. A fellow like that would have gone well in the pot. Made a few good meals he would.'

Sarah looked at him aghast, 'How like a man to think only of his stomach. Can't you see the beauty of such a creature running free?' Brown eyes glared at him, burning with indignation.

'Not when I'm hungry, I can't!' he teased.

Sarah glared disdainfully at him then turned away to peep coquettishly at him a moment later from beneath lowered lashes. Laughing, Patrick stepped up behind her, pulling her against him. Closing his arms cosily round her, he wrinkled his nose against the tickling of her hair.

They stood like that, motionless, for many minutes, drinking in the gentleness of the day and the view, revelling in their closeness.

Looking at the pile of dried peat, Patrick thoughtfully rubbed his chin. 'I hope you're feeling strong, Sarah Fayle, for you've a lot of mans' work to do today,' he told her, his hazel eyes sparkling mischievously.

Sarah shook her head happily. 'Not me. I'm a lady. I just came as a spectator.'

'You'll do your share, Madam. If you know what's good for you!' Patrick glared threateningly, failing to hide the twinkle in his eye, or the good-humoured upward tilt to the corners of his lips.

'I will *not*!' Sarah replied defiantly. 'I'm not your slave to be ordered around, Patrick O'Malley. Nor will I ever be!' She faced him, hands on hips, eyes glowing.

'Is that so?' He took a step toward her and with a squeal of delight she wheeled about and ran off, giggling.

Patrick bounded after her, catching her quickly, grasping her around the waist as he tripped and fell. Pulling her down with him, he twisted so that she landed, laughing excitedly, on top.

Struggling to pull away from him Sarah's gaze held his. Her giggles ceased abruptly at the intensity she saw in his gold-flecked eyes. When the laughter went, a speculative look came into those eyes. Sarah saw a strange animation had come to his face, a keen anticipation, and butterflies flapped wildly inside her at the sensations he stirred in her. Looking down at him, she knew her eyes concealed nothing. They clearly told him of her delight at being alone with him — the excitement she felt in the nearness of him. She was consumed with a passion stronger than any she had experienced before and had never suspected desire could be so overwhelming.

All her strong, turbulent feelings, she was sure, were reflected in her eyes and she couldn't have hidden them even if she had wished. But she did not wish it, for his eyes showed the same desire. Heart brimming with an awesome tenderness and a sudden need to touch his skin, she put a hand to his face. Wondering at the sensation this act stirred, she ran her fingers down his cheeks to his lips. Thrilling when he gently kissed their tips.

Patrick's hand tangled in her hair, pulling her lips to his and in a moment, she was drowning in her desires. They melted together in a prolonged trembling embrace that became almost unbearable in its intensity.

Patrick's hand wandered over Sarah's body, his fingers plucking at the row of tiny buttons on her bodice. In moments he had freed her breasts, holding her away from him slightly to where he could feast his eyes on them. Then gently he pulled her close, taking a nipple between his lips, playing his tongue on it.

A shiver of pleasure ran down Sarah's spine, but at the same time a sudden fear made her recoil. Looking at his tangle of red hair, bent to her breast, she wanted at the same moment of confused emotions to both caress it and push it away.

Her breath caught in her throat at the wonderful sensations in her nipples. His hands urgently tugging at her skirts, filled her with an overpowering, wanton craving. A tiny voice in her head told her this was wrong. That she should be saving this until after she was wed. But she wanted his love making so much. Needed it!

Patrick's hand was above her knee now and gentling itself slowly higher before Sarah came to her senses. Angry with herself for acquiescing so easily, she took handfuls of his hair, pushing herself away from him.

Patrick looked up, puzzled and hurt, screwing his eyes against the glare of the sun.

Sarah sat up, looking down at him, his chest bare where she had tugged the shirt buttons open. His trousers half undone also her handiwork, she admitted to herself. Then she noted the state of her undress. With anyone else it would have been unthinkable to have her breasts exposed in this fashion. To sit half-naked in the warm sunlight with Patrick's eyes on her was unbelievably exciting.

Sarah knew suddenly that despite any misgivings or self-doubts she might have, there could be no stopping. Patrick must choose for her what they would do. Her own feelings smouldered, her hands shaking with a need to touch him, to discover him for herself. Curious to experience him. Anyhow they would be married soon, so surely it was not very wrong. For a moment she held back, then with a shuddering sigh, lay down beside him, feeling him shiver with ecstasy when she slid her hand onto him, wonderingly exploring his maleness.

Gently he removed the rest of her clothing, then stood to admire her, his eyes hungrily seeking every little curve of her lithe, perfect young body. Sarah, to her own surprise, felt no shame or embarrassment, but her insides blazed with anticipation when he hurried out of his clothes, to stand in full-blooded excitement before her.

With a sharp intake of breath, Sarah's eyes widened, nostrils flaring. She had seen her brothers naked many times but hadn't imagined a man could grow to be like this.

When Patrick laid beside her, she clutched him to her, gasping as he slid his thigh between hers, plaiting their limbs together until their bodies were as one. No part separate from the other. Mouths, tongues, breasts merged.

In a sudden moment of fear, Sarah tried to imagine what was before her. All she knew of it really was what she had learned listening to the ribald stories of the women on the washing-floors.

Patrick felt her tense and, pulling away from her slightly, let his hand move gently to tease her pubic area.

All fear suddenly vanished, and Sarah pulled him to her again. 'Please,' she whispered, her eyes closed tightly, willing him to take her.

'Are you sure?' Patrick asked throatily, just praying he could stop if she wished him to.

Words failing her, Sarah nodded breathlessly.

Patrick moved to lean over her, arranging himself and moving gently into her.

Sarah took him into her with love, almost unaware in her passion, of the pain of his first thrust. She felt like a different person beneath him. Holding him as an extension of herself, feeling his weight upon her, the surge of him within her until together they reached a pulsating climax.

Afterwards they lay locked together, naked and breathless in the sunshine for a long time. Then when Patrick was able, they repeated it more gently, but every bit as pleasurably, enjoying it even more.

It was with reluctance they lazily replaced their clothing, as the sun was low in the west. Then after filling the sledge with peat they stumbled off down the hill hand in hand as they pulled the load of peat.

Sarah felt a new glow about her afterwards. An aura of fulfillment. She felt older, somehow. Wiser. The birdsong seemed sweeter, the butterflies brighter, like a mad artist's pallet. Skirting a tangle of undergrowth, she pushed aside an overhanging bough, allowing it to snap back in place behind her. A startled woodpecker flew up, winging into the sunlight in an angry flurry of black and white and crimson.

They stopped at the crest of the last slope to the croft, wanting the excitement of a final passionate embrace. There was a gentleness in the smoky splendour of Autumn, with the trees glowing russet and golden; the grass withered to a pale straw.

Certain her new status must show; Sarah feared her mother must notice. If she did, Judith said nothing.

Surprisingly, though she had an exciting feeling of

wantonness, Sarah felt no shame. It had just seemed so very right.

Chapter 17

George stood on the slopes of Snaefell, looking down on the scattering of white-painted houses far below.

He couldn't quite see the wheel from where he stood and was not sure if it was hidden by trees or an outcrop of land. He had never seen Laxey from this angle before and could not help but be breathless at the beauty of the glen, with the sea shimmering beyond. George felt a million eyes upon him, hidden in the gorse and bracken and the heather. All God's creatures, content and without a care, save to wonder from whence the next meal would come. A handful of seagulls swirled, mewing overhead.

'My, but it's good to be home,' he told the birds and the bees. A lone rabbit watched him, twitching its whiskers, but disappeared rapidly into a warren when he turned to look its way.

Sitting on a clump of dry bracken to regain some energy and rest his worn feet, George contemplated the future. Well, it had taken him almost three weeks, but he'd done it. All was organised — a cottage and a job.

The cottage was a little small, but it would do until they could find something better. Only one small room, but it had a cupboard bed, which though tiny, would be cosy for Judith and himself, while he wasn't at the fishing that was. There was a loft for the children, and with Sarah staying in Laxey there would only be four to bed there. They were already used to sharing a loft. *Yes. It would do.* He smiled to himself in smug satisfaction.

The wind picked up, blowing round the mountain, whipping at his hair. Hoisting himself to his feet, he prepared to face the last leg of his journey. The day had seemed short, though the sun now hung low in the domed ceiling of sky. The wind had grown cold and he still had some distance to go.

Reaching his arms upward, he stretched his stiffened muscles, watching for a moment the cotton wool puffs of white cloud chase each other over a clear, cloudless sky.

Taking a deep, refreshing breath, he continued his journey, treading carefully, for the heath was full of rabbit burrows and a broken ankle was something he could well do without at this juncture.

What a journey it had been too, for he'd had to walk all the way from Peel. Harry had been continuing on southward after he dropped George at Peel and had no sort of idea of when he would be back. All he seemed sure of was that he would be travelling north by way of the east coast and Douglas, so was unable to offer George a ride home.

At first it had appeared quite a hopeless task in Peel, looking for work, but always on edge with the fear that someone might recognise him. Then in the end he had spotted a skipper he knew and felt sure he could trust and had dared approach him. It had been a lucky gamble, for the man, Andrew Stark, was in need of a good crewman and glad to take him on. By the time he went looking for a house, Andrew had made him known in the town as William Fargher.

Having settled his business and with one month until he could move and take up his job, he set off to walk home. The roads seemed a long, tedious route so he had come cross country, following animal tracks for the greater part of the journey. He'd found it an arduous trek, but pleasant in comparison with his run with Jos across the north of England.

Jos! It was a long time since he'd thought about the lad. 'Hope you made it alright, boy,' he muttered, gazing toward the mainland.

Shaking his head sadly, he set off slowly, limping on blistered feet, down the hill.

Judith received his news with mixed feelings. 'I'm pleased, really. But sorry we'll have to leave Sarah behind. Sorry to leave Laxey too. It's been a pleasant place to live.' Aye, she thought bleakly, and more pleasant it would have been if she had not been ill so much of the time. Perhaps it would be a good thing to move to where she wasn't known. Even now, she knew people still called her the crazy woman of Agneash.

'It will be for the best and we will have a busy time ahead now,' George reminded her quietly. 'For apart from the move, there's a marriage to arrange.'

Sarah greeted the news with mixed feelings. It would sadden her to see them go but pleased there might be a home for her and Patrick. She had not at all been looking forward to sharing a house with his ill-tempered landlady.

The time had come, they decided, to tell the children that George was home. The school was on holiday for another two weeks, so they prayed that if they swore the children to secrecy, they would not let it slip. Richard, they felt was a safe bet, but Alexandra, Elizabeth and Louisa could perhaps be loose cannons.

Their reactions were mixed.

The younger three were playing a card game on the floor and looked up, puzzled at this stranger their mother had brought in.

Alexandra was reading and only glanced up then returned to her book.

'This is your Daa,' Judith said nervously.

Richard was the first to respond. '*Daa!*' he screeched. Leaping to his feet, he ran to throw himself into his father's arms. 'I knowed you would come! I just knowed it! I knowed they was wrong when they said you was dead! An' I wouldn't talk to the Constable when he came looking for you!'

'And pissed his pants!' Alexandra added spitefully, looking up from her book at last.

Richard burned scarlet. 'Well it stopped him asking me things,' he said defiantly.

'He's a real scaredy,' Alexandra sneered. 'He pisses hisself all the time!'

'That's enough, Alexandra. Richard can't help it, it's because of the fever he had. You should just be happy he didn't die like the others. And there's no call to be vulgar either. You're not so free of faults yourself!' Judith glared at her second daughter.

No, Sarah thought, *and how well it is that Mam does not know just what dreadful faults you do have. Her heart would be truly broken. And Daa's.*

Six year old Louisa had only the faintest recollection of her father. Shy by nature, she hid behind her mother, clinging to her skirts, peeping timidly at him through fearful, limpid green eyes.

Elizabeth, a bare year younger however, friendly and boisterous as ever, was quick to warm to him, though she remembered him not at all. Soon she was on his lap, giggling while he played 'this little piggy' on her toes.

This was all too much for Louisa, who was very soon at his side, unsteadily lifting a foot toward him and pleading, 'Me too, Daa.'

Sarah sat at the table, her chin on her hand pensively watching the homely scene. The warmth and security of a complete, real family again was almost overwhelming. This was the way it should be. The way it always used to be.

'I want you all to listen to me very carefully,' Judith said, when all the excitement had died a bit. 'We are going to move to Peel soon, where no one knows your Daa and we will have to have a different name. Our name will not be Fayle, it will be Fargher. Until we go it is very important that none of you tell any soul that your Daa is back. The Constable thinks he is dead, and it must stay that way. If you tell anybody Daa is here, the Constable might get to hear an' he will be taken back to jail in Liverpool. So please, if you are talking to your friends, think very carefully about every word that comes out of your mouths.'

Three solemn little faces looked up at their mother and three little heads nodded.

Patrick arrived at this moment. George and Judith smiled their welcome and he went to sit by Sarah.

'Sarah will not be coming with us,' Judith continued. 'She will wed Patrick and they will be staying here, in this cottage.'

Alexandra had shown no interest in her father's return apparently from the dead and now glared at her parents. 'Peel, did you say?'

George nodded. 'I cannot stay in Laxey, for I am known here. I have work in the fishin' and have found us a cottage in Peel.'

Alexandra looked on her parents with raw hatred in her eyes. 'Well I won't be going with you!' she said stamping her foot to emphasise her point.

'You'll go where you're told, Madam!' George's eyes flashed dangerously. He'd heard from Judith how rebellious Alexandra had become and he was not going to permit it.

'I'm *not* leaving Laxey! You can't make me!'

'We can and we will!' Judith was no less determined than her husband.

'Sarah's staying!'

'Only because she's being wed.'

'I'll stay with Sarah then. If she and Patrick get this croft, they'll have room for me.' Alexandra's eyes blazed, her nostrils flaring with temper.

Patrick's head jerked up and he felt his heart give a leap, then plummet to his boots. How could he possibly explain why he and Sarah could not board the dreadful child? But most certainly it would be too dangerous a situation to have her living with them.

'You will come with us, my girl! Now I'll hear no more argument.' Judith was adamant. It was bad enough Sarah had to stay. She would leave no more of her children behind.

Patrick heaved a silent sigh of relief.

Without another word Alexandra turned on her heel, storming up to the loft. They heard the thump as she threw herself angrily onto the straw mattress.

When she failed to come home from school the following evening, no one was too concerned. Obviously, the silly child was still held by a sulk and, no doubt, trying to teach them a lesson.

'When she does come home,' George growled, 'I'll make sure she gets a lesson she should have had long ago. It's my feeling she got a bit out of control while I was gone.'

When she did not come home at all they tried to tell themselves she was staying with a friend for the night. But as time wore on their worry increased.

'I'm sure she'll be alright,' Sarah tried to comfort them, though all the while in her mind she was picturing the sort of person her sister was probably with.

By morning Judith was completely distraught, reduced to a trembling, red-eyed wreck. George could bear it no longer.

'I'm going into the village!' he announced suddenly.

Judith jumped to her feet, alarmed. 'No, George! You must not!'

'I have to find her and bring her home.'

'But what if you're recognised? You'll be gone back to Liverpool!'

'Sorry lass, but it's a risk I must take. I have to find her and bring her home,' he said desperately.

'I'll go, Daa.' Sarah was on her feet, reaching for her shawl.

George thought about this for a moment, then nodded his head. 'Aye, you can come with me and ask at the police house. I'll look around the village.'

Judith watched, fidgeting agitatedly, watching from the door until well after they had disappeared from view.

'You go in and ask, love,' George instructed when they reached the police-house. 'I'll wait for you outside.'

The Constable eyed Sarah appraisingly until she felt almost as though she stood naked before him. 'Aye, I know the one you mean. The spitting image of you only not so tall.'

Sarah nodded hopefully. 'Have you seen her?'

'Not today. She may have gone off on the coach to Douglas yesterday. I saw her hanging around the coach station in the morning.'

'Are you sure she got on it though?"

The man shrugged non-commitally. 'I just saw her there. I should have thought you'd be glad to have her gone — a doxy like her.'

Sarah regarded him in panic, remembering her father outside the open door. Praying he wouldn't overhear and come storming in.

'Well, th–thank you,' she stammered, backing toward the door.

'Mind you, I suppose there will be many a miner sorry to see the back of her.'

'If you knew that was going on why didn't you put a stop to it?' Sarah asked angrily, knowing her father would already have heard if he was within earshot.

The man shrugged again. 'It wasn't none of my business.'

'She's only a child! Surely that makes it your business?'

'Didn't look like a child to me. I thought she was older'n you.'

Sarah shook her head in despair. 'She was only thirteen years of age! Couldn't you see that?'

The Constable shook his head. 'No. I couldn't.'

Sarah turned and ran from the building, her face burning with anger and humiliation.

George was slumped against the wall, his face ashen, his stomach in spasms and hands clamped over his face. Sarah thought she had never seen such anguish in her life.

'You heard?' It was more statement than question.

George nodded; his eyes haunted. 'I was listening, on the chance he might have news her.'

'News you would have been better not to know,' Sarah said quietly.

'You sounded as if it was no surprise to you?'

Sarah sighed and shook her head sadly. 'Nor was it.'

'Have you known for long?'

'Does it matter?'

George was silent for a moment, his tortured mind turning the question over. 'Aye, to me it does, lass. I don't know why, but I have to know.'

'I've known for most of this year. Many of the miners and the women gave me a bad time for they thought I must be the same.'

George stared at her, stunned. Disbelieving. His face almost grey now. 'So long?' he asked, his voice cracked and dry. 'Why didn't you tell me?'

'It would have made no difference. The damage was done. There was nothing to be done that could have stopped her. I tried to talk to her, but she wouldn't listen. And I saw no sense in you being hurt too. I just prayed you would never have to learn of it.'

George closed his eyes, as though to shut out reality and pain, shaking his head sadly. 'And you suffered all the more to protect me?'

'Telling you wouldn't have helped. And Patrick always stood by me. I had his shoulder to cry on.'

'He knew too?' For a moment George looked as though his knees would buckle. 'I still love her you know,' he said presently. I'll bring her back and somehow we'll save her from herself.'

They learned at the booking office that a girl answering Alexandra's description had left on the previous morning's coach.

'Told the driver she would make a lot more money in Douglas than she ever would here,' the clerk cheerfully informed Sarah.

When told, Judith took the news better than Sarah expected. Although tearful, she appeared more relieved than anything else, just to learn that the girl was alive and had left of her own free will.

'I'll bring her back!' George stood up abruptly,

Judith looked up; her eyes frightened. Dazed. 'Bring her back? How?'

'I'll go to Douglas and find her!' He picked up his coat, moving decisively toward the door. 'I'll catch the afternoon coach.'

'No!' Judith was on her feet, clinging to his arm. 'You can't go to Douglas. You'll be caught.'

'I'll be cautious. But 'tis a risk I must take. Alexandra's but a child and I can't leave her in whatever mess it is she's got herself into. I must fetch her home.'

'But in Douglas? How will you find her?' Judith was torn between fear for her husband and love for her daughter, wanting them both safe with her.

'It's not such a large town. If she's there I'll find her.' Gently, George prised his wife's fingers from his sleeve. 'There's nothing to fear, love. I'll come home with Alexandra,' he promised. Then he kissed her and hurried to catch the coach.

'Well, it's almost full,' the booking clerk studied his list, 'but I can fit you on as long as you don't mind sitting up top.'

'I don't mind where I sit,' George replied thankfully, 'just as long as I get to Douglas today.'

It was an eternity until the coach came, with George stalking back and forth, becoming more agitated by the minute.

Bounced and jolted on top of the coach, the journey seemed almost longer and more arduous than George could bear. Time passed agonisingly slowly, and he could feel the heart running out of him in rivers of misery.

His eyes scanned the hills as they travelled, but they stayed out of focus, seeing other things. Seeing Alexandra. Thirteen years old! Merely a child — naked with dirty, raucous, miners. What sort of men, he wondered, would fornicate with a child? Sick men. Men unfit to live on God's good earth. Even less on God's own beautiful island! Men such as those should be castrated, he concluded. Or boiled in oil. Or both! And then hung up by their privates!

He saw nothing of the beautiful, rugged coastline. The sea crashing in endless agitation almost matching his own against the rugged rocks and pitted grey cliff faces.

The closer the coach came to Douglas, the angrier he grew

and the more turmoiled his mind became. He would find the child and bring her home. If he had to gag and bind her and drag her all the way, he would get her there. And make sure she never had the opportunity to return to her self-destructive ways.

Suddenly he was aware that someone had hold of his sleeve, tugging it.

'We're in Douglas, Mister. Unless you want to go back to Laxey you'd better come down.'

George looked blankly at the man for a moment, then shook himself back to awareness.

'Sorry,' he said sheepishly. 'I must have dozed off for a moment.'

Climbing down from the coach, he went to the booking office, described Alexandra and enquired of the clerk whether he had seen her.

The man smiled, nodding. 'The lass from Laxey you'll be meaning. By God, she must be good if you fellows are following her all the way to Douglas!'

George stiffened; his hand balled in a fist. 'I mean my thirteen-year-old daughter,' he hissed through clenched teeth.

The man blanched. 'Sorry, mister. I didn't know. Probably a different lass you're looking for.'

George sighed, shaking his head tiredly. 'I fear it's the same girl,' he admitted flatly.

The clerk caught his breath, looking at him sympathetically. 'Well, the young-er lady asked me about rooms, and I suggested that for a short term she might try the Market Hotel. It being a reasonably priced establishment, you understand.'

George nodded, thanked the fellow, then hurried from the office toward the hotel. His heart lifted slightly in hope. Perhaps Alexandra was not going to be so hard to find after all.

Striding to the desk in the foyer, he grasped the wooden handle of a large brass bell, ringing it loudly. After what felt like hours, and several more furious shakings of the bell, a harassed looking man scurried through a curtained archway from the bar, wiping his hands down the side of his pants.

'Sorry to keep you, but we're busy at the moment, and the barman hasn't turned up for work. Is it a room you're looking for?'

George shook his head. 'No. I'm looking for a girl. She ran away from Laxey yesterday, and I've been given to understand she might have taken a room here.' He went on then to describe Alexandra.

The man eyed him suspiciously, his teeth thoughtfully scraping his lip. 'We've got a girl staying here what looks like that. But we don't allow none of that sort of behaviour here you know! This is a respectable hotel!' he finished.

George felt his fists clench and a cannon-ball lodged in the pit of his stomach. 'She's my daughter!' His voice was an almost inaudible hiss and a shuddering sigh shook his body.

'Sorry,' the other man studied his feet shamefacedly. 'She's out, at the moment. She went out with——no matter. Look, why don't you wait in the bar? Have a couple of ales and I'll tell you when she comes back.'

George nodded mutely. 'I'll do that. Thank you.'

'Would you like a bite to eat? We've a good herring stew?' The man asked kindly.

George looked at him dazedly for a moment, not immediately comprehending. 'Oh–no. No thanks. Just an ale will do.'

Making his way through the curtained arch to the smoke-filled room beyond, he seated himself on an empty stool at the corner of the bar, knowing he would wait all day, or longer, if he had to.

Huddling on the stool, his mind registered nothing of the

buzz of conversation in the busy room. An occasional explosion of raucous laughter brought him back to the present momentarily. His eyes, clouded and sunken, failed to notice the wisps of blue smoke curling ceilingward, moving fretfully in every draught that invaded the hot, sweat-smelling bar.

Suddenly, with the opening of the outside door, the smoke moved irritably. George idly glanced toward the new arrivals, A rough-looking man and a woman with brightly painted lips and make-up that would take a hammer and chisel, he thought, to remove.

They stood just inside the door, the man with his arm slung across the woman's shoulder, hand hanging, idly caressing her breast. The woman laughed up into his eyes, moving to rub her buttocks against him, while he leered down at her.

George watched the scene, his insides in a whirl of disgust. God, he thought painfully, I must find Alexandra and get her away from here before she becomes like that whore!

The woman turned, caught George's eye and, putting a hand to her face, took a step back away from him.

In that moment, like a life-shattering blow to the heart, George recognised his daughter and was forced to accept she had sunk every bit as low as he had been led to believe.

For a dreadful moment George's vision went black, he felt himself swaying on his stool and tasted the sourness of vomit in his mouth.

Heaving himself from the seat he staggered, half blind with heartbreak and fury, toward the couple.

Alexandra tried to turn and flee from his advance, but her companion, mistaking the purpose of her wriggling, merely held her more tightly and thrust his hand down the inside of her bodice.

With a howl of rage George hurled himself forward, his arms

flailing wildly. Grabbing Alexandra's arm, he pulled her from the man's grasp, swinging her away with such force that she was sent stumbling backwards, landing in an ungainly heap against the bar.

George paused briefly, his eyes following her flight and in that instant of inattentiveness, her companion swung his fist, catching him a solid blow to the side of his head, stunning him momentarily.

'Find your own strumpet, old man!' The fellow sneered.

George stood for a moment, half bent, watching the man warily, sensing others around closing in on him. He glared at his adversary, letting the anger and fear mingle and grow within him until it became a white rage.

Employing the animal cunning he had learned in prison, he feigned defeat. Then, without warning, he leapt on the other man, swinging his fist, snapping the devil's head back with a crack that told him his neck was broken.

The body folded to the floor, looking no more human than a pile of old rags.

George saw a large, red-faced man lunge at him from his left, with a bottle in his raised hand, swinging it toward him and knew it would be close.

Moving quickly to his right, he took advantage of his speed to swing his fist to the man's temple, sending him staggering on rubbery legs. With a quick kick he caught a second adversary in the mid-section sending him reeling away, doubled over, retching and gagging.

Others who had thought of joining the fray, backed away from the wild look they saw in his eye.

Seeking Alexandra, George ordered her to his side after finding her standing as though in a trance, transfixed, her eyes glued to the body on the floor. Her face was drained of all colour, the bright lipstick now just an ugly gash in a face vulnerable in its youth.

'Come!' George commanded again and with a dumb nod she began to obey.

'Hey, Mister, this is no way to get yourself a whore,' one man started to protest — a weedy little blonde fellow with pale eyes. 'You can't take 'em by force, you know!'

George silenced him with a look that withered the man to his soul.

Just as he reached to grip Alexandra's wrist, the door swung open and George looked up, to find himself confronted by the Sergeant of Police.

'What's the disturbance here?' His eyes wandered the room, settling on George, who had half turned away. Nobody spoke at first, though all eyes in the bar flitted between the policeman and George, drawing attention to him.

'I–I think that fellow,' the weedy man nodded in George's direction, 'Has killed this one!' He then indicated the pile of bones and rags on the floor.

The crowd shuffled aside slightly, leaving the body in a space, looking grotesque and ugly, its head at an unnatural angle, tongue and eyes protruding as though there was no room inside the head for them.

The policeman spared the body only a brief glance, then transferred his eyes to look searchingly at George. This man was familiar, wasn't he? Take away the beard and who would he have? He had a good memory for faces and he had seen this face somewhere before. Where was it? He faced George, staring into his eyes and suddenly saw the face of a man who had been on a wanted poster. Escapee from Liverpool jail, and presumed dead. Here he was alive! The sergeant's eyes lit with the glint of a hoped-for promotion.

'I know you, don't I?' he asked triumphantly. 'George Fayle. By all that's holy, we thought you was dead. An' you turn up here, right under my nose!'

George squeezed his eyes shut for a few moments, to bring his thoughts into order. Opening them he impaled the sergeant in their implacable gaze, almost haughtily daring the man to try to catch him.

The man was wary, having seen around him the damage his quarry had already inflicted. He would not be trapped as the others had been. Without taking his eyes from George's, he started to withdraw his truncheon.

'I hope you're going to be sensible and not force me to use this.' His voice lowered in volume as he spoke, gaining in intensity, his eyes almost hypnotic. He was a big man and as he moved into the room it seemed to shrink in size, the crowd of faces around him diminishing to an insignificant background in his presence. He stared unblinkingly at George.

Knees shaking, George glanced at the cosh in the other man's hand, his face blank. Thoughts of his years in jail flashed through his mind. Terrible memories.

'I won't go back to prison,' he said quietly and saw the sergeant's hand tighten on the haft of his weapon.

Tightening his leg muscles, George became, suddenly, an uncoiling blur. A dark shadow shooting through the dim light of the tavern, trying to duck under the outstretched arms of the policeman.

The man swung his arm back and, reacting instantly, George raised his arm to defend his head. The truncheon crunched down on his fist with agonising force and George felt, rather than saw, the spattering of blood appear as the skin split and tore.

He then spun, bracing on one foot and, using his free leg, slammed the sole of his boot into the policeman's groin. The sergeant staggered, off balance, collapsing to his knees with a grunt.

With a quick sideways jump, George leapt past the policeman seeing him from the corner of his eye struggling to his feet, his face more fearsome than ever, black as furious thunder now.

Reaching the door, George turned for a moment to look pleadingly at Alexandra. She stared back, fingers to her lips, her face stark with shock. Then he saw the sergeant coming at him and plunged out into the night.

Turning toward the harbour, George fled with all the speed his tired legs could muster. Close behind he could hear the hue and cry of the mob from the hotel who, lent courage by the presence of the Sergeant, had joined in the chase. The sound of the police whistle seemed to be drawing closer as he reached the market corner, raced around it and across the road to the water's edge.

The rabble followed, baying like a pack of hounds and George found himself cornered between his pursuers and the dark waters below.

The mob stopped, silent and deadly now, not one of them prepared to risk closing with him. Spreading into an arc, they advanced slowly, driving him back until his feet scrabbled on the harbour's edge. Breath rasping from him, he defied the pursuers, his face a blanched, frozen mask, lips pulled back in a grimace of fear.

Trembling, George eyed them, then glanced behind him to where fathoms of green water swelled and sucked, alive with the riotous growth of the sea.

'Well, either I live, or I die,' he muttered, 'but I shall not again be imprisoned, and that is the sum of it.' Then spinning about as the first hands reached for him, he dived into the sea.

Pulling to the harbour floor, he swam along it, staying under water for as long as his breath would permit. His lungs burning and feeling his body like a dead weight, he hauled upward. Struggling against a force and a weight that seemed inordinately heavy. Strange lights flashed in his brain and he could feel time slipping away beneath him.

In a thrilling moment of relief his head broke the surface and, gasping in great lungsful of air, he opened his eyes.

Just a few feet away, and closing fast, was the bow of a trawler. Before George could open his mouth to shout it was upon him, hitting him resoundingly on the head.

There was no pain, and as blackness took him, he had a wonderful, floating sensation of peace.

Chapter 18

<hr>

Sarah had very mixed feelings about Alexandra's departure. Part of her was glad. Relieved, anyway that the dreadful business was out in the open at last. No matter how hard she had tried to keep her sister's behaviour from her parents, in her heart she had always known they must find out some day. There had been times she had seen Alexandra, when she had thought no one was watching, leering hungrily at Patrick, her eyes almost stripping him.

Sighing, she watched another wagon tip its load of ore down the sloping bunker onto the revolving table for sorting.

The day was chill, the sky turbulent with a roiling mass of purple and black clouds and the possible threat of a storm to come. Sarah shivered with a sudden sensation of foreboding, as though a ghost had passed close by.

Mary looked up at her, frowning. 'Are you alright, love? You look a bit peaky.'

Sarah nodded. 'Aye, I just had the strangest sensation. Look how angry the sky is. It looks as though we could well have a thunderstorm. Maybe it's a warning that winter's not far off.'

'I suppose it is not so far away really. But look on the bright side — by the time it does set in you'll be long since wed and settled and your Mam and Daa will be safely away where no one knows them.'

Sarah looked thoughtful. 'I wonder if Daa has found Alexandra yet. If he has, how will he persuade her to come back? I'm sure she won't just come because he tells her to. And I can't imagine that he would return without her.'

'Now don't you go worrying about that one,' Mary said firmly. 'Let's just hope he'll manage to talk some sense into the girl. Make her see she's going to ruin her life. Going to Peel could be a fresh new start for her too you know. Not a body there will know her past.'

'I hope you're right. You know, sometimes I feel it might be best if she refuses to come back, or he cannot find her. If she does come back and carries on the way she has been doing it will only cause all sorts of heartaches. And I really don't think my Mam is strong enough to bear much more. She is in the most awful state of agitation now, worrying about my Daa being in Douglas. Fearing he will be seen and recognised. It really was not wise for him to go. I have this dreadful feeling about it!'

Mary, studying her friend from under lowered lids, could see the strain in Sarah's face. 'I'm sure your Daa will be safe. He'll stay as well out of sight as possible and the police think he's dead, so they won't be looking for him now.'

They waited in vain that evening for George to come. Judith, sitting tensely on the edge of her chair jumped to her feet and rushed to the door every time there was the slightest sound from outside. Usually it was just the wind soughing in the trees, shifting their branches. A magpie, chattering in the garden, brought her to her feet several times, to leave her sagging limply when she realised what it was she had heard.

Sarah tried hard to make small talk, as did Patrick, but to no avail, for neither could think of anything sensible or reassuring to say. By mid-evening they too had become as forlorn and melancholy as Judith, their eyes often creeping warily to the door.

The three younger children, prey to the tension, huddled in a corner conversing in whispers as they watched the grown-ups through wide, frightened eyes.

Later in the evening, just as Patrick was preparing to leave, the wind increased in intensity. It brought with it the first smattering of rain, which quickly grew to a steady downpour, whipping and lashing angrily against the front of the cottage. Within minutes the sky was alive with forks of lightning and the ominous rumbles of thunder.

'You'll not walk all the way to Baldrine in this, Patrick,' Judith said, looking up at him with dull eyes. 'Stay here the night. There's Alexandra's mattress in the loft you can use. She won't be needing it this night.' Laying her arms on the table, she let her face flop onto them and burst into tears, her body racked with heaving sobs.

With a tear in her own eye, Sarah moved to give her mother comfort. Her dark eyes, seeking Patrick's across her mother's back, were haunted and beseeching.

A gentle knock came out of the storm so unexpectedly that everyone in the cottage started, every eye turned toward the door. Judith leapt to her feet as though scalded and was at the door in an instant, jerking it open.

On the threshold stood a bedraggled young man, tall and muscular with fair hair, which was plastered to him, as were his clothes.

Judith froze, staring at him wide–eyed, her mouth sagging open for a moment. 'Yes?' She managed finally.

'I–um–I.' He started, not quite sure how to find the words he wanted. 'Do I have the pleasure of addressing Mistress Fayle?'

Judith nodded faintly. 'And who ...?'

'I'm Josiah Panter.' He paused as though expecting some sign of recognition.

Judith eyed him warily. 'Should I know you? Oh, look you'd better come inside.' Suddenly she had realised that while they talked, he was still being rained on.

'I'm soaked. Dripping water,' the man said apologetically.

'No matter,' Judith shook her head dismissively. 'This floor's had worse than rainwater!'

Sarah smiled quietly, remembering Richard's problem which, she realised suddenly, had vanished since his father came home. As the stranger moved into the cottage, she noticed he limped badly, one leg quite twisted and shorter than the other.

'Have we met before?' Judith asked.

'Well, no. Now I'm here I'm not sure if I should have come.'

'Well now you are here, why don't you tell us why?' Patrick asked abruptly, eyeing the man suspiciously.

The stranger looked at him, almost fearfully, as though realising for the first time that there were others present. His eyes quickly circled the room and Sarah noticed how startlingly blue they were.

'Well ... because ... George told me to come,' Josiah stated hesitantly.

Judith's hand went nervously to her mouth, her eyes lighting up. 'Have you seen him? Are you a friend of his?'

Jos looked puzzled. 'We were friends. But no, I haven't seen him for many months. We–um–we escaped from jail together and George was bringing me here. I had a fall, broke my leg badly.' At this he tapped the deformed leg with a rueful smile.

Sarah pushed her chair back from the table and stood up,

moving toward him. The flame of interest that flared in the lad's blue eyes did not escape Patrick's notice. He moved quickly to place a proprietorial arm around Sarah. His own eyes blazed an unspoken message of warning.

'You haven't seen my father today, then?' Sarah asked quickly.

Josiah frowned, not understanding. Shaking his head as though to clear muddled thoughts he said gently, 'Sorry, but I thought you would know. They told me in the village he was dead.'

'Dead?' Judith put a hand to her head, her voice no more than a harsh whisper.

'Aye,' Josiah shuffled uncomfortably. 'I went to the tavern to enquire the whereabouts of the Fayle family and they told me there, amongst other things, that George Fayle had drowned trying to sail alone from England.'

Judith started laughing then, an unearthly, high-pitched sound that startled them all. Helping her to a chair, Sarah sat with her, holding her hand.

Josiah watched apprehensively for several minutes, remembering the other stories he had been told in the tavern about Judith Fayle — the crazy woman of Agneash.

When Judith was calmer, Jos looked apologetically at Sarah. 'I'm sorry, I didn't mean to cause an upset. It's just that I owe my life to your father. When I fell and shattered my leg he looked after me. He could have run off and left me, as most would have done. If he had, I would have died but he risked recapture himself to drag me along with him. Although I told him to save himself, he refused to leave me until he knew I would be found. He thought it was prison officers who were just yards behind us.'

'Why are you not in prison now, then? If you were recaptured?' Patrick asked suspiciously.

'As it turned out, the men were not pursuers, but smugglers

who happened to be using the same trail as us. They had with them a pet dog, which we'd heard, and thought was a tracking hound. Thanks to George they found me and cared for me. The last thing your father said to me was that if I ever came to the Isle of Man, I must look him up.'

'So here you are,' Sarah said quietly.

Jos turned those startling blue eyes upon her, nodding slightly. 'Yes. Here I am. I'm truly sorry to hear about George. He was a good friend. I owe him my life!' He eyed Judith apprehensively, unsure of how such a statement might affect her, hoping he hadn't hit a raw nerve that might spark some violence. Remembering what he had been told of her in the village, he stood nervously, ready to jump if she should come at him. Remembering his friend, a wetness came to his eyes.

Sarah studied the stranger, wondering if he could be trusted. True, she did recall her father talking of the lad who had escaped with him. He had expressed a hope on occasions that the boy had been properly cared for and would not have too many more years to spend in prison. George had never said his name, though this fellow's description fitted — especially the crippled leg.

After another few awkward moments, Sarah told him the true story, omitting the part about Alexandra's immorality. Telling only that she had run away from home and that George had gone after her.

'I'm glad I came then,' Jos said sincerely. 'When they told me at the tavern of George's drowning I almost left again. But then thought I owed it to him to see if his family needed help. So here I am. If there is anything I can do, to assist in any way at all, please just ask.'

'I really think we can manage well enough thank you.' Patrick said quickly, before Sarah had a chance to reply.

'It's very nice of you to offer, Mister … um … sorry–I've forgotten?' Sarah stumbled to a halt.

'Josiah Panter, Jos.' He smiled at her, his eyes like a sunlit sky.

'With luck my father should be home tomorrow and I'm sure he will be delighted to see you, Jos.'

'You must stay here tonight, Mister Panter,' Judith said quietly. 'This is no weather for you to turn out again.'

Jos looked down ruefully at the puddle his dripping clothes had made on the slate floor.

'Thank you, but I have a room at the tavern, and dry clothes. The storm sounds to be dropping off a bit now, so if you'll pardon me, I'll take my leave of you now and return tomorrow if I may?'

Jos left then, turning in the doorway to bow deferentially to the two ladies. There were a few moments of thoughtful silence after he had gone, broken by Patrick volunteering, 'I don't trust the fellow.'

'I did,' Sarah said absently. 'His story precisely matched all Daa told us about the lad who escaped at his side. Daa will enjoy renewing the friendship and seeing Jos is alive and not too badly crippled.'

Unseen by Sarah, Patrick scowled at her unthinking use of the stranger's given name.

Judith spoke suddenly. 'I liked him. And your Daa must have thought a lot of him to risk his freedom to save him.' Wearily she struggled to her feet. 'Now I think it's time we all went to bed. You will stay, Patrick. 'Tis no weather to be walking all the way to Baldrine. Get yourself up to the loft'

Sarah lay awake for hours listening to the howling darkness. Feeling the storm ripping around the cottage, pushing into every nook and crack. At times the gusts were so strong she could feel the house shake, as though gripped by giant hands.

What if Patrick is right, she wondered after a while, and Josiah Panter was not to be trusted? It was beyond her, thinking in the darkness, to understand why she had told him, a stranger, that George was still alive, when the whole world thought him dead.

Sometime in the early hours she heard movement on the stepladder from the loft, the tread of bare feet across the floor and Patrick's hand gripped her arm, shaking her slightly.

'Sarah. Are you awake?'

She kept her eyes closed, pretending to be asleep. This was neither the time nor the place for whatever Patrick had in mind.

'Wake up, Sarah,' he persisted, attempting to squeeze into the tiny cupboard bed with her.

'Not tonight, Patrick. Not here. Mam will hear us.' She tried to resist, but he pushed her over, crushing her between himself and the wall.

'I only want to talk. I couldn't sleep. Your Mam will be asleep and if she wakened, she wouldn't hear us for the storm.' He tightened his arms around her, tilting her head back to accept his kiss.

A few minutes later, feeling the movement and hardness of his arousal against her stomach, she pulled away from him as far as the little bed would allow. 'You said you only wanted to talk,' she accused. 'What's to talk about that is so urgent?'

'That fellow tonight.'

'Jos?' As soon as Sarah spoke the name, she felt Patrick tense in annoyance. 'What is there to say about him that couldn't have waited until morning?'

'I don't trust him.'

'You said that already. Now please will you go back to the loft, so I can get back to sleep. And before Mam catches you here, for she won't be sleeping too soundly with her worry about Daa and Alexandra on her mind. She'd never believe we were only talking, and I don't want her to be any more upset than she already is.' She put her hands against his shoulders, trying in vain to push him away.

'I don't trust him with you either. Not just with the truth about your father. There's something about the man. The way he looked and smiled at you. I didn't like it!'

'Now you're being silly.'

'That's as maybe, but if I am it's because I love you to distraction.' He pulled her close to him, kissing her again, his tongue prying her lips apart, seeking and finding her tongue, exploring it, causing wild explosions around her insides.

Sarah tried to fight him at first, wriggling and pushing at him, her thoughts on her mother in the next room. His probing tongue, and gently caressing fingers, quickly overpowered her. Despite her misgivings, her body took control of her mind and she found herself responding eagerly to his urgent love making.

When the violent wave of their mutual climax had passed, Patrick rolled carefully on his side, moving Sarah with him.

Desire still high, Sarah turned, limbs locked around his. Staying pressed close to him. Wanting to hold him inside her forever.

And so, without meaning to, they slept. The first light coming in the tiny window wakened Patrick. Realising where he was, feeling a new arousal starting, he tried to pull away. Sarah's limbs, still around him, held him and with a quiet groan, he submitted to nature.

Sarah, waking with the feel of him moving inside her, responded instantly and passionately, unheeding of where she was.

Just as they climaxed Sarah heard a gasp. Her eyes flew open and to her horror she saw her mother framed in the doorway, a hand half covering her ashen, shocked face.

Sarah tried to push Patrick off, but unconscious of Judith's presence, he held her tightly until he was spent.

Judith, seeing him holding down her apparently struggling daughter, driving into her, could think only of stopping what appeared to be a rape. As she rushed past the hearth, she grabbed the coal shovel and brought it down on Patrick with all the force she could muster.

Luckily for him it missed his head, catching him only a flat, stinging blow on the shoulder.

With a muffled curse, he leapt from the bed, rounding on Judith, his eyes blazing, fist raised. Realising in an instant whom he was facing, and the ridiculous state of his nakedness, he swept his trousers from the floor and battled to keep his balance as he struggled into them. His shoulders sagged, and he had the look of a man who was about to become violently ill.

'Beast! Filthy, fornicating *beast*!' Judith screamed, her eyes burning with a wildness that Sarah had seen before and hoped was gone for ever. A look that made her shudder with foreboding.

Judith raised the shovel again, swinging it toward Patrick's head, mustering all the strength she possessed into the blow.

Sarah screamed, and Patrick grabbed Judith's wrist, with the weapon just inches from his face, jerking it violently away. The shovel flew from her hand, crashing against the far wall with a resounding clatter, then skittered across the floor.

'I gave you shelter from the storm!' Judith screamed. 'I let you stay to protect you and under my own roof you attacked my daughter!' Judith dashed toward the fallen shovel.

Leaping from the bed, Sarah dragged down the hem of her nightdress, caught her mother's arm and pulled her toward the table. 'Sit down, Mam.'

While Judith's back was momentarily turned, Patrick quickly buttoned his trousers.

Judith obeyed her daughter but went on glaring venomously at Patrick. Finally turning her gaze to Sarah, her eyes softened. 'Are you alright, love? Did I stop him in time?'

'In time?' Sarah asked, puzzled.

'Yes, love?' Judith nodded. 'Was I in time to stop the rape?'

Sarah felt sick. 'It wasn't rape, Mam. I allowed it. Patrick and I are to be wed remember?'

Two blank, empty eyes looked up at her.

'Not rape? No, I don't believe that. You're trying to protect him. But it won't work because you're too clean a girl to allow that when you're not wed. And you won't be wed. Not to him! I won't have you marry an Irishman!' Judith's shoulders heaved with her sobs and a flood of tears ran down her cheeks, to drip onto her nightdress.

'Oh, Mam,' Sarah said despairingly, her eyes misting. Kneeling, she put her arms round her mother.

'Mistress Fayle. Please allow us to explain ...' Patrick started weakly, but the hatred and disgust on her face when her eyes met his stopped him in his tracks.

'You'd best leave,' Sarah said quietly, her lips quivering.

'I can't just walk out and leave you to face her alone!' Quickly realising that comment might cause Sarah even more trouble he whispered, 'God, but I do some stupid things sometimes. To go and make love to you under your mother's roof. It was only seeing the way that man looked at you. It had me stirred up and jealous. I must make amends for upsetting her so.'

Sarah drew a weary hand over her face. 'Just go! We can't discuss it now. Leave. I'll try to sort things out.' Sarah was suddenly acutely aware of three small faces peering in terror over the edge of the loft.

With a helpless shrug, Patrick turned, and climbed the ladder to get properly dressed. When he was ready to leave, he hesitated at the door, looking beseechingly at Sarah. 'Please let me make things right,' he pleaded.

Sarah, who was still trying to calm her distraught mother, gave a slight shake of her head, then looked pointedly at the door.

Calling himself every bad name he could think of, Patrick left, his body shaken by a deep, shuddering sigh. Just when things were going so right, and Judith had warmed to him, his lust and jealousy had spoiled it all. How in heaven's name could he ever make things right again?

A magpie swooped overhead, making its strange cry that sounded to him like mocking laughter. A lone magpie. Patrick was taken, for a moment, back to his childhood, and the memory of his adoptive grandfather telling him a lone magpie was the herald of misfortune.

'Well, you could not be more right,' he murmured, watching sadly as the bird took flight.

Chapter 19

◆──────◇──────◆

Mary groaned, sighed and shook her head crossly. 'Why? Why? Why in your own house no — your mother's house? And just a few feet away from her. *And* in the morning when she was likely to be awake to hear you?'

Sarah shrugged miserably. 'You can't say anything I haven't already kicked myself for. It should not have happened. But it did! And Mam caught us at it. That's all that really matters. She was dreadfully upset, thinking that he was ... you know. Just when she'd grown to trust Patrick. Now we're back where we started, with her hating him.'

'I'll talk to her if you like. Try to make her see it's not the end of the world. 'Specially as you're to be wed in two weeks in any case.'

'Would you please, Mary?' Sarah heaved a tremulous sigh. 'She might listen to you. She likes you. Maybe when Daa comes back she'll be better. She's at her wits end worrying about Alexandra and my Daa at the moment.'

'How was she when you left her?'

'Much calmer, but still very upset, I'm afraid.'

Another wagon load of ore slid down onto the washing table.

The women rubbed their numb, wet hands to try and bring some circulation, then set about sorting the metal ore from the rubbish, their chatter muted for the time being.

Patrick, still distressed and highly embarrassed, waited on the viaduct when they finished work. 'I must come home with you and see if I can make amends,' he pleaded.

Sarah and Mary exchanged questioning looks, the older woman frowning thoughtfully.

'I'm not sure it wouldn't be best if you just stayed out of the way for a while. How could you be so senseless and insensitive? There's some excuse for Sarah, because she's just young and in her own bed. But you're seven years older and forced your way into her bed. Surely you should be at an age by now when you should have a modicum of self-control. I hope you are thoroughly ashamed of yourself.'

Patrick gave a shuddering sigh. 'Indeed, I am, Mary. That's why I wish to talk to Mistress Fayle now. Things must be put right.'

Sarah dreaded going home, particularly with Patrick along, but it had to be faced. The sooner the better too, she realised, so she set a smart pace up the hill, with Mary struggling to keep up.

At the corner they saw Richard, obviously distressed, running toward them.

'Come quickly,' he cried as soon as he spotted them. 'Mam's ill!' Tears streamed down his dark young face, streaking the dirt, and he trembled uncontrollably.

Sarah broke into a run, her heart thundering. 'Oh, dear God! What's wrong? What's happened?'

Richard scurried along beside her. 'That man came. That other man.'

'Which one?'

'The one what came last night. The limping man,' Richard puffed.

'What did he do? Has he hurt Mam?' Sarah could feel panic clutching at her breast.

'No. He picked her up and put her to bed after the policeman came!'

'Sarah stopped dead, staring, horrified at the boy. 'The policeman?' she rasped.

'Aye. He came and said my Daa was drownded, then Mammy screamed and fell on the floor. The limping man said I should get you.'

Sarah burst through the door into the tiny cottage, finding herself immediately confronted by Josiah Panter.

'What's happened?' She leaned on the doorpost trying to catch her breath and gather her scattered wits.

'I think maybe you'd better sit down,' Jos suggested kindly.

Sarah stumbled to a chair and sat looking up, pleading in her eyes. Patrick came to stand behind her, his hands on her shoulders, as though he could lend her his strength.

'I came to see if your father was home safe, and the Constable came,' he paused, choking back a sob.

'Tell me?' Sarah knew already, but she needed to hear him say it. Until he did, she would cling to the slender thread of hope.

Jos took hold of her hand and she felt Patrick's grip on her shoulder tighten.

'I'm sorry, but he said your father died.'

'How?' Sarah's question was a barely audible breath, her voice having deserted her. 'How did he die? Are they sure this time?'

Josiah nodded bleakly. 'This time they do have his body. I am not sure how to tell you this, but the Constable said he killed a man in a fight over some doxy, then dived into the harbour to evade capture. He was hit on the head by a boat and went under. His body was found washed up on the beach in Douglas Bay this morning. I–um–I asked him — the policeman, that is to arrange to have his — um,' Jos winced, 'his body brought home. He said he would. I hope I did right?'

Sarah nodded mutely. 'We must give him a proper Christian burial. And what of the girl? What news is there of her?'

'Disappeared,' the Constable said. 'Ran off and no one has seen her since.'

'Alexandra!' Sarah said bitterly. 'He found her and tried to bring her home. And died for her! Oh Mam, what have we all done to you?' Crying out in anguish, she leapt from the chair and ran into her mother's bedroom.

Judith was sitting on the far corner of the bed, her legs curled in the foetal position, arms wrapped round them, leaning against the wall.

'Mam. I'm sorry. So sorry,' was all Sarah could find voice for, and that caught with the tears that burned in her throat. She sat on the edge of the bed, hoping her nearness would give her mother some slight comfort.

Judith stared at her daughter over her knees. Her eyes were blank, lifeless and without hope. To Sarah it was an all too familiar vacantness.

When Sarah took her hand, it was icy, and Judith gave no response to her affectionate squeeze.

'Mam, I'm with you. I'll help you through all this,' Sarah promised, tearfully.

There came not a glimmer of acknowledgement.

Patrick edged into the room; his eyes concerned. 'How is she, Sarah?'

Wordlessly Sarah shook her head, biting her lip to hold back the tears that threatened. 'She doesn't even seem to know I'm here.'

'Mistress Fayle,' Patrick moved to stand by Sarah.

The dead eyes moved slowly to focus on him, then as recognition dawned, they lit with a sudden blaze of hatred. With unbelievable speed and agility Judith uncurled, like the release of a tightly coiled spring, to launch herself from the bed, hands reaching for Patrick's throat.

Just in time, he grasped her wrists, holding her away from himself with great difficulty, while she kicked viciously at him. Like a captured animal, she tried to bite his hands to break his grip.

'Fornicating *pig*!' Judith screamed. '*Rapist*! *Murderer*! *Irish* murderer! You killed my husband!' Her cry came in a blood-curdling scream.

'No, Mam. Not Patrick. It was another Irishman, Sean Casey who took Daa smuggling,' Sarah said shakily.

With Mary's help, she pulled her mother away from Patrick, and led her back to the bed.

Jos had followed Mary through when they had heard Judith's scream and he now lingered hesitantly in the doorway.

'Get *that one* out of my house,' Judith spat, her eyes no less wild. 'He murdered my husband.'

'No, Mam, it wasn't Patrick. I'm promised to Patrick, remember? We're to be wed in two weeks.'

Judith's despairing cry had a sound not quite human. 'You will not marry an Irishman. It would be over my dead body if you did. It was an Irishman killed your father and one is as bad as the other. If that man comes in my house or near you again, I'll be the next one to do a murder. *This I vow*!' She pointed a shaking finger at Patrick.

Sarah stood up, clutching at Patrick's sleeve pulling him toward the door. 'You'd best leave. I'll talk to her when she's calmer. The shock still has her just now.'

Patrick nodded and left without argument; his shoulders slumped. It seemed that nothing could ever go right in his relationship with Sarah. But he *would* win her. No matter how long it took. He *would* win her.

Sarah sat with her mother until she fell into an exhausted sleep, her breathing fitful and noisy. Exhausted, she stumbled through to the parlour. Sitting at the table, she put her face down on her arms and wept.

Mary came to stand beside her, gathering the girl in her arms, cuddling her to her ample bosom, like a child.

'It will all work out, my love,' she promised. 'We'll fight this together. I'll help you get your mother well.'

'I hope Alexandra rots in Hell!' Sarah said with sudden vehemence.

'There, there, love. Those sorts of thoughts aren't going to help anyone,' Mary soothed. Then added with a touch of bitterness, 'But she probably will — God willing! We all get our comeuppance sometime before we leave this world.'

'Alexandra?' Jos frowned in puzzlement.

'Her young sister. She's the doxy George was fighting over,' Mary said simply.

Jos winced and sighed. 'The one he went to fetch home? Is there anything I can do to help?'

'Not at the moment, I don't think. Are you going to be in Laxey for a while?'

'If I can be any use at all here, there's nowhere more important I have to be.'

'Well if you care to, you're welcome to move in with James and me. The accommodation is not great, I'm afraid. There's just a truckle bed in the parlour, but it must be better than a hotel room.'

Jos hesitated for a moment. 'Has Sarah told you I'm an escaped convict?'

Mary smiled warmly. 'Aye lad. But so was George, and we were the ones he was brought to when he struggled back to the island more dead than alive. If you're a friend of his we won't hold your past against you. I have just one concern though.' Mary paused for a moment, while Jos waited apprehensively. 'Will it be safe for you to be here? What if the Constable sees you?'

Jos smiled. 'My crime was committed in Manchester. They are unlikely to be looking for me in the Isle of Man. The scars on my face from the fall have changed my looks quite a lot. And they won't be looking for a cripple.'

Mary nodded her satisfaction.

The day had come and gone when the wedding was supposed to have taken place. Now, Patrick reflected, there seemed less chance of it ever happening than there had been on the day the *Lady Isabella* was set in motion.

He had repeatedly cursed himself for every kind of a fool, but it didn't help much. No amount of self-recrimination could alter the facts, and the clock could not be turned back.

Sarah wondered if Alexandra might hear of her father's funeral and turn up to pay her respects and feared the effect this might have on her mother. However, there was no sign. It seemed she had simply vanished.

George, for whom he had grown to care deeply, was buried without Patrick's presence, for try as they all might, Judith would not forgive him. He had attempted several times in the three weeks since the tragedy, to talk to her, but her reaction became more violent and hate-filled each time. She regarded him as the ravisher of her daughter and murderer of her husband and would not be swayed from that view.

He knew, because Sarah had told him so, that she spent all her days now huddled, curled in a tight ball at the back corner of her bed. Sometimes still; sometimes rocking. Her mind seemed to have gone completely now, her eyes mostly blank and staring. But sometimes they became wild and blazed with an insane hatred. That was when she came to life ranting and screaming, calling all the powers of some black God to strike all Irishmen dead.

Walking up the dark, damp adit to the shaft head with his three pitch mates, he remembered with horror the effect his visits had had on Judith.

Each time she had roused quickly and violently from her stupor. On the last occasion she had bounded to the table, grabbed the cleaver Sarah had been using on some herring. With a blood-curdling scream she had leapt at him with it raised. Luckily that convict fellow, had been there to hold her. For some reason Patrick couldn't understand, Josiah seemed to have more control over her than anyone.

Even Josiah had tried, Sarah assured him, to talk Judith around to accepting Patrick again. But that had only served to make her leer at him suspiciously through half-closed eyes and ask if he, Jos, also had Irish blood.

Patrick puzzled about Josiah sometimes. What was his stake? Why he was hanging around, trying so hard to help? Or was it just to impress? He said he owed it to George, seeing as how he had saved his life, to help his family. But Patrick couldn't help but wonder if perhaps his intention wasn't perhaps to help himself to George's daughter.

He even found himself wondering about Sarah. He hardly saw her now, for she said she had no time. Always rushing away because she had to look after her mother. And Josiah was very often there, supposedly helping. Doing what though?

Patrick knew the younger children were no longer living in the house. Fearing what might happen if they were left with Judith, they had been moved down to Mary's where Josiah was also supposed to be living.

It must be crowded in Mary's cottage, he found himself thinking, with four extras to be bedded! Or were there always four? Did the cripple always sleep at Mary's? Or did he sometimes stay at the croft to help with Judith? And so, Patrick wondered about Josiah, torturing himself.

He swung himself onto the ladder that led a hundred and twenty feet down to the second level. A rung, green and slimy, half rotted and loose, turned under his hands, causing his heart to jolt with fear as he grabbed quickly at the next, more stable spoke.

Things were never going to work out between himself and Sarah. That became more obvious with every day that passed. At times he wondered if he had already spent too many years nursing his obsession for her. Maybe Robert had been right when he'd said the best thing to do would be to go to Australia and forget her. But could he face life without her? Now, to give up and know he would never see her again was unthinkable.

He sighed emptily and continued down the treacherous ladder. Hand after hand. Foot after foot.

From far above him came a muffled, terrified cry followed by a few moments of scrabbling and confused shouting from other men in the shaft.

'*Look out!*' someone yelled, while another voice screamed.

Instinctively, moving like lightning, Patrick looped one arm over a rung, pushing it behind the ladder as far as his elbow. Gripping for dear life to the rung below, he pressed himself in as hard as he could against the spokes, bowing his head forward, pressing it against the ladder.

In an instant a body hurtled past him, brushing the back of his head and landing full weight against his shoulders before hurtling on downward to crash with a solid thud on the level now about twenty feet below.

Knocked loose from his perch by the force of the blow, he found himself hanging only by his elbow, swinging and scrambling to get a foot and handhold again. He felt, with frightening clarity, the aching void at his back. Having at last achieved a grip, he climbed down, heart thundering wildly, at all speed to reach the fallen miner.

Letting go of the ladder, he jumped the last few feet, taking care to land on the resting platform, which was only about six feet square. A breeze caught his candle, which guttered and died. Not daring to move without a light, from where he stood, he waited for Robert, the next man down and rekindled his wick.

Together they knelt beside the injured miner, moving him gently back from where he lay, dangling halfway over the edge of the next shaft. Patrick heard, with a shudder and an upheaval of his insides, crepitus, as the broken edges of bones ground together.

'Hell!' Robert's hands shook as he examined the man. 'It's Percy! I don't think there is much he hasn't broken!'

The miner's face was a jellied mass of grazes and contusions, with half the left side of his face torn away. Splinters of bone protruded from his jaw and skull, his left eye hanging on his cheek. Blood oozed thickly from every orifice, his breathing stertorous and irregular.

'God Almighty!' Was all Patrick could find to say.

A continuous stream of miners shuffled down the ladders, many of them gathering on the small platform, crowding it dangerously.

'You'd better all carry on down,' Patrick told them, shakily taking command. Moving to the foot of the shaft, he tipped his head back, calling out, 'Pass the message up for them to send down the dead box!'

Returning to kneel beside Percy, he heard his order repeated several times, in different voices, each more distant than the one before.

After an eternity, a rough wooden box was lowered down the shaft. Patrick shouted a message to let the folk at the top know it had reached the required level.

Thanking their Maker that Percy was unconscious, Patrick, Robert and Caesar, set about the sickening task of moving their broken workmate. Caesar opened the lid of the box while the other two lifted Percy into it. Their stomachs churned with the unpleasant sound and sensation caused by the unnatural movement of his bones. With the greatest of care, they placed him on the seat of the dead box, strapping him firmly in position. Before they closed the lid on him, Patrick took one last shocked look at the shattered body that flopped bonelessly in its harness.

Having called to the miners at the top to haul the box up, Patrick climbed the ladders alongside it, guiding it to prevent it catching and fouling the rocky walls of the shaft.

Groups of miners stood at each level, waiting before their next descent to leave the ladders clear for him to pass.

At one stage Percy started an inhuman groaning and a gurgling in his throat, which chilled the blood of everyone who heard it.

The mine's surgeon had been summoned and was waiting at the top of the shaft. As soon as the dead box had been lifted clear of the black chasm and placed safely on solid ground, he asked for the lid to be opened and before Percy was moved, was checking for signs of life.

A clutch of fearful, wide-eyed miners stood around, watching tensely, hardly breathing. Patrick studied the faces, seeing reflected in them his own feelings and terror. Not a sound was heard, bar the far away thud and drone of the water pump deep below their feet, while the surgeon made his examination.

Looking up finally, his eyes sought Patrick's. 'I'll check properly when we get him outside. But I am quite certain he has gone.'

Patrick watched, as though in a nightmare, the body lifted carefully from the box. Then it was laid awkwardly on a stretcher and carried toward the outside world which, Patrick thought with a sudden sick calmness, Percy's sightless, staring eyes would never see again!

Oh Hell! Percy's family were going to have to be told. Suddenly the full impact struck Patrick and he found himself trembling uncontrollably.

Shaking his head sadly, he started back down the ladder. Taking more care than ever. Securing a tight grip on each rung, before releasing the other hand. Wedging each foot as hard onto the rungs as was possible. Knowing, more certainly than ever now that his life depended on caution.

It took him longer than his usual hour to reach the lowest level, then he stumbled nervously along the roughly hewn tunnel toward his pitch. With only the dim glimmer of one candle to show the way, he stumbled in the blackness, feeling his way along the wall like a blind man, knocking his head frequently on sharply protruding rocks, glad of his hard cap. Sweat slickered like rain on his face, running in rivulets down his back. Until this day, he realised, he had never known real fear.

Robert and Caesar looked up when he shuffled into the core, their eyebrows raised questioningly.

Patrick drew a deep breath, holding it for a moment. Then shaking his head, he let it out on a sigh.

All three men removed their hats and stood for several minutes with their heads bowed in respect for their dead friend.

Patrick worked for hours, his thoughts in a turmoil. With George dead and Judith's mind now completely gone, he feared there was no possible hope for Sarah and himself for the future.

Pulling Robert aside he asked quietly, 'What are your plans for the future? Do you still intend to sail for this new country to look for gold?' he asked as they changed back to their street clothes that night.

Robert nodded enthusiastically. 'Indeed, I do. More than just plans. I have made up my mind. I am definitely going!'

Patrick nodded thoughtfully. 'When is it you leave?'

Robert's face lit up. 'Another two months at the most, I hope. I have the fare saved and will be making the booking in the next few days. All I have need of now is sufficient savings to set me up until I find work or some gold there.'

'Let me know when you're to make the booking. I have decided to come with you. After what happened to Percy today, I've thought a lot. And I've realised this deep core mining is too dangerous. The wages are only a pittance. I like the sound of gold to be found near or on the surface. I'll risk my life no longer in these depths and for so little reward.'

'What about your maid? Will she agree to go?' Robert tried, but could not hide his surprise.

Patrick shook his head sadly 'No. She will agree to nothing that will take her away from her mother. And the woman has gone completely insane now. When she sees me, she tries to kill me, so there is no chance Sarah and I shall ever be wed.'

'I'm sorry,' Robert lowered his eyes in genuine sympathy, for he knew just how strong Patrick's feelings had been.

'It's best if I leave. Then we can both get on with our lives. For Sarah's sake as well as mine. I certainly can't continue as I am. So, count me in. I'll be glad to come with you to Australia.

Together we'll be rich!' Patrick tried to summon a laugh but didn't quite succeed.

Just a short few hours ago, he remembered, Percy had been laughing with them. Telling a tale of some mischief one of his children had been into. Now he was gone; never would he see their amusing antics again. Never would they see their father again! Nor his wife her see husband. How fragile this life is, Patrick thought. And how precious!

Chapter 20

Sarah heard the accident warning siren sound at the mine and immediately felt panic twisting her insides. Her eyes strayed nervously up the glen to where she could see the stark buildings huddled beyond the big wheel.

People were running toward the main adit. Running. Shouting. Arms waving. Panic seemed to be the order of the day.

Captain Rowe appeared in the doorway of the mine office, then hurried up toward the adit. A little while later Sarah saw the mines' surgeon arrive in his trap, his horses at a sweaty canter. Jumping down almost before the carriage had stopped moving, he grabbed his leather bag. Leaving the horse in the charge of one of the office workers, he too sped to the mine entrance.

A ripple of agitation ran through the women on the washing-floors. They all stopped work, standing like statues, looking toward the mine through frightened eyes. They looked at each other, murmuring nervously as they returned to their chores, for most of them had husbands, sons or brothers working under ground.

Sarah, possibly because the whole world seemed to be working against her these days, was convinced ill had befallen

Patrick. Terror took her and immediately she felt the harsh talons of loss clawing and twisting at her heart.

Life seemed to be closing in on her, crushing her head, stopping her breathing. Her stomach clenched in sick anxiety. A cold sweat breaking out on her face, she felt the earth swaying, spinning, turning black.

Then Mary was holding her. Helping her to sit down. Comforting her.

When the attack had passed, she found herself hot and cold at the same time, trembling uncontrollably. Mary watched her, understanding the girl's fear, her eyes grave.

'Don't get yourself in a state, love. There are hundreds of men down there, you know. I just thank God my James is not on shift.'

Sarah nodded mutely, turning waterlogged eyes to her friend. Her throat ached with unshed tears. When strength returned to her legs, she was about to resume working, when she saw the supervisor approaching. Clutching a hand to her mouth, she sagged against the table.

The women all stopped and turned to watch him, each one heavy hearted and dreading what he would have to say. As he neared, he shook his head.

'I'm sorry ladies, but I have nothing to tell you. I know a man has died in a fall, but I have not yet been made privy to his name. As soon as I know, I promise I'll come and tell you.'

With another sad shake of his head, he turned and re-traced his steps.

No one settled to work properly for the rest of the shift. Every woman had the same fear — that it was her man who had died.

The fact that no official came to the washing-floors to inform any of the other women of the death of her man, made

Sarah's fears all the greater. By the time the working day finished she was quite ill and weak with fear.

The girl dashed up the path after work, determined to go to the mine office for information. Mary ran behind, puffing and blowing like an old dray horse with too much weight to pull. Patrick was waiting on the viaduct, his face ashen and drawn.

With a sob of relief Sarah ran to him, wanting him; needing him to take her in his arms. To hold her tight and prove to her that he was real, and alive, and unhurt. But he stood, shoulders slumped, head bowed and arms hanging limply at his sides.

'Thanks be to God you're alright,' she sobbed, her voice catching in her throat. 'I was so scared it was you who had died.' She clung tightly to him but evoked no response. Looking up at him then she saw his eyes were dull and lifeless. Even the gold flecks, usually so brilliant were almost indiscernible.

'What's wrong?' Her heart thudded with apprehension at what she saw in his face.

'Did you know of the accident this morning?'

'Aye.' Sarah's eyes flooded again. 'I have feared all day that it might be you.'

'Perhaps worse than me,' he said, almost inaudibly. 'For I have no family. No one to miss me or care if I die!' This last was spoken with a trace of bitterness.

Sarah's eyes blazed with a combination of guilt and indignation. '*I* would care! *I* would miss you!'

Patrick looked speculatively into the brown eyes he loved so much. 'Would you, Sarah? Would you really?' His question was quiet and frighteningly cold.

Looking at Patrick, Sarah saw a tremor at the corner of his lips. 'It was Percy who died,' he said with a sob.

'No! Not Percy!' Was all she could manage to say.

'And him with all those childher,' Mary said, shaking her head sadly.

'Thank God it wasn't you,' Sarah said feelingly.

Patrick made no reply but fell into step beside the women when they headed off toward Agneash. His hands were dug deep into his pockets and he looked at the ground as he walked, kicking absently at the odd stone.

It was obvious to Sarah and Mary that he was having some sort of inner battle. Something was weighing heavily on his mind.

More than just Percy's death, Sarah thought. She looked up at him questioningly and in the absence of an explanation, glanced at Mary, who raised her eyebrow and shrugged.

'What's wrong, Patrick? It's more than just what happened to Percy that's bothering you isn't it?'

He remained silently thoughtful. The only sign that he had heard her, a slight twitching of his shoulders.

Sarah shrugged helplessly, then walked on in silence.

'We must talk, Sarah!' Patrick's voice came suddenly, startling her. 'Things cannot continue as they are, and the time has come when decisions have to be made.'

'What sort of decisions?' His tone and the cool determination in his voice brought a sudden fear to Sarah's heart.

'About our future. We must make up our minds what we are to do with it. I will no longer tolerate being kept dangling, to be manipulated at your whims like some mindless doll at the end of a string.'

'I haven't done that!' Sarah retorted indignantly.

'Oh? Really? What name would you give your treatment of me then?' There was a note of sarcasm in his voice.

'Treatment? I love you. I want to marry you!'

'Why don't you then? I have asked you often enough.'

'You know why. Because of my Mam. The way she is. She will

not abide me marrying an Irishman. Just now that is. But she'll get better. Then we can marry.'

'Some time — never,' Patrick said bitterly. And in the mean time I may not see you!'

'It has to be this way. I must be there to care for her. And it would upset her too much to know I was with you. The fewer upsets she has the sooner she will get better.' Sarah was trembling — torn between her two loves.

'How long do I have to wait for that to happen? And what if she never gets better? What then? Am I expected to hang around here forever in the hope a mad woman might become sane again? Or waiting for her to die so I may make a decent, life for myself? And while I wait that other man, that crippled fugitive is hanging around. Ingratiating. Smiling. Conveniently helping care for your crazy mother while he earns your gratitude and worms his way into your affections!' His eyes blazed with a cruel, scornful anger.

'No! I don't know! Don't you dare call my mother crazy. She's just ill. She'll get better. She did before, when everyone said she wouldn't. And she will again. How can I tell you how long it will take? And it's not like that with Jos. He wants to help because Daa saved his life.'

'So he tells *you*!' Patrick snorted derisively. 'Well you have a decision to make now. And if it's the wrong one for me then you will be quite free for him to win. You will be at liberty to go to him.'

Sarah's heart rattled painfully against her ribs and she felt sick. Her head spun dangerously. 'I don't want Jos. I want you. I love you.'

Mary saw the colour go from Sarah's face and beads of perspiration appear on her brow. Gripping the girl's arm, she steered her toward the door of her cottage.

'I think it would be best if you two came in and talked this over inside. Now, sit down and talk not fight. Anger and insults will do nobody any good. I'll make us all a drink of hot camomile while you two talk. And I don't want to hear any raised voices. I refuse to referee a bout of fisticuffs!'

Patrick pulled out a chair for Sarah and when she was seated, sighed and lowered himself onto the chair across the table from her.

'I'm sorry, Sarah,' he said quietly. 'But I cannot go on waiting and hoping for something that will never happen.'

Sarah felt her mouth dry, her tongue cleaving to its roof. 'What do you plan then? What is it you're trying to tell me?'

Patrick was unspeaking for a moment, his brow furrowing thoughtfully as he gave careful consideration to his words. 'Robert has asked me to go to Australia with him. If you do not consent, now, to wed me, in spite of your mother, as soon as it can be arranged, then I intend to go with him.' He spoke quietly but firmly.

The cottage was possessed by a deathly hush. The grandfather clock, ponderously ticking away the seconds in the corner, sounded unnaturally loud. It grated discordantly on Sarah's ears and nerves. She sensed an intense consciousness of Mary, half bent over the hob, frozen like a statue, caught in the act of raising the kettle.

'Australia?' She mouthed, the question no more than a breath.

'Aye.'

'Australia? Where? That's not on the island is it? It's somewhere far away isn't it?'

'No. Not on this island. It is a new country around the other side of the world.'

'How far away is it? How long does it take to get there? When would you be back?'

James came through from the kitchen from where he had been overhearing the conversation.

'I've heard of it. Isn't that a convict settlement? I heard that is where they send all the convicts that are too bad to stay in prisons in England and Ireland. Doesn't it take about six months to get there?'

'Aye. About that unless I'm lucky enough to find passage on a fast ship.'

Sarah felt herself on the edge of hysteria. 'But it's so far, Patrick! Six months away!' She felt the void almost as though he'd already gone, and a strange awareness of Mary straightening from the hob to dazedly fill the mugs.

'Aye. I reckon that's how far I must go to be able to put you out of my mind. Though God knows I'll never forget you completely. The choice, though, is entirely yours.'

'Choice?'

'Of whether or not I go!'

'Can I stop you?'

'Easily. Just marry me right away and I shan't go. All you have to do is say 'yes'!'

'But my mother!"

'The choice, Sarah, is yours. If your mother will not accept me as your husband, then you must choose between us!'

'Then I must stay with my Mam,' Sarah quavered after a few moments. 'You can manage without me. My Mam cannot!'

'So be it.' Patrick stood up, nodding solemnly. 'If that is the way it's to be, then I'll take my leave now. I expect you won't see me again, for we'll be gone soon.' He swallowed a sigh to hide the tremor in his voice.

Looking uncomfortable, James sidled toward the door. 'I'll just go pick some veggies,' he mumbled.

Sarah remained seated, her legs having not the strength to support her.

Mary suddenly came alive, darting forward to catch Patrick's arm as he reached the door.

'Before this business goes beyond redemption, can we at least try to put things to rights?' Before either could speak, she continued. 'I can see both sides of the argument. And Sarah, while I understand your commitment to your mother, I also have a good notion of how Patrick must feel. You say you cannot marry him, and he cannot be expected to go on living as he is at present. To be fair, I don't think I could have taken as much of this nonsense as he has already.'

'What can be done, Mary? The situation seems impossible.' Sarah's voice was harsh, barely carrying on the choke of a sob.

'Please, Patrick,' Mary pleaded. 'At least allow me to make one last effort to talk Judith into accepting you before you dash off around the world.'

Patrick fiddled with the door handle, looking morosely at it, but a faint glimmer of hope had come back into his eyes. Gulping in a huge draught of air, he nodded his assent.

'Then wait for me here — both of you and I'll go straight away to talk to her.' Mary hurriedly threw her shawl around her shoulders, pulled an outdoor bonnet on her greying hair and hurried out. At the door she hesitated, throwing a glance back over her shoulder ordering them, smiling, not to fight while she was gone.

Patrick returned to his chair, then he and Sarah sat, staring into the fire in an uncomfortable, embarrassed silence. Neither could think of anything to say that did not sound either silly or trite or would not rekindle an argument.

When James came in from the kitchen garden, filled with bluff goodwill a few minutes later, it was a great relief to both Patrick and Sarah. Prattling on about manure, vegetables, slugs and hedgehogs, he broke the tension in the atmosphere.

'Try not to worry. If anyone can sort this thing out it will be my Mary,' he said reassuringly.

The grandfather clock ticked off the seconds, grinding and clanging at every quarter hour, noisily gonging away every hour. Each time it made a sound the three people in the cottage stared at it as though seeing it for the first time.

The click of the door-latch, when it finally came, startled them all with its suddenness.

All three jumped to their feet and spun to face the door. All spoke at once.

'How did you get on?' James raised a quizzical eyebrow.

'What did Mam say?' asked Sarah.

'Is she going to allow us to wed?' Patrick's voice held a mixture of hope and doubt.

'I think I've made quite good progress,' Mary said cheerfully as she collapsed into a chair to recover her breath. 'There's a stiff, cool breeze tonight. Blowing straight in my face it was. Fair blew the breath back inside of me.'

No one wanting a weather report, Sarah gripped Mary's cold hand, shaking it impatiently, as though she could wring the information out more quickly. 'What happened with Mam?'

'Well, I pointed out to her, over and over again, how much you love Patrick, and desire to marry him. Tried to make her see that Patrick did not even know your father before he went smuggling, so could not possibly be to blame, in any way, for anything that has happened. I even reminded her that Patrick had helped when George was brought home, nearly dead, by Harry. That all those months your father was in hiding Patrick could have, but did not, inform the police.'

'And?' Sarah prompted when Mary stopped for breath.

'Well Jos was there too.'

Patrick started at the name, his face darkening. 'What was he about?'

Mary scowled. 'Now, Patrick, you've no call to be antagonistic toward him. He's working hard on your behalf to make Judith see your side of it.'

Patrick snorted. Unbelieving.

Mary raised her head, fixing him with a cool, direct look. 'I was getting nowhere,' she said quietly, 'until Jos pointed out that she was going to ruin Sarah's life if she continued her grudge against you. He, it was, who pointed out to her the anguish she was causing and persuaded her to at least try to make friends with you again.'

'Does that mean ...?' Sarah's colour returned; her eyes hopeful again.

'Aye, lass, she says she'll talk to Patrick. It would be best to go just now, while she is in a receptive mood. I'll come with you, for if there is any disagreement, she might listen better to me. We can only pray.'

'Should I come too?' James asked and at his wife's grateful nod, he donned his coat.

The night was damp and chill, with a stiff wind blowing in off the sea. Sarah shivered in the unfriendly darkness as the door of Mary's cottage closed behind her.

There was an awful, empty, scared feeling squirming like worms inside her. Fear dragged her feet, tripping her on the stony path and several times she almost fell. It was only Patrick's arm, tensely supportive, that saved her.

The next few minutes, she thought, could be the most important of her life.

At the door of the croft she paused to take a deep breath and collect her scattered wits.

Make or break time. Decision time! Either her mother would accept Patrick as her son-in-law, or Sarah would have to send him away to travel the world.

With a trembling hand, she lifted the latch and stepped hesitantly over the threshold.

Judith was at the table, watching the door, calmer now, her eyes still dead and expressionless. Ever so slightly she rocked backwards and forwards with a monotonous rhythm, like the slow pendulum of a clock that needs rewinding.

Jos sat close by, watchful and alert for her every movement, wondering just what was taking place in her unfathomable mind. Her unpredictability frightened him at times.

When the door opened, and Sarah stood there, pale and apprehensive, Judith started, and her face softened. There was the look of the woman she used to be. The gentle loving mother Sarah used to know.

'Sarah, I don't mean to hurt you. The last thing I want is to ruin your life. Nothing is more important to me than your happiness.' Her face crumpled, ugly and lined, and she was overcome by a noisy storm of weeping, so violent she was retching.

'Mam!' Sarah ran to her, kneeling on the floor to take her in her arms. 'I know, Mam. I love you. But I love Patrick too.'

Judith nodded, her face darkening at the mention of his name. Sarah could see she was trembling with her fight for self-control.

Looking around, Sarah saw Patrick lingering hesitantly in the doorway. Mary and James were just behind him, their faces pale and ghostly and floating in the dim candlelight that escaped from the croft.

Patrick took a tentative step over the threshold, the movement catching the corner of Judith's eye. She watched warily while he approached, much as a mouse would watch a snake. Her breathing was heavy and controlled, but her tremor increased. Anxiously, Sarah took hold of her hands and found them like ice. Judith inclined her head slightly.

'Patrick,' she whispered. 'Welcome back.'

Letting out the breath he had been unaware he was holding, Patrick moved further into the room. Extending his hand, he leaned toward Judith, saying, 'Thank you, Mistress Fayle, for your forgiveness.'

In a blinding flash, Judith saw, in her mind's eye, a picture of this man with her daughter pinned under him on the bed. Saw him, again, standing naked before her with raised fist.

'*Beast!*' she screamed. Leaping from the chair she made a lunge at his face, drawing her fingernails down it and leaving deep gushing channels of blood.

Patrick staggered back, clutching his injured cheek with trembling hands while James and Jos leapt to take hold of Judith, forcing her back to the chair.

Sarah, who had been knocked to the floor in the scuffle, sat ashen-faced where she had fallen. Shock brought it home, cruelly, that her mother was never going to be well and that she, would not ever be free to marry.

Looking up at Patrick with stunned, pained eyes, she said, 'You had better go,' she paused, unable for a moment to continue. Finally, with a sob in her voice she continued, '... with Robert to Australia ... we shall never be a couple.'

Patrick nodded miserably said haltingly, 'Then ... this must be goodbye, Sarah.' At the door he turned to look at her one last time then reluctantly he stumbled from the cottage that he had once thought would be their home.

Tears of heartbreak and despair ached in his throat and flowed in rivers down his cheeks.

Chapter 21

❖

Judith pulled her legs up, heels on the edge of the chair and wrapping her arms round her shins, she glared over her knees at everyone in the room. Her eyes, flicking from one to the other, glittered with a look of maniacal triumph.

Sarah huddled on the floor motionless. Her body rigid, her weight on outstretched arms, she let her head hang. Her world had just shattered, and she could think of no way to put it back together.

Mary, watching with the most awful tearing feeling in her own heart, felt she had never in her life seen such utter defeat and dejection in anyone. It brought back to her memories of the agonising misery she had suffered with each of her lost babes.

'Come on, love. Come and sit on the chair,' she said quietly. Bending, she gripped her friend's arm to gently help her to her feet.

Sarah stayed unmoved, apparently oblivious of the other woman. Tears streamed down her cheeks to spill, unnoticed, leaving dark splashes on the floor.

Mary looked up at her husband, a silent plea in eyes that gleamed with unshed tears. James, reading her mind, moved to Sarah's other side and between them they gently eased her to her feet, guiding her to a chair.

Judith watched impassively, still curled up on the chair in the foetal position, rocking gently back and forth. The last thread that had held her to sanity seemingly snapped.

Mary made a pot of hot camomile tea, pressing a mug of it into Sarah's hands. 'Come on, love. Drink this up and it will make you feel better.'

Sarah looked up, her eyes distant and unrecognising for a moment. Then she shook her head, as though trying to jolt her thoughts into some sort of order. Biting down on trembling lips she said, 'We shouldn't have brought him here, Mary. We should have known.' Sarah looked at her mother, then closed her eyes, shutting out the pain of what she saw.

'We couldn't have known. She seemed alright and appeared to understand how important it was. Her consideration was for you. Your happiness. She told me to bring him, didn't she, Jos?' Mary looked up at the young man, who nodded unhappily.

'Well the damage is done now.' James quietly took control. 'There is no point in self-recriminations. What's done is done. Not one of us could have foreseen it. What we do have to decide is what's to be done now.'

'It's best if Patrick goes to Australia. Feelings fade with time and distance. He'll get over me.' Sarah's voice shook, her brown eyes brimming with tears. Pushing her thick mass of brown curls back from her face, she held it with both hands pressed to the crown of her head while she struggled to control her emotions.

'But what of you?' Mary asked gently.

Sarah shrugged. 'I shall stay here and look after my mother,' she replied emptily.

'This is no life for you. A young girl trapped here wasting her life caring for a–well for her!' Mary waved a shaky emotional arm in Judith's direction. 'You should have a husband and family and happiness. You deserve that!'

'No. I must put my mother first. She cared so well for us all these years; I must do the same for her. Besides I missed my flux this month, so I think I might have Patrick's child to care for too. If I can't have him, at least I'll have a part of him to love.'

This was spoken in such a matter-of-fact manner that it brought the room to total silence. All eyes were on Sarah. Shocked, wondering if they had heard correctly, or whether she might not be serious about it. The only person seemingly unmoved was Judith, though her head twitched a couple of times and Sarah wondered if perhaps she was taking in some of the conversation.

'Then you must send your mother to hospital and marry Patrick if that is the case.'

There was, Sarah thought, almost a trace of relief in Mary's voice.

'No. I cannot leave her, and Patrick cannot come here to live. Mam would be unable to look after herself in her present state. I must stay and care for her here. I fear that if she was taken away, they would lock her in Castle Rushen with the other–with the lunatics and evil people. I couldn't do that to her.'

Mary nodded understandingly. 'No. I would never have been able to treat my mother so. But something must be done. Patrick must know about the child.'

Sarah shook her head vehemently and refused to allow them to tell Patrick. It would be unfair for him to know, she told them, for then he would refuse to leave. He would waste the rest of his life waiting and yearning for something that could never happen. If he knew nothing of the child he could go off to Australia, get rich and find happiness. His life must not be ruined too.

In the end they all promised, though reluctantly, that Patrick would not learn of her pregnancy.

'I wonder,' Mary said hesitantly, 'if it might be safer for the childher if they were to come and live with James an' me until your mother is stronger in her mind.'

Startled, Sarah studied her friend for a moment. 'Do you not think they are safe here?'

Mary lowered her eyes and shuffled her feet in discomfort. 'I think it is possible your Mam might become violent if one of them said the wrong thing. With you at work all day they would have no one to protect them.'

Sarah thought about it for a moment, then nodded. 'Yes. It is possible. But what about James?' She looked up questioningly at James, who smiled and nodded.

'I think Mary is right. They would be safer with us for the time being. We get on well with them and I enjoy their company.'

With that agreed, the children's few meagre belongings were packed up and they moved down the hill to crowd into Mary and James' homely cottage.

If Judith noticed, she made no objection.

With the mines prospering, Jos easily found himself a job on the washing-floors, shovelling ore. For although one leg was weak and twisted, his back and arms were powerful. Still lodging with Mary, he walked with her and Sarah to work each morning, always offering friendship and encouragement. In the weeks that followed, Jos often went to the croft. It pained him to see what had befallen George's family and he enjoyed helping in every way he could, working hard in the fields and with the livestock to boost their income.

From the wages he earned in the mine, he paid Mary, not

only for his own expenses, but also for those of the three young Fayle children, which he suspected Mary undercharged for. If, indeed she charged anything.

What little was left of his wages he gave to Sarah to help her pay the rent for the croft. Reluctantly, but with gratitude, she accepted all he gave her and dearly valued his friendship. When she tried to tell him that he should be spending his wages on himself, he merely laughed.

'What would I do with money?' he asked. 'Like your father was until his death, I am a fugitive. Although I'm not known on the island, I dare not appear too much in public. I cannot go to the tavern, for instance, for fear someone might come who recognises me. So, I am happy to be here, where I am, useful I hope, liked for myself, and need not live in fear.'

'Even though you are trapped in a strange situation with a pregnant, unwed girl and,' Sarah shot a glance at her mother then finished with a sigh, 'with a mad woman?'

'Not mad — sick and unfortunate,' Jos corrected. 'And not trapped. Here by choice. Part of a family for the first time in my life. Albeit a strange one!' He finished with a rueful smile.

What a wonderful comfort and support he was, Sarah thought. He reminded her of her elder brother, George, who had been lost to the fever — was it only five years ago? What disasters had befallen them in such a short period of time.

One evening Jos and Sarah sat talking over a jar of jough. Judith had seemed more lucid that day, her eyes a little less vacant. But later she had withdrawn back into herself and now sat in the chair, curled into a tight ball.

'Do you think her mind might be mending?' Sarah watched her mother speculatively.

'We can only pray,' Jos replied without taking his eyes off Sarah. 'I saw Patrick today, you know.'

Sarah nodded, her heart slowing, beating with ponderous discomfort. Even the mention of his name still caused agony. 'I saw you talking to him.'

'He told me he was finishing at the mine today and leaving for England in ten days' time. He sails from Plymouth four days after that. He's suffering, Sarah. And I think it is made worse by his suspicion that there is something between you and me.'

'I can't help that.' Sarah drew in a shuddering breath and her vision blurred with unshed tears.

'He asked how you were.'

Sarah bit on trembling lips. 'You didn't tell him, did you? About the baby, I mean.'

Jos drew his breath in an angry, frustrated sigh. 'No, Sarah, I did not tell him. But only because I had promised you I would not. I really think he has a right to know, though. How do you think he will feel if he ever finds out he has a son or daughter and was not given the choice to stay here and get to know it? To help and have a say in its upbringing. To be a father. Do you not think he has that right?'

'I think he has a right to be happy, but he never will be that if he stays here. Besides, from what I'm told, gold mining is much safer than the search for lead and silver. He'll be far better off in Australia.' Her voice caught in her throat in a sob.

'Sarah ...' Judith's voice was a mere whisper.

Startled, Sarah looked round, to find her mother, her face an anguished mask, reaching a thin, trembling hand toward her. A tear trickled down her cheek, stopping at the corner of her mouth, and her tongue came out slowly to lick it away. A huge, racking sob shook her body and suddenly Sarah realised how painfully thin she had become.

'What is it, Mam? What's wrong?'

'I'm sorry, Sarah. So sorry,' she mumbled, then she fell again into her trance.

When Jos was leaving that night, he stood twisting his cap in his hand in the doorway, seeming unwilling to bid her farewell. 'I have an offer to make, Sarah.' He spoke quietly so that Judith would not overhear.

Sarah said nothing, but stood quietly waiting, while Jos shuffled his feet, trying uncomfortably to find the words he was seeking.

'I realise I'm nothing great,' he started, 'Being lame and a fugitive, but I'm not known on the island, so there is little risk I'll ever be recognised. And I wondered … well I hoped you might consider marrying me.' He finally raised his head to look into her eyes.

Sarah was startled for a moment, but quickly recovering her wits, she asked, 'Why, Jos?'

'Because I care for you. We get on well with each other. I think we could live happily together. I feel it would make life easier for you if we were wed and save you the embarrassment of a bastard child. That's not my thought, but the way other people will see it.'

Sarah smiled gently. 'One thing you did not mention was love.'

Jos shrugged, colour rising from his neck to his scalp. 'I said I cared for you.'

'The sort of feeling a brother has for a sister. The same way I care for you. Not the type of love that makes a marriage.'

'That might come with time.'

'Then if it does and if I feel the same about you that is when I shall marry you, and not before. Thank you though, for caring enough to offer. It means a lot to me.'

Jos nodded and smiled. 'Well the offer will always be there,' he said quietly.

When Sarah and Mary left work the following day, Richard was waiting for them on the viaduct looking agitated.

'This is an honour,' Mary joked as they approached him. 'A gentleman waiting to escort us safely home.'

Richard rushed toward them, an anxious look on his face. 'Mammy came to see me at school today,' he said as soon as they were close enough.

'Mam did?' Sarah felt her heart sink. This was the first time her mother had left the croft since George's funeral. 'Why did she go to the school? Where is she now?'

Jos joined the group, seeing from their faces that something was badly amiss.

'I don't know where she went.' Richard's eyes were dark and frightened. 'But she told me to tell you she's sorry and that she is going to make everything alright.'

Sarah felt her heart constrict with an almost overpowering stab of fear. Looking at Mary and Jos, she read concern in their eyes too.

'Did you see where she went when she left the school? Was she going home?' Sarah had gripped Richard's shoulders and he winced as she dug her fingers in a bit too hard.

'That hurts,' he complained, pulling away from her. 'I didn't see where she went, but I know it was not home because I can see the road from my classroom window.'

'She must be in the village then, unless she's gone home while Richard has been waiting here,' Jos said thoughtfully. 'Look, you go and see if you can find her in Laxey. I'll run up to the croft and look there.'

Being such a tiny village, the search of Laxey took no time at all. They had looked in the shop, the cafe and the tavern, without finding a trace. A few of the villagers they asked said they had seen her but were unsure of which direction she had taken.

'Perhaps we had better call at the police house, in the event that she has caused a disturbance and been arrested,' Sarah suggested forlornly.

Mary pulled a face. 'Is that likely? I don't like that Constable!'

'Neither do I!' Sarah agreed feelingly, remembering the attitude he had taken when Alexandra had gone missing. 'I think I must go there and ask though.'

'Aye.' Gritting her teeth, Mary glumly followed her friend to the police house.

'Every time I see you you've lost someone, girly. It would be the crazy woman from Agneash you're looking for this time would it?' The Constable leered over the desk at them.

'I'm looking for my mother,' Sarah said through clenched teeth, only just managing to stop herself clawing his eyes out. 'And she happens to be very sick — not crazy!'

'Looks crazy to me, the man sneered. Passed me a couple of hours ago. Talking non-stop and no one near to hear her.'

'You saw her?'

The man nodded, laughing to himself at the memory.

'Well where was she going? In which direction?'

'Out on the Douglas road. She's mebbe gone after that doxy!'

'Douglas?' Sarah and Mary looked at each other in puzzlement. 'Walking or by coach?'

The Constable laughed. 'You don't believe they would ever let that one on the coach, do you? If you do, you're as mad as she is.'

'Why would she be going to Douglas? And what did he mean about the doxy?' Sarah asked when they were back out in the street again.

Mary shook her head. "Tis beyond my understanding. But she told Richard she was going to make everything alright for you, so perhaps she thought she would go off to Douglas so that you could live your own life. He probably just mentioned Alexandra because he knew she was your sister.'

'Run away from home, you mean?' asked Sarah incredulously. Thoughts of Alexandra quickly washed from her mind.

Mary shrugged helplessly.

'Then if she has, we must go after her. There is no possibility she would be able to cope alone.'

At that moment they saw Jos running toward them, a look of horror on his face, waving a piece of paper.

Catching his panic, Sarah ran to meet him. 'What is it, Jos? What's wrong?'

'She–um, she left a note, Sarah.'

'A note?' The girl could already feel a black foreboding closing in. 'What does it say?' she whispered hoarsely.

'Simply that she knows what a mess she is making of your life. So, she is going where she can be happy and at peace to join your father and her other four children.'

Sarah stared blankly at him for quite some time unable, or unwilling, to comprehend. When the brutal truth struck home, she turned to look along the road that led to Douglas. Her stomach clenched in sick anxiety.

'The cliffs!' Sarah whispered with certainty. 'She's gone over the headland!'

'Maybe not.' Mary said without conviction, moving to put her arm around her friend. 'Don't go jumping to conclusions.'

'We must find her and bring her home,' Sarah said calmly. Mary eyed her a little uncertainly, until she added, 'We can't leave her lying out there. Will you tell the Constable please, Jos?'

Forgetting for the moment his fear of the law, Jos obeyed.

*　*　*

After the funeral, Sarah stood looking at the mound of earth, with the little wooden cross Jos had made. He had polished it and burned her mother's name into it.

'It looks well,' she said quietly, smiling up at him. 'Thank you so much.'

His dark blue eyes looked anxiously back. 'Are you alright, Sarah?'

'Aye. Thank you. But why do you ask?'

'You have seemed so unnaturally calm since your mother's death. Cheerful almost. I know how much you loved her though. You were prepared to sacrifice everything for her. Yet you have never shed a tear for her; nor even shown much sign of distress.'

Sarah thought about it for a moment. 'No, Jos. Nor shall I. For if the truth be told, I'm relieved! I miss her, and I'm sorry she had to leave so violently. But I'm pleased for her sake. Fate had turned her into an unhappy, empty shell, and there would have been no happiness in the future for her. I know she would never have recovered — and so did she. So, she took herself to join my father and my brothers and sisters. She will be with them by now, and she will be happy again. All we put in the ground was the empty shell. I'm glad they're all together again. Mam loved them so much.'

'I'm relieved you can see it that way. It makes it so much easier for you to bear. I brought someone with me today who wants to talk to you.'

'Who?' Sarah frowned up at Jos.

'Over there.' Jos pointed toward the horse-chestnut tree in the corner of the grave-yard.

There stood Patrick, nervously stripping bark from a thin branch with his thumbnail. He straightened as she approached unconsciously tugging his coat into a tidier shape.

'Hello,' was all she could think of to say. Suddenly she felt unreasonably shy with him.

'Sarah, I had to come when I heard,' his tone almost apologetic. 'How did you know?'

'Jos told me. He walked over to Baldrine this morning. I didn't come into the church because I wasn't sure how she would have felt about having an Irishman there.'

'I'm so glad you came. I've wanted you so.' Sarah moved close to Patrick and with a groan of pleasure, he drew her into his arms.

For a fleeting moment, from the corner of her eye, she caught a glimpse of a figure in the far corner of the cemetery. She turned her head, but whoever it was had melted into the trees.

Sarah and Patrick sat in the cottage kitchen a few hours later.

'I know it is early days, and not long since you buried your mother, but I have not much time to make up my mind about the future. I am very sad for you that she has gone, but I also need you. I love you with all my heart and I need to know if you will marry me. *Please*?' He held her hands and looked pleadingly into her eyes.

'Oh, Patrick!' Sarah's love shone back at him. 'I love you too, but there are so many things to think about and you are leaving for Australia in a few days.' She shook her head in bewilderment. 'And there is something else I have to tell you before anything can be decided.'

'Yes?' Patrick waited, watching warily, trying to read what was on her mind.

'I'm sorry, I hope this is not too much of a shock, but I have thought about this a lot and I have to tell you I am with child.'

Patrick drew a sharp breath. Stunned into silence for a moment. 'With child? How? When?'

'Well, you know how, and I think you probably know when.' Sarah looked anxiously into his eyes. 'The important thing is how do you feel about it?'

'How I feel? You are going to make me a father and you ask

how I feel? There is only one way I can feel. Excited! Joyful! That's two ways isn't it? It's wonderful! Now you *must* marry me! We shall be a family!' Drawing her into his arms he kissed her.

'But what about Australia?'

'What about Australia? I want you to come there with me. It would be a whole new start for us. Away from all the troubles and nastiness we would never be able to escape if we stayed here, on this small island with all its gossipmongers.'

'Oh, Patrick I would love to come with you, but there are the childher to consider. Would we have the money to take them all?' Sarah's heart was leaping with joy, but also apprehension. There were so many things to consider.

Patrick sighed and shook his head. 'I don't know. I have no idea of how much their fares would be.'

'What's this about the childher?' Mary came bustling into the room, trying to look as if she had not been eavesdropping. A mention of the younger Fayles was more than she could let pass.

'Patrick wishes to wed me immediately and carry me off to Australia with him. But I can't go off and leave the children,' Sarah cried in anguish.

'Yes you can, you silly girl. You can leave them with us. They can be the childher James and I have always yearned for and could never have. We are all fond of each other and get on well together. If Patrick can arrange passage for you at this late date — go. You'll be there before the child is due, won't you?'

Patrick's head snapped up. 'I hadn't thought of that; I've heard tell it can be a six-month journey. We can leave it a year or two if you like?'

Sarah adamantly shook her head. 'It's now or never, Patrick O'Malley. I don't want you down that lead mine again.' Turning to Mary, she quietly asked, 'Are you sure about the children? I know they love you.'

'And I, them. I have never been surer of anything in my life.'
'And James——?'
'Will agree with me!'

<h1 style="text-align:center">Chapter 22</h1>

J ames looked up in surprise as the little party trooped into the cottage.

'What's all this then?' he raised his eyebrows questioningly.

'Well, to cut a long story short, Patrick has yet again asked Sarah to marry him and he wants her to go skylarking off to Australia with him!'

James' nodded his agreement. 'What a great idea,' he enthused. 'You would have a far better chance of happiness away from this village and its gossips.'

'An' I told Sarah we would be happy to have the childher, so they wouldn't have them to worry about. You're alright with that are you?'

James' face lit up. 'You know I am. More than just alright. Thrilled! This place has always lacked the laughter of childher — until now! We will love to have them.'

'We'll send you money whenever we can,' Sarah volunteered.

'Indeed, you will not!' James said sternly. 'We have always put money aside for the childher we would have one day. Now we will have them. You youngsters will need all the money you can get.'

'Well, now all that's settled, the lass quite rightly wants to know a bit more about this wilderness full of convicts he wants to take her to. You've heard quite a lot about it, so I thought maybe you would tell her what you know,' Mary encouraged.

James nodded and drew a deep breath. 'Aye. I don't know a lot, but I'll tell you what I'll do, Sarah. You can ask me questions, but I don't promise to be able to answer them all.'

Sarah shrugged and gave a rueful smile. 'I don't know where to start, James. So please just tell me what you do know, and some questions may come to mind.'

'Okay then,' James took time to fill and light his pipe before putting in place his best storytelling face. Rubbing his chin thoughtfully, he started. 'It was discovered by a Captain Cook, who was wandering around the world charting the oceans. They reckon this Cook fellow was probably the best seaman in sailing history. Anyway, I think Australia was called New Holland then.'

'Why New Holland?' Patrick broke in.

'Well, I heard as how the Dutch had already discovered it, but they didn't want it. Then this Captain Cook found it, in about the year 1770, I think. Being as how the English think they have to own every piece of land they set their eyes on, they said, "this is ours now" and grabbed it.' He broke his narrative for a moment to have a satisfying drag on his pipe and to ask Mary to make him a cup of camomile, the talking being thirsty work.

'Anyway, he'd been about three years charting oceans and he just sort of stumbled across the east coast of Australia. Endeavour, I think his ship was called. He landed, on the 29th April in a place he called Botany Bay, planted England's flag on the beach there and claimed the country for England.'

'Wow! I heard it was full of convicts. So, what about them? Where do they come into it?' Patrick asked, his brow furrowed in a frown.

'Well you see, England had more prisoners than they had jails for an' they used to ship them off to America to get rid of them. Then there was some big revolution over there in, I think it was about 1776. After that they couldn't send their prisoners over there no more and the jails got terrible overcrowded. Then in 1779 this fellow, Sir Joseph Banks, had the bright idea to start a substitute penal settlement in Botany Bay and send thousands of convicts over there to get rid of the overcrowding in the jails.'

'There must be a lot of crime in England if the jails are so overcrowded,' Mary tutted, shaking her head.

'Well you've got to remember, lass, that you can be thrown in jail for stealing a little bit of food just to keep yourself alive. That's why a lot of the folk were locked up. In them days if you stole anything worth more than thirty-nine shillings you got hanged. Well — men did — they burned women at the stake!'

When his audience all gasped and paled, James felt perhaps he had given just a bit too much information. 'Now where was I?' he quickly continued. 'Anyway, it took a few years, but in 1787 the government agreed to send their excess convicts to this new colony. I think the idea was that they could be put to work to help free settlers to build their houses, make roads and prepare land for farming. And to help with the farm work and any other kind of labour they may be needed for. Then when their sentences was finished, they could apply for a grant of land and get on with their own lives.'

James' audience were held in thrall, watching him wide-eyed. He was always good to spin a yarn, so no one was quite sure just how close to the truth his story was.

'Next thing was, because they were short of space in the jails, they started holding the prisoners in the rotting ships that were no longer fit to go to sea. They were kept in shackles, in the depths of the ships. Long rows of these rotting, dismasted ships there were; right near London Bridge, an' some in Portsmouth too, I think. There was the most awful stench coming from them. And they reckoned the cries from the prisoners inside them were like sounds from Hell. 'The Hulks', they called them. There were rats and lice and fleas. The prisoners were wet most of the time and with no heating even in the middle of winter. Stands to reason a lot of them died while they waited for the ships to be ready to take them to Australia.'

Mary shook her head and tutted again. 'Those poor people,' she said quietly.

James nodded his agreement, then went on with his story. 'In April 1787 a Captain Phillips, what had been chosen to be Governor of this new colony, set sail with a fleet of eleven ships. Some of them of them was merchant ships, hired by the government for only ten shillings per ton per month. There was about fifteen hundred folks on those ships. Some were marines and their families. Crewmen of course an' nearly eight hundred of them was convicts, mostly in shackles in the hold. It took them eight months or more to get there and quite a lot of them died on the way. A few babies were born on the way too!'

Sarah shuddered at the thought of that. Eight months chained up in a creaking, rolling ship! It hardly bore thinking about.

'When they got to Botany Bay Captain Phillips didn't like the soil. It wasn't as rich and fertile as he had been led to believe, so he went a few miles north and found a nice river with richer soil and decided to start the settlement there. Sydney, I think it's called — the settlement.'

'Oh, dear God! All those months chained up in the belly of a ship!' Patrick's eyes were moist. 'No matter what they did against the law, they didn't deserve that.'

James nodded. 'They did not, indeed. And many of them

were not much more than children, locked up for stealing a loaf of bread just to stop from starving.'

Sarah started sobbing at this revelation and Patrick moved to put his arm around her.

'I heard they kept on sending convicts out there for about thirty-five years or more. So, a lot of the people living there are descended from convicts. A lot of them was rough alright, but most probably many had done next to nothing wrong. A lot of prostitutes were sent out too, so Sydney was a pretty rough place for a long time. An' the regiment that was sent out to keep order was called the 'Rum Corps' on account of there was no money for a long time. Rum was the revenue an' that's what they were all paid in. Yes, a rough place!' James clamped his lips together and nodded his head.

Sarah sat in stunned silence for a moment then, shaking her head, she said, 'Oh, Patrick, I don't think I want to go to such a place.'

Patrick was also looking shaken. 'I didn't know it was so bad,' he finally managed to say. 'Where did you hear all this, James?'

'Friend of mine, Jack. His father's uncle, or such likes, was sent out there for something and nothing. Well his uncle reckoned a lot the convicts on his ship perished on the voyage because the captain was a devil of a man and hardly gave them any food. At times they was left chained to corpses for days before they was taken away and chucked overboard. They were all those months chained in the bowels of the ship and never saw a chink of daylight in all that time.'

The people in the room stared at the floor in shock. None of them able to meet the others' eyes.

'The country has grown a lot since then,' James broke the silence. 'You wouldn't have to go to Sydney. There are quite a lot of other places to go.'

'Robert and I were going to go to a place called Ballarat to look for gold. I guess that will probably be well away from Sydney, would it not?'

James drew his lower lip between his teeth and thoughtfully chewed on it. 'Well, Jack was talking about the gold mines too. He reckoned they's rough places. They live in tent towns and beat each other and kill sometimes if they know one has found gold. The only women there are prostitutes the miners have taken there to give them their comforts.'

Patrick drew in a deep, shuddering breath. 'I'd never heard any of this before. Are you sure your friend wasn't just making it up?'

James looked offended and shook his head. 'Nope! And on top of all that they have what they call bushrangers. We would call them highwaymen here, I suppose. They're likely to stop you on the road and rob you. Or shoot you!'

Mary tutted and stamped her foot in anger. 'Then a goldfield is no place to take Sarah. No better than Sydney, by the sound of things, 'specially with a little one on the way!'

'No. I can see that,' Patrick agreed. 'I must find out if there are safer places in the country to go, where I could find work.'

'Well, Jack said something about a new colony, further west, which has no convicts. The folk there are all free settlers — respectable people. And he said there were copper and silver mines there. That might be worth finding out about. South Australia, they call it.'

Patrick's spirits lifted. That sounded a promising prospect. 'Thanks, James. I'll have to look into that. And tomorrow I'll have to tell Robert I won't be going with him.'

Immediately the atmosphere in the room lifted. 'I'll put the kettle on,' Mary said cheerfully, 'and drink a toast to the bride and groom to be.'

'And I must cancel my booking to Sydney and start gathering information about South Australia. It sounds a far safer place to be than Sydney or the goldfields.'

Patrick watched for Robert arriving in the morning and pulled him aside. 'I have news for you,' he said quietly, 'and I hope it won't disappoint you too much.'

Robert looked at him quizzically. 'I think I might know what you are about to say but go on.'

'You know they buried Sarah's Mam yesterday?'

'Aye.'

'Well, her Mam was the only thing stopping her from marrying me. Now she has agreed to wed.'

Robert's face lit up. 'That's great news. Will she come with us to Ballarat?'

Patrick shook his head. 'No. Please keep this to yourself, but she tells me she is with child. I feel it would be unsafe for her to give birth while we're at sea, so I will have to delay my voyage until after the babe is born.'

Robert frowned. 'But your passage is booked. If you don't go the Australian government might make you pay the fare. Then they might not allow you free passage in the future.'

With a shrug, Patrick told him, 'Well if that's the way it must be then I shall just have to stay here until I have saved enough for three fares.'

Shaking his head Robert said, 'I thought with that doxy being back you would want to get out of Laxey as quickly as possible.'

'What doxy?'

'Sarah's sister! Alexandra was it?'

'Alexandra! Back in Laxey? How do you know?'

'I saw her a night or two ago hanging around outside the inn. I thought you would know.'

Patrick felt his stomach clench. *Alexandra back?* How could she dare show her face, knowing that she had been responsible for her father's death?

'Oh, dear God! Sarah can't know about this or she would have told me. How will she feel? I will have to make sure to avoid her sister.'

'Perhaps you would do well to think again about whether to sail when we planned to. If we speak to the agent, he might be able to arrange for Sarah to come with us.'

Patrick shook his head. 'No, I would love to take Sarah away from this place right this minute, but I can't risk her life, or the babe's. I must stay and just make sure I keep well away from Alexandra.'

Robert pursed his lips and gave a slight shrug. 'I guess I can see your point, but I'm sorry you won't be with me on my big adventure. I was looking forward to us getting rich together. You wouldn't think of coming to Australia with me as planned and coming back for Sarah and the child when we have struck gold? he asked hopefully.

Patrick gave a determined shake of his head. 'No. I cannot leave her when she will have most need of me here.'

Robert gave a rueful smile. 'I suppose I would have thought less of you if you had said yes, but I'll be saddened to go without you.' Giving Patrick a friendly punch on the shoulder he added, 'We must keep in touch and maybe some time in the future we can meet up again.'

'Aye,' Patrick agreed. 'There's nothing I'd like better.'

Sarah, when told of Alexandra's return, lost all colour and collapsed into a chair. 'You're sure it was her? Have you seen her?' she asked in a hoarse whisper.

Patrick shook his head. 'I have not seen her myself, but Robert has. He had no doubt it was her.'

Sarah was thoughtful for a moment. 'I have just remembered, after my Mam's funeral I thought I saw someone right over in the far corner of the graveyard. It was only for an instant and she had vanished before I was even sure. I wonder, now, if that could have been Alexandra.'

Patrick nodded mutely, and his heart sank ever further. Why, he wondered, had that little demon returned? Surely, she must know how the last remnants of her family must feel about her? The sooner he and Sarah could escape from Laxey the better. Unfortunately, that could not be for some time.

Patrick went to see the migration agent, John Quirk, who had arranged his and Robert's passages to New South Wales. The agent was not too happy about his change of heart, but seeing the possibility of future business, he took it well and went out of his way to try to be helpful.

From John, Patrick obtained a lot of promising information about South Australia.

'Yes,' John told him. 'There is a fairly large colony called South Australia, which is growing quite rapidly. The city, if you would call it such, is called Adelaide. It's quite a new city.'

'Is it populated by convicts too, do you know?' This was really Patrick's main concern.

'No, from what I've heard no prisoners at all were sent there. There are convict settlements I know in Swan River, at the western end of the country, and on an island called — em — I think it's Van Diemen's Land — or something like. By the time South Australia was founded they had stopped sending convicts out there. It is free settlers who form the population of South Australia. From what I have heard it is a happier, safer and more settled place than any of the other colonies.'

It seemed to Patrick that John was quite enthused by this infant state.

'I believe they are keen to have tradesmen and farmers, to build the state into a worthwhile community and from what I've heard they seem to be making a pretty good job of it,' John chattered on happily.

'How about mines and miners? Are there any gold mines there and, if so, what are the living conditions in the mining communities?' Patrick was starting to get good feelings about South Australia.

John scratched his head and looked thoughtful. 'I don't know about gold, but I've heard tell of copper, silver and lead. But now I think of it I think I did hear there was a gold mine there at one time, but I don't think there was much in it. Might still be going, but there was no big rush there like there was in the east.'

Patrick nodded thoughtfully. 'Thanks, John, that gives me plenty to think about. I'll talk it over with Sarah and see how she feels about it all. I should imagine she'll like the sound of that better than the goldfields in Victoria.'

Patrick stepped out of John's office, excited and in a hurry to get home to tell Sarah all he had learned. This sounded like the right place for them to go.

A hand grabbed his arm as he stepped down from John's doorway.

'Hello, Patrick. Have you missed me?'

He looked down and his heart missed a beat before it plummeted down into the depths of his belly.

'Well. Aren't you going to talk to me?' Alexandra smiled up at him.

Patrick shook his head vehemently. 'I have nothing to say to you, Alexandra. Nor does any of your family.'

Alexandra shrugged. 'I'm not interested in any of my family. Just you.'

Patrick snorted. 'I have no interest in you whatsoever. So just stay away from me. And from Sarah!'

Alexandra grasped his shirt and pushed herself hard up against him. 'I could make you interested. You were once before, and you would enjoy me more than that lump of ice you think you love.'

Patrick felt the bile rise in his throat. Gripping Alexandra's wrists he tore her hands free of his shirt and pushed her roughly away from him. 'Stay away from us, Alexandra,' he snarled. Turning quickly, he hurried away.

'You will be sorry!' Alexandra screamed behind him. 'I'll make you sorry you ever turned me away!'

Shaking, Patrick strode angrily up the hill to Agneash. He wouldn't, he decided, he *couldn't* upset Sarah by telling her of the encounter. The sooner they got out of this God-forsaken village the better he would like it.

Patrick was right. Sarah did like the sound of South Australia. In fact, she got quite excited at the idea of it. A new life. In a new country, where no one would know anything of her past. Where no one would know she was the daughter of the crazy woman of Agneash.

Mary was visiting with Sarah when Patrick arrived and listened as he enthused about South Australia. She sat looking thoughtful for a while. 'Just think well first,' she advised. 'Don't go rushing headlong and maybe find yourselves in trouble. Remember you've got a babby due in six months, and it takes a long time to get to this new land. It wouldn't do to be in the middle of the ocean, maybe in a storm, when the babby comes along!'

Patrick and Sarah looked at each other in thoughtful silence.

'And first things first,' Mary continued. 'First of all, you've got to get wed. So the sooner you sees the vicar gets that fixed up the better! Then you've got to decide whether you go before the babby or after.'

Patrick nodded. 'Aye. I'll see the vicar in the morning and get it fixed for as soon as he'll do it.'

After Mary had gone home, Sarah and Patrick talked long into the night. They would both have loved to pack their few belongings and leave straight away. Laxey had too many unhappy memories for Sarah and she would be relieved to put the place behind her.

Patrick, however, had his feet more firmly on the ground. 'No, love,' he said quietly. 'We've got to remember you're with child. The voyage will probably be at least four months, even if the winds are favourable. And the high seas are not a safe place for a pregnant woman. Not a safe place for you to bring a child into the world, and even less safe for the baby. Even if we left straight away it would be too big a risk.'

'I know you're right, Patrick, though it would just be so nice to get away from here. Especially now Alexandra is back.' Sarah still felt sad at times when she thought of Alexandra. She had loved her little sister once and wondered how she could have gone so far wrong. What had happened to twist her mind so? Did she still love her? Sarah wasn't sure, but she didn't think so.

Bringing her thoughts back to their conversation she agreed, 'Yes, I think we must stay until after my confinement.' Sarah nodded and in her eyes was excitement mixed with a little shadow of fear.

'Well, when I come to think of it, it is likely we wouldn't get booked on a ship for some months to come anyway,' Patrick said thoughtfully. 'I'll see the agent again tomorrow and see what more I can find out.'

Sarah nodded, her eyes glowing with hope for the future.

'Maybe we had best wait until the babby is a few months old. Give it time to get a little strength before the long voyage.'

Patrick smiled and took her in his arms. 'In the meantime, my love?' He looked toward the bedroom. Sarah smiled, and nodded. After kissing her soundly, Patrick picked her up and carried her to bed.

The marriage was held two weeks later, with only Mary and James, the three young Fayles and a handful of friends in the chapel. Mary put on the wedding breakfast and afterwards the happy young couple walked up the hill to the croft in newly wedded bliss.

A shadowy figure watched from just beyond the tree line. Her pretty face made ugly by a mask of jealousy.

* * *

Sarah and Mary trudged up the hill in a steady July downpour. Mary could see that Sarah was exhausted, so took her arm to make sure she did not slip and fall on the rough road. With the baby due in just a month, it would not do to take risks. Mary and Patrick had both tried to persuade Sarah to give up work; it was too heavy a job for a woman in late pregnancy; but the girl had insisted they must save as much money as possible toward their new life.

'Aye, well, money's not everything,' Mary kept grumbling, with her lips clamped tightly between her teeth. She looked at Sarah now, not liking what she was seeing. The girl looked worn out and looked to be carrying a large baby, very low.

Sarah rubbed her back and stretched. 'I'll be stopping work in a week. I'm getting too tired to stay on my feet all those hours every day,' she said wearily.

'Aye, and heavy work at that!' Mary eyed her warily, concerned about the looks of her. 'You go on inside and put your feet up. I'll bring you down a bowl of broth in a while.'

Sarah stumbled wearily into the cottage and dumped her bulk in the worn-out old chair. Only a month to go, she thought, then this burden would be out for her to love. A sudden sharp pain made her catch her breath. It had her wincing and worrying. Just a bit of a twinge, she told herself. It couldn't be the babby yet. It was too soon. *Just a twinge.*

Suddenly, the door was flung open and to Sarah's horror Alexandra stood there looking down at her with a sneer on her face.

She looks old, was her first thought. Old and hard. Life has not treated her well. 'Why are you here?' she asked angrily. 'You were responsible for Mam and Daa's death. You are not wanted here. Leave my house.'

'I'm here to do you a favour. To let you know what sort of a man you have married.'

Sarah felt another twinge, which kept her sitting while her sister stood over her. 'I know what sort of man I married. The best, the kindest and most loving man that walks God's earth. So, whatever you have come to say, leave it unsaid and take it away with you. This minute!'

Alexandra gave a harsh laugh. 'Well, I just thought you would want to know that before I went away Patrick caught me in the lane and forced hisself on me!'

At that moment Mary arrived with the soup and overheard. She saw Sarah, her eyes wide with horror and shock. Dumping the bowl hurriedly on the table, she turned on Alexandra. Grabbing her by her hair, she dragged her outside.

'You evil, lying little monster. Stay away from Sarah. Stay away from Patrick and get out of this village. Get back to Douglas! If I see you anywhere near here again, you'll be the next one to go over the cliff!'

Alexandra faced up to her for a moment but when Mary took a step toward her, she turned and fled.

Mary watched until Alexandra was out of sight, then went back into the cottage. She found Sarah curled in the chair almost chewing on her knuckles and rushed to kneel beside the girl and pull her hand from her mouth.

'What is it my lovely?'

'What Alexandra said——.'

'Was a pack of lies and you know it as well as I do.'

Sarah nodded sadly. 'Why did she do it? Why did she say those things?'

'Because she's jealous, my lovely. Because you have what she would like and knows she will never have. You have Patrick, you have his love and very soon you will have his babby.'

Sarah looked at her through frightened, tear-filled eyes. 'The babby!' she said, 'I think it's coming, but it's too soon.'

'Dear God!' Mary gripped her hand. 'When will Patrick be home?'

'Not for many hours,' Sarah sobbed. 'He'll be on the bottom.'

Mary drew in a deep breath. 'Well he can't be reached then. How near together are your pains?'

'About ten minutes apart. I'm scared, Mary!'

'No need to be,' Mary, sensible as ever, took charge. 'I'll send your Richard to find Voirrey Crellin, she's a good woman. Had about ten of her own and delivered dozens of others.' She rose to leave.

'Don't leave me, Mary!' Sarah cried in terror and tried to grab her arm.

'Hush, my lovely,' Mary reached to give her hand a reassuring squeeze. 'I'm just going to send Richard. I'll only be gone minutes.'

'What's all this about?' A large lady exploded into the room half an hour later. 'Got a young lad here who arrived banging on my door in a panic.'

'Thank heaven you're here, Voirrey, and thanks for coming so quick,' Mary heaved herself to her feet and waddled to meet the newcomer. 'You know Sarah, do you?'

'I've seen her about.' Voirrey moved to kneel beside Sarah. Laying her hand on the girl's sweating forehead she said gently, 'There's no need to be frightened. I'll see you through this.'

'It's too early. It's not due for another month,' Sarah's breath caught on a sob and tears scorched in her throat.

'Well, you know, babby's can't read calendars too well. They come when they're ready,' Voirrey said matter-of-factly. 'They don't know nothin' about dates. Now let's look at you. I'll help you to the bed, so I can better see how far on you are.'

Mary had already prepared the bed for the delivery and had plenty of water boiling on the stove.

Voirrey had a quick look, then nodded knowingly. 'Not too far away. Let's have a bit of a feel then.' Putting her hands on Sarah's distended belly, she squeezed and kneaded gently, but enough to make Sarah groan.

Stepping back, Voirrey frowned and shook her head.

'What's wrong?' Sarah read her expression and felt a stab of panic.

'Well, we've got a bit of a problem, but I reckon I'll be able to fix it. Babby's wrong way round and coming bottom first. So, I've got to turn it. It won't be comfortable, so you'll have to be brave.'

Turning to Mary she said quietly, 'We've got to get her bottom in the air. Find anything and everything you can to put under her bum to raise it.'

'Now, little lady,' she turned her attention back to Sarah, 'I've got to push this little 'un back up where he's coming from and turn him right way round, 'cos he can't come out folded in two.'

Using sheets, towels, pillows and clothes the two women

quickly raised Sarah's bottom. With strong, well-practiced hands, Voirrey worked between the contractions to push the baby back and turn its head down.

Sarah bit on the cloth Mary had put between her teeth, crushed Mary's hand and tried hard not to scream.

After what seemed a lifetime of agony, the baby was in the right position and within minutes it slid into the world. It was tiny boy. Blue and limp!

Mary put a hand to her lips and whispered, 'Oh dear God!'

Voirrey picked the baby up by its legs and swung it, as Mary had seen shepherds do with lambs. Then pressing her lips to his, she blew gently into his mouth.

Sarah and Mary watched in horror, hardly daring to breath. Instinctively trying to breathe for the baby.

Voirrey continued patiently for several minutes until, finally, the baby gave a quiet cough, clenched his fists and tried a tired cry.

Sarah burst into tears and Mary whispered, 'Thank you God. Thank you, dear, dear God. And thank you Voirrey.'

'He's so tiny,' Sarah murmured. Suddenly she drew in a breath and groaned. 'The pain is back!'

'That will the afterbirth coming,' Voirrey said confidently. 'On second thoughts,' she continued cheerfully, when she had examined Sarah, 'It's another babby! Double trouble, my lady.'

The second baby, to everyone's relief, arrived head first and without any trouble. It vented its anger on the world quite lustily the moment it entered it.

'Pigeon pair!' Voirrey whooped happily as she cleaned the howling baby girl and laid her gently in her mother's arms.

Sarah looked, with a mixture of anxiety and joy, at the two tiny babies she held. 'So tiny,' she whispered. 'I didn't know a baby could be so tiny.'

Six hours later Patrick staggered in, exhausted from a long shift underground, to find himself confronted by three smiling women and two tiny babies.

The boy, who was named George Patrick weighed in at just over three pounds and the girl, Judith Claire at just under five pounds.

George was a sickly baby at first, but slowly rallied and in time he started to catch up with his robust, lively sister.

For a time, until George's health started to pick up, all thought of Australia was shelved. In October, with the twins thriving Patrick and Sarah felt the time was right.

Richard and the two girls were happily settled with Mary and James, so Sarah had no qualms about leaving them. Except, of course, that she loved them and would miss them terribly, though she knew that her future now was with Patrick and the twins in Australia.

Patrick talked with John Quirk and asked him to find out what ships there were going to Australia early in the next year.

John quickly came back with the news that there was one, quite a good-sized ship — *Tantivy*, a 1040 tons burthen — sailing from Liverpool on the 25th February 1857.

Both Sarah and Patrick were excited by this. It would be so much easier to sail from Liverpool instead of having the long and tiring trip to London or Plymouth. So they were upset and disappointed when John Quirk told them, a few days later that there were no berths remaining untaken on the *Tantivy*. The next ship that would be sailing to Port Adelaide would be a much smaller one — the 493-ton *Navarino*, which would be sailing from Plymouth in April.

After a long discussion and a lot of soul searching, Sarah and Patrick decided they had put this new future off long enough and it was time to bite the bullet. They did not much relish the journey to Plymouth, but it could be a long time before there was another sailing to Port Adelaide from Liverpool.

With a mixture of fear and excitement they booked their passage and started making their preparations.

Chapter 23

✦——◇——✦

The *Navarino* was due to sail on the 8th April. John Quirk got their bookings in place then laughingly presented Sarah and Patrick with a long list of do's and don'ts.

The young couple read it and shook their heads, while Mary and James fell about laughing.

'Is this a joke? They can't really be serious, can they?' Mary asked.

'It says,' started Patrick, 'That I must find my own outfit and I have to have at least six shirts, six pairs of stockings, two warm flannel shirts, two pairs of new shoes or boots, two complete suits, strong exterior clothing, four towels and 2lb of marine soap! That's more clothes than I've ever owned in my life! And where am I going to find marine soap? And what is it anyway?'

Sarah took the sheets of paper from him and drew a deep breath. 'And I must have six shifts, two flannel petticoats, six pairs of stockings, two pairs of strong boots or shoes, two strong gowns — one of which must be made of a warm material — four towels and 2lb of marine soap.'

'They must think you're going to get awful dirty,' Mary giggled.

'Oh, look,' Sarah continued, 'It says here that if we can't find any marine soap, we'll be able to buy it at the depot when we get there. And it says too, Patrick, that it would be a good idea if you got a few coloured shirts and I should take an extra supply of flannel for myself and the twins.'

Mary, still laughing, took the papers as she wiped the tears from her eyes. 'Did you see how much luggage you're permitted to take? You can only take twenty cubic feet each, however much that is, and it's not to be more than half a ton in weight. It must be closely packed in strong boxes or cases no more than fifteen cubic feet each. If you take any more than you're allowed you have to pay extra for it. And you're not to take mattresses, feather beds, firearms, offensive weapons, wines, spirits, beer, gunpowder, percussion caps, Lucifer matches or any dangerous or noxious articles!'

'They reckon that before you embark some fellow from the Land and Immigration Commissioners office comes and checks to make sure you have everything you should have and nothing that you should not!' Patrick went on.

Mary had stopped laughing now. 'It all sounds so–so–I don't know what word I'm looking for!'

Sarah clamped her lips between her teeth. 'It's a bit frightening really, because they won't let you on the ship unless you have a notice to say you have been approved on inspection and have an embarkation order from the Land and Immigration Commissioners. And you must be in a fit state of health too.'

'Wow!' James shook his head. 'So, it's possible you might get there then be left, standing on the dock with nowhere to go!'

'Oh, don't!' Sarah cried. 'Then what would we do? It would just break my heart if we had to turn around and come all the way back from Plymouth.'

Patrick put his arm round her. 'That won't happen, love.

We'll make sure we have everything we're supposed to have and that we're all healthy.'

Sarah gave a wan smile and nodded. 'I suppose it will be worth it all when we get there.'

The following few months were hectic. Patrick was working extra shifts in the mine to make up for Sarah being unable to work. Sarah was trying to fit in sewing and packing between feeding and caring for two demanding babies.

Patrick managed to scrounge some strong wooden crates from the mine manager and between them Mary and Sarah wrapped and packed the few pieces of furniture and dishes and pans that were worth taking with them.

Many a time Sarah was hit by a wave of foreboding. A stream of 'what ifs' slithered through her mind. What if the ship sinks? What if the children take ill in the middle of the ocean? What if we get there and hate it? What if anything happens to Mary and James? Who would take care of Richard and the girls then? Their only family would be at the far end of the earth with no way of getting back to care for them! *What if?*

Sarah said nothing to Patrick of these fears. When she voiced them to Mary, her friend merely tutted and brushed her fears aside.

'Away with you, girl. Nothing is goin' to happen to us. We love having the childher an' you know they are happy with us. Don't you be worrying' about the childher — or a about us. We'll all do well together.' Mary gave a brisk nod of her head to emphasise her point.

Sarah smiled fondly. 'All I can do then is thank you yet again.'

In better moments she looked forward to her new life. A life away from being labelled the daughter of a crazy woman and the sister of a whore. A life where the wayward Alexandra could not reach her!

The day for leaving came upon them all too swiftly. The first day of April, all fools' day, washed in on a typical spring shower. To everyone's relief this dried up and the sun shone before Harry the Knife arrived to take them to Douglas.

Harry stood scratching his head. 'I didn't know you was going to have this much stuff! How's we going to get it all in the cart?'

Sarah's heart sank as she looked on in despair. What if they couldn't fit it all in the cart? What then? Would they have to leave a lot behind? If they did not have all that was on their list, they would probably not be allowed on the ship. This day was hard enough to bear without any more problems. Today she had to leave Richard, Lizzie and Jess, probably never to see them again. And Mary and James. They were like family now. Much more than just friends. Tears ached in her throat.

Patrick put an arm around her. 'Don't you worry, my lass. We'll get it all to Douglas if I have to carry it there myself.'

'Let's get my tools off the cart, then we may have a chance,' Harry decided.

He, Patrick and James heaved his grinder and all his sharpening paraphernalia off the cart and made a careful loading. Everything was placed to fit as closely together as was possible and eventually, after a lot of puffing, heaving and cursing the last piece was fitted in and secured with ropes.

Sobbing uncontrollably, Sarah hugged and said a shaky farewell to her siblings, then to Mary and James.

'Oh, Mary,' she started tearfully as she gave her a hug.

Mary gently pushed Sarah from her. 'Get on with you, lass. Harry and Patrick are waiting. Get away to your new life. I'll look after the childher well.'

Seeing the tears that brightened Mary's eyes, Sarah nodded mutely and moved to join her husband and children.

Harry and his four passengers would have to squeeze up on a seat meant for two, but there was no way around that. Mary held the twins, while James handed Sarah up into the cart. When Patrick was settled, the babies were handed up to them and Harry clicked his tongue at his pony, Junket. She put her weight against the traces, then turned her head, to look disapprovingly at Harry.

'Aye, girl. I know it's a heavy load, but you'll manage it with a bit of help.' Harry encouraged.

The little cart, with its mountainous load, set off down the rough track, swaying precariously, while the three Fayle children ran alongside. They stopped at the corner and Sarah turned for a last look and a wave to her siblings and the best friends she could ever have wished to have.

It was a fraught trip to Douglas. Not a great distance, but a hilly one and after the rain, the track was slippery. The load was too heavy for Junket on the steep hills, so Patrick and Harry had to climb down and push. Sarah walked behind carrying the two babies. It had been a wise move, Sarah realised, to leave Laxey so early, for the journey had taken them a lot longer than anticipated.

Her heart bounded with relief when the little party rounded the headland at Onchan, and they could see Douglas below them. It was all downhill from here — things were looking up.

The sea glistened below them in the sunlight. It seemed to Sarah to be bidding them farewell. Drawing a deep, tremulous breath she realised that this was almost certainly the last time she would see this scene. The unknown she was going to suddenly became quite frightening.

Sarah sat on a box at the docks, with a baby in each arm, gazing around in awe. Huge crates and nets full of heaven-knew-what cargo swung high above her head and onto the deck of *Mona's Queen*. There was noise and clatter all around her. Hustle and bustle that made her dizzy.

The twins, wakened by the noise, wanted to get down and crawl around, but Sarah deemed it too dangerous. They grumbled a bit at first, but soon all the activity around them held them in thrall and they settled happily on her lap.

The ship towered above her, moving slowly as the tide lifted her then let her fall. To Sarah's relief she looked enormous. The girl had only ever seen her in the distance, from the headland at Laxey. At that distance she had looked so small and inconspicuous, like a cork bobbing on the ocean.

Patrick and Harry busied themselves heaving all the crates and trunks onto the dockside. A docker came along with a cart and cheerfully helped them to lift all the luggage. Then whistling happily, he wheeled it away to where Sarah watched it being dumped onto a net to be swung up and onto the ship.

After a while the call came to board and they had to say farewell to Harry. Sarah's heart tore apart as she held his hands and gave his cheek a last kiss. Her final goodbye to her last Manx friend! Tears flowed down her cheeks as she turned away from him to follow the other passengers up the gangway.

When the steam engines grumbled into life and the ship began to shudder, Patrick and Sarah went on deck. They watched with a mixture of sadness and excitement, when the huge hawsers fell away. As the ship set sail, they held each other and their children, standing for a long time until the island shrank away into the distance and finally disappeared. Such a beautiful island, but they would never see it again. Nor Mary. Nor James and probably not Sarah's three younger siblings.

A great heaviness settled on Sarah's heart and she struggled to hold down her sobs. Patrick put a comforting arm around her and gave her a gentle squeeze.

'It's for the best, love. A better future for both us and the children. A future away from all the Laxey gossips, and where Alexandra can never do us harm.'

Unable to find her voice, Sarah merely nodded.

Finally, seated at last, she was able to put George and Judith on the floor. Patrick had all the baggage they would need for their long voyage on the *Navarino*.

The twins became fretful in the confines of the ship. They could not be allowed to crawl freely, for there was the ever-present danger of someone staggering and stepping on them.

The journey, which had started out peaceably enough, became rougher as the voyage went on. A wind blew hard and set the seas boiling, rolling the *Mona's Queen*. Sarah's stomach heaved a bit and she prayed the children would not be sick. For once luck was with her. If anything, they seemed to enjoy the sensation, giggling and clapping their hands in glee at every slap of the sea against the hull.

Due to the delay the storm had brought, it was very late when they arrived in Liverpool. Sarah started to panic at the thought of trying to find somewhere to stay for the night, but to her great relief they were told they could stay on board the *Mona's Queen*. There would not be a bed for them, but they could sleep on the floor if they wished.

Sarah and Patrick found a corner and laying the babies against the wall, they lay in front of them and managed to get a few hours of fretful sleep.

First thing in the morning Patrick went to ensure all their belongings were unloaded, then he hired a carriage to take them all to the steam railway station.

Liverpool was not like anything Sarah had ever experienced. The noise was incredible and at times quite frightening. The carriage driver shouted and swore at anyone and anything that held him up. They came close to injuring a few pedestrians, but eventually reached their goal without mishap. All their trunks and assorted luggage were unloaded onto a trolley and a porter disappeared toward the back of the train with it. Patrick followed to ensure nothing missed being loaded.

Sarah sank thankfully onto the hard wooden seat in the train. Patrick took George from her and after flexing her back she settled for the journey to Birmingham, where they were to change to the Plymouth train.

Arriving in Plymouth, after what seemed like a lifetime with two bored toddlers, they were faced with having to find accommodation for the night. On the recommendation of the stationmaster, they found a room in a boarding house.

'Lady that runs it is my cousin Millie,' he told them proudly. 'She runs a good clean house and if you tell her Gilbert sent you, she won't mind you coming so late.'

Cousin Millie was indeed friendly and welcoming. She cooed and clucked over the twins. After showing them their room — which was plain, but clean, warm and comfortable — she promised to make a nice hot meal.

'Call me Millie,' she told them cheerfully as she sat them down to the best meal they had tasted for ages.

It was with great sadness that they left in the morning, but they dared not stay longer for they were to report to the migrants' depot to be checked.

They left early and took a coach back to the railway station, where Patrick checked that all their belongings, which had been stored overnight at the station, were loaded on to the coach. As they travelled Sarah realised, with damp eyes and a lump in her throat, that this was the last journey they would ever make in Britain. Soon they would be off into the unknown.

Another uncomfortable, bumpy coach trip found them

finally in the migrants' depot in Plymouth. To Sarah's eyes, it all just seemed like noise and confusion. There were people everywhere and at least half of them seemed to be children — most of whom were shouting or screaming. Harrowed parents tried to control them, mostly without success.

'Dear God, what have we come to?' Sarah muttered, her ears splitting.

Men who were obviously some sort of officials were struggling to get things into a semblance of order and forming the mob into an orderly line.

In front of Sarah and Patrick was a family with several children. Some of them had the most dreadful coughs and Sarah tried to keep them at a distance to keep the twins safe.

When eventually, a migration official came to the family in front of them he looked searchingly at the children and drew his lips in. Turning, he beckoned to someone in the distance. Sarah watched curiously as a rather dignified man approached.

'Mr Goullett, these youngsters is coughing bad. I think you'd better check them,' the migration officer suggested.

The newcomer bent down to check the children. Standing, he looked at the officer and shook his head.

'Whooping cough! They can't go.' he stated apologetically.

A long, tearful and heated argument followed. Arms waved; the father of the family actually raised his fists on one occasion. Standing as far away as possible in the crush of people, Sarah and Patrick could only make out bits of the conversation. It was clear though that the family were being refused passage.

'We *have* to go!' the father said angrily. 'We have left everything, and we have nothing to go back to. No home, no job, no nothing!'

The official drew a weary hand down the side of his face. 'You have my sympathy, believe me. But with the crowded conditions we have on these migrant's ships, the disease would quickly spread, and we'd lose half the passengers before we'd gone far.'

'We'll keep the children away from everyone,' the mother promised.

The migration officer shook his head. 'I'm sorry, that's not possible. We can't take you now, but once the children are well, we could arrange passage for you in the future.'

'But where will we go now? We're from Yorkshire. We have nowhere to go until the children are better!'

The man shook his head sadly and shrugged his shoulders.

'You said, or your bosses said, they were taking us on this ship, and we have given up everything!' the father raised a fist.

Starting to lose his patience the official pointed out that it had been clearly set out in the conditions of passage they received, that they had all to be in good health. 'And clearly your children are not in good health!' he finished.

The family were then led away, sobbing and gesticulating, by another official.

It was now their turn to be examined and Sarah found herself trembling and in terror. What if the same were to happen to them?

The migration official smiled and offered his apologies for the scene they had witnessed. They were examined, and all found to be healthy. Next to be checked were their trunks and boxes. When, to Sarah's relief, they were found to have all they should have and none of the banned items, they were finally handed their embarkation order and led away to the migration accommodation, where they would spend the next few nights, until the ship was ready for boarding.

Both Patrick and Sarah stopped in astonishment when they were taken into the room where they were to sleep. It looked to be a cold, comfortless place. There must have been two hundred or more people there, some laughing, some crying and many just looking too shocked for words.

It was like a huge dormitory, such as they had never seen before. All these people were to sleep in the one room, Patrick and Sarah discovered. Down both sides of the room a wide shelf stretched the full length of it and about four feet from the ground. On this were planks about two feet high and three feet apart. The lower tier, underneath this shelf was similarly divided. This tier was for the children. The partitioned boxes were only about six feet long and three feet wide. They were allocated one on the upper deck for themselves and one on the lower for the children. These were their beds, Sarah realised with horror and they were like rocks.

There was such a complete lack of privacy that most people could not look their neighbour in the eye. They were all sleeping within sight of each other. Lights were never doused but luckily, they were so dim that they could hardly see more than a few feet.

Sarah feared for her babies if she put them in the lower bunk alone. They were far too young and might crawl off on their own at night. So, she decided to take the lower one with Judith, while Patrick would share the top with George. Sarah's bed smelled so awful that she was sure it had not been cleaned after the previous migrant. She only prayed that whoever had preceded her had not suffered from some dreadful disease.

The provisions they were given were adequate, but not good enough to make up to the families trapped there, for the torment of the conditions they were living in.

Sarah and Patrick quickly befriended a couple about their own age who had a baby just a few weeks old. They introduced themselves as Alison and Jeremy, 'And this here is little Billy,' they said proudly.

'We're from Leeds,' Alison told them excitedly 'and we can't half wait to get to Australia. We've been livin' with my father in one room and he's drunk most of the time.'

'We're from Laxey, in the Isle of Man,' Sarah replied, happy to have found a friend. It made the voyage ahead seem a little less daunting.

They got on so well and were all not much looking forward to trying to sleep on the hard bunks, so they talked long into the night. To their further dismay Alison and Jeremy had been given only one three-foot-wide bed space for themselves and the baby.

Sarah was brought suddenly awake in the early morning by a terrible screaming. Scrambling to the front of her bunk, she saw Alison slumped, trembling, on the floor with little Billy lying limp in her arms. Jeremy crouched beside her with his arm round her.

'He's not breathing,' Alison gasped when she saw Sarah. 'We must have laid on him in the night. We've smothered him!' The baby was blue, his eyes wide and staring. They tried shaking him gently, then blowing into this mouth. Everything failed, and his little body just hung limp and blue.

A migration officer took the heartbroken parents to town in the morning to arrange little Billy's funeral. They returned alone later, with empty arms and tear-streaked faces to continue their journey.

At last, after three nights in the hellhole, the order came for them to board.

It was a tired, weary, but thankful procession of passengers who trailed up the gangplank. Patrick carried all the bags containing their change of clothes and cooking utensils. Sarah, bone weary and apprehensive, staggered along behind with both twins, who were getting heavier by the minute.

When they reached the deck a smiling, though harassed-looking migration officer took George from Sarah's arms and told them he would take them to their berths.

As they crossed the deck Sarah glanced toward the quay and saw a huge mountain of luggage, of all shapes and sizes, piled there waiting to be loaded. There were also rows of buckets and barrels, Sarah presumed for the use of the ship.

Around her, in the procession of steerage passengers, she heard grumbles and loud oaths as the person behind walked a bit faster and trod on the heels of the one in front. Children screamed and whined as they were knocked about or stood on in the crush.

The migration officer led them to a hatch and down a companionway to what he told them was the Between Decks or *tween decks*.

Sarah stopped dead in her tracks as she stepped through the doorway into what she had expected to be a cabin for herself and her family. 'What's this?' she asked, frowning.

At first it was so dark, with only a few dull lanterns hanging. As her eyes adjusted to the gloom, all Sarah could see was a huge room full of what looked like two tiers of large wooden boxes. It looked little different from the room they had left in the depot; just smaller. There were barrels, bags, cooking utensils and heaps of assorted baggage littering the deck. Above her head were huge beams — a danger to taller men — and ringbolts.

The officer looked around. 'It's the accommodation for families travelling steerage,' he told her nonchalantly.

Sarah looked at Patrick in despair. 'But I thought we would have a cabin!'

The man shrugged apologetically. 'Only the full-paying passengers have cabins, ma'am. But steerage gets this.' He swept an arm. 'Follow me an' I'll show you your beds.'

He set off, wending his way between the clutter on the deck and a milling horde of children. Stopping halfway along the large crowded cabin, he stopped beside some empty boxes. 'These are yours. Parents on the top and children on the bottom. Gotta go now. Got other folks to sort out.' he told them cheerfully before handing George to Patrick and hurrying away.

Sarah studied the scene through tear misted eyes. 'I can't believe this,' she whispered miserably. 'Has this really to be our home for heaven knows how many months?'

With a hand over her mouth, she studied what were to be their beds. They looked to be about six feet long by three feet wide, like the hellhole they had just left. The bottom ones had planks about half the height of the space and the upper ones had planks part way up dividing one bed from the other. There would be no privacy whatsoever for the whole voyage as the person in the next bed was only one plank's width away from you as you slept. This was worse than any nightmare she had ever had. It was not better than the depot! Worse if anything, for at sea there would be danger.

Patrick put an arm around her shoulder. 'Sorry, love, but there's nothing we can do to change it. Just try to bear it and think about the good life we will have when we reach Australia.'

Sarah nodded and attempted a watery smile as she gazed around in abject misery. 'I can only hope you are right,' she said miserably.

Tables ran the entire length of the room, with fixed seats on either side of them. Beneath the tables were plate racks and battens to hold the small casks that contained the daily allowance of fresh water. Hanging shelves were secured between the beams for their cooking utensils. There were seats also fixed at the outer edge of every bed-place. Anyone sleeping on the lower level would have to climb over these seats to reach their beds.

Counting, Sarah could see there were forty-eight bed places for married people above and for their children below. The stanchion at the end of each bed was furnished with a peg on which to hang their clothes.

Miserably she sank on to the seat at the end of what was to be her bed. *So, this was it!* This lack of privacy amongst this noisy, chaotic mob of men, women and apparently uncontrolled children. Would she survive it, she wondered, or would she have been better to stay on the island and tolerate being known as the daughter of a convict and a mad woman and the sister of a prostitute?

Then she thought of her children and realised that the mud that had been sticking to her would have stuck to them and darkened their lives too. So, better for them to go to this new world where no one knew anything of her.

Lifting her chin, she smiled up at Patrick. 'Well,' she said bravely. 'We must just make the best of this and it will really take only a few months out of our lives!'

Patrick drew her into his arms and gave her a long, tender kiss. 'It will all be worth it in the end. I promise you.'

Chapter 24

More and ever more bodies seemed to crowd into the cluttered room, which seemed so dark, and which closed in on them. Friends and relations were allowed aboard to say their farewells. To Sarah and Patrick, the chaos this brought to their dark, dreary *tween decks* cabin became unbearable. Accustomed to the freshness of the Isle of Man, the air in this little prison, fetid to start with, turned their stomachs and they soon fled up the companionway and onto the deck.

A crewman showed them which part of the deck was for the use of steerage passengers and made it very clear that the other areas were out of bounds.

'Pass that barrier on fear of death,' he told them dramatically. 'Cap'n will have you in irons if you do!'

They stood on the deck for a long time with the twins securely clutched in their arms. Sarah's insides churned as she thought of what lay below them. She did not think she would ever get used to living with so little privacy. But she would have to manage would she not? There were months of it ahead of her. It was too late to change her mind, so she had no choice. This would be her life for the next four months or more.

They watched with no small amount of envy as the better-dressed cabin passengers boarded.

Sarah drew in a huge sigh as she watched them, 'I wish——' she started, but Patrick put a finger to her lips.

'If wishes were horses, love, but they are not! We had not the money for a cabin.'

Sarah nodded and managed a brave smile, 'I know, my love. I know. We'll be alright.'

Below on the quayside, the last of the mountain of baggage was being winched aboard. All the buckets and barrels were gone. At the depot they had been given canvas bags and told to put enough clothes for a month in them. All the other boxes and trunks were to be put in the hold and could only be taken out once a month to exchange dirty clothes for clean ones.

What little money they had; Patrick had fastened securely in a belt under his shirt. Some of his fellow passengers, he felt, looked a bit rough and he wanted to take no chances.

The activity on the deck increased. Men scuttled everywhere and the noise around them grew into a deafening din.

The area of deck the steerage passengers were allowed was a seething mass of men, women and children all pushing to try to reach the rails. All the visitors had long since left the ship and many were now lined up along the quay.

It was late in the afternoon when the huge hawsers dropped away and three tugs, one at each side and one ahead, started to move the ship. Looking down they saw the gap widening between the quay and the ship and Sarah shuddered at the sight of the black water below. She felt her heart constrict then lurch. This was it then. There could be no change of mind. *No way back!* Tears misted her eyes, but she choked them back into her throat.

The rails were lined with passengers, some laughing and excited, but most with long faces and many of the women in tears. Flags were waving, and a brass band was playing a tune Sarah did not know.

When they were well clear of land the tugs left them. Full sail was set, but there was just a light breeze that only partly filled them.

People started to drift away, but not keen to return to what seemed like a prison, Patrick and Sarah stayed on deck. They watched until England disappeared into the light mist. They would never see it again and both had very mixed feelings about it.

There was a slight roll to the ship, which Sarah found to be not unpleasant. *If it stays like this*, she thought, *the voyage might be bearable.*

The twins were becoming a bit fractious, and as there were no longer many feet tramping the decks, they were allowed to crawl around for a while. Finally hunger took over and they were forced to return *tween decks*.

For three days the calm weather held. With a light breeze, the ship did not make much headway. Sarah and Patrick spent as much time on the deck as they could, which was greatly encouraged by Mr Goullett, the ship's surgeon.

Dressing and undressing was an embarrassment. Not so bad for the men who could pull their trousers on while lying down, provided their wives would allow them more than their allotted eighteen inches of bed space. Not so easy for the ladies with their voluminous garments. Luckily the lanterns were dim.

All that made it liveable was the presence of a *windsail* — a large tube that was divided into two compartments, which was fairly well protected from the weather at the top. This tube passed from the main to the *tween decks*, the heated air passing up through one compartment, while the cold, fresh air descended through the other. To Sarah's relief this was close enough to their bunk to make things a little less unpleasant.

They found there was just one closet at the hatch end of the room, but that was for the use of the women and children only. The men had to go to an upper deck.

Sarah noticed with absolute horror, that many of the males, especially at night, made no attempt to go to the upper deck as they were supposed. Instead, many used the dishes which they, or more likely someone else, would later use to eat from. With grim determination she made sure she kept her utensils on her bunk at night and well out of harm's way.

The surgeon-superintendent, Mr Arthur Goullett made it clear that he felt it appalling that decent married couples should be confined together as though they were animals. With only a very thin mattress, and no sheets as there was no way of washing them.

Mr Goullett tried to encourage the emigrants to bathe as often as possible. Sarah and Patrick were glad to do this. Sarah in a bath room near the single ladies' quarters and Patrick in a tub provided for the men in the fore part of the ship.

George and Judith had their share of exercise, crawling around the deck. With their parents constantly plucking them out from underfoot, they thrived. Their skins were turning to a healthy gold. Had it not been for the dreadful, cramped living conditions, Sarah would have been happy.

It couldn't last, of course. On the fourth day the wind started to strengthen. The seas, which until then had rolled gently, churned and heaved. Huge waves towered almost to the deck of the ship and white water blew from the top, spraying the full length of the decks.

There were hens in cages firmly tied on the deck. The owners hurried to get them to safety when the storm struck. Some of these poor creatures were lucky, but those that were not were either swept overboard or drowned by the force of the sea-water.

Captain Robert William Morgan ordered all passengers, for their own safety, to stay in their cabins. To make sure this order was obeyed, the hatches to the *tween decks* were battened down, and the steerage passengers imprisoned. The side glasses had been shut and fastened as soon as the weather blew up, so there was even less light and air.

Sarah and Patrick huddled together at the far end of their top bunk, clinging tightly to their frightened children and the timber dividing the bunks. All around them was noise — people screamed; men, women and children alike. As the boiling ocean threw the ship around, they were tossed about in their bunks like rag dolls.

Many times, Sarah felt herself lifted from the bunk as she clung to Judith. Then she would crash down painfully on the thin mattress. Patrick held desperately to both George and Sarah. And they all prayed.

All the pots and utensils that hung over the table swung wildly against each other. Many flew off their hooks like missiles. The clanging from these added to the screams and moans of pain, made the whole scene an unholy nightmare.

The huge seas crashed deafeningly onto the deck above their heads, making the ship shudder and roll. Water seeped past the edges of the hatch, ran into the cabin and sprayed down the windsail, soaking Patrick and Sarah. They tried to protect the children by covering them with a blanket, but soon that was also drenched.

The storm lasted forever, it seemed to Sarah, but it was in fact just over a day.

No one had dared try to make it to the water closet, so the deck and everything on it was awash with human waste, including vomit, and seawater. All sweeping backward and forward with the movement of the ship.

The surgeon came to treat the multitude of cuts, abrasions and broken limbs. The more seriously injured were taken to one of the two small hospitals which had been set up. While he was there Patrick asked him about the wet mattress and clothes.

'I'll get you permission from the Captain to take them up on deck and get them dried. I'll send a crewman to show you where you can spread them.'

Exhausted and hungry, for they had not been able to eat, the migrants set to cleaning up as best they could.

Their quarters was now a foul-smelling prison. It had become airless and was poorly lit with just a couple of dim lanterns. The stench could not be got rid of.

Swing stoves and hot sand were brought in to dry out the decks, which had to be cleaned without water, using only holystones and dry rubbing.

When they had finished the cleaning and with a good meal inside them, the migrants all settled down to sort out their belongings.

Sarah and Patrick were just beginning to recover from the ordeal of the storm when George started to cough. At first it seemed like nothing too bad. The following day Judith was sounding raspy too and the young parents started to become concerned.

'Should we send for the surgeon?' Sarah asked uncertainly, as George's cough worsened.

Patrick thought about it for a moment. 'Perhaps we should wait another day. Mister Goullett is very busy at the moment with all the injured,' he replied thoughtfully. 'Let's see how he is in the morning.'

The lower bunk was too close to the still damp and smelly deck so, with their mattress now washed and smelling fresher than it ever had, all four squeezed into the top bunk to try to sleep.

Sarah rested, but could not sleep. George's coughing, which grew worse through the night kept her awake and frightened. By morning the poor child had a raging fever as well as the cough.

'I think it might be the whooping cough,' Sarah said fearfully.

Patrick nodded. 'Aye. I had been thinking the same. We'd best take him and Judith to the surgeon's sick parade this morning'.

Mr Goullett nibbled thoughtfully at his lower lip. 'I'm sorry, but you would appear to be correct. Both children have whooping cough. I had to refuse some families passage because of it. I fear your children might have picked up the germ at the migrant's depot.'

Sarah shook her head helplessly, tears burning in her throat. 'You sent the family in front of us away because of whooping cough. My babies will be alright, won't they?'

Mr Goullett nodded thoughtfully. He looked at her kindly and laid a gentle hand on her arm. 'I hope so, but I can make no promises. I'll have to admit them to the hospital until the worst of the illness has passed.'

Sarah sat on the hospital bunk and looked around in dismay. It was hard to believe how quickly the twin's health had deteriorated. One day they had seemed a picture of good health, as lively and cheeky as ever — enjoying the warm air on deck. Then in the next, they seemed at death's door. She lost all track of time as she huddled there with her children cuddled against her. Every cough, she knew could be their last as they struggled and whooped to try to draw in a breath. George was by far the worse of the two and Sarah had never witnessed such distress and such pain. So much she wanted to help them. So much.

She had never felt so helpless and frightened in her life. There was nothing she could do for them; nothing at all. Her only comfort was to hold them tight against her to let them know she was there and to let them feel her love. She could only hope and pray her strength would be greater than the devil that was trying to take them from her.

Patrick sat beside Sarah, his arms around her and his two beautiful children, feeling every bit as helpless. He had never been overly religious, but he mumbled an endless, fervent prayer as he sat there. What else could he do?

For four days, which felt like four lifetimes to Patrick and Sarah, the twins coughed and fought for breath. On the fifth, Judith started to breath more easily and the surgeon declared her out of danger.

George, who from birth, had always been the weaker of the two, was hit hardest by the disease. His parents watched with growing horror as his breathing continued to worsen. Sarah found that as he struggled and whooped she was drawing in great gulping deep breaths, breathing for him. Willing him to keep going.

Without warning the fight became too much for poor little George. He gave a strange little gurgle and gave up.

'*No!*' Sarah screamed. Eyes wide with horror, she shook him gently.

No response.

Patrick, who had been dozing, took him from her, held him up by his feet and slapped his back, as he knew they did with new born babies to start them breathing.

Still no response.

Sarah snatched him back and, putting her mouth to his, blew gently.

Patrick watched in shock for a moment, then he leapt from

the bunk. 'I'll fetch the surgeon,' he said as he fled from the room.

Her face awash with tears, Sarah kept to her task of breathing life, she hoped, into her tiny son. *Blow. Press on his chest to expel the air and blow again.*

Judith, as though sensing she must behave, sat quietly on the bunk watching her mother fight to save her brother. She made not a sound, just sat watching, wide-eyed.

Blow. Pause. Blow again. Sobs heaved at Sarah's body. Keep calm, she told herself. I must stay calm. Calm and blow. *Pause and blow again.*

Where was Patrick? He had been gone forever. Why had he not come back with the surgeon? Keep calm. Blow. George lay limp and unresponsive in her arms. But she would not give up. Blow. Keep blowing. Keep putting air in his lungs and he will waken. However long it took, he *would* waken.

Mr Goullett came striding into the hospital room, with Patrick hot on his heels. Bending, he took George from Sarah's arms listened, to his chest and felt his pulse.

Straightening, he shook his head. 'I'm so sorry, but your son has gone.'

'*No!*' Sarah screamed, 'He can't be dead. I won't let him be! Give him back to me!' She reached out for her son's body and Mr Goullett put him gently into her arms.

'He *is* gone,' he said quietly. 'I'll see Captain Morgan to arrange his funeral.'

Sarah sat on the bed in stunned silence. In her arms she held the tiny limp body that looked so much smaller in death than it had in life. So small. So still and he looked so peaceful. After all the dreadful, pain-filled days and nights of fighting for breath, he looked so peaceful.

Sarah, her eyes filled with tears and her heart filled with

pain, kissed the tiny cold cheek and looked up at Patrick. His pain, she saw, was as great as hers.

'I'm sorry,' she said. 'So sorry. I've lost your son! I tried so hard to keep him alive. But I let him die. I lost him. I'm so sorry.' Her whole body shook with her sobs.

Patrick put his arms around her and drew her to him. 'I know how hard you tried, but it was impossible. His fight for breath had stopped his little heart. You didn't lose him, love. You did not let him die. God took him. I know how much this hurts you. I just wish there was some way to make it easier for you. He was only on loan, you know. Children are always only on loan from God.'

Sarah looked up at this wonderful, gentle giant of a man she had married and loved him more at that moment than she ever had. His suffering was as great as hers, yet his first thought was for her.

'You just have,' she said quietly. 'Made it easier, I mean. God tried to take him when he was born, did he not. But he relented and gave him back to us, for a short while. He let us have the joy of him for nine months.'

Patrick smiled gently and wrapped his arms around his two special ladies.

The following morning, as the ship scudded along ahead of a stiff northerly wind, the burial service was held for George.

Patrick and Sarah had said their goodbyes and kissed their son's cheek for the last time. A seaman had made a little sailcloth cradle and stitched George's body inside it with a weight to make sure it would not float.

As Captain Morgan read the service and said the last prayer, most of the steerage migrants were crowded on to the deck. Quite a few of the cabin passengers stood silently on the poop.

'Unto almighty God we commend the soul of our brother departed, and we commit his body to the deep,' Captain

Morgan's strong voice was raw with emotion, 'in sure and certain hope of the Resurrection unto eternal life, through our Lord Jesus Christ; at whose coming in glorious majesty to judge the world, the sea shall give up its dead; and the corruptible body of those who sleep in him shall be changed, and made unto his glorious body; according to the mighty working whereby He is able to subdue all things unto himself. We hereby commit the body of this child, George Patrick O'Malley to His care. God bless you my child.'

Sarah and Patrick were vaguely conscious that a pipe was playing as the flag covered platform was tilted. They watched in numb disbelief as, in slow motion, the little sail-cloth bundle slipped out from under the flag and fell into the sea. Looking over the rail they saw it sink quickly beneath the waves.

'Goodbye, my angel,' Sarah whispered as her first born child disappeared into the dark depths of the sea. 'Mam! Daa! Look after him for us. Don't let him be alone.'

Patrick took her in his arms and clinging tightly together, they wept.

Sarah felt a hand on her shoulder and, looked up into the moist, sympathetic eyes of Alison Knight, with Jeremy standing just behind her.

'All I can think of to say is that I know just how you feel,' she said quietly. 'If there is anything we can do ...'

Alison left the sentence unfinished when Sarah nodded and whispered her thanks.

When Alison and Jeremy had gone Sarah turned to Patrick. 'It's only now I really realise how hard it must have been for them to lose little Billy. They only had him a few weeks and were left with empty arms. We had George for nine months and we are lucky enough to still have our beautiful daughter.'

Patrick nodded and tightened his hug. 'Then we must give

them more of our time. Now, let's go and fetch that beautiful daughter from the hospital. Mr Goullett said she is well enough for us to take her today.'

Chapter 25

For a long time, the little family felt utterly lost and adrift. Judith, even at such a tender age badly missed her twin. She kept looking reproachfully at her parents with a puzzled little frown.

Sarah and Patrick had never felt such pain and could not have imagined such agony and such emptiness. All that kept them going was Judith. It was only now they realised the full extent of how Alison and Jeremy had suffered. But it could not be changed. The clock could not be turned back, and neither could they. There was no choice for them, but to continue their journey and hope they survived.

As day followed endless day the temperature soared and conditions in their wooden dungeon grew constantly more unpleasant. The ever-present stench of sickness, stale sweat, and sour baby napkins and a myriad of other odours pervaded and clung in the air rendering the cabin almost unendurable.

Watching the sailors working in the rigging, hoisting and lowering sails fascinated Patrick. He befriended one of the crew men, Lennie, who, when he had the time, would answer Patrick's questions.

Peering up at the rigging Patrick asked, 'What type of ship is this?'

'This is what they call a barque rigged ship,' Lennie said knowledgably. 'It has three masts, as you can see, that are square rigged except for the stern-mast, which is fore-and-aft rigged.'

'Sorry, you've lost me. What does that mean?'

'Well, the square sail always takes the wind from the same side of the sail and it's at its best when sailing before the wind. Not so good beating against a wind though. The fore-and-aft can take the wind from either side of the sail, depending on the direction of the wind.' Lennie nodded, as if pleased to have aired his knowledge to a know-nothing landlubber. 'And it is about four hundred and ninety-three tons burden,' he added as an afterthought.

The ship ploughed on at a good speed for several days, sailing before a fair wind. Each day seemed warmer than the day before and most of the passengers spent much of their days on deck. This was greatly encouraged by the surgeon, who told them their best chances of staying healthy were to escape the confines of their putrid cabin and catch as much fresh air as possible.

A flurry of a gale blew up quite suddenly.

Sarah and several of the other ladies were scrubbing the deck in the cabin when a huge wave came down the hatchway onto them. Many screamed in fright and anger and there was a pretty scene all at once. It fairly set the place afloat. The beds on the bottom berths were soaked. Sarah jumped up on a water keg balancing herself with a mop.

Terrified the ship was going to sink, there was a scramble for the stairs. They all climbed on deck as quickly as possible for fear they might be drowned. It was little better there, for the waves washed over the deck and soaked them.

Sarah scrambled to join Patrick who was huddled, clinging to some rigging, trying to protect Judith.

'What shall we do?' Sarah shouted. 'It is dangerous here. We might be swept overboard. But it is flooded in the cabin and if the ship should sink, we would be trapped.'

They could hear Captain Morgan shouting instructions through his bullhorn, but could not hear what he was saying.

Lennie came slithering along the deck. 'Cap'n says all passengers has to go to their cabins. There's a real gale coming, and you'll get washed away if you stays here. I'll give you a hand to get Mistress O'Malley and the little 'un down.'

Clinging tightly to any handhold they could find, they finally made it to the companionway and almost fell into the hold. Once all the passengers were below deck the hatches were battened down. Even so, water seeped in and down the companionway.

'I was talking to the mate,' Jeremy said in a frightened voice. 'He said there's not enough boats for everyone. So, if the ship sinks only the paying passengers will be taken off!'

A hum of disbelieving murmurings simmered round the cabin.

'What about us then? Are we just going to be left locked in here to go down with the ship?' One man asked fearfully.

'What else is there? If there's not enough boats, we can't swim, can we?' Jeremy's question was a mixture of fear and desperation.

Anger was building in the room and Patrick started to fear some sort of a riot. That would do nobody any good.

'The Captain's a good man,' he said placatingly. 'I'm sure he wouldn't do that. My reckoning is it would be women and children first.'

'Aye,' a few of them nodded, but many still looked doubtful.

'Anyway,' Patrick added. 'This is a good, strong seaworthy

ship. It's not going to sink!' He just wished he felt as much confidence as he was trying to imbue.

'We can only pray you're right. But I too, feel the Captain is a good man. And the surgeon. It's his duty to look to the wellbeing of the passengers, no matter what class they are in.' Jeremy added weight to Patrick's opinion.

The smell of fear was now added to all the other odours in their dark damp room.

There followed the most terrifying night, a regular night of horrors. The wind blew at hurricane force and often the ship seemed to go right under water. It poured down around the edges of the hatch and down the wind sail in a deluge. It was then that Patrick and Sarah were glad to have a top bunk, for some of the people in the lower bunks were washed out of their beds. The screams of the people as each wave broke over the ship was enough to make even the strongest hearts tremble. Many of the women fainted with the shock of it all. Men, women and children alike crowded onto the top bunks as the lower ones went under water.

Patrick tried to climb from his bunk to see if he could help anybody, but Sarah held him back.

'There is nothing you can do. I need you to help keep Judith safe,' she told him.

'I thought perhaps I might bail,' he told her. 'With all the water coming in through the hatch and down the windsail the cabin is filling up.'

Sarah shook her head. 'But where would you bail it to?'

'Well, I thought if we formed a bucket-chain we could empty it into the closet.' All the men who were well enough manned the buckets and between them, managed to get some sort of control over the flooding in the cabin. They could hear the rumble and thuds of the ship's pumps struggling gamely.

The wind kept up all the following day, but at least the sea was no longer breaking over the ship and the hatch could be opened to let in some fresh air. The passengers had to take their meals in their berths. Nothing could be left standing by itself for a moment or it took a leap to the other side of the ship. They had to work hard to save themselves following it, by clinging to the posts.

The wind was right against them and the vessel rocked and creaked like an old cradle.

Some of women were handing cans of water and oatmeal up the hatch to have it made into gruel, when the ship gave a sudden lurch and some of them went down, with both oatmeal and water all over them. They were lucky enough not to be hurt but were covered in the gruel. Some of them were caught in the lying water, and rolled from side to side of the ship, unable to find a grip to stop themselves. By the time they managed to regain their feet, the other steerage passengers had been well entertained.

When the storm had finally passed, the surgeon, Mr Goullett, came down and told them to take all wet mattresses, blankets and clothing on deck.

Patrick and Sarah thankfully dragged theirs up, yet again. The deck was not a pretty sight, adorned as it was with dozens of sodden articles.

Their *tween deck* cabin was finally pumped clear of water and the hot sand and swing stoves were brought in again to dry it out.

Three weeks or so after sailing, the wind dropped away completely. Full sail was set, but the *Navarino* just bobbed around gently on the placid water and went nowhere.

Sarah and Patrick leant on the rail looking down into the clear dark water. Judith played at their feet, happy to be free to roam. She was just finding her feet, pulling herself up on her mother's skirt and standing for quite long stretches of time.

'She'll be walking by the time we get to Australia,' Patrick commented. 'I wonder if she'll be able to walk on land that isn't constantly moving under her feet.'

'At this rate we won't ever get there anyway,' Sarah quipped. 'I don't think we've travelled a mile today!'

'I was talking to Lennie earlier. He said this area is called the Doldrums. We are getting close to the equator, whatever that is, and often because of changes in the atmosphere the wind drops away completely. Sometimes for weeks. We'll not make much headway until it picks up again.'

'You mean we could be stuck here in this unbearable heat for weeks?' Sarah asked despairingly.

'It probably won't be as long as that,' Patrick consoled. 'But if it is, we'll just have to put up with it I'm afraid.'

Sarah thought of the horror of the nights. Days were bad enough, but at least they could get out into the fresh air. Even if it was unbearably hot and made breathing hard, at least it smelled freshly of salt sea air.

The nights were dreadful though. Almost too much to bear. They were told the daytime temperature was reaching over eighty-five degrees. The side glasses were able to be opened because of the calm seas. But even with those and the hatch and the windsail to allow in air, the room still smelled putrid. Most of the men slept with nothing but their underwear, but it was indecent for the women to do the same, obliged to wear their long nightdresses. So, Sarah left Judith and Patrick to share the top bunk and she took the lower. It smelled, but she thought it would smell more by the time she had sweated on it. It was still more comfortable than being crushed in a three-foot space with Patrick and Judith.

'Tonight, as it's so calm,' Sarah told Patrick, 'I shall sleep on the deck.'

'And I shall join you,' Patrick agreed. Anything had to be better than the stinking oven *tween decks*.

In the distance, Sarah saw some darker humps against the brilliant blue of the sea. 'Look,' she pointed, 'is that land?'

Patrick peered into the distance. 'Yes, I think so.'

The purser was passing and had overheard. Stopping for a moment, he nodded and said, 'Those are the Cape Verde Islands.'

That was all they saw of them and eventually they faded into the distance. If nothing else, it let the passengers see the ship actually *was* still moving.

Each day seemed hotter than the one before. The ship drifted sluggishly on leaden wings. Trying to find shade wherever possible from the blazing sun, the steerage passengers crowded the decks during the day, huddling wherever the sails cast a shadow.

Navarino drifted along ahead of a murmur of a breeze for eight days, during which the passengers, cabin and steerage alike, grew ever-more distressed.

There were a few of the steerage passengers who could play a musical instrument or sing a bit. One of them, Col Jenkins, was a copper miner from Cornwall, who suggested that to try to lift everyone's flagging spirits they should hold a concert. They consulted the surgeon, Mr Goullett, who thought it was an excellent idea and said he would seek permission from the Captain. He returned grinning from ear to ear.

'Good news, my friends. Captain Morgan agrees that it would be a good thing. But he says to do it soon, on the deck, for the breeze is starting to freshen and we'll soon be out of the Doldrums. And I'd like an invitation to your concert, if you please.'

There was a loud cheer and a chorus of 'thank you sir' and 'of course you must come.'

All the steerage passengers with musical ability put their heads together to plan a program for a concert to be held that same evening.

Everyone — man, woman and child — cleaned themselves up as best they could and climbed up on to the deck as the sun lowered itself toward the horizon.

Word had spread in steerage that there was to be a concert. The single ladies and single men came out to crowd the deck and mixed together a bit — something that the surgeon would not normally allow.

Patrick had the first place and played some Irish songs on the penny whistle. All the Irish passengers sang along with him and were joined soon by all the other passengers. Those who did not know the words hummed along and tapped their feet.

Next came the Cornish miner on a concertina, then a farm labourer with a flute.

Several passengers sang solo, some very well and some not so well, but however they sang they got a rousing cheer.

After nearly three hours, when all the children had fallen asleep on the deck, a Welsh miner got to his feet. He was a giant of a man, standing at least six feet and six inches tall. When he started to sing, all three musicians accompanied him. He sang *Home Sweet Home*, in the most powerfully moving voice. To Sarah it seemed the song had come from his heart and gave the lasting impression he was saying a final farewell to a dearly loved country. He had a tear in his eye when he finished and many of his fellow passengers wept along with him.

On hearing the music start, most of the cabin class passengers had come out on to the poop deck to listen and had stayed for the whole concert. Their cheers were as loud as anyone's when the concert was reluctantly ended.

It was a rip-roaring success and had succeeded in doing what had been intended. When the steerage passengers squeezed into their narrow, hard little boxes that night they were in better spirits than they had been in since they had arrived at the depot in Plymouth.

Mrs Goodfellow, who had been appointed matron in charge of the single steerage ladies rounded up all her charges and locked them into their cabin.

Watching her count heads to ensure there were none missing, Sarah shook her head.

'Do you know those poor girls have to share a bunk the same size as ours? And most of them were strangers to each other before they boarded this ship?'

Patrick looked at her in amazement. 'How awful that must be for them.'

Sarah nodded. 'I would hate that. It's different for the men. I was told it was not thought decent for men to share a bunk, so they are given a two-foot wide one each. The men are given so much more freedom too. That large lady, Mrs Goodfellow, was appointed Matron by the surgeon. She has to lock the young ladies in at night, to make sure no men, either crew or passenger can reach them. It seems so unfair.' Sarah shook her head in irritation.

'Yes, it does, doesn't it?' Patrick agreed. 'It must be most tedious for them, but I suppose it is for their own protection.'

'Yes, perhaps,' Sarah conceded, 'But I should hate it. Though some of the men do seem rather rough, don't they? And there are a few men in the crew who frighten me a bit. I'm just very thankful I have you here to protect me.'

Patrick agreed. He had noticed that the surgeon, whose job

it was to look after the safety of the young ladies, had been keeping a very wary and protective eye on them.

The wind picked up by the following morning and the *Navarino* cut through the waves at a spanking rate. That improved morale amongst the passengers almost as much as the concert.

On a scorching hot day, the ship crossed an invisible line which Lennie said was the Equator. 'It's the longest line round the world,' He told them airily. 'There will be a big do today. You just watch. The weather's good, so it'll be a bit of fun.'

'What's it all about then?' Patrick asked, his interest sparked.

'Well it was started hundreds of years ago; they reckon to test the new men in the crew to see whether they're fit to stand their first voyage.'

Hustle and bustle increased on the deck, so Judith was not allowed to crawl around lest she get stepped on.

There were sailors dressed as bears, one as King Neptune, a judge, one as a surgeon wielding a huge knife, as well as several other strange looking characters. In addition, there was an almost carnival atmosphere alive on deck. The passengers were gathered on the forecastle, the steerage having been given permission to mix with the cabin passengers for once. Excitement grew as several strange creatures were hauled over the bows. These were led by an apparition wearing false hair and with what seemed to be seaweed hanging around its clothes. This ugly creature wore a paper crown and was carrying a wooden trident in its right hand.

The passengers squealed with laughter when the strange figure declared it was King Neptune, ruler of the deep. It swaggered across the deck, claiming kisses from the ladies it passed.

'I am Neptune, king of the deep!' it declared in a loud voice, 'And this ship is passing the equinoctial line into my kingdom.

All who enter for the first time must pay tribute. Rum and sugar from the Master and the ship's name shall be entered in my log!'

Crossing the line was always an occasion for horseplay and high spirits, which relieved the stress and boredom of a long voyage. A canvas pool was rigged up and bilge water pumped into it. The younger members of the ship's company, including officers were then lined up alongside older officers, who were supposedly Neptune's nymphs and neroids, their faces painted red. Each struggling victim was seated on a stool, his face lathered with a dreadful mixture of tar and tallow. This was then scraped off with a large piece of wood shaped like a razor and the stool was then upended to give Neptune's new subject a dunking.

Captain Morgan presided over the festivities with a barrel of rum from which, grinning cheerfully, he was generously rewarding the participants in the ceremony.

Some of the single women were grabbed by the revellers, but Surgeon Goullett soon put a stop to that.

Toward the end of the ceremony Sarah noticed the surgeon striding over to where some of the sailors were talking to the single girls.

Mr Goullett slapped away the hand of a sailor who was holding the arm of an upset looking girl. Sarah saw arms waving and a sailor raise his fist. His face black with fury, the surgeon knocked the man's fist away, stabbed his fingers into his ribs and pointed toward the bridge.

'You get below now and leave the ladies alone or I'll report you to the Captain!' Mr Goullett shouted.

Digging an elbow in Patrick's ribs, Sarah said, 'There's trouble over there, look.'

The Captain, having noticed the altercation, hurried down on deck. 'What's to do?' he demanded.

'This scoundrel was forcing his attentions on this young lady,' the surgeon said angrily, 'And as you know, it's my place to care for the welfare and morals of the single ladies.'

'Indeed, it is, Mr Goullett,' Captain Morgan agreed. Turning to the mate, who stood nearby, he told him to clap the man in irons for twenty-four hours. 'Maybe that will teach him a lesson. If not, it will be the cat-o'-nine-tails next time.' he added.

The mate led the sullen sailor away to be chained, and the line-crossing ceremony continued.

Chapter 26

◈⋯⋯◇⋯⋯◈

'*Land ahoy!*' the cry went up from the lookout, at the head of the mainmast.

Shading her eyes, Sarah looked up, seeing not much more than a tangle of rigging. As her eyes adjusted, she could just make out the tiny figure of the man high above her. Following the direction of his pointing arm, she saw nothing but white-capped rolling waves.

Patrick stood beside her, holding tightly to Judith. 'It will be lovely to see land again won't it?'

Sarah nodded; her eyes bright with excitement. 'After all these dreary weeks trapped in that little box it will be nice to know the rest of the world is still there.'

Patrick laughed, his thrill matching hers. 'Aye. After a while you get to feel it must all have sunk from being! I can hardly remember what it feels like to walk on solid land!'

It was well over an hour before they saw a darkening on the horizon. It was no more than that at first, but slowly grew until they could recognise it as land.

'That there's Cape Town,' Lennie told them. 'It's the southern-most point of South Africa. It's the last land before Antarctica.'

The names meant very little to many of the steerage passengers. All that mattered was that it was dry land. Proof that the real world did still exist.

'Will we be allowed to go ashore?' Sarah asked hopefully. It would be so wonderful, she thought, to walk where the ground wasn't constantly moving and likely to sink from under her feet.

Lennie stroked his chin thoughtfully. 'Well, I shouldn't think so, Missus. The cabin passengers might, but not the steerage I don't think. British Government paid a lot to the shipping company to bring you all out. If we let you ashore some might run off because they don't want to go back to sea. Then there'd be a hell of a lot of trouble for Captain Morgan.'

'No one would do that, surely?' Patrick frowned in disbelief.

'Has happened. People have a few scares and they don't want to go no further. So, they jump ship first chance they gets.' Lennie shrugged. 'And the worst of the voyage is still to come,' he added ominously.

'Oh, don't say that! Surely it can't get any worse than we've had?' Sarah was shattered by the thought.

Lennie nodded enthusiastically. 'It can too. Much worse. We'll be sailing right far south in the Indian Ocean, where we've got to look out for icebergs. And there will be hard frost and maybe snow too. It's winter down this end of the world you know! Storms worse than you've ever seen as well, no doubt!'

Sarah felt her knees trembling. This got worse by the minute. Wasn't that last storm bad enough? 'What's an iceberg?' she managed shakily.

'An island of floating ice. Some of them is massive, miles long, and others is not too big. But there's a lot more underwater than you can see above. The lookout must be extra careful, for the ice can easily tear the bottom out o' the ship!' Lennie was enjoying his story telling; Sarah prayed he was exaggerating.

They lay at anchor in Cape Town for two days while stores and some sheep and hens, for fresh meat and, they hoped, a few eggs were loaded.

The cabin passengers were allowed ashore and enjoyed being free of the ship. When told they were sailing the following day, they pleaded with Captain Morgan to stay a few more days.

Their pleas, to the relief of the steerage passengers, fell on deaf ears as the Captain was determined to make the voyage as short as possible. 'Can't do that,' he said gruffly. 'I've got to get you lot safely to Australia as soon as I can. And I'll wager any money none of you want to be at sea any longer than you have to!'

No one disagreed.

Well, the steerage passengers certainly did not. As Lennie had predicted, they had not been permitted to go ashore. Despite that, they enjoyed watching the hustle and bustle on the quayside, spending most of each day watching at the rail. In all the daylight hours there was activity on the dock, which was much better than looking at endless, empty ocean all day, every day. Judith happily crawled around the deck at their feet.

They listened with pleasure to the sounds of the workers shouting, and varied animal noises. Whistles blew, horns blasted. They also enjoyed the spectacle of the cargo, particularly the live animals being taken onboard.

One of the sheep slipped on the gangplank and, to Sarah's horror, fell between the ship and the quay. There were a frantic few minutes while men with boat hooks and ropes jostled and shouted to each other as they tried to rescue the fallen animal. At last, to everyone's relief, the mate was lowered and managed to get a rope on it. The poor thing was dragged, kicking and spluttering onto the quay, then carried up the gangplank to be dumped unceremoniously while protesting loudly, on the deck. After all that, Sarah was saddened to think that the poor creature's fate was to have its throat cut and be served up on the passengers' dinner plates.

It was with mixed feelings they eventually heard the order to weigh anchor. There was some relief to be underway again, some sadness and, for many, a great fear of what lay ahead.

Sarah heaved a great sigh as the hawser dropped and two tugs drew the ship away from the quay.

As Cape Town and its huge flat mountain — which they had been told was called Table Mountain — faded into the distance, Sarah watched from the rail. Patrick held her hand and Judith sat on the deck watching the sheep.

The tablecloth descended on the mountain as if farewelling them.

'So that was South Africa,' Sarah said sadly. 'And we'll never see it again.'

'Nay, lass. Nor shall we.' Patrick agreed. 'The next land we'll see will be Australia.'

'And what's to come before we reach there, I wonder? I didn't like what Lennie said about those — what did he say they were? Ice islands was it?'

'Icebergs, he called them. Well, he's a bit of a storyteller, isn't he? Let's not worry about that until it happens. *If* it happens.' He put his arms around her and gave her a reassuring hug.

Sarah nodded, a bit doubtfully and nibbled on her upper lip. Her heart beat a mighty tattoo against her ribs. How she dreaded the next few weeks.

The weather became colder as they sailed south, with a good tailwind most of time. The vessel scudded along joyously, and Captain Morgan was well pleased with the progress they were making.

It had been so hot in Cape Town — nearly one hundred degrees they had been told. The steerage passengers, trapped on board, had fought a losing battle in trying to stay cool. They had been constantly wet with perspiration. Now, within just a few days of leaving, the cold was such that they had had to change into their warm winter apparel.

The small amount of entertainment the passengers had were the schools of flying fish they saw occasionally. Sometimes a pod of dolphins or porpoises broke the water, leaping as though in dance.

One day Sarah saw a huge fountain of water shoot high in the air nearby and cried out, pointing. Her heart racing with fright she gasped, 'What's that?'

Lennie, who had been chatting to Patrick, looked around laughing. 'Why, 'tis only a whale. The largest creature God made; I reckon.'

They all watched in amazement and fear as a huge body heaved itself out of the water. It could not have been more than one hundred feet from the *Navarino* and looked to be just as large. It slapped back down into the water, close enough to rock the ship and to set many of the passengers to screaming.

Squealing with delight, Judith bounced in her father's arms and pointed excitedly to where the creature had been.

'If it comes up under the ship it will sink us,' a man standing next to them said gloomily. 'We're doomed!'

The passengers on deck had all rushed to the larboard side of the ship where the whale had been spotted, all watching nervously. A few minutes later it was spotted quite a distance further away. A communal sigh went up and people turned away to resume their conversations.

The following week the temperature had dropped so low that, try as they may, the passengers just could not get warm. Many of the days were sunny, but there was always a strong, bitterly cold wind. It was a tailwind that kept the ship moving briskly.

That at least was some relief, for it meant their dreadful voyage would be over so much sooner.

It seemed to Sarah that time was flying on leaded wings. All there was to see in every direction was turgid grey waves, with white spray blowing from their crests. A most boring and, often frightening scene. There was nothing with which to fill their days with almost no entertainment of any sort.

Now and again the musicians would start up and they would have an impromptu concert in the *tween decks* cabin. This lifted their spirits for a short while. It was too cold to contemplate even a repeat of the lovely concert they had held on deck a few weeks earlier.

A hurricane blew up with a sudden squall. There was a flurry of hailstones to start with. Stones the size of large pebbles fell, which sent all on deck falling over each other in a scramble to get to shelter.

That turned into the most miserable day Sarah could imagine. The hatch and windsail were shut to keep out as much of the cold and the sleet as possible, and as the storm grew, the cold intensified.

The steerage passengers had to stay in bed all day. Sarah, Patrick and Judith cuddled up tight together, with their few thin blankets wrapped around the three of them, to keep them all as warm as possible.

Fearing for Judith, who still had a bit of a cough but otherwise seemed to be thriving, Sarah dressed her in all the winter clothes she had in the cabin. She wriggled and whined constantly, as did most of the other children, but it had to be. They had to be kept snuggled in their bunks. There was no other way to keep them from freezing to death. Still they shivered, and their hands turned blue.

Going to the closet was a torture. The men took to using

it, though they were not supposed to. But it was too cold and dangerous to go to the heads. And who would tell anyway?

Sarah watched Judith like a hawk, determined to keep her healthy. If anything happened to her remaining baby, she was sure she would not be able to survive it. Losing George had knocked the heart out of her.

Many a time she berated herself for having come on this God-awful voyage. If they had stayed safely in Laxey, George would not have died. She tried not to think this way but could not help herself. Then she would shake herself mentally. Many children died of diseases in the Isle of Man too and he might easily have caught an illness there. Had not four of her siblings died of diseases there? And poor George had always been a bit frail since birth.

They crept out of their bunk at meal times, with blankets wrapped around them. Then straight back to their bunks. As well as the blankets from both bunks, which they guarded jealously, they laid as many of their clothes over themselves as they could. Still they felt the icy claws of death reaching out for them.

The night to follow was the most dreadful night they'd experienced. Hardly anyone got a single moment's rest as the ship was rolling and heaving like a creature in pain. She repeatedly rolled her bulwarks right under water. It was as much as the terrified passengers could do to keep to their beds. Waves were felt to batter the ship from every side. It seemed to many as though at any moment with the pure weight of the water landing on the *Navarino*, they should be engulfed and sunk.

The wind increased during the night and whistled through the rigging.

Sarah and Patrick clung to each other, wrapping themselves protectively around their baby. They tried but could not shut out the sound as the sea broke over the ship with crash after thundering crash.

Would they ever survive this? Sarah wondered. It seemed impossible. Her heart was heavy. What if the ship foundered? She thought of the boats. How few there were of them. There could not possibly be room for all the passengers. Would the steerage passengers be left to drown as someone had told them? Even if they did get in a lifeboat, she thought, they would never survive the cold and the wild sea.

Giving herself a mental shake, she tutted angrily. Of course, the ship would not sink! She must not think of such a thing! *Of course, it would not!*

Sarah heard a yell and a splash and saw that Jeremy had been thrown out of his bunk. He cracked his head on the post, leaving a nasty gash and rendering him unconscious. The surgeon was called, but after a careful examination he said poor Jeremy was probably only concussed. Whatever that meant! Sarah thought scornfully.

The ship was tossing too much to try to move him to the hospital, or to stitch the wound in his head. This would be done when the storm had abated. In the meantime, Jeremy was lashed to his bunk and Alison scrambled up and lay weeping beside him.

Sarah would have liked to go and comfort her but dared not venture from her own bunk. Instead she called to her and could only hope Alison could hear her words of comfort above the storm.

The assault lasted for five days. The condition *tween decks* was something beyond description. Throughout the gale the steerage emigrants were battened down below for their own safety. There was almost no light, no heating and no fresh air as the windsail was also closed. Even so, icy water ran into the cabin and again all the mattresses were soaked. The lower bunks were unusable, so all the passengers now huddled into the top bunks, clinging together and sharing in each other's misery.

Everyone was worn out in both mind and body through fear and lack of sleep. When they went to sleep most of the passengers felt certain that they would not see the light of another day. It seemed impossible to them that the ship could survive such a battering. Although they had almost no food in this time, the passengers were too frightened to feel much hunger.

The wind blew, and chains and ropes rattled. The ship rolled and pitched like a live thing trying its best to add to their discomfort. What a clatter the pannikins made flying through the air like cymbals, with slop pails and buckets rolling and jumping all over, women groaning and screaming, babies yelling and even some men crying.

Sarah often had to cover her ears to shut out the frightening noise of it all.

The icy seas reached a height, at times, of forty feet. Huge waves rolled in the direction of the wind, with higher peaks and crests produced by crossing waves. The violence of the storm blew off the lighter summits of the foaming crests. It seized upon the roaring peaks of mountainous seas, cut them off and drifted them away. When the waves slammed against the ship it made it tremble, with a crash like cannon firing, when it fell on the deck.

When, after ten lifetimes — or so it seemed to the heart-weary passengers — the storm stopped, and they were mustered on deck. Sarah felt she would never forget the poor, sickly looking creatures they were when seen out in good daylight. She had no idea the cold weather and close confinement could have had such an effect. Their eyes were red-rimmed and empty, their skins yellow. All looked devoid of any hope.

When they were brought up into the fresh air some of the women were praying while others were dumb with despair. Throughout the storm they had all been aware that in event of a wreck there were not enough boats to take them all.

Looking around, through frightened eyes, Sarah could see a lot of damage had been done to the *Navarino*. Several of the boats were destroyed and lay in splinters that hung on the side of the ship. Some of the wooden davits were smashed. Ropes were in tatters threatening to break, where they had beaten against the mast. The sails had all been taken down, so she hoped that they would be undamaged.

Still, she told herself, despite it all we have much to thank God for. That we are all still alive and that we are all in reasonably good health and that the ship has not been disabled more.

With all the noise they had heard when they were trapped below decks, they had quite expected to find they had lost their masts. It seemed a miracle they had not.

All the mattresses had to be brought up on deck for a thorough cleaning and to be dried out. There was only salt water for this but that was better than nothing. At least it rid them of all the unpleasant bugs that had been residing there and left them smelling much fresher.

The day was bright, but cold and brittle; too chilly to stay on deck for long. Mr Goullett ordered lime juice for everyone, which was the best drink onboard and very welcome. As soon as the surgeon had finished his examinations, and removed one or two to hospital, they all returned in misery to their bunks. He put some stitches in Jeremy's head, and told him he would bear a scar for life.

The wind had abated quite a bit by the following morning, and they were able to take a turn on deck. It had snowed very hard during the night and was many inches deep on the deck.

It continued all morning and the rolling of the ship created several large snowballs. The sails and the rigging were stiff from the frost.

There was a hearty family on board with whom Patrick and Sarah had become quite friendly. There were about twenty of them — uncles, aunts, sisters, brothers, cousins, mothers and fathers. They were mostly miners from Cornwall. No matter what the weather and the seas threw at them, they managed to stay cheerful. Their bright chatter and laughter often lifted the spirits of the other migrants when everything looked black and hopeless.

They told Sarah and Patrick stories of copper mining in Cornwall, while Patrick recounted tales of the silver, zinc and lead mines in Laxey. Like Sarah and Patrick, they too were heading for the copper mines of South Australia.

With the seas now calm they were sailing a little steadier, and very fast. There was a good tail wind and all sails were set.

The *Navarino* was sailing as far south in the Indian Ocean as it was safe to be, Lennie told them. Right on the ice line.

Just before daybreak one morning the lookout atop the mainmast gave a panicky shout. '*Iceberg! Dead ahead!*'

The passengers awoke to shouted orders and running feet thudding across the deck above them. They heard Captain Morgan shouting into his bullhorn giving the order to turn the ship.

This was followed by the screech of the rigging as the sails were hurriedly taken in.

Patrick, Sarah and many of the other passengers wrapped blankets around themselves and clamoured up to the deck.

In horror they saw, in the light of a full moon, a mighty ice island towering close to the bows of the ship. They held their breaths as the ship slowly, ever so slowly, started to answer the helm.

Knowing that hundreds of lives, as well as his ship, depended on him, Captain Morgan wanted the decks cleared. He ordered the passengers to return to their cabins. Those who heard him disobeyed. If the ship was holed, they did not want to be trapped below decks.

A feeling of panic was rife as the sailors raced about their tasks, unceremoniously pushing aside any passenger who got in the way.

To everyone's relief, after what seemed a lifetime, the ship turned. The iceberg still looked a good distance away as the *Navarino* skimmed along parallel with it. Suddenly there was a bump that threw the ship around. There was a terrifying ripping sound as the ship grated against ice.

Many of the passengers screamed and ran around in panic, certain the ship was holed and about to sink; knowing there were now so very few boats.

Sarah gazed up in awe at the mountain of ice that towered over her. She could think of nothing that could describe it. Frightening though it was, she was enchanted by the strangeness and splendour of the sight.

She reckoned it must have been many hundreds of yards or more in length. From the ship she could not see either end of it. And it would have been several hundred feet in height. It appeared to turn slowly and to rise and fall like a cork bobbing on the water.

The waves heaved and creaked against its base, to freeze and line its lower reaches with a white crust. There was a deafening sound as the ice mountain cracked. Huge pieces broke away to tumble down and slide under the sea.

Looking into the main body of the iceberg, Sarah could see it was a deep indigo colour, shading at the edges to snowy whiteness.

More passengers rushed in a panic onto the deck, thinking the ship was about to be wrecked. Seeing the ice mountain towering over them, they were frozen in horror for a moment then there was a din of noise as many of them started screaming.

Captain Morgan ordered all the passengers to their cabins. Some obeyed, but many of them had to be forced down and the hatches closed over them.

Then the ship was checked and by some miracle there was no damage. Nearly all the sails had been taken in and were to be kept reefed until they cleared the iceberg dangers.

The following morning, they found they were surrounded by sheet ice and there was another iceberg not too far distant. The ship still had to make very careful way with very little sail.

Thinking about it later, Sarah realised that not in her wildest nightmares could she have imagined anything as awful as the torment they had been through. Yet at the same time she had seen such breathtaking beauty. The iceberg, with its vivid contrast of colours and the sharp, cracking noise as sheets fell away from it had to be seen and heard to be believed.

Lennie saw Patrick and Sarah and came to ask if they had fared without too much fright. 'I have a funny story for you now the danger is past,' he told them. 'One of the single men complained to the surgeon about one of his cabin companions who was in a filthy condition and never washed himself. The surgeon sent for the man. On examination he was found to be both lousy and filthy. Mr Goullett told him to go and wash himself immediately in the tub near the forecastle. The first man came back, soon after, to say that the fellow refused. Mr Goullett then ordered six of the single men to strip him and scrub him all over. They filled a tub on the deck and threw him in it and gave him a good washing. He was shivering and near blue with the cold, but it gave us all a bit of a laugh.'

'Oh, the poor man!' Sarah was horrified.

Lennie shrugged. 'Had to be done, Missus. There's a lot of trouble amongst the single men with body lice. Grey backs we calls them. Fellow wouldn't wash himself — so someone had to. It's the only way to make them all keep clean. The surgeon has to do his best to stop them lice spreading.'

As the ship sailed north and the temperature rose, life became more bearable.

Judith had finally shaken off her cough and by a miracle, seemed a sturdy bundle of good health. She was testing her legs at every opportunity and her proud parents were certain that had it not been for the rocking movement of the ship she would be walking.

The little family spent as much time as possible on deck, talking to the other passengers, many of whom had become good friends during the voyage.

Several of the sailors, they noticed, were quite blatantly trying to force their attentions on the single ladies. The ladies tried to ignore them, as far as possible, but they became an irritating nuisance.

Sarah saw the surgeon come on deck. He stood grimly watching the antics of these sailors for a few minutes, his teeth clenched. Shaking his head angrily, he stormed over to the men and ordered them to leave the ladies alone.

They swore at him at first, then slunk off muttering amongst themselves. As soon as Mr Goullett was out of sight, they returned and started their pestering again.

Lennie had told Patrick that three of the seamen had been causing trouble throughout the voyage. They had been caught *tween decks*, near the single ladies' accommodation and had been reprimanded for it. He said the Captain reckoned they had only engaged onboard the ship for the purpose of causing a disturbance and forcing their company on the women.

On the 9th of July the three main troublemakers were again found *tween decks* by one of the Constables. The captain and surgeon were summoned, and they ordered the men back on deck. Using threatening language, the men refused to go.

This altercation was heard clearly in the emigrants' cabin and the passengers huddled in their bunks exchanging frightened looks.

Captain Morgan then grabbed one of the men and wrestled him up on deck. Once there, the whole of the starboard watch stood against him to prevent him taking the man aft. Aided by his officers he made his way through them, but they followed him to the quarter-deck, threatening him.

'We'll knock your bloody brains out!' Sarah heard one man shout. Trembling, she grasped Patrick's hand.

'Neither you nor the surgeon won't live to see Australia!' another voice said.

'What if they harm the Captain and take over the ship?' she asked fearfully. 'They're evil men!'

Patrick put his arms around her and gave her a gentle hug. 'It won't come to that, my love. There are too many of us on the captain's side.'

An hour or so later Captain Morgan sent word that he would like all the male emigrants to go on deck. He had a request to make.

'I have no doubt you will have heard that we have had something of a mutiny conducted by some of our crew. They have been behaving in a totally unacceptable manner toward the women on the ship. Neither Mr Goullett nor I are prepared to tolerate this.'

The men assembled before him nodded and voiced their agreement.

'Therefore, the troublemakers have been confined to their

quarters, rendering the ship undermanned. I am asking for twenty-four volunteers amongst you to aid in the working of the ship. I know most of you will not have had any experience in running a ship, but I'm sure if we all pull together, we will manage admirably.'

The male emigrants almost unanimously volunteered and the selected twenty-four most able looking, Patrick included, were chosen to work in two shifts of twelve men.

When told, Sarah was both proud and apprehensive. 'Oh, Patrick, it is good you're going to help. It will be an interesting experience for you.' While saying this she couldn't help wondering how she would cope alone with Judith if there was another storm.

Two days later Patrick returned from his shift with a stout piece of timber in his hand.

'The mate informed us today that it had been discovered the mutinous crew were going to attack the volunteers. So, we were advised to arm ourselves.'

Sarah gave a little cry and clapped her hand to her mouth. 'Did you have any trouble with them?' she asked worriedly.

Patrick shook his head. 'No. Some of them were glaring at us pretty angrily. But there were more of us than them. In the end they gave themselves up and the Captain has them in irons now. They'll make no more trouble and they'll be handed over to the constabulary when we reach harbour.'

At 7 a.m. on the 16th July the passengers were shocked by the discharge of three guns, which seemed to make the ship tremble in the water.

Racing on deck, they found they were in thick fog and could see no more than a few yards past the rail.

Sarah sniffed at the air. 'I can smell land,' she said excitedly.

Patrick gave her a sideways look. 'How can you smell land?'

'Oh, I can! I can! It is not the smell of the sea. It's the smell of flowers and grass. Surely you can smell it?' She clapped her hands excitedly.

Patrick shook his head. How he hoped she was right. For several days they had spent much time looking for land; knowing they were close, but not knowing just how near. *Please God, let Sarah be right.*

A large blue butterfly, of a type they had never seen before, hovered over the ship's rail. Sarah put out a joyful hand and it alighted on it.

'This is no sea creature,' she said with joy. 'This proves we are near land.'

The fog took several hours to clear. When it finally lifted, the emigrants were excited to see land in the distance. Houses and civilisation. They could see Port Adelaide.

In the distance, through a blue haze, they could see hills. On the highest there looked to be a smattering of snow.

They had made it! They were alive! Despite the dreadful conditions, and much due to the great care of the surgeon, Mr Goullett, most of them were in reasonably good health. The only lives lost had been George and another, newly born infant.

Sarah's heart lifted with joy, but there was sadness too, that poor little George could not have lived to share it.

Chapter 27

As they drew closer to the first land they had seen since Cape Town, the sails were taken down.

The little family stood at the rails, along with most of the other passengers. They watched with interest as a pilot boat came out to meet the *Navarino*. In it were emigration and customs officials, doctors and a troop of Constables.

All the adult passengers were interviewed and given information about what was expected of them in South Australia. The doctors checked everyone for any signs of illness or infection and congratulated Mr Goullett on the good health of his passengers.

While this was going on the Constables dragged the seven mutineers up on deck, an atmosphere of sullenness and fear pervading the group. They were then manhandled, none too gently, down to the pilot boat to be taken to jail.

The emigrants were told they would be allowed to sleep aboard ship for up to fourteen days, or until they could find accommodation on shore. They were given addresses where they might find accommodation, and where to arrange transport to the mines.

When the pilot boat, officials, Constables and mutineers had left, a steam tug towed the Navarino up the Port River to the jetty.

'How do feel about staying onboard?' Patrick asked, looking a bit doubtful.

'I feel we have spent more than enough time here. It might be alright to stay for a day or two, but I really feel I would like to get ashore. It would be nice to start our new life as soon as possible.'

Patrick nodded his agreement. 'It might be best if I go alone into Adelaide to see what I can find out. I'll have to see if I can sort out some accommodation until we can get transport to the mines.'

'Yes, that would be best, I suppose,' Sarah replied a little doubtfully. She did not much fancy the idea of being left on the ship without Patrick, but it seemed that was how it must be.

In the evening all the mining immigrants got together on deck and decided the men would all go to Adelaide the following day to sort out some transport and, if necessary, temporary accommodation organised. They left first thing in the morning and rode on a horse-drawn bus to the city.

Sarah and the other miner's wives had an anxious two days waiting for their men's return. The children fretted, fidgeted and were noisy and hard to control. They had been cooped up and bored for far too long. All they wanted to do was escape the confines of the ship and run around freely.

The women just wished to escape the cramped confines of their *tween decks* cabin. They all desired nothing more than just to make a start on the rest of their lives.

It was during these two days that Sarah felt movement deep in her belly and realised she had not had her monthly curse in all the time she had been on the ship. Life had been so confusing and frightening that she had not even thought of it. Now she was certain. It was not what she would have chosen, with life so unsettled, but she could have no regrets. It would be a child. Hers and Patrick's. Not to replace George — that was not possible, but to fill their lives with more love and to help heal the pain of George's death.

There was great excitement onboard when the bus finally drew up beside the ship. Women and children alike crowded noisily down the gangplank to welcome their men. A sailor made a feeble attempt to stop them going ashore but was cheerfully brushed aside.

The men arrived with good news. Patrick and the other miners, including the large Cornish family who had stayed so cheerful throughout the voyage, had managed to hire a train of bullock wagons to take them and their belongings to Kapunda.

'They are coming with the wagons tomorrow. It will take the best part of the day to get everything transferred from the ship to the wagons. So, we hope to leave here early the following morning. As it means only a couple more nights on the ship, I thought it was best if we stay here. It will save us having to pay for accommodation.'

Sarah wrinkled her nose but nodded in agreement. 'How far is it to Kapunda?'

'About forty-five miles, they say. It should take us about five or six days.'

'Five or six days? Where will we sleep? Are there towns on the way?' Sarah was full of fearful questions.

'Well, they told us to buy tents. Not just for the journey, but it is possible we might need them at first when we get to Kapunda, until we can find a cottage to rent. The tents will come with the wagons tomorrow.'

'Tents?' Sarah was not happy with that idea. 'We'll have to live in a tent?'

'If we do have to, it would not be for long. The draymen reckon there will likely be a lot of cottages standing empty up there. But we will also need the tents for stops along the way.'

'Will there be work? What if we get there and there is no work?' Sarah's fears were growing.

'We were told when we were granted assisted passage that there would be plenty of work. Otherwise the government would not have paid our passages out here, would they?'

'Well, no. I suppose not,' Sarah agreed doubtfully.

'Anyway, the migration officer who came onboard said a lot of the miners had left to go to the gold diggings in Victoria. So, the mines here are desperately short of workers. They need us to keep the mines operating.'

'Well, let's hope you're right because I have some news for you. I hope it will please you,' she said nervously.

Patrick raised his eyebrows questioningly. 'News? What news is that?'

Sarah drew a deep breath and behind her back her fingers were tightly crossed. 'I just realised yesterday that I am to have another child!'

Patrick regarded her for a moment in stunned silence. 'A child? You are with child? How? When?'

Sarah laughed. 'You asked me those same questions the last time I was pregnant. It must have happened just before we left the island.'

'So — another little Manxie!' He let out a huge roar of joy, which caused the others to look at him in astonishment. 'Listen! Everyone! We're going to have a baby! My beautiful wife is with child!'

There was a loud cheer and a few ribald comments, then one of the men went off to beg some rum to celebrate.

Very early on the morning of the 21st July, with over a dozen bullock drays loaded up, the little procession straggled away from Port Adelaide docks, carrying a lot of excited, but nervous passengers.

Their bags and boxes were piled in the wagons along with the tents the men had bought. Their supplies and cooking utensils were within easy reach at the rear.

Many of the children, with months of bottled up energy in them, climbed down frequently to run beside the plodding bullocks. Then, exhausted, they would climb back aboard and fall asleep.

It was a clear, bright winter's morning when they left. They had been surprised at how cold it became overnight, for they had been told it was always hot in Australia. However, the sun shone, and the day soon warmed up to what would have been regarded as a very nice summer's day in the Isle of Man.

The land they travelled through was very flat until they reached the northern side of Adelaide. Everywhere was a brilliant, lush green, but too level to remind Sarah and Patrick of the island they had left behind.

Sarah had made a comfy little bed in the corner of the wagon for Judith. She and Patrick sat beside the driver, Ted. He was a friendly fellow who had travelled this road often and seemed very knowledgeable.

Gazing around, Sarah said, 'I have never seen such vast stretches of level land. Are there no hills in Australia?'

Ted laughed. 'Get on with you, Missus. If you could see past all the muck the carts are kicking up, you would see there were hills ahead of us. The Mount Lofty Ranges, they call them. They're pretty hard work for the bullocks, but they're strong and willing animals. They'll get us over.'

Sarah peered ahead but could see nothing but dust.

The bullock team plodded along, making steady time, until

they reached the foothills. The ground rose quite sharply, and the poor animals had to lean hard into their traces. At times, with the gradient as steep as one in three, the adults had to get out and walk. By the time they reached the top everyone was exhausted.

'Will there be many more like that?' Sarah asked plaintively.

Ted shook his head. 'That's the worst. We just have to get down the other side now.'

'Can you tell us much about the mines at Kapunda?' Patrick asked. 'We were not told much, except that they mine copper and there will be plenty of work for us.'

'Aye, that there will. A lot of the miners upped and left when they discovered gold in Victoria.' Ted replied.

'Yes. We heard that. That was our bit of good luck.'

'That was a few years ago now, though there is still a lot of gold-mining going on. Some struck it rich, but not many,' Ted continued. 'A few came back, but most did not. Probably a lot died. It's tough and dangerous in the gold areas. You find some and everyone wants to steal it from you. So, you have to keep your mouth well shut.'

'I had a friend, came out over a year ago, but I've heard nothing from him since. I guess I would have if he had struck it rich. Maybe he was too busy to write. Or his letter could have passed us on our travels.' Patrick was silent for a moment, looking into the past and thinking of Robert. He found he could hardly remember, now, what his best friend looked like and prayed he was not one of the ones who had died.

'For most of the gold hunters it was a fool's errand. Anyway, you asked about the mines at Kapunda. Well, the first copper there was found by a couple of lads, Francis Dutton and Charles Bagot, in 1842. They held the land on leasehold at the time and had the sense to keep quiet about their discovery.'

'Smart fellows,' Patrick agreed.

'Well,' Ted continued, 'They sent a sample to England to be assayed and it was found to be 22.5 per cent pure, which was the richest source of copper in the world at that time.'

'Wow! Good find! So, what did they do next?'

'Well, they said nothing about it until they had managed to purchase eighty acres of land. And all they paid for it was a pound an acre! Mining started there about two years later. The ore was on outcrops on the surface. At first it was all mined with picks and shovels.'

'Surface mining!' Patrick said enthusiastically. 'I like the sound of that!'

Ted shook his head. 'That was in the early days. There was a lot of it though. The first load that was sent to England was seventeen tons and it was 26.5 per cent copper. They got 21 pounds and ten shillings a ton. It was all taken to Port Adelaide by bullock carts and in the first year, six hundred tons was shipped out to Swansea in Wales.'

'Those two fellows, Dutton and Bagot must have been laughing. How clever that was of them. You say it's not surface mining now though?' Sarah's hopes had been high for a moment. She still was not excited by the idea of Patrick having to go underground again.

'No. About the end of 1844 the government started bringing out miners from Cornwall and began tunnelling.'

'Most our group here are from Cornwall,' Sarah said. 'We're from the Isle of Man. Patrick used to mine zinc, silver and lead.'

'Been to the Isle of Man once,' Ted beamed at her. 'When I was a nipper we went there for a holiday.' He paused for a moment, smiling as he remembered his holiday. 'The mine here all grew quite quickly after the Cornishmen came. A horse whim was installed.'

'A what?' Patrick asked.

'A sort of round thing pulled by a horse. Poor thing must have got dizzy walking around in circles all day! It was used to bring the ore up from the shafts. Then the Welsh came out to help with engineering and do the smelting. All sorts of people came out after that. Irish did a lot of the labouring and Germans to help the Welsh with smelting. They did quite a bit of tree felling, too, for the boilers and smelters at the mine. Changed the look of the countryside a lot, they did.'

'It must have been quite a big operation by then,' Patrick said thoughtfully. 'Must have been as good as a gold mine for the fellows who found it.'

'You bet. They got richer than most of the men who went looking for gold. The Germans were hard workers too. They used to do quite a bit of farming. You would see their wives walking into town with wheelbarrows full of produce to sell. Still do!'

When a halt was called to stop for lunch there was a sigh of relief all round. The weary travellers spread blankets in a clearing and thankfully settled down to satisfy their hunger with the cold fare they had prepared before leaving Port Adelaide.

Some of the children started to run around, but the wagoners warned the parents to keep them within the clearing. 'They can be lost in a minute in the bush and may never be found,' one said ominously. 'And there are snakes in the bush too! Tread on one they'll get bit!'

Sarah looked at Patrick in horror. 'Snakes?' she asked. She had heard of the creatures but knew nothing about them. There were no snakes in the Isle of Man.

Ted nodded. 'They usually won't attack unless you scare them. But nippers running around might stir them up a bit.'

'Are they dangerous?' Sarah asked, her eyes wide with apprehension.

'Can be. Most of the Australian snakes are poisonous, some more than others. Best to stay out of their way and you'll be safe enough. If you leave them alone, they'll leave you alone!'

Sarah looked around, nervously as though expecting to see them all lined up around the clearing.

With the meal over and everyone rested, the bullocks were hitched to the carts, and heads counted. Everyone clambered aboard, and the little procession moved on.

The road was reasonably passable, and it was a beautiful calm, sunny day. Most of the travellers found it just warm enough to be comfortable.

With a half hour stop every three hours, to rest the bullocks and allow the travellers to refresh and relieve themselves, they made good time on that first day.

The entire company, man, woman and child was so excited at finally being on dry land that they felt nothing could dampen their spirits.

How wrong they were! By late afternoon darkness was falling and the wagoners decided it was time to call a halt for the day.

'It's looking like rain,' the head wagoner, Luke, said. 'We'd best get the tents up before it starts. Then maybe we can get a fire going. I shot a kangaroo this afternoon, so we'll have some good, fresh meat.'

Mouths started to water at the thought of fresh meat of any kind, though not many of them knew what a kangaroo was. The men started, with gusto, to erect the tents. The Cornish singing as they worked.

The wagoners quickly had a good fire going and the kangaroo was skinned, cut up and put on a makeshift spit to roast. The miners' wives soon had vegetables prepared and a hearty feast was promised.

Huge black clouds rolled over the hills and before the meal

was cooked the heavens opened suddenly. Icy rain sheeted down and by the time everyone had grabbed their children and pushed them into the tents they were all soaked to the skin.

The fire quickly died under the half-cooked meal.

'I don't believe this,' Patrick said. 'It has been such a beautiful day!'

'Until now,' Sarah said glumly. Realising suddenly that their bags of clothes were still in the dray, she ducked out of the tent and ran. She heard Patrick shout, but kept going. She had to get the clothes before they too were soaked.

But which wagon? Which wagon was theirs? Sarah looked along the line in despair. She felt the water running down her back in rivulets.

There was a sudden blinding flash, followed almost immediately by an explosive crash of thunder. With a scream, she turned to flee back to the tent. But which tent? They all looked the same! There was another flash. Sarah felt her feet going from under her and she was flat on her face in the mud, with rain beating on her back. Stunned for a moment and terrified, she lay where she fell.

Strong hands slipped under her and she was lifted into strong comfortable arms. Patrick carried her into the tent and dumped her unceremoniously on the straw mattress.

'What the *hell* were you thinking of?' he asked angrily. 'Running out into a thunderstorm like that.'

'I was going to get our bags of clothes before they too were soaked. We need to change out of these wet things. And it wasn't a thunderstorm when I went out,' she finished defensively.

Patrick shook his head. 'You gave me a scare. Don't ever do that again. When the rain stops, I'll go out and get them. Maybe there will still be some dry ones.'

The rain did not stop. It continued to batter down on the

tent and the noise of its torrent on the canvas was deafening. During the night it turned to hail for a while, then back to rain and the thunderstorm returned.

When morning broke, the rain had not lessened. The camp was swamped and most of the travellers had had a sleepless night, slumped miserably in pools of water.

A fierce wind blew, thrashing the branches of the huge eucalypt trees that hung over them.

The air was suddenly rent by a thunderous roar, accompanied by a tearing, splintering sound.

Alarmed, the men rushed outside, to find that the tent of one of the Cornish families had had vanished. In its place lay a huge branch, ripped from a tree by the storm.

There was frantic activity while the men, as one, put their shoulders to the branch. It would not be moved. The drivers brought a team of bullocks in and fastened chains round the log. Gradually, with a lot of shouting and cracking of whips, they managed to drag it clear of the tent. The ripped canvas was pulled away and the saddened men stood shaking their heads.

One of the Cornish ladies, who had been watching the rescue efforts, rushed over and threw herself on the sodden ground. Sobbing out the names of the tent's occupants, she looked in horror and pleaded with them to reply. Gathering the limp body of a young child in her arms she screamed, 'No! Oh no! It cannot be! Dear God, we did not come all this way to end our lives!'

Some of the other ladies came and lifted her away. 'Come now, Bronnie, they're gone. They're at peace now and they probably felt nothing.'

Bronnie wept endlessly. She was inconsolable. Her son, daughter-in-law and three grandchildren had been wiped out, just like that.

The miners and their families all stood looking in stunned

disbelief. This could not happen. To endure and survive that dreadful voyage, then to perish in such a way on only their second day on shore. It could not be true.

Sadly, it was true. A whole family had been wiped out in seconds.

The wagoners said they hoped to reach a town called Gawler that day or the next. It depended on what the roads were like after the rain. There was a church in Gawler, they said, and the minister would give the poor deceased a good, Christian burial.

The load from one of the wagons was divided between a few others and the five bodies were gently laid on the floor.

It was a sad and very frightened band of travellers who took to the road that day, still in torrential rain. For each of them knew it could just as easily have been they who were laid out in the wagon.

They all sat in dejected silence as the bullocks struggled, hooves slipping to pull their loads. Rivers ran down the side of the road and in the ruts, making things even more difficult. When they came to any kind of a steep slope the bullocks could not cope. With so much weight to carry their hooves would not grip, so the men had to get down and help to push the carts.

Torrents of water ran down their faces, necks and in their ears, but they had to keep going. Everyone was soaked to the skin, with no way of getting dry and no dry clothes to change into.

So much time was lost with the weather that they did not reach Gawler that day. Some of the men wanted to keep going, but the wagoners refused.

'Them beasts have done a good job for us today, but they're more exhausted than we are. If we try to push them any further, we'll lose some of them. Can't do it. They've got to rest.'

'We all have to rest,' Patrick sided with them. 'We've all

pushed ourselves too hard today. We can only hope tomorrow will be a better day.'

The wet tents were pitched again. The travellers ate whatever food they had, mostly raw vegetables, then lay down in their wet clothes to sleep the sleep of the utterly exhausted.

In the morning they awoke to sun shining on the tent and to bird sounds they had never heard before — the strange warbling of the Australian magpie and the raucous, mocking laughter of kookaburras.

After they had broken their fast it was a subdued, but slightly more cheerful crowd who set out that morning. They had all taken a change of clothing out and laid them out on top of the wagons. So, while they sat in clothes that were still sodden, they knew that soon they could change into dry.

It was nearing noon when they came to a ford and the wagoners stopped, stroking their beards and conversing quietly amongst themselves.

'Gawler is just across the ford, but the water has risen, with all that rain,' their spokesman said eventually. 'We want to have a go at getting one of the wagons across. If it is too deep, we'll have to wait here until the water level falls again.'

'This is the South Para river,' Ted said quietly, 'and this crossing is called Dead Man's Pass.'

Patrick frowned. 'Why so? That sounds a bit ominous.'

'Well, way back an exploration party found an exhausted man an' gave him shelter. He fell asleep and when they stopped here, they checked and found him dead. They had no shovels for a grave, so they stood him upright in a hollow tree. Later another lot of travellers came along an' found him. They wrapped the body in clay in the tree. It was the nearest they could come to burying him.'

Patrick shook his head sadly. *What a strange tale.*

How long will it be before we can cross?' one lady asked. 'We need to bury our dead.'

'I know, I know,' the wagoner sympathised, 'But if the water is too deep, we can't cross. The wagons would be swept away. I promise we'll get you across as soon as we can.'

The bullocks held back, nostrils flaring and eyes rolling, refusing to face the fast-flowing stream. Six of the wagoners went into the water, three on each side. The front men, though they had sticks in their hands, talked quietly to the animals. Not one of them used their stick but quite soon they had managed to coax the animals into the water. Taking it very slowly and holding on to the yokes to stop themselves being swept away, they reached the centre of the flow. The cart became a bit flighty but did not float and eventually they made it safely across.

Having seen the first bullocks cross safely, the others followed without too much trouble and in about two hours they were all safely on the northern side of the ford.

One of the children fell over the side and looked like being swept away, but Patrick shot out a large hand and grabbed him by the scruff of the neck as he sailed past him.

It was a miserable, wet party that straggled into Gawler.

The townspeople, seeing the state of them, came rushing to offer help. A minister was sent for and, after promising a funeral for the following day, said a prayer for the dead.

The weary travellers were taken into homes to be warmed, given hot nourishing food and privacy to get changed into dry clothes. They were all offered a bed for the night by the friendly, sympathetic townsfolk.

In the morning a simple, but moving funeral service was conducted and the poor little family was interred, all in the one grave.

'At least they'll all be together, forever,' Bronnie said, bravely stifling her sobs.

'What will become of Bronnie now?' Sarah wondered. 'All her family gone and in a strange country.' She need not have worried. The Cornish looked after their own. In a way they were like one large family; Bronnie would always be well cared for.

After the funeral the miners assembled, preparing to continue their uncomfortable trek. The innkeeper generously gave a few pannikins of rum, 'to help them warm the rest of their journey'. Once again, they were on their way to this unknown and frightening future.

In an effort to keep his own and his passengers' minds off the tragedy, Ted continued his history of the Kapunda mines.

'I was telling you about the mines, wasn't I?'

Patrick nodded, glad of the distraction. 'Yes. Please tell us more.'

'Well, in 1846 Francis Dutton sold his share of the mine to some English company — 16,000 pounds he got for it, so they tell me. I think he went back to England for a short while. When he came back, he went into sheep farming.'

Sarah gasped. 'It's hard to imagine so much money isn't it?'

'Yeh. 'Tis. Charles Bagot had fifty-five per cent ownership of the mine by then and they called him 'Captain Bagot' because he was manager. A year of two after that they brought in a steam engine, the Cornish beam engine, but had a lot of trouble with that, so got a different kind. Smelters were built, so they're able to send the refined copper overseas. The ships that take it to England bring back coal from Newcastle-upon-Tyne to fire the smelters. So, it's all pretty well organised.'

Sarah felt cheered by all this information. It made her feel less as though she was coming into the completely unknown.

Weary, but rejoicing, the wagon train and its miners trailed into Kapunda a week after they had left Adelaide. Thankfully there had been no more disasters, no more rain and the rest of their trek had been uneventful.

Chapter 28

⸻ ◈ ⸻

From quite a distance away the band of weary travellers saw the huge mine chimney. It pointed to the sky like a welcoming finger. It was the flue system, they realised, for the pumping and winding engines. Though it was late afternoon and almost dusk, it still belched smoke. To the miners and their families, it was like coming home.

A murmur of excitement whispered its way along the line of carts. As one, their thoughts were transported back to the mining towns and the families they had left behind. It seemed so long ago now, that they had started on their big adventure. So much had happened since and they were all far stronger for their trials on the voyage, and more determined to take the future by the throat and make a good life for themselves, no matter what might be thrown at them. This was what they had come for. To help in the building of a new country and, they hoped, a more prosperous life for themselves and their children.

Within minutes they saw the first buildings. Rows of neat stone cottages, with smoking chimneys. There was a shop and a tavern. A blacksmith. To their joy it appeared to be quite a good sized and tidy looking town.

'Oh, Patrick,' Sarah said, looking around with moist eyes. Past the tears that ached in her throat, she continued, 'It is not at all what I was expecting. It is different — but better. We are home!'

'Aye,' Patrick agree thoughtfully. 'I don't know what I was expecting, but this will do me just fine. It looks a good place to rear our Judith — and the little bump!'

Ted smiled his agreement. 'I'm sure you'll be happy here. 'Tis a nice friendly town. You'll find quite a few of the natives wandering about from time to time. Sometimes they're naked, but mostly they wear old clothes the townsfolk give away. They're friendly enough, though. Keeps to themselves mostly.'

'Naked?' Sarah was not so sure she liked the sound of this.

Ted laughed. 'Yeh! But not too often. You just have to look the other way — or give them some clothes to put on!'

A man wandered out of the tavern and stopped to look in surprise at the scruffy, grubby looking collection of people sitting wearily atop carts. Children hung from the sides, gazing timidly about them.

The man approached Patrick's wagon. 'Who have we here?' he asked, and they could see he was trying to suppress a grin.

'I brought you a load of miners, mostly from Cornwall,' Ted said cheerfully.

'Cornish miners, eh? Well we could be doing wi' them. Mines are producing well but running a bit short of labour these days. I'll go fetch the Captain; he'll know where to put you all. Take yourselves into the tavern and get a bite and a drink. You'll be made welcome.'

He strode away, stopping long enough to throw open the tavern door and shout, 'Get yourself ready, Justin, you've got a huge mob of hungry and thirsty miners coming in!'

The families, sighing with relief, climbed stiffly down from the carts and dusted themselves down as best they could. When the stragglers had arrived, they all shuffled into the tavern together. A wood fire blazed — a relief to everyone after their long, chilling journey.

'Sit yourselves down. Anywhere will do. The children can sit on the floor!' Justin, the landlord, shouted. 'Get yourselves organised, let me know what you want, and I'll have it for you as soon as we can manage. Just as long as it's stew and ale. I think we can manage some milk for the youngsters too.'

Patrick sat Judith on the floor and took Sarah's hand. 'Well,' he said, 'What a wonderful welcome. It seems like a nice friendly town.'

'It does, indeed,' Sarah agreed, gazing around wide eyed. It was so cosy, and she had forgotten what it felt like to be warm. She thought the fire the most beautiful thing she had ever seen. 'I think we will be very happy here.' Her heart was doing little somersaults.

Judith pulled herself to her feet, holding on to her father's trouser leg. She looked up at him with a cheeky smile. Balancing herself carefully, she let go of her father and, with a look of determination, took her first three steps. Bumping down onto a well-padded backside, she grinned proudly up at them.

'That has to be an omen,' Ted said quietly. 'Three small steps into a prosperous future.'

'I hope you're right,' Sarah said, laughingly. 'I really do hope you are right.'

Justin and a couple of serving girls brought out large bowls of something that looked and smelled delicious. 'Kangaroo stew,' he announced. 'We got word you were near so Jessie, my missus, made enough stew to feed an army.'

Travellers shifted uncomfortably, some brought back in memory to the awful night when they had been roasting a kangaroo and the storm had taken the lives of five of their friends. With tears in their eyes, they picked up their spoons and started eating.

A few minutes later the tavern door swung open and an impressive looking gentleman stood there. For a minute or so he studied the weary looking people, then he smiled.

'Welcome to Kapunda,' he said genially. 'Captain Bagot at your service. I'm told you're all copper miners. We will be very pleased to have you. Things slowed down a bit here when half the miners took off to search for gold. However, we've got the mine up to full production again and we can always use experienced miners. None better than the Cornish, I've found.'

In the days that followed the newcomers were found accommodation and made very welcome in the friendly town. The men started work straight away and the wives began to make homes of the cottages they had been allocated.

Sarah was overjoyed to find the previous tenant of their house had left some furniture. It was home-made, obviously by a man proud of his craft. There was a bed, a table, a cupboard and a couple of chairs. Not a lot, but it gave them a good start. Added to the bits they had brought with them; it turned the cottage into a home. Anything else they needed; Patrick would make when he had the time.

Their biggest problem was fleas. The cottage had been unoccupied for quite some time and was over-run with the nasty, biting creatures.

Sarah bought large quantities of Lysol from the shop and frequently scrubbed the floor, walls and furniture with the smelly stuff. It took about two months, the cottage stank, but in the end, she won the battle, and they were finally itch-free.

They quickly settled into a happy lifestyle, though Sarah still always worried when Patrick was underground. The mine seemed to be well made and there were no accidents of any note. Still, she worried.

Sarah was happy to learn there was a resident doctor in town. Doctor Blood, she was told his name was, which amused her. Doctor Matthew Blood, whom she learned had about nine or ten children.

'Well, if he has nine or more children of his own, he should know what he's doing,' she gleefully told Patrick, 'I should be well looked after if I have any trouble with the delivery of this little bundle!' she fondly patted her swelling belly.

'Don't go looking for trouble,' Patrick growled. 'It was only because there were two last time, and one of them wrong way 'round at that ...' he paused for a moment to fight for control, 'that George had trouble ...' he finished with a sob in his voice.

Doctor Blood estimated, when consulted, that the baby would be due around about Christmas. 'Not the best time of year,' he said thoughtfully, 'With the heat there is then. But as long as you're sensible you should not have any problems.'

As she awaited the arrival of this new little life, Sarah threw herself into establishing a vegetable garden. There were some fruit trees already growing well, though they were very overgrown and needed a lot of tender, loving care to bring them to good health. They recovered well, so the little family ate healthily and cheaply. Now and again one of the men would shoot a kangaroo, and it would be shared amongst the families. Any of Sarah's produce that was surplus to their own requirements, she carried into town and sold to Graham and Linda who ran the shop.

'Would you like some hens?' Graham asked one day as he was paying her for some cabbages.

'I would love some, but I don't know where I could buy any,' Sarah replied.

'Well, you leave it with me, lass. I know some of the German farmers' wives have hens. I buy eggs from them, but they can't supply as many as I need. I'll ask about it next time they are in the shop. They're friendly ladies, so I'm sure they'll be glad to help. Yes, you leave it to me. I'll find you some hens.'

'Oh, thank you. I would be most grateful' Sarah's eyes sparkled with excitement at the prospect. 'I would let you have any extra eggs I have. If I have any.'

'I'm relying on you for that lass. I'll let you know as soon as I find any birds for you.'

'I would be so grateful if you can,' Sarah said excitedly. 'My dream is to save enough money to buy some land of our own. Then Patrick could give up mining and become a farmer instead!'

''Tis a long, hard step from mining to farming, you know, lass. You got to know what you're doing.'

Sarah nodded. 'I know, but Patrick grew up on a farm, so he should know what he's doing.'

Graham nodded, slightly doubtful. It was one thing to grow up on a farm, he thought, but a different thing to run one in Australia!

So, it was that Patrick found himself, a couple of days later at the far end of the garden with a hammer, nails, wood and wire, constructing a chicken run. Two weeks later they had a dozen fat healthy hens.

Any money she made for her produce Sarah put in a tin that she hid under a loose slate in the far corner of the cottage. One day, she told herself, if she was careful, they would have enough to buy a few acres of land. Then they could build their own home. They could then grow more produce, keep more chickens and maybe a goat for milk. It was an exciting prospect and not one they could ever have contemplated in the Isle of Man.

Now and again when she was walking to the shop, Sarah would see some of the natives. Usually they stayed at a distance, watched her warily, but were unsmiling. She was not sure what to make of them because she had heard so many conflicting stories. They often carried spears and another kind of weapon Patrick told her was called a boomerang. Though she never felt they looked threatening, she still found she was nervous of them. Perhaps that was because they were black, and she had never seen a person with black skin before. To her, it made them look rather ferocious.

Patrick had made her a little cart to carry her produce. A handy object, also, when Judith tired of the long walk to the shop and back.

One day, as Sarah walked into town, a group of four adult natives and a handful of children walked toward her. They kept well over on the other side of the road and eyed her openly as she approached.

Sarah smiled and one of the women, with a baby hitched on her hip, smiled back. The rest of them remained stony-faced.

Suddenly a little boy of about three ran toward her, his arms outstretched. One of the men shouted something, but the child ignored him and kept running. Tripping on the rough ground, he landed on the hard road just in front of Sarah. Without a moment's hesitation, she bent to pick him up. Taking a handkerchief from her sleeve, she dabbed at a bleeding graze on his knee.

The woman who had smiled came over and shyly held out her arms for the crying child, while the man spoke rapidly and unsmilingly in his own language. Sarah tried not to appear frightened, but nonetheless did find him a bit intimidating.

Sarah wiped the child's eyes, handed him to his mother, then gave her also a handful of plums, indicating they were for the children. The woman smiled and nodded, then the group went on their way, chattering loudly in a tongue that was very strange to Sarah's ears.

Sarah smiled to herself, then carried on to the shop and thought no more about it.

The following morning when Sara opened the door, she found a dead parrot on the doorstep. Puzzled, she looked up and down the street, but there was no one in sight. The ants and flies had got there before her, but they would wash off. She had found that parrot pie tasted very similar to pigeon pie, so this was a very welcome gift — whoever it was from.

When questioned, none of her friends knew anything about it, but in the weeks following a few more titbits were left including, on one occasion, a small snake. Sarah happily accepted these treats. At first, she was a bit doubtful about the snake, but when asked, Graham assured her it was quite edible. Well, she could not afford to waste anything, determined as she was that one day, she would have enough money to buy her piece of land. So, the snake found itself in the stew pot and made a very tasty meal.

Flies were a constant pest, which Sarah found very hard to bear. They were everywhere and inescapable. They relentlessly attacked mouths, eyes and noses. At times she felt almost panicky as she tried to brush them away from herself and Judith. As fast as she swatted them away, they came back. In the end, just to keep herself sane, she bought a length of fine netting from Linda and attached it to the front of their hats. Judith rebelled against it at first but gave in in the end.

Walking to the shop with a cart full of fruit, vegetables and eggs, Judith, eighteen months old and now quite steady on her feet, was toddling a good distance in front of her.

Some natives came toward her, including the mother and her little son. As they neared, the man stopped then suddenly, with his eyes on Judith, raised his spear.

Sarah stopped, rooted to the spot, for a moment, puzzled. What is he doing? She wondered. Why is he looking so intently at Judith?

Suddenly he moved. His arm swung forward, and the spear was just a blur as it sped toward Judith. Sarah screamed and started running to her little daughter, seeing the weapon speeding toward her. Seeing it land only a foot or two in front of her. The man was running too, faster than Sarah could in her advanced state of pregnancy. Screaming at him to stop, she stumbled on.

The man reached Judith and swept her into his arms.

'No! No! Please give her to me!' Sarah screamed. In a frightened corner of her mind she was aware of other people running and shouting. Then she realised in her panic that the native man was bringing Judith to her, holding her out to her.

Sobbing, Sarah took her sweet child from the man, burying her tear-stained face in Judith's hair.

Suddenly the native woman was beside her, pointing to where her husband was retrieving his spear.

Sarah looked, and it was then she first saw the huge snake — an ugly brown thing. Its head was fastened to the ground by the spear that impaled it. Its body still thrashed wildly, until the man took his knife from his waistband and decapitated it. Still the body moved. Sarah shuddered and averted her eyes. Slumping to the ground, she sobbed her thanks and hugged Judith so tightly the little girl grumbled and tried to push away from her.

'Thank you! Oh, thank you so much,' she sobbed, not knowing if the native girl understood her. She only hoped they did not realise she had thought the spear had been aimed at Judith.

Other people were there then. White people asking her if she was alright. Friends. Neighbours. People she didn't know, helping her to her feet. Dusting her down. Asking what had happened.

Gasping for breath, still stifling sobs, she told them the wonderful Aboriginal man had saved Judith from a snake. When she looked round, the natives had melted away. The snake was gone too!

The following morning, when she and Judith went to wave Patrick goodbye, she found a good-sized portion of snake on the doorstep. Now she knew who had been leaving her gifts — and knew she had made some very precious friends.

From that day on Sarah frequently left a box on her doorstep with some eggs and whatever fruit and vegetables were seasonal. Sometimes the box would be empty in the morning, on others it would contain a parrot or some native vegetable. She never saw the Aboriginal people come or go, but was thrilled with their strange, distant friendship.

Sarah wakened in the early hours of Christmas morning with a tightening in her lower belly. Ten minutes later it was repeated. The time had come for 'the bump' to make its way into the world.

It was early stages yet, she decided, so no point in depriving Patrick of his sleep. When he did wake, and she broke the news, he was like a dog chasing its own tail. Not knowing whether he should call the midwife, call the doctor, or just sit there waiting. He was relieved that it was Christmas day, so the mine was closed. In horror he remembered that he had been down the mine and had not been there for Sarah during the dreadful trauma of George's birth. This time he would not leave her and would hold her hand all the way through, he determined.

Sarah persuaded him to just sit quietly and wait. She would tell him, she said, when it was time to go for the midwife. That was as successful as telling a hungry tiger to lie still while an antelope walked past its nose. Patrick paced endlessly and asked, every few minutes, if he could go for the midwife.

In the end, and to get him out from under her feet for a while, Sarah agreed.

Twenty minutes later Patrick was back, with a breathless, red faced Mrs Mills.

'Now then, what's the panic here?' Mrs Mills asked as she waddled her heavy body into the room.

'No panic at all,' Sarah assured her. 'Not from me anyway.'

Mrs Mills nodded. 'Yes. They all get like that. The ones that care do anyway. I'm used to it my girl. Now I'm here, you get on the bed and I'll take a look.'

'Hours away yet,' she pronounced.

'Is everything alright?' Patrick asked anxiously. 'You see last time—.'

'This is not last time though, is it?' Mrs Mills cut him off sternly. 'This is *this* time and each time is different. This time she is only having one. And a big one at that with a heartbeat like a jungle drum. Now, make yourself useful and go and boil some water.'

Patrick nodded, picked up a bucket and went outside. Mrs Mills followed him out.

'Now then, boy,' she told him, grim faced. 'Either you stop frightening that girl, or I'll chuck you down the mine shaft. Childbirth is enough for her to concern herself with without you putting a scare into her. Is that clear?'

Patrick nodded.

'Right then, get a smile on your face and keep it there no matter what happens. Sarah needs supporting not frightening. Got that?'

'Yes,' Patrick said shamefacedly.

Mrs Mills glared at him; lips clamped tightly together. 'Just remember!' She nodded abruptly, gave him a half-friendly cuff across the side of his head, then stomped back into the house.

'Now then,' she said cheerfully, 'You've got a nice fire going here, girl an' I've only an empty house to go back to, so I might as well stay with you. Saves me huffing and puffing up that damned hill too.'

Sarah was more than glad to have her there.

It was not a long labour, as labours go, but too long for Sarah and Patrick. Mrs Mills chattered away cheerfully, checking on Sarah now and again to see how the labour was progressing.

'All's well,' she pronounced. 'This one's going to be a live wire. She'll keep you on your toes, alright!'

'She?' Patrick questioned. 'Could be he.'

Mrs Mills shook her head decisively. 'Nope! She!'

Without any problems Emily Mary O'Malley slipped into the world, protesting loudly at seven o'clock that evening.

Mrs Mills prescribed a large stout for each of them, herself included, to help them all recover from the rigours of labour.

Chapter 29

Sarah stood in the shop with Graham and Linda. They all watched anxiously as hot dust hissed against the window pane. A fierce wind whipped the tree branches to a frenzy and Sarah's face glowed with the heat radiating from the glass.

Graham shook his head. 'I don't like the look of it. It's real bushfire weather!'

Sarah took a backward step. 'Is a bushfire really bad? I have heard tell of them, but I've never seen one.'

Graham chewed on his lip. How much to tell the girl? She had to be made aware of the danger, he decided, but he didn't want to frighten her too much.

'Pretty bad,' he said finally. 'If we're going to be hit by a bushfire, my guess is it could be today. We haven't had a really bad one here, but it can happen any time. I don't think I've ever seen a more dangerous day!'

Linda nodded and glanced fearfully toward the window. 'With the day so hot. And this wind so fierce.' A shudder shook her body.

'You can see the heat coming up off the ground.' Graham continued, 'The smallest spark today and with a wind like this it will run like wildfire. I'm not a pessimist by any means, but I reckon there's a disaster out there just waiting to happen!' He nibbled his lip a bit more and shook his head again. 'All we can do is cross our fingers and pray.'

Linda took another long look out of the window, sighed and nodded. 'Yes. It's not looking good. This wind is getting wilder too.' Shaking her head, she added, 'I'm not trying to get rid of you, Sarah, but you'd best get on home. There's a lot of dust blowing around already. It wouldn't do to have the babies out if it gets worse. You're right on the edge of town so keep a good eye open though in case of fire. Come back to us if anything does happen. Don't stay up there on your own.'

Sarah nodded, wide-eyed and frightened. Bundling the two little girls into her cart, she hurried home. The fierce wind and the dust it carried stung her skin and she told the girls to keep their eyes shut.

For a while she stood nervously at the window looking out through eyes clouded with fear. With a shake of her head she tried to drag her thoughts back to the matter in hand. Best get on with peeling the potatoes, else Patrick would be home and there would be no tea for him.

Outside, the wind suddenly wrenched the lid from a bin that rolled and skittered noisily along the road, clattering against every stone. Twigs rattled on the roof as they fell and skittered across it. There was an earth-shaking crash as a nearby eucalypt surrendered a giant branch to the wind. It crossed her mind that someone had once told her they called those trees 'widow makers' because of their habit of casting branches without warning.

Startled, Sarah glanced at the window again, tense, anxious and with a terrible sense of foreboding. With her mouth feeling as though it were full of dry straw, she prayed the huge tree at her back fence was not close enough to drop a branch on the cottage. It would come straight through the roof! Looking toward the roof (and heaven) she sighed and whispered 'Please, God'. She remembered only too well the tree branch that had killed the Cornish family.

Fourteen-month-old Emily took fright and started crying as a flurry of gravel hit the window. Sarah picked her up and cuddled her. 'Hush now, it's only a lot of noise. It won't harm you.' she comforted, while praying she was right.

'What was that awful banging, Mammy?' Judith asked, wide-eyed.

'It was just an old bin lid. We'll get it back when the wind stops.'

Borne on the wings of the blustering wind, gritty red dust, scorched dry by months of drought, was picked up and driven against the cottage. It beat against the windows. Swirling, it piled into miniature dunes in sheltered corners and crept under the doors. Sarah put rags on the floor to keep it out. They did little good, for the wind under the door immediately blew them aside. She had been told about the ferocious bushfires they had in Australia. *It's this wind that makes it worse,* she thought nervously. *I don't remember when we last saw rain. Everything is tinder dry. It will only take one spark to send the countryside up in flames.*

There was a distant rumble of thunder and Sarah's heart leapt with joy. *Rain!* Surely thunder meant rain was coming! Didn't it? God knew it was badly needed.

No rain came though Sarah waited and prayed, almost not daring to breath. It had been a dry lightning storm, far in the distance. She had been told about them and how often they started fires when the land was brittle dry.

'Please God, don't let that happen,' she beseeched silently.

'The farmers are just ready to harvest their crops. The fields are full of ripe wheat. It would destroy some of the smaller farmers,' she whispered.

It had been a growing spring. A very warm and wet one that had lasted a while and got the wheat-fields off to a good start, to the delight of the farmers. While their crops had been developing into a bumper harvest, though, so too had the weeds. They were shoulder high along the roadside and throughout the bushland.

Then summer had arrived — unendurably long and hot. Hardly a drop of rain had fallen for nearly five months. Now, in mid-February, as well as the wheat, a dry tangle of grass and scrub covered the countryside, the hills and the forests.

Unconsciously Sarah still gripped the potato knife as if her life depended on it. She wandered aimlessly back to the parlour. Through the window she saw the trees bent low, flailing in the grip of the gale. Red dust whipped the glass like tongues of flame, hissing and crackling against it. Visibility outside was virtually zero. The cottage seemed to tremble with the force of it.

Shaking her head, Sarah took a tremulous breath and wandered back to the kitchen and her potatoes.

Gradually a new smell crept into Sarah's nostrils. Smoke! Was it? 'Oh, dear God, no! Please no!' Heart pounding, she dashed outside and looked frantically around. From the back garden she could see nothing. There was a dark haze over the sun. Was that smoke? Or was it just the dust?

From the front of her cottage on the edge of town, Sarah peered toward the far distant hills. Raising a hand to shade her eyes she thought she could see a whiff of smoke. It was a long way off and did not look too bad. Not much more than an impression; perhaps just a wispy grey cloud. Hard to tell with all the dust. Maybe rain would come. *Please let the rain come.*

Neighbours came out to stand beside her, all braving the stinging dust to gaze to the hills.

'Aye. 'Tis smoke. Gawd help us if it comes this way!' One of the older women said.

They all watched worriedly as the smoke swirled up toward heaven. Yes, there was no doubt now. Smoke rose quickly to scramble swiftly across the sky. Sarah could see no flames but knew they must be there. No smoke without fire! Sarah thought, frightened. Just smoke so far though.

On the wings of the wind it raced along the ground, disappearing into a gully that had a stream running through in winter, but now was bone dry. Nothing there to stop any flames. For a few minutes the smoke seemed to die, and Sarah's heart lifted a little with hope. But then she saw it again as it flew up the near side of the gully, whirling like some mad creature.

It had happened suddenly. So suddenly. Sarah's very worst nightmare had become reality. Everyone's worst nightmare!

It seemed not much more than just wind and dust and smoke for a while. Then it reached a distant stand of eucalypt trees and now Sarah could see the flames.

They exploded from the crowns of the trees, showering flames and burning leaves high in the air. Carried on the wind, these started new fires until a vast stretch of land was a wall of flaming fury. It was wildly dancing, orange and yellow and blue, with billowing grey and black smoke. It writhed like an angry demon before Sarah's frightened eyes. It was still a long way off but galloping like a frightened horse.

The sight was awesome. Terrifying! Even from a long distance and as far as the eye could see, the scene was of fire, smoke and total, burning devastation. Flames, like deadly tongues from Hell leapt several hundred feet into the air. Fed by the ripe crops, they raced, swirling ahead of the wind at terrifying speeds.

Sparks and burning leaves took flight, spinning like drunken fireflies amongst the flames, many landing miles ahead of the main blaze and starting secondary fires. The wind whipped these up and made new fires much closer to the town than the main one.

There were many fires now, still a long way off, but getting closer every second. And the town was right in their path.

The inferno raged through the tree-tops, crowning, exploding and tossing flaming branches and leaves to the ground and other nearby trees. It seemed that the whole world was on fire.

It was coming so close now that Sarah could hear the crackling and the roar of it.

Men were running past her now with branches, blankets, anything they could think of to beat the flames. Too close. It was coming too close to the town. Sarah could feel the blistering heat of it now and the air was too thick, almost, to breathe.

Patrick arrived, the men being all brought up from the depth of the mines to help fight the flames. He put a hand on Sarah's shoulder and shook her out of her terrified trance.

'Get the girls and go into the centre of town! It's not safe for you here!' he shouted above the crackling. 'Stay there and out of danger until we've stopped the fire!'

'Be careful, Patrick. Oh, please be careful,' Sarah pleaded, clinging to his arm.

'Go now. Go! Get the girls and go. Quickly!' He gave her a gentle push toward the house.

Sarah nodded. Heart pounding, she turned and ran into the house. Grabbing her two daughters she dumped them unceremoniously into her little cart. Her heart banging loudly in her ears, she fled down the road toward the town centre.

It seemed most of the women and children were there, all looking as frightened as Sarah felt. They huddled together, eyes wide with fear as they watched the blackness fill the sky and blot out the sun.

Suddenly Sarah remembered her hens. If the men could not stop the fire, her house was one of the first it would destroy. Her chickens were there, penned up, with no chance of escape. Rushing into the shop she gasped, 'Please, Linda, look after the girls for a few minutes.'

'Why? Where are you going?' Startled, Linda's head jerked up and she frowned at Sarah.

'My hens. I must set them loose and at least give them a chance.'

'No! Bugger the hens! Don't go back up there. It's not safe. The fire is too close.' Linda grabbed at her arm.

Sarah jerked her arm free. 'I must. I can't just leave them penned up to be roasted alive. I must give them a chance. Please look after the girls,' Sarah pleaded.

Linda nodded. 'God speed, then,' she called as Sarah turned tail and fled up the road.

The fire was very near now, the smell of it acrid and the sounds angry, snarling and snapping. As she came close to her home, she could feel the heat of it scorching her skin. Heart pounding painfully, she raced toward home.

The roadway was alive with kangaroos, lizards, an emu family and a myriad collection of native animals Sarah could not identify. There were rabbits by the score. As they raced to escape the flames, several of the kangaroos nearly bowled Sarah over in their haste. A possum sped past with its fur on fire.

There were snakes everywhere, which Sarah nervously avoided standing on, but they too were intent on outrunning a fiery death and had no interest in her.

The men were beating down the wheat in front of the fire in the hope that would slow it. It was a hopeless task, Sarah saw.

They were being driven before it, having to run for their lives at times.

Sarah reached her house, with the flames now only a few hundred yards away. Running to the chicken coop, she unfastened the gate. At first, they would not move. They huddled in the back corner, frozen there with fear. She ran in, waving her arms, screeching at them, pushing at them with her feet until she had forced them out through the gate. Once free from the pen, they seemed to come to their senses, and all flapped out of the garden and squawked off down the road.

Spluttering and choking on the smoke and with the heat burning her lungs, Sarah raced after them. The flames by then had almost reached the end of her garden. As she fled, the huge eucalypt just outside her back fence exploded in a shower of burning branches and leaves.

Sarah felt hot embers land on her head, burning into her scalp. Panicking, she brushed frantically at her hair. Her face blackened and smeared with perspiration, she stumbled into the crowd outside the shop. It seemed every woman and child in the town was there, looking fearfully up the street.

'The fire is at my fence — I'm going to lose my house,' she gasped to Linda. Her mouth tasted of smoke and her throat and lungs felt scorched.

Linda came and put an arm round her. 'You have your children safe and that's all that really matters. A house can be replaced. An' they'll stop the fire before it gets here. There's not much to keep the fire fed once it gets to the town. Come into the shop and I'll make us a nice cup of tea.'

Sarah nodded. *Aye*. The children were safe. But what about Patrick? He was out there somewhere, fighting the fire. Her heart stammered with fear for him. She struggled to hold down the tears that scorched her eyes.

Linda was right. The worst of it was over.

They did stop the fire before it got right into town. The five houses at the top end of town were razed, but it could have been so much worse.

When the fire was under control the men straggled wearily home, leaving a few beaters on guard in case it flared up again. Two men had been badly burned and Doctor Blood did not hold out much hope for them. He was a good doctor but lacked the equipment and facilities to treat such severe injuries. Nor would they survive the journey to the infirmary in Adelaide. Many of the men were burned, Patrick included, but not severely. Only a few were not fit for work the following day.

Sarah and Patrick's little cottage had perished, with everything in it. All they had left was the clothes on their backs — and their children. The most precious things in their lives; their beautiful, dearly loved daughters.

When it was cool enough to return, Sarah and Patrick stood hand in hand surveying the wreckage of the place they had called home for the past three years. It was a miserable sight. All that still stood were some blackened stone walls, which looked none too safe, and the stone chimney.

White streaks ran down Sarah's cheeks where the tears had washed away the soot. It was all gone. Her cosy little house. All the furniture Patrick had put so much love into the making of. Suddenly she remembered the little tin she had hidden under the slate in the corner. If the fire had got to that her dream of a little farm would be set back several more years. So many more years Patrick would have to spend in the mine!

With a sense of dread, Sarah rushed to the corner and raked through the ashes. The tin was there, under the slate and apparently undamaged. She dragged it open and gave sob of relief when she saw her meagre savings had survived.

'I hope Alinga, Mullyan and Mogo and the rest of them are alright,' Sarah said worriedly as she surveyed the heap of blackened rubble.

'Who?' Patrick looked puzzled.

'My Aboriginal friends. Mullyan was the man who saved Judith from the snake. I hope they weren't caught out there in the fire.'

Patrick nodded. 'Well you probably don't have too much to worry about. From what I've heard they are experts when it comes to fires. Do you know they often deliberately start fires? It enriches the soil and does the countryside good. But they know how and when to do it without causing any damage or danger. I reckon we could probably learn a lot from them, you know.'

'You don't think they started this fire, do you?'

'No. I'm sure they didn't. They would have more sense than to do that in this wind. They say it was a lightning strike. There was a thunderstorm up in the hills where the fire came from, but no rain. That would be what set it off.'

'Well, if they didn't start it, I hope they were not in the way of it.'

Patrick nodded. So did he. He knew how fond Sarah had become of her Aborigine friends.

'And just look at my garden!' Sarah said, with tears stinging her eyes. 'My vegetables have all perished. The fruit trees are burned. My hens are gone. My little business has gone! I have nothing to help us save for our own piece of this country. To get you safely out of the mines.'

'We'll get more hens. Plant more vegetables. The trees may recover. We'll build a new house and I'll make new furniture. The important thing is we have each other, and we have the girls. We are all safe, apart from some very small burns. We have everything to be happy about. So, wipe those tears away and let's see that beautiful smile.' He drew the back of his hand gently down her blackened, smeared cheek and thought she had never looked so beautiful.

Sarah nodded. Patrick was right. Of course, he was right, — they did have so much to be thankful for. She just prayed her lovely black friends were as lucky.

The neighbours were all wonderful. As in any small, young community they had all become close friends and clung together to give help and support wherever it was needed. None of the large Cornish family who had sailed with them from England had lost their homes. Without hesitation, they took Sarah and her daughters under their collective wing. They took them into their home, to stay for as long as it took for their cottage to be rebuilt.

Clothes appeared as if by magic. Some fitted, some were several sizes too large. Those were easily altered, and all were welcome and accepted with gratitude.

Patrick and the other four men whose homes had burned slept under the stars. There were many disoriented snakes around, making the ground unsafe, so the men threw mattresses on the back of bullock carts and slept there. No great discomfort in the hot summer nights.

Many of the townsmen banded together to rebuild the burnt houses. They worked cheerfully and quickly, completing the cottages in a surprisingly short time. When they were ready for occupation, the families were lent whatever pieces of furniture their friends could spare until they could restock for themselves.

To Sarah's delight, the day after they moved back in, all but one of her hens wandered home. Patrick quickly rebuilt their pen and within days they had settled and started laying again.

The new house seemed, to Sarah, to be better than the old.

Most of the stones from the old house had been used, with quite a lot extra brought in from the quarry. It was roomier, fresher and at least there was now no more danger of any lurking flea eggs hatching! Though her friendly neighbours had been kindness itself, it was with joy she moved back into her own home. Lovely to have privacy and her own space again. The cottage was sparsely furnished, and she and Patrick had to make do with a borrowed mattress on the floor, but it was their home and they were together again.

Patrick dug the garden and cut all the burned, dead wood from the fruit trees. They would probably not have fruit the following year, but thankfully most of the trees would survive.

Sarah sowed a variety of vegetable seeds and in no time, they had germinated and were looking healthy. She knew it was the wrong time to be growing them but hoped to get a bit of a crop before winter arrived. She knew too that the burning would have made her land more fertile.

One day, to her great joy, she found a dead parrot on her doorstep and knew her friends had survived. Parrot pie had never tasted as good as it did that night.

Patrick came home from work one day, very quiet and subdued. Although he played with the girls, reading to them, as he always did, Sarah could see his mind was miles away. He seemed to be off in another, not too pleasant world.

'What is it love?' she asked once the girls were out of earshot.

Patrick looked up, startled. 'What is what?'

'What is it that's worrying you? And don't say 'nothing', as you were going to. I know you too well to believe that!'

Patrick sighed. 'I was just trying to think how to tell you. Not good news, I'm afraid.'

Sarah nodded. 'I'd guessed that. So just tell it to me straight. Fancying it up won't make it any easier to stomach.'

Patrick nibbled at his lip and sighed again. 'I just heard today that the mine is starting to wind down. They're getting toward the end of the seam.'

Sarah thought that over for a moment. 'Does that mean the mine is going to close?'

Patrick nodded. 'Not right away. They're not taking on any new men and soon they'll be starting to pay off. Eventually the mine will close. I don't know how far away that will be though.'

'So, what shall we do? Wait 'till it closes, then hope we've enough saved to buy some land an' go farming?'

Patrick shrugged and chewed thoughtfully on his lip. 'I don't reckon we'll ha' near enough saved to buy our own land. It maybe depends on how long this mine keeps going. I have heard there is a new mine north of here somewhere. A place called Moonta. We might have to move up there.'

'And go mining again?' Sarah shook her head sadly. 'I hate you having to go down the mine.'

'I know it worries you, my love. I don't much like it either, but it's all I know. Apart from farming, but it's not likely that will be a choice.'

Sarah nodded mutely. If only she had managed to save more.

Nine months to the day after they had moved into their new cottage, James Robert O'Malley made a very noisy entry into the world. He was a bouncing ten and a half pounds in weight and so greedy they could almost see him grow.

Cheerful Mrs Mills attended the birth again. She had told Sarah the baby would be a king-sized boy.

'Well. I told you did I not?' she grinned smugly. 'I said it would be a big 'un and a boy. Got it right again didn't I? On both counts!'

Sarah and Patrick could only smile, laugh and agree with her. Sarah was thrilled that she had given her husband a son this time. Patrick couldn't care less. All that mattered to him was that Sarah and the baby were well.

'Shall we call him James Robert, for our two dearest friends?' Sarah asked tentatively.

'I can think of nothing better,' Patrick agreed. 'I wish I had tried harder to keep in touch with Robert after he left the island. Things just got a bit hectic and I never got around to it. Lazy of me.'

'There were two to blame on that score, for he never wrote to you before we left to sail here.'

Patrick nodded. Sarah was right, as she usually was. Still, he should have tried. Robert had been a good friend to him through the troubled years.

On the day following James' arrival a tall stranger knocked on the door.

Mrs Mills, there to check on mother and baby, opened the door. 'Yes?' she asked guardedly.

'I hope I've got the right house,' the stranger said. 'I'm looking for Patrick and Sarah O'Malley.'

'You've got the right house. But I don't think they're expecting no one.' Mrs Mills eyed him suspiciously and folded her beefy arms across her mighty bosom. 'An' Patrick ain't here. He's down the mine!'

'Is Sarah here then?' The stranger raised a questioning eyebrow.

'Aye. But I don't know as she's up to seeing anyone right now.' Mrs Mills glared at the man.

'Who is it?' Sarah called out.

'A man. Don't know him.'

Sarah arrived at the door behind her friend and looked closely at the man.

'I don't believe it,' she said, her eyes wide. 'Is it really you, Robert?'

The stranger smiled. 'Yes. It's really me. I've crossed the country on horseback to find you.'

'But how? Why?' Sarah shook her head in bewilderment. *Robert — here!* He was the last person she had expected to see. 'Oh. Come in. Come in,' she said, remembering her manners at last.

'Mrs Mills, this is Robert Kelly, a friend of Patrick's from the Isle of Man, where we came from.'

Mrs Mills eyed the man a bit doubtfully but stepped aside to let him pass.

'What are you doing here and how did you find us? I can't believe you're here! It was just last night we spoke of you.' Sarah was still trying to get her breath back. Seeing Robert standing on her doorstep had been a shock, but a nice one. She well knew what good friends he and Patrick had been.

'Well, I've done a lot of wandering, and prospecting of course, since I got here. Ballarat, Bendigo and a few other places besides.'

'Did you get rich like you said you would?'

Mrs Mills was listening to this exchange with avid interest.

Robert laughed. 'Well I found a bit of gold here and there. Enough to keep me comfortable and buy myself a good horse. But I didn't get rich. I met up with some bushrangers a couple of times.'

Sarah's eyes widened. 'Bushrangers? Did they rob you? Did they hurt you?'

"Nah. I'm still in one piece — as you can see. I had no more than a little bag of gold dust on me. They went through all my things, but when they were sure how little I had, they left me with it. I guess I was lucky I didn't meet up with any real bad ones.'

'You look well, anyway,' Sarah nodded her approval. 'How did you find us?'

'I wrote to Mary and James, just hoping they were still there, and they told me where you were at. 'They said you had a couple of daughters now.'

Sarah laughed. 'Aye. A real pair of little mischiefs. And a son too. Born yesterday.'

At that moment James decided he was hungry and started squawking lustily.

'Patrick's a very lucky man,' Robert said feelingly. 'One of these days I hope I'll meet someone as nice as you and have family of my own.'

Sarah, feeling shy about feeding the baby in front of Robert, excused herself and went into the bedroom, leaving him to Mrs Mills' tender mercies.

Chapter 30

'Wait until I tell you what I heard today—'Patrick began as he stomped into the cottage. He stopped short, frowning when he saw Sarah had a visitor. 'Oh! Sorry! Didn't know we had company.'

Robert leapt to his feet. 'I'm not just company! Now don't tell me you've forgotten your old friend already. It hasn't really been so long has it?'

Patrick peered into the gloom of the cottage, his face splitting in a grin when he recognised the visitor.

'Robert! By all that's holy! Where did you appear from? What brings you here? How did you find us? 'A million questions tripped over each other in his mind. The two men then engaged briefly in a hand-crushing and shoulder-slapping contest.

'Sit down and let me get you an ale. No doubt you've met my family.' Patrick waved an arm, vaguely encompassing the cottage.

At that moment the girls, having heard their father's voice, erupted through from the bedroom. Amid squeals and giggles they launched themselves at Patrick. It took a while to settle them to quiet play before Patrick was able to pour the promised ale and start a sensible conversation with Robert.

'First question? How did you find us?'

'Good old reliable Mary. I wrote to her about a year ago to ask of you. I'd moved on since, so it took until a month ago for her reply to catch up wi' me. By the way,' Robert turned to Sarah now, 'Mary sends her love and to tell you the childher are all well, happy and doin' good at school. She can't read or write, of course but she says she'll get James to write to you soon.'

Sarah smiled and nodded. 'I have a letter from them from time to time, with all the news of the childher. I've likely had one since the one she wrote to you. Mary is the best friend any-one could ever have. She thinks the world of the children an' is a proud of them as any mother could be. Had it not been for her kindness and her love of the childher — and theirs for her — Patrick and I could never have left the Island. Mary could not love them more if she was their real mother. Aye, an' James too.'

'Aye. I remember what a support she was to you when you were having such a bad time with your poor mother.'

A cloud crossed Sarah's face as the black memories returned. Remembering the family she had left behind, and probably would never see again. And Alexandra. She had not always been bad. Something must have jarred her mind to make her turn the way she did. Sarah's eyes filled with unshed tears.

'What brings you here then, Robert?' Patrick quickly changed the subject. He leaned forward in his chair, eager to hear his friend's news. 'Have you come to boast of your riches?'

Robert gave an ironic smile. 'I wish that I had, but sadly that's not the case. I found enough gold to live on and a bit left over, but sorry to say, I'm not by any means a rich man, but I'm not poor either! Most of the gold is taken by the big companies. The lone prospector only gets the leftovers.'

'When you left the island didn't you say you were going to some place called Bally something? Did you get there?'

Robert laughed and shook his head. 'Ballarat, it was. Long before I got there, they'd had some sort of a riot.'

'What was that about then? Were they fighting over the gold? We heard there was so much of the stuff it could just be picked up off the ground.'

Robert nodded, then shook his head. 'That's what I heard too. But when I got to Ballarat there were so many diggers, about twenty-five thousand they reckoned, there was hardly room to sit down. The government had brought in licences. You had to buy one before you were allowed to dig. Whether you found any gold or not you had to pay for a licence. A lot of the miners were not finding enough gold to even pay for this piece o' paper. Then they put the price of them so high most of the diggers couldn't afford one.'

'What did they do then?" Sarah asked. "Did they have to give up digging?'

'Some did, most did not. They just went on digging and no one bothered them much. Then in June 1854 a new Governor, Hotham by name, came to power and set up a licence check twice a week.'

Patrick sat spellbound. He'd heard some whispers of trouble in the goldfields but knew little about it. Some of the copper miners had gone looking for gold, but little had been heard of them after they had left Kapunda.

In the background the girls whispered and giggled as they played.

'Go on,' Patrick urged.

Robert was really getting into his story now and feeling pumped up and important with all his knowledge.

'Tempers ran high as opposition to the licences increased. Then there was a problem wi' corrupt officials too. It all came to a head when a group o' men beat a Scottish digger to death.

The local hotel keeper, name of James Bentley, was one of that group, but because he was a friend of the magistrate he wasn't prosecuted.'

'That's dreadful!' Sarah stamped her foot angrily. 'He should have been hung for murder!' She clapped a hand over her mouth and looked apologetically at Patrick.

Robert nodded. 'Of course, he should but 'tis rough justice on the goldfields. Anyway, the other diggers agreed wi' you an' in October that year they held a meeting to try to find a way to bring the killers to justice. I don't know what they decided, but soon afterwards a bunch of the diggers burned down Bentley's hotel.'

'Good. No less than he deserved!' Patrick nodded enthusiastically.

Robert nodded again. 'Trouble was that three of the diggers were arrested and thrown in jail for burning down the hotel. A couple of weeks after that about ten thousand diggers had a meeting. They demanded that the three prisoners be freed, licences be abolished, and all men given a vote. They also formed a group, the Ballarat Reform League, to negotiate or fight for miner's rights. Around the end of November there was another, even bigger meeting, and the diggers decided to publicly burn their licences.'

Patrick drew in his breath. 'Wow! I'd heard there was some sort of trouble on the goldfields, but I didn't really know much about it. I didn't know it was all that bad.'

'What happened to the miners who had burned their licences?' Sarah asked, wide-eyed.

Robert chewed on his lip for a moment. 'At that meeting,' he continued, 'the diggers made their own flag, based on the Southern Cross star constellation. They call it the Eureka flag now. In response to the meeting the Gold Commissioner ordered a licence check.'

'Well, the diggers weren't going to take that lying down, so there was another mass burning of licences. Under the leadership of a man called Peter Lalor they then marched to a site called Eureka, where there was a deep lead of gold being mined. They built a rough wooden barricade there, closing in about an acre of the goldfields. Inside this stockade about five hundred miners took an oath on their new Southern Cross flag. In the next two days they gathered what firearms they could and forged pikestaffs to defend their stockade.'

Patrick and Sarah sat, speechless, as they listened to this narration.

'Well,' Robert continued, 'the next thing was that three days after the diggers barricaded themselves in, third of December I think it was, the authorities attacked the stockade. They already had the 12th and the 40th Regiments standing by to help the police troopers.'

'It must have been quite a fight,' Patrick cut in eagerly.

Robert shook his head emphatically. 'Not at all. The diggers were hopelessly out-numbered, and it was all over in about twenty minutes. At the end of it twenty-two diggers and five police troopers lay dead. An' many more injured. The Southern Cross Flag was pulled from the flagpole and taken by the winners. Peter Lalor escaped, but he was badly injured and later his arm had to be cut off.'

Sarah and Patrick sat silent for a while, unable to take in the enormity of it.

Sarah drew a deep, shuddering breath. 'I thank Our Lord Patrick never went looking for gold then,' she said feelingly.

'So, what happened after that?' Patrick asked after a while.

'Well, a few days after the uprising, martial law was declared and a Commission to the goldfields was appointed to look into it all. Thirteen, I think it was, of the diggers were arrested, but they were all acquitted when it finally came to trial. It seems it was a fair-minded Commission because when its report came, it was on the side of the diggers. All their recommendations were passed, and all the diggers' demands were granted. The vote was given to all who possessed a miner's right, which by then cost only one pound. Before that the licence had cost eight pounds per year.'

'That sounds alright. Is that what you had? Tell us all about it.'

'Well, of course, it was all sorted long before I got there. All the trouble was over, and everything had settled down. By then, though, all the best claims had been taken. There were only the scratchings left.'

'What did you do?' Patrick was leaning forward, elbows on knees, eager not to miss a word.

'I bought myself a miner's right, okay. Bought a tent and everything the storekeeper said I would need — tents, pots and pans and even a horse. I'd never ridden one before, so had a bit of fun an' a lot of bruises learnin', but the main thing I needed it for was to carry all my gear. I'd no idea how far I would have to go to find a claim and I couldn't have carted all that on my back. In the end me an' the horse came to an agreement and we're quite good friends now. Most of the time anyway!' Robert gave his rump a dramatic rub.

Trying to imagine his friend on a horse, Patrick gave a shout of laughter. 'That'll be the horse that's eatin' Sarah's spuds I suppose!'

Sarah squealed and ran to the window. Seeing nothing, she picked up a tea-cloth and swiped Patrick with it.

Robert laughed, scowled at Patrick, then continued, 'Men tried to sell me their claims, but you had to be careful because there were a lot of charlatans around. Some didn't have claims to sell, just trying to diddle you out of your money. Others did have claims but were trying to sell them because they hadn't produced much — if anything.'

'Sounds tough,' Patrick put in.

Robert nodded. 'Aye. It wasn't the easy 'get rich' I had expected. I scratched around for months, but only came up with enough grains of gold to keep me in supplies. Then I met a lad called Dandy. That's what he called himself anyway. He was anything but a dandy. He was a poor little skinny bit of a lad an' had something wrong wi' him. He told me he'd had some sort of an illness when he was a lad that had crippled his legs, so he can't walk proper. Had to swing his body and drag his legs to get around. One time I was in town buyin' supplies I saw a gang of louts knocking him around an' jeering at him. I had a spade in my hands I'd just bought, so I jumped between Dandy and the bullies. They saw I meant business an' backed off. After that Dandy pleaded with me to take him with me to my claim. Promised he'd work hard with only his food for payment.'

Sarah shook her head sadly and wiped a tear from her cheek. 'So, what did you do? Did you take him?'

'Well, my first thought was that he'd be more hindrance than help. I reckoned I'd end up feeding him and get next to no work out of him in return.'

'So, did you just leave him there?' There was a sharpness of disapproval in Sarah's voice.

'In the end the poor little bugger was just about on his twisted little knees begging me to take him with me. I could see the bullies hanging around on the corner. I knew if left him there they would come back and be twice as hard on him. Even kill him, maybe. So, I shook my head at mysel', then pulled him up on the horse behind me and took him wi' me.'

Patrick eyed his friend thoughtfully. He knew what a soft heart Robert had. 'Good decision or bad?'

'The best I ever made. He'd been pushed around and bullied all his life. No one had ever stood up for him before and he'd have worked for me for nothing,' Robert replied without hesitation. 'He was a game little runt though. Never complained, he didn't. Worked like a slave, without me having to ask and had a heart the size of Laxey Wheel! From sunup to sundown every day he was out diggin'. Worked twice as hard as me, he did. For months we only found a few small nuggets, which kept us in supplies, but not much more. Then one day he came sauntering into camp looking right down in the dumps. He gave me an eye, then nodded toward the tent an' went an' crept into it.'

'What was wrong?' Sarah asked worriedly. Already she cared about this poor little fellow.

'Well, I followed him in to see what was up with him, you know. He put his finger to his lips, took his hand out of his pocket an' it was full of nuggets. More gold than I had seen in all the years I had been in Australia.'

'Wow!' Patrick leaned forward eagerly.

'It was a fortune to us. Luckily Dandy had been around the goldfields long enough to know not let drop a hint that we had struck lucky. There had been a flood a few days before and Dandy had the sense to go diggin' around roots above the usual water line. That's where he found it. Must ha' washed down in the flood.'

In the days that followed we went back to the river together and fossicked around roots at the high-water line. Between us we found quite a few more nuggets. Mind, we had to make sure there was no one else around to see us. We didn't dare leave them in the tent while we were out, so we dug a hole under a heavy rock and kept them there. Then when we stopped finding more, we decided we had to get rid of what we had.'

Robert stopped talking for a moment while he wetted his dry throat with a swig of beer.

'We talked loudly enough for others to hear, about goin' into town for supplies. Then we both scrambled up on the horse, left all our camping gear and rode away. When we got to the rock, we collected our gold and headed for town. The most perilous part was after we picked up the gold, but luckily we made it to town without meeting up with any bush rangers.'

Patrick pursed his lips. 'I've heard about them. I heard they were just as likely to kill you even after they'd robbed you.'

'Some did, but most of them would leave you alive if you gave them what they wanted. We met a couple after we had sold the gold at the assayers. Luckily Dandy had had the sense to open up the stitching on the saddle and put our money in there. By the time he sewed it up again you would never have known he'd been at it.'

'Didn't they rob you of anything then?' Sarah asked, concerned.

'I had a little gold dust in a bag in my pocket an' I gave them that. It wasn't worth much. They searched us, and the saddle bags then let us go.'

'You were lucky then. And you didn't go back to the camp?'

'Nope. We were finished there then. Someone would have our tent and all our gear within days. They'd figure out we'd either given up or been killed. I'd had the letter from Mary by then and we were both fed up trying to find gold. It was a dangerous game too. We thought we'd head off and try to find you.'

'So here you are! I'm pleased you reached us in one piece.'

Robert laughed. 'Not half as pleased as I am. Probably wouldn't have made it if it hadn't been for Dandy. He was my lucky mascot from the day I found him.'

'Well what has happened to Dandy? Where is he now?' Sarah leaned toward Robert, her face a picture of concern.

Robert heaved a shuddering sigh and his lips trembled. Shaking his head, he said quietly, 'poor little bugger got bit by a snake. We'd just set up camp an' he went for a pee. Next minute I heard him scream. I did all I could. Cut his leg an' tried to suck out the poison. Everything! But it didn't work. A stronger man might have survived. Sadly, Dandy was not a well boy, but he was a brave one. He knew he was dying, but he took it calmly. He thanked me for being such a good friend and making his last years so happy. He had no family. Said I was the closest he had to that. He told me to have his share of the money and the bit of gold we had dug up on our way over here looking for you. Said to make a good life for myself with it. Then he just drifted quietly off to sleep! Didn't wake up! I buried him under a tree by a lake. In his memory I must do something really good with our joint savings.' A tear ran down Robert's cheek as he finished his story.

Sarah took his hand in hers and pressed it to her cheek. Robert gave her a watery smile of gratitude.

'Where are you staying?' Patrick asked to make a sudden, needed change to the conversation.

'I found a nice spot near a billabong just out of town. I'll set up camp there.'

'No, you will not!' Sarah glared. 'You will set up your tent in our garden. It's a good size and there's plenty of room. Safer too, than out in the bush.'

Robert nodded. 'Thanks, lass. It would be nice to be here. Are you sure it wouldn't be too much of a bother to you?'

'Ach, what bother could you be? Better close to the house than out under a dusty hedge somewhere! Go now and fetch your stuff. Patrick will be wanting to do a lot of talking too!'

It was less than an hour before Robert arrived back and enthusiastically set up his camp in their garden.

414

Chapter 31

Patrick dumped himself heavily into 'his' chair. He had listened avidly to the tales Robert told of his adventures. Some he had found exciting, but many were just downright horrifying. The fact that his friend had survived to reach Kapunda was nothing short of a miracle.

'So, now you're here, what plans have you got? There's no gold around here, though I think I heard there was a small mine somewhere in the valley, down toward Gawler way. Not much there, I don't think. If the mine is even still open!'

Patrick had just come off shift and was weary beyond words. He was delighted to see his friend but could not think of anything that was likely to keep him in Kapunda. He would be sad see Robert leave though.

'Well, as I said, I've decided luck's been with me so far. And lucky I have been. But it won't hold forever. I was starting to feel it must soon run out. So, time perhaps to find something a bit steadier an' safer. I thought I might see about getting a job in the mine with you. I'm getting a mite tired of wandering.'

Patrick pursed his lips and shook his head slowly. 'I don't think a job in the mine is too likely. Not here anyway, I'm afraid.'

Robert frowned. 'Why not? You know I'm a good miner.'

Patrick nodded and chewed on his lip. 'There is a big problem though. The mine here is running down and they're starting to pay the men off. I doubt they would even gi' you a job.'

'You're jokin' surely?'

Patrick shook his head sadly.

A flock of galahs flew overhead, looking like a misty cloud of pink and grey but, sadly, sounding like a cacophony from hell.

"Fraid not old friend. The year we came over, the mine made its greatest profits ever. In total over four thousand tons of ore was reached that year. It had been closed for about four years because most of the miners raced off to join the gold rush. Then by the time we arrived it was up to runnin' at full strength again.'

Robert whistled softly.

'It was going so well that a couple of years ago the smelters were extended so they could produce refined copper. That year, 1861 it was, they produced nearly six hundred tons of copper.'

Robert frowned thoughtfully. 'So, what has gone wrong then? From what you say it sounds as if it was going well.'

'It was. But now the ore near the surface has been mined. The deeper diggin's are so costly that the mine is losing money. Everyone is worrying. What do we do if the mine closes?'

Robert nodded thoughtfully.

'Sarah and me's been doing a lot of talking, trying to decide what we must do. There is another copper mine opened quite a distance to the north. Moonta, the place is called.'

Robert nodded thoughtfully. 'I think I've heard mention of it somewhere.'

'Aye. Well they reckon it's a big one, wi' top quality ore and should run for many a long year. We've had thoughts o' moving up there, but there's a lot against it too.'

The two men sat for a while, deep in thought. They watched

puffy white clouds drift across a perfect blue sky. In the distance a willy-willy picked up dust and dry leaves as it whirled and danced, like a mad Dervish, across the landscape.

Eventually, with a sigh that shook his whole body, Patrick said, 'There are so many things to be considered. This is our home. A place we have grown to love. All our friends are here. The Cornish are more than just friends. They're family. We shared a cabin — if you would call it that — on the ship that brought us here. We've laughed with them. Cried with them. Mourned with them. They built this house for us after our old one was burned down in a bushfire. When we were left without a roof over our heads, they took in Sarah and the girls. Lent us clothes. Then when the house was rebuilt — by them — they lent us furniture until we could get our own. It would be a terrible wrench to leave them.'

Robert drew a deep breath. 'That must ha' been frightening. I've heard a bit about these bushfires. Pretty fearsome I should think.'

'Aye, it was,' Patrick agreed. 'Apart from the fire everything has gone well for us the six years we've been here. Anyway, whether we like it or not, I expect a lot of our friends will move to Moonta. There's a lot of talk about it, though no one really wants to go. It's a lot further from Adelaide. No trains out there! Very isolated. I–we would miss them badly if they left and we stayed. If the mine shuts it will tear this whole community apart!'

Robert rubbed a grubby hand across his hot face, leaving a muddy red streak. 'Aye. I understand.'

'When we landed in Adelaide there was no steam railway. There was one being built an' if we had come a few months later, it would have been running an' we could have come as far as Gawler on it. But it wasn't runnin' then and we had to come here by bullock cart. It was a wagon train, wi' all the Cornish miners an' their families. It was a hard trip and one family died when a tree fell on their tent.'

'Sounds rough.'

Patrick nodded thoughtfully. 'Aye it was. And there are the children. The girls have started at school here. There may not be one at Moonta. An it's a rough trek for such young ones in a bullock cart. Specially the boy. He's only just out of his mother's womb. And we've lost one son already!' His eyes were suddenly wet, and he flicked a hand to swipe the tears from his cheek.

Robert nodded sadly. 'Aye, I heard. Mary told me. That must have been the hardest thing you've ever had to bear.'

'Just as hard, and maybe worse, was seein' what it did to Sarah. She fought an' fought to keep the babe alive. Long after he was dead, she was still trying to breathe life into him. She couldn't — would not — let him die. But die he did. It's a wonder she didn't get the whooping cough too. Then she wrapped his little body in a shawl with his favourite toy. The crew bound him gently in sail canvas an' put a weight in, then they had a little service on the deck an' slipped him into the sea. Sarah stood there lookin' into the water 'til long after he had sunk from sight. I couldn't see her suffer like that again. Not ever! But I must have work and soon there will be none here for me. Then there is a very good doctor here. He'll come, no matter what time of day or night. An' there's no knowing if there is one at all at Moonta. It's a very new community. These are all things we have to think about.'

Robert looked thoughtful for a moment. 'Is there no other way than movin' to this Moonta place. Are you sure there is no other work you can do around here?'

Patrick shrugged and sighed. 'Sarah hates me working in the mine. She fears for my life every day, but there is nothing else for me. Ever since we got here, she has been saving pennies. Caring for her hens and her vegetable garden and selling what she can spare to the local shop. They are good people there and give her a good price. Every penny she has made there she has squirreled away because she has it set in her heart that one day, we might buy some land and have a little farm that will pay well enough to support us. That time's a long way off though. If it ever comes!'

Frowning thoughtfully, Robert nodded and sat gazing into the distance. 'She's a good girl, your Sarah. I wish I could find someone who could care so much for me,' he said wistfully.

In the days that followed Robert spent a lot of hours in the garden. If he couldn't get a job in the mines, he determined he would pull his weight by helping Sarah with the garden. He could see that with a new babe her days were full. No matter what the heat, he toiled endlessly digging more and yet more earth to give Sarah more planting space. He went to the store with Sarah's little cart and struggled back with it laden with timber and poultry wire.

'I'm going to make that chicken run much bigger, so's you can enlarge your flock an' get more eggs,' he told her proudly.

Sarah smiled sadly. 'I do appreciate what you're doing, Robert, but you might be wasting your time. We may have to leave here quite soon if Patrick gets his ticket from the mine.'

Robert shrugged. 'We'll have thought of a way, before then, for you to stay here. This is where you belong.' He sounded so confident that Sarah almost believed him.

'How I wish it could be. An' I worry about you because you are working too hard out here in this terrible heat.'

Robert laughed. 'No need to worry, Sarah. I've worked hard all my life. In hotter places than this. This is easy graft compared with the diggings.'

Sarah studied him and chuckled. It was easy to see why Patrick had always thought so highly of him.

'Anyway,' Robert continued cheerfully, 'We're going to have the best vegetable and chicken farm in Australia. So, get used to the idea, Missus!'

When Robert was not working in the garden, he spent hours every day trekking around the neighbouring farms trying to find some sort of employment. Sometimes he found a few hours of work, but most times it was a fruitless task.

However, in no time almost the whole garden, front as well as back, was either chicken run or vegetable patches. All sorts were planted, some of just about everything they could get seeds for.

Robert even found a goat from she knew not where. It supplied most of the milk the family needed. The girls quickly named it Jessica, though no one knew why. Jessica spent much of her time tethered by the roadside tidying up the verges, so it cost them next to nothing to feed her.

'Letter here for you, my girl,' Robert announced when he arrived back from town one day.

To Sarah's delight it was from Mary. Excitedly she ripped it open, read it, then with a tear in her eye handed it to Patrick.

'It sounds bad,' Patrick said as he handed the letter back.

'What can we do?' Sarah asked, tears stinging her eyes. 'We must help them. They have done so much for us.'

'What can we do?' Patrick sighed and shook his head.

'But James sounds so ill. Mary fears that another winter down the mine will kill him. She thought the pneumonia was going to get him last time. It has weakened him badly.'

'Aye,' Patrick shook his head sadly. 'They've been the best friends we could ever wish for, but they are months away from us. And James knows no other kind of work.'

'If anything happens to James, it would break Mary's heart. What would become of her? And the children. Richard is working in the mines now, though Mary and James don't like him to. But not Lizzie and Jess. I suppose they could work on the sorting beds, but neither Mary, James nor I would want that for them.' Sarah clenched her teeth on her lip to hold back the tears.

They showed the letter to Robert, who agreed they must do something to help their friends. Sadly, no one could think of what that might be. They were a whole world away, out of reach!

In the days that followed Sarah noticed, in puzzlement, that Robert spent increasingly more time at the far end of the garden, a pot of beer to hand. With a thoughtful look, he gazed into the distance.

Sarah worried that he was planning to leave and was saddened. She was sensible enough to realise that he needed to find a real job. He was too proud a man to not be gainfully employed. It would be a sad day for all of them if he left, she thought. It was bad enough having this worry about James and the family.

One evening Sarah and Patrick sat on the veranda watching Robert. He sat on a log at the far end of the garden. His elbow was on his knee, his chin cupped in his hand as he looked thoughtfully up at the night sky.

'What is he thinking about?' Sarah asked.

Patrick merely shrugged. He had no more idea than she.

Finally, Robert rose and wandered, to the veranda where they sat.

'I've been thinking,' Robert started.

Patrick nodded and said quietly, 'We've noticed.'

Sarah thought, 'Here it comes. He's going to tell us he's leaving. God, how I'll miss him!'

'Well, you see, it's like this,' Robert continued. 'I have all this money and some gold. Just lying here doing nothing, it is. An' we're all sitting aroun' here worrying about the future an' about trying to find work without having to up sticks an' move into the middle of nowhere. An' we're fretting about how to help James and Mary. Right?'

Sarah and Patrick nodded warily.

'I can't spend all my life just wandering about the country. So, I was thinkin' that we all like the outdoor life. We'd all enjoy being our own bosses. Patrick has been a farmer in a past life. So why don't we pool our money? Sarah's savings and mine and buy some farming land together.'

Patrick and Sarah stared at their friend in stunned amazement.

'I–I–I, well we,' Sarah finally stammered. 'We thought you were making plans to leave!'

Robert gave a great roar of laughter. 'Nothing is further from my mind. I'm too well looked after here. But what do you think of the idea?'

Sarah sat dumbfounded. Patrick just grinned. 'By all the Gods,' he said eventually. 'Nothing would please me more. But would we have enough money between us?'

'Well, if you're happy with the idea, that's something we'll have to find out. I suggest we start right away and look into the cost of land. In addition, we'll need enough money to bring Mary, James and the family out, too.'

It had taken three months for Mary's letter to reach them. They knew that if they were to get their friends away from the Isle of Man before next winter they would have to act quickly.

While Sarah sat in open-mouthed shock, Patrick nodded enthusiastically. 'Aye. But it's not just the land we would have to get a price on. We would need the tools to work the land. Probably bullocks and a cart. Maybe a horse or two.'

'We've got one horse already,' Robert reminded him.

'We'd have to build a house. And we'd need enough money left to keep us in food until the farm was producing,' Patrick pointed out.

'Well, I'll get down to the assayer's office in Adelaide an' sell that bit of gold I have. That should buy quite a bit of stock.'

'Well, thanks to all Robert's hard work in the garden, we're growing a lot of fruit and vegetables here. And the hens for meat and eggs. That would help us through,' Sarah pointed out.

The conversation ran on long into the night and gained enthusiasm with every minute that passed. Like a snowball on a steep slope, the idea grew quickly. By the time they all retired, exhausted, to bed it had been decided that Robert would get started on the pricing process the following morning.

First things first, he would have to take his gold to Adelaide to sell before they would know exactly how much money they had to work with. This decided, Robert cheerfully boarded the train to the city the following morning.

The following day he arrived back jubilant. The price of gold had risen, so he came home with much more in his pocket than he had anticipated.

Sarah also had news. When she had taken her produce to the shop that morning, she had discussed their plans with Graham and Linda. They had been very sensible and good friends all the years she had lived in Kapunda and she valued their opinion.

Both were enthusiastic. They knew how much Sarah wanted Patrick out of mining and how hard she had worked and saved toward that end.

'Well,' Graham began thoughtfully. 'I know of a farm that is to be sold, but have no idea of the asking price, or how much money you will have.'

Sarah leaned forward eagerly. 'Go on,' she coaxed. 'Where is it?'

Graham nodded thoughtfully. 'Well, it's not far from town. Do you remember that German farmer, Gustav Kreig?'

'Yes. He had an accident and died, didn't he?'

'Aye. Fell from his hay loft and broke his neck. Well his widow doesn't want to keep the farm. She wants to take her children back to her family in Germany.'

'So, it's definitely for sale?'

'That's what she told me a couple of days ago. You should go and see her. Find out what she wants for it. I don't know much else about it. Size or anything. She might have some animals and farming tools too. I know she has some hens.'

Sarah rushed home, to wait impatiently for the men to return — Patrick from the mine and Robert from Adelaide.

When she had them all seated after tea and had listened to Robert's story of his successful gold sale, she excitedly told them her piece of news.

'Sounds good. It will depend, of course on how much land there is and what price Mistress Kreig is hoping for. First thing tomorrow we'll get ourselves over there and have a talk to the good lady. Find out exactly what she has for sale,' Robert suggested.

Everyone nodded, but Sarah thought perhaps they should not all go in case such a deputation scared the lady.

'I have met her once or twice in the shop, so best I go — and Patrick — not any strangers to her.'

The men both agreed, so first thing in the morning Sarah and Patrick set off. The children were left with Robert so there would be no distractions during their conversation, or so they thought. They had overlooked Mrs Kreig's large brood of noisy, farm-bred children.

Mrs Kreig was feeding her chickens when they arrived but gave them a cheery wave. Securing the chicken run behind her, she wiped her hand on her apron, then offered it for a handshake.

'You're the girl from this end of town, aren't you?'

Sarah nodded. 'Sarah O'Mally and this is my husband, Patrick.'

'I'm Mena. Have you come for some eggs?'

'No thank you. We have hens of our own. I hope you don't think us cheeky, but we came to ask about your farm,' Sarah said hesitantly.

Mena Kreig frowned. 'The farm, what about it? Oh, look, you've had a long walk in this heat. Come on in out of the sun.'

They all trooped into the house, battling their way against a tide of squealing children who were chasing each other out.

Though taken by surprise Mena made them very welcome, sat them down and gave them a stein of her late husband's home-made beer.

After the long walk from home both Sarah and Patrick gratefully took a long slurp of the welcome beverage.

'It's not often I get visitors out here. It's nice to see a grown-up face sometimes and have some proper conversation. Now what was it you wanted to ask about the farm?'

'Well, we are looking for some land to farm, and Graham in the shop told me you might be thinking of selling yours. I hope you don't mind us coming to ask.'

Mena looked from one to the other of her visitors and her face lit up in wide beam. 'Mind? I should think not. I have been trying to decide how best to go about selling it. I can't manage it and the children on my own. It will just go to ruin and be worthless if I don't sell it soon.'

Sarah nodded sympathetically.

'We had such plans,' Mena continued wistfully. 'It was to be our future. Ours and the children's'. We hoped one day we would be able to buy more land and have a really good-sized farm.'

A tear fell on her cheek and she brushed it away impatiently.

'Can you tell us the size of the farm please? How much land does it have?' Patrick asked quietly.

'It's a square mile. Otto cleared quite a good acreage in the years we were here. But he had to do most of the work himself, so a lot of it is still scrub.'

'We — I have two shire horses. They're quite young and Gustav trained them well. Good workers, both of them. There is a good strong iron plough and there are ten oxen to pull it. Also, I have a mullensing harrow Gustav made. It has iron spikes and is strong and it is pulled by the shire horses.'

'I'm not too familiar with farming tools,' Patrick confessed. 'The plough I know about, but what does the mullensing harrow do?'

'Well the plough is much stronger than most as it breaks up the hard, virgin soil. Gustav used to cut down the trees, use what he needed of the larger wood, then sell the rest as logs. The small stuff he just burned. Then he threw the wheat seeds on the ground. The harrow grubbed out the scrub, broke up the soil and buried the seeds.'

Patrick took a deep breath. 'Well, that all sounds quite impressive. It seems it is just what we are looking for, but of course we will have to discuss a price, then talk with our partner.'

Mena nodded. 'Of course. Now would you like another beer?' German hospitality was second to none, Sarah had found.

'What will you do, though, if you leave here?' she asked gently.

Mena heaved a heavy sigh. 'Well, I did think of going back to Germany, but I'm not sure that would be a good idea. My family are all there, but my friends are here. This is home to the children. We left Germany because of the persecution and that will still be there. If I'm to be sensible there is not really much for us to go back to. So, I think I will probably just buy a little house in town. Or maybe it must be a big house for all my children!' She gave a hearty laugh.

When Sarah and Patrick left about an hour later, they had a price that sounded reasonable to them, to discuss with Robert.

'It sounds just right,' Robert agreed enthusiastically. 'It will give us a good start, until we know what we are doing. 'If it's not enough we can possibly buy more land later.'

'Aye, and it's near enough to here for us maybe to keep this cottage on for a while. Seeing it's in the town you two could stay on here and I can live out on the farm.'

Patrick frowned. 'It will be a long walk out there for me very day. I'll be pretty tired before I get there.'

Robert gave a loud shout of laughter. 'You will have to learn to ride my horse then! I meant only until we have found our feet and you can give up the mining.'

The following day the riding lessons began, and a conveyancer was found to draw up the transfer of title papers. Settlement date was to be in two months, to allow Mrs Krieg time to find a large enough cottage in town.

A letter was sent to James and Mary inviting them, rather — begging — them and the children to join them on their farm at as early a date as they could arrange. Money enough was enclosed to pay for cabins for them all on the ship.

Eight months later, on the 7th December 1864 Sarah stood with her children on the platform at Kapunda railway station. She watched anxiously as the steam train pulled to a halt and doors started to open.

Robert stepped down, followed by a man who could only be James, but looked much older. Then came plump Mary.

Tears fogged Sarah's eyes as she ran toward them, James clutched to her chest and the girls running behind. As she hugged Mary, she saw a handsome young man step down on to the platform. Surely this could not be Richard, she puzzled. But he had Richard's beautiful blue green eyes. *I bet he doesn't piss his pants now!* the rogue thought crept in.

Richard was followed closely by two excited and beautiful young ladies. 'My little girls. My little sisters,' Sarah's eyes widened in wonder. In her mind her three siblings had always been as they had looked when she last saw them.

Another person stepped down from the train and Sarah gasped with pleasure. Holding out an arm, she invited him to join the group hug.

Jos gave a slightly embarrassed shrug. 'I hope you don't mind. I heard this country was full of convicts, so I thought they might not notice another one,' he said sheepishly.

'You are more than welcome,' Patrick smiled and extended the hand of friendship.

Mary had not told Sarah they were bringing Jos. That had been left as a surprise but, Sarah thought happily, the family would not have been quite complete without him.

T H E   E N D